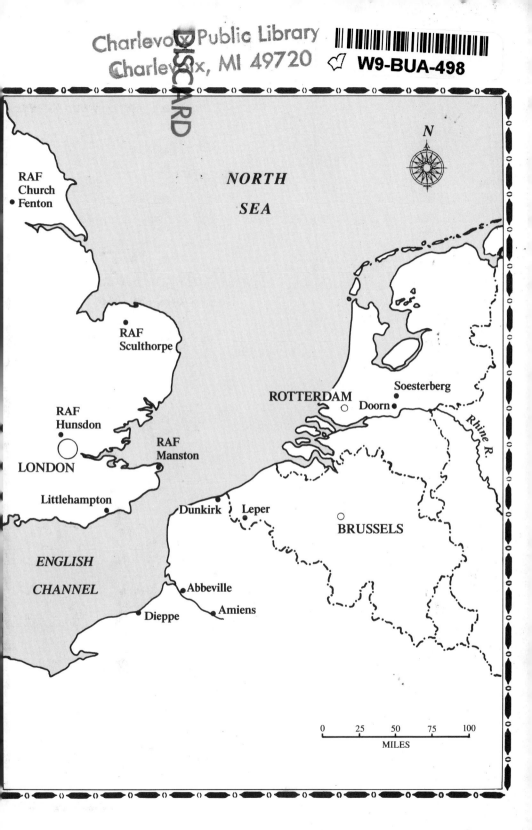

N

NORTH

SEA

RAF
Church
• Fenton

RAF
Sculthorpe

Soesterberg
•

ROTTERDAM   Doorn •
○

RAF
Hunsdon
•
○

RAF
Manston
•

LONDON

Littlehampton
•

Dunkirk   Leper
•

BRUSSELS
○

ENGLISH

CHANNEL

Abbeville
•

Amiens
•

Dieppe
•

Rhine R.

0   25   50   75   100

MILES

CALL TO
DUTY

Also by Richard Herman, Jr.

The Warbirds

Force of Eagles

Firebreak

CALL
TO
DUTY

RICHARD HERMAN, JR.

WILLIAM MORROW AND COMPANY, INC.
New York

Library of Congress Cataloging-in-Publication Data

Herman, Richard, Jr.
Call to duty / Richard Herman, Jr.
    p.   cm.
  ISBN 0-688-11438-5
  I. Title.
PS3558.E684M67   1993
813'.54—dc20   92-19121
                                        CIP

Printed in the United States of America

First Edition

1   2   3   4   5   6   7   8   9   10

BOOK DESIGN BY PAUL CHEVANNES

For Sybil,
my mother-in-law,
who lived through it all
and endured with hope and grace

AUTHOR'S NOTE

Although this is a work of fiction, much of it is based on fact. The 1st Special Operations Wing, Delta Force, and the United States Special Operations Command exist and function much as described in *Call to Duty*. Similarly, many of the historical personalities appearing in this novel lived and made their mark on history in World War II. The raid on Amiens prison was led by Group Captain Percy Charles Pickard and he was shot down with his friend and navigator, Bill Broadley, on that legendary mission. With the exception of the protagonist of *Call to Duty*, his navigator, and John Maitland, the names associated with the Amiens mission are factual. The film from the mission can be seen today at the Imperial War Museum. General Adolf Galland was not flying nor was Fips Priller shot down that day, but both were part of Jagdgeschwader 26, "the boys from Abbeville."

And the de Havilland Mosquito, "the Wooden Wonder," was the most versatile aircraft of World War II. It was probably the safest Allied bomber and it did perform like a fighter. What it did is not fiction and *Romanita* did exist.

I would like to acknowledge the help given me by the men and women of the First Special Operations Wing at Hurlburt Field, Fort Walton Beach, Florida; the staff at the Imperial War Museum; Mr. David Lawrence of the Royal Air Force Museum, who took the time to let me crawl over a Mosquito and trusted me in its cockpit; and Peter Waxham and Ian Thirsk of the Mosquito Aircraft Museum, Salisbury Hall.

Many thanks are due to the two pilots who introduced me to the wonderful world of helicopters: Ken Fritz and Charles "Chip" Hall.

To the two very elegant ladies, Ingeborg Wright and Ellen Butcher, who showed me the reality of life in wartime Germany, thank you.

I owe a special debt of gratitude to three individuals who were willing to trust a complete stranger: Jack Eskenazi, for the journey through wartime Germany; John S. Gerrish, who flew the Mossie during the Second World War and made it come alive; and to one of "Jerry's Kids," who gave me a glimpse of what special operations are all about. I only hope I can do the power of their memories and experiences justice.

GLOSSARY

Abwehr: German Military Intelligence in World War II. The Abwehr was commanded by Admiral Wilhelm Canaris, who was often at odds with the Gestapo, the SS, and Hitler.

AFCOM: Air Force Command.

AFSOC: Air Force Special Operations Command. The Air Force command that is part of USSOCOM.

ANVIS-6: A type of night vision goggles worn by aircrews.

C4: The modern version of plastique explosive.

Combat Talon: The MC-130E flown by the 1st Special Operations Wing.

CSM: Command sergeant major.

DCI: Director of central intelligence. The individual in charge of all United States intelligence agencies and functions. Heads the CIA.

DEA: The Drug Enforcement Administration.

E-boat: A German World War II motor-torpedo boat.

ETA: Estimated time of arrival.

FLIR: Forward-looking infrared.

GCI: Ground-controlled intercept. The interception of an aircraft that is directed by a radar site.

GPS: Global positioning system. A worldwide navigation system utilizing satellites. The receiver is about the size of this book, rugged, and accurate to eighty-two feet.

Have Quick: A radio that uses rapid frequency hopping to defeat jamming and monitoring.

Hilton: A British-made lightweight, multipurpose, single-shot weapon that is easily converted from a twelve-gauge shotgun to a forty-millimeter grenade launcher.

HUMINT: Human intelligence. Old-fashioned spying or exploitation of human weaknesses for wine, women/men, money, and drugs to get information.

IP: Initial point. A well-defined, easily distinguishable geographical feature that points to the target or objective.

ISA: Intelligence Support Activity. A secret group that conducts special operations and counterterrorism.

KIA: Killed in action.

LZ: Landing zone.

Magellan: The name of the NA1000M GPS receiver/monitor.

Met: The term for the meteorological or weather section used during World War II.

MP5: An excellent nine-millimeter submachine gun made by Heckler and Koch.

NKVD: The name of the Soviet secret police during World War II; now known as the KGB.

NMCC: National Military Command Center. The Pentagon's "war room."

NSA: The National Security Agency. The United States intelligence agency responsible for monitoring communications and breaking codes.

NSC: National Security Council.

NSPG: National Security Planning Group. The President's chief advisers on matters relating to national security.

Pave Low: The MH-53J helicopter flown by the 1st Special Operations Wing.

R/T: Radio/telephone. The British term for two-way radios during World War II.

RTB: Return to base.

SAS: The Special Air Service. The elite British counterterrorism unit.

SITREP: Situation report. A report transmitted immediately after, or during, the action to update higher headquarters on the existing situation.

SOE: Special Operations Executive. The British organization responsible for carrying out sabotage, subversion, underground activities and assassinations during World War II.

Special Activities Center: The Air Force organization responsible for collecting HUMINT.

Spectre: The call sign given to AC-130 gunships flown by the 1st Special Operations Wing.

STU-III: A portable, key-activated, plug-in-anywhere telephone that scrambles conversations.

System 4: The highly classified computer system the NSC uses to monitor United States intelligence activities and operations.

USSOCOM: United States Special Operations Command. The unified command headquartered at MacDill Air Force Base that is responsible for all special operations conducted by the United States military.

WIA: Wounded in action.

Zulu: The phonetic alphabet for the letter Z. When used after a time, it means Greenwich mean time.

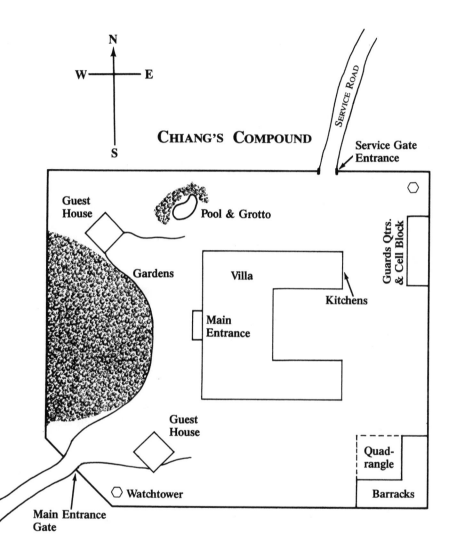

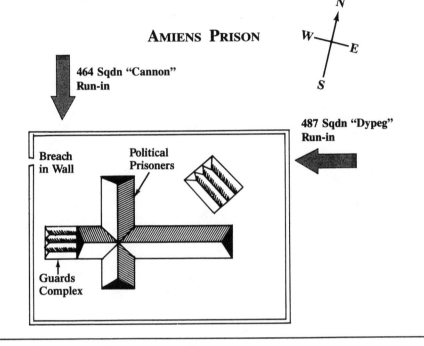

AMIENS PRISON

N
W — E
S

464 Sqdn "Cannon"
Run-in

487 Sqdn "Dypeg"
Run-in

Breach
in Wall

Political
Prisoners

Guards
Complex

ALBERT — AMIENS ROAD

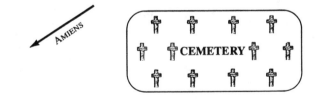

AMIENS

CEMETERY

PROLOGUE

1942

RAF Church Fenton, England

The driving rain propelled the sergeant through the door of the officers mess. He saw the man he was looking for and walked quickly across the large room. "Mr. Ruffum," he said, catching the young RAF officer's attention. "The weather prophet says the rain is lifting and you should be able to take off in thirty minutes. You best find Mr. Pontowski."

Flight Officer Andrew Ruffum gave the middle-aged sergeant his most disinterested look. "Right," he said and tapped the crud out of his pipe. The twenty-year-old ex-university student thought the combination of Royal Air Force uniform and big pipe gave him a mature look and the pipe had become his constant companion, clenched firmly in his teeth. He went in search of his pilot. Another navigator pointed him in the direction of the room where they stowed their flying kits.

"Yank," he called from the doorway, "you in here?"

"Back here," a voice said from the far corner where a light was glowing. Ruffum worked his way past the parachutes, heavy flying jackets, boots, helmets, and other paraphernalia required to fly a British night fighter over the North Sea. His pilot, Matthew Zachary Pontowski, was stretched out in a deck chair with a small reading lamp perched beside him.

"Whatever are you reading now?"

Matthew Zachary Pontowski gave him a crooked smile and held up a leather-bound volume. "A history of your Anti-Slavery Society. I found it in a used bookstore in York."

"Ah, William Wilberforce," Ruffum replied. "Not very fascinating stuff in this day and age."

"I had no idea how bad it was," the lanky American said. "Did you know they packed them into the slave ships buck-naked. Men and women."

"Sounds lascivious," Ruffum replied.

"Not if you were one of them."

Ruffum put on a serious face. "Sorry to interrupt your education about human bondage, Zack, but Met says the weather is lifting. Time to go." Zack Pontowski closed the book and followed his navigator as they collected their flying kit and headed into the rainy night.

"Hello, Falcon. This is Red One. Any trade?" Zack Pontowski's distinctive American accent was easily recognizable over the radio/telephone as he entered his assigned patrol area over the North Sea.

"Sorry, Red One," the controller at Ground Control Intercept answered, his clipped British words in sharp contrast to Zack's California-bred accent, "I have nothing for you at this time."

Zack returned to his battle with the blind-flying instrument panel on his Beaufighter, trying to decide which of the instruments were lying to him. Probably the artificial horizon, he decided; it always gave up first. He cross-checked the air speed indicator, altimeter, rate of climb, turn and slip, and direction indicator. Why can't they call the DI a directional gyro like everyone else, he thought. As usual, the ways of the Royal Air Force both puzzled and amused him. Pay attention to business, he reprimanded himself. You went to a lot of trouble to volunteer for this war.

"Set course one-three-five degrees," Ruffum said over the intercom.

"Got it," Zack replied and turned to the new heading, establishing them on the first leg of their first night patrol over the

North Sea. He glanced outside the cockpit, surprised at how bright it was. Then he realized they were skimming along in the top of a cloud deck. He pulled back on the control column and climbed twenty feet before breaking out on top. The bright moonlight gave him a distinct horizon and he felt better. The blind-flying instruments had not been lying to him. Zack Pontowski forced himself to relax as they droned through the night.

"It's gorgeous above the clouds," Ruffum allowed, taking in the night from his perspex dome mounted on top of the fuselage, halfway between the cockpit and tail. Flying Officer Andrew Ruffum, known simply as Ruffy, had been with Zack since Cranfield, site of the operational training unit where they had both been sent to train on the twin-engine Beaufighter. Ruffy had taken massive amounts of good-natured ribbing about being teamed with a "Yank" but had taken it all in his easygoing way and they had become good friends.

In the air, the two were an ideal match and complimented each other perfectly. Zack was a superb pilot and a natural at the controls of the blunt-nosed tanklike Beaufighter, while Ruffy took to the cantankerous Mark IV airborne intercept radar set with an instant affinity. They rapidly surpassed their instructors and then, in one of its rare moments of sanity when it came to personnel assignments, the RAF assigned them as a crew to 25 Squadron, currently on operations at RAF Church Fenton, an airfield ten miles south of the old city of York.

"Time to reverse course," Ruffy said over the intercom, bringing Zack back to the moment. The pilot banked the night fighter to the left, away from the coast, and traced a northward track in the box they had been assigned to patrol. He cross-checked his instruments when he rolled out and again scanned the night. Above the clouds the visibility in the moonlight was excellent.

It was in June of 1941 on a night flight like this one, Zack remembered, that he had decided that the war in Europe was also his war. Hitler's blitzkrieg had rolled over Western Europe, the Battle of Britain had been fought, and Russia had been invaded the day before. He had mentioned it to his flying instructor and was given a phone number and the name of one Ernest W. Bellway. "Bellway's the guy to call," his instructor had said, "if a pilot wants to join the Royal Air Force."

It had been deceptively easy. When Ernest W. Bellway discovered that Zack had a pilot's license, money for a one-way train ticket to Ottawa, Canada, had magically appeared. It started to get complicated in Chicago, where he, and two of his fellow-pilot traveling companions, had to change trains. The FBI was waiting with orders to enforce the Neutrality Act and had arrested the other two pilots while he was purchasing their tickets. He had seen the commotion, slipped away, and boarded the train to Ottawa. There he was met by a car that took him to an RAF group captain who sent him on to Halifax. Six weeks later, he was on the *Duchess of Richmond* sailing for England.

In England, after still another delay, Zack was assigned to an OTU, operational training unit, that had been set up to rapidly evaluate and process pilots into the RAF. Things turned sour when the engine of the Avro Tutor biplane he was training in quit in mid-flight and nothing he did could get it restarted. He had to deadstick it in for a landing on a freshly plowed field. It didn't work and he crashed, killing the instructor and badly breaking his right leg. It was months before he could fly again and, by then, the RAF had decided to send him through an extensive flight training program. He had endured the needless repetition until he found himself assigned to the OTU at Cranfield where he had met Ruffy.

"Hello, Red One. This is Falcon." The GCI controller's voice was much more rapid. Zack acknowledged the call. "I have a customer for you," the controller said, "vector one-eight-zero. Buster." Zack turned to the south, bumped up the propeller speed controls and shoved the throttles forward.

"Anything on the box?" Zack asked Ruffy, hoping for an early pickup on the radar set.

"Nothing yet," Ruffy answered.

Zack knew the GCI controller had to get them within four miles of the customer, or bandit, for their radar set to acquire the target. The airspeed indicator was hovering around 230 miles per hour. He made a mental adjustment for altitude and temperature and came up with a true airspeed of 280—four and a half miles a minute, probably with an overtake of 60 miles per hour, so it would be a while before Ruffy could paint anything on the radar. He flicked on his sight and moved the gun master switch up, activating the six Browning .303 machine guns in the wings and the four 20-millimeter Hispano cannons fixed in the underside of the forward fuselage. He selected the machine guns for firing. He mashed the button on the yoke, testing the guns. The Beaufighter had an awesome amount of firepower, if it caught anyone.

Control your breathing, Zack cautioned himself. This may not be the real thing. He swept the horizon hoping he might see a vague shadow, anything to tell him that he had finally met the enemy. This will be something, he thought, action on our first patrol. Not what they had told me to expect.

Their sector had been quiet for the past few weeks and the crews were bored, longing for some action. The squadron's intelligence officer made it worse by constantly updating them on the action farther to the south, where the night fighters seemed to be constantly engaged with Heinkels and Junkers.

"Red One, this is Falcon," the GCI controller transmitted. "Your customer is on your nose, moving southward, range twenty miles."

"It's turned into a tail chase," Ruffy said.

Zack checked his engine instruments, not ready to give up yet. All were fine and the big fourteen-cylinder, 1,590-horsepower, Hercules XI engines were humming smoothly. The sleeve-valve radial engines were amazingly quiet. "Red One, Falcon," the GCI said, "bandit now turning to the east and descending. Vector one-three-five." Falcon was turning them to a cut-off heading.

"Hope he doesn't go too low," Ruffy said. Below five thousand feet, ground clutter blotched up his radar and it was impossible to break out the target. "If the bugger doesn't change course, intercept in four minutes." Ruffy had worked out the geometry of the developing intercept.

Zack glanced at his watch, noting the time and when four minutes would be up. He wished the clock on his instrument panel had an elapsed minute hand. He made a mental note to mention it to the maintenance officer, but he wasn't worried—Ruffy would back him up. Ahead of him, he could see the end of the cloud deck below them and the night became beautifully clear, right down to the surface of the North Sea.

"Red One, bandit turning south," Falcon said.

"Turn to one-eight-zero," Ruffy said. They were in a tail chase again.

"Red One, vector now one-eight-zero," Falcon said, reacting slower than Ruffy to the bandit's heading changes.

"Red One," Falcon said, "the bandit has dropped from my coverage. Maintain your current heading."

"The bastard's taking advantage of a break in the clouds," Zack said over the intercom. "He's dropped below Falcon's radar coverage and running for home on the deck." The flickering of a light on the horizon caught his attention. "Ruffy, get your binocs on that light at ten o'clock." He waited for his navigator to rotate his seat forward and focus the binoculars he always carried.

"Can't tell much," Ruffy said. "Maybe a fire. Hold on ... I believe it's growing. Yes ... much bigger now. Definitely a fire on the surface."

Zack relayed the information to Falcon. "Red One," the GCI controller answered, "Air-Sea Ops reports a sweep in that area." Zack acknowledged the transmission. The RAF had its own fleet of small, very fast launches known as the Air-Sea Rescue Service that operated in the waters around Britain, rescuing airmen forced down in the sea. If one of their boats was on patrol, that fire could mean trouble.

"Ruffy, I'm going to check it out." Zack radioed his intentions to Falcon, retarded the throttles, nosed over, and headed straight for the glowing beacon. He descended to five hundred feet and slowed as they circled the brightly burning fire, sizing up the situation and not closing. Now Zack could clearly see a burning boat and rafts in the water. He gauged the boat to be about sixty feet long—the right size for an Air-Sea launch.

A stream of tracers reached out of the night, slicing across the dark directly in front of them. Zack's reflexes were razor-sharp and he wrenched back on the yoke and ruddered the Beau around, easily avoiding the tracers. "At your four o'clock," Ruffy shouted, "on the surface, another boat."

Out of the corner of his eye Zack caught a dark movement in the water—the source of the tracers. The shape took on a harder definition as he circled and maneuvered until the unknown boat was between him and the moon. "I think it's an E-boat," he said, climbing to three thousand feet. "Falcon, Red One," he transmitted over the radio. "We are in contact with what looks like an E-boat and a smaller launch that is burning in the water."

"Red One," Falcon answered, "I hold you in the area where bandit last observed."

A warning signal started bonging inside Zack's head, jolting his emotions. Without thinking, he hauled back on the control column and firewalled the throttles. At the same time he sawed back and forth on the rudder pedals. "What ... " Ruffy said over the intercom, the sudden erratic maneuver throwing him around. A dark shape materialized out of the darkness, skidding across the sky beneath them.

"A Junkers Eighty-eight," Zack said, breathing hard, working against the heavy control loads. "Night fighter. Where the hell did he go?"

"Tallyho!" Ruffy shouted. "At your three o'clock. Low." Zack rolled the Beau and pulled down to his three o'clock position. He caught a glimpse of the German plane as he turned, its nose on him and climbing. He skidded the Beau to the right and jabbed at the gun button. A short burst of tracers reached out for the Junkers as he passed under the German, going in the opposite direction. He missed. Now he pitched back after the German, trading his airspeed for altitude.

"Falcon," Zack radioed, "help please." He wanted to know where the Junkers had gone.

"The bandit is to the north," came the immediate reply. Zack turned northward and continued to climb.

"I have him on the box," Ruffy said, his voice amazingly calm. "Four miles, slightly left and above you."

"Contact," Zack radioed to Falcon as they entered the cloud deck. "Christ! We're in the clouds," he told Ruffy.

"It's okay, he's not maneuvering," Ruffy said. "Come left five degrees; we're closing." Zack followed Ruffy's directions as he played the throttles. They slowly closed. "Range, half mile," Ruffy said.

The cockpit filled with light as they broke out on top of the cloud deck, directly behind and underneath the Junkers. Zack drove in closer. The German filled the lighted gun ring on his reflector sight and he selected the cannons. His right thumb brushed the firing button but he hesitated, wanting to close. Suddenly, the Junkers skidded to the right and pitched into a steep dive. The German crew wasn't going to be surprised.

Zack hauled the Beau around, following, determined to get the Junkers, and chased him down into the cloud deck. Now they were in a sixty-degree dive in the clouds. "On the nose, two hundred yards," Ruffy said. "Lost him in the ground clutter. Sorry."

The engines howled and the fuselage shook as Zack pushed the dive past 350 miles per hour. He concentrated on the instruments. "Come on, baby," he coaxed, hoping the artificial horizon wouldn't give up. He was sweating from the strain of muscling the ten-ton fighter through the sky. Again, that internal warning screamed at him and he hauled back on the control column and raked the throttles aft. The warnings grew louder and he pulled back harder while he spun the elevator trim wheel with his right hand, feeding in nose-up trim. He used both hands to pull back on the yoke, forcing the nose of the plane to lift. Slowly, the nose came up and the wind noise quieted down.

They bottomed out of their dive as they broke out of the clouds, two hundred feet above the choppy surface of the North Sea. The Junkers screamed by them, going straight down. "What the hell," Zack shouted as the German crashed into the sea, "we overshot him in the dive." He pushed the throttles forward and circled the sinking wreckage. Silence. An empty feeling that had replaced his stomach and a weariness from hauling the Beau around the sky mauled his emotions. Then it hit him: Only that eerie warning, that strange sixth sense he had never experienced before, had saved them—twice. He wondered about that. Another thought occurred to him. "Did we get a kill?" he asked, more to himself than to Ruffy.

"Looks like Sir Isaac got him," Ruffy allowed.

"Beg pardon?" Zack asked, confused.

"Sir Isaac Newton. Gravity."

Zack returned to business and headed south, hugging the surface and staying below the clouds, returning to where they had last seen the burning boat. When they broke free of the clouds, they could see a glow on the surface in front of them. "Got it," he told Ruffy. As they approached, the pilot could make out the silhouette of the E-boat, motionless on the surface. A burst of tracers reached out from the boat toward them and Zack hauled the Beau around, staying out of range. "What the hell . . . " he muttered.

"I've got the glasses on him," Ruffy said. "He's picking up survivors still in the water."

For a moment, Zack considered attacking the E-boat—a strafing run with the twenties. But an attack would drive the E-boat off and leave the men to their fate in the frigid waters of the North Sea. "How long do you think they can last in the water?" he asked.

"In December?" Ruffy answered, "Not bloody long." He was thinking the same thing. "Why don't you drop it in Falcon's lap? Let him make the decision." Zack agreed and climbed above the E-boat, staying out of range. He could see it start to move while he established contact with GCI. Falcon asked him how certain he was that it was an E-boat and Zack admitted that he could not be positive as it was night. Falcon gave them a vector back to their patrol area and said he would pass the sighting on to

Coastal Command and Air-Sea Ops. "It could be one of ours, old chap," the controller told him.

"You think it might be Young Ernst?" Ruffy asked. Young Ernst was the name Intelligence had given to Ernst Hofmann, a twenty-four-year-old E-boat captain whose reputation had reached legendary proportions as he worked at will along the British coast, sinking targets of opportunity with impunity.

It all came together for Zack. "Ruffy, I'll bet you a pint that Junkers was working with that E-boat."

"Flying cover?"

"Perhaps. Maybe finding targets. The Jerries might have come up with a new tactic." He made another mental note to mention it when they debriefed Intelligence.

An hour later Falcon told them to return to base and they headed back to land.

THE PRESENT

The Andaman Sea, Between India and Malaysia

The girl's head popped above the coaming of the cockpit and her eyes blinked, driving the haze away. Nothing had changed from the day before—the water's surface was mirror smooth and the sails hung empty in the still, unbelievably clear morning air. Frustration clouded her eyes and she refused to accept the lack of motion, the sense of nothing happening, a world at rest. She kicked out a long leg and banged her foot against the lifeless wheel of the sixty-five-foot sailboat. The only response was a sharp pain in her ankle.

Roll with it, Heather Courtland told herself as she rubbed her foot. So you're becalmed in the Andaman Sea, about two hundred miles north of nowhere. She studied the horizon, trying to see the coast of Malaysia or Thailand to the east. You can't get any further out of it, she moaned to herself. Why did I ever do this? The haze was threatening again, moving onto the shoreline of her awareness.

Again, she swept the horizon, wondering how far she could see, looking for the telltale signs of a wind stirring the sky or water. Nothing. Then she caught a smudge on the horizon but dismissed it. Probably a freighter sailing between Singapore and

Calcutta, she thought, or maybe a supertanker headed for the Straits of Malacca on its way to Japan. She was too lazy to reach for the binoculars hanging from the compass in front of the wheel. A mistake.

The top of Troy Spencer's mass of tangled blond hair appeared in the dark of the cabin's companionway and hesitated as he stumbled up the ladder. Then the rest of his head appeared in the sunshine. He scooped up the bottom of her bikini and tossed it overboard when he reached the deck. She watched without comment as it drifted beside the boat before sinking. They were a matched pair: naked, skinny, blue-eyed, and with blond hair that reached to their shoulders. Even the single diamond earring that dangled from their pierced nipples was part of a matched set that had cost over four thousand dollars on Rodeo Drive in Beverly Hills. Only their tattoos differed. His was a bold spiderweb on the right shoulder, hers a small coiled snake and impossible to see unless she wanted to show it. That was one of the many deferences paid to her father—something they both understood.

"You still with it, babes?" he asked.

"No way," she groused. "I need a blast. Gimme a bullet." Troy Spencer grunted and disappeared back down the companionway.

She slapped the teak deck surrounding the cockpit as she waited impatiently for him to return. She drew her fingernails across the well-oiled teak, not caring about the beautiful sloop that belonged to Ricky Martel and Nikki Anderson, the other couple with them. The sailboat was a masterpiece of yachting perfection with its gleaming varnished woodwork and polished brass fittings. Down below, the cabins were comfortable and the boat was packed with the latest electronic gear for communications and navigation. Only the constant attention of the professional crew, Mark Livingston and his wife, DC, had kept the boat in tiptop shape and in good order. Heather wasn't sure which of them, Ricky or Nikki, owned the sailboat and doubted if they really knew or cared. Ricky Martel and Nikki Anderson had made a small fortune from their heavy-metal band, Poison Pig, and its number one hit song, "Cock the Bitch Silly." Not that they needed the money, since both came from wealthy families.

Heather wished she had never let Troy, Ricky, and Nikki talk her into flying to Mombasa, Kenya, to board the boat, which Mark and DC had sailed down from Cannes, France. But Troy had promised her an endless supply of good coke and that had been enough. Once at Mombasa, Ricky and Troy had purchased a kilo of coke from a contact Troy knew and they had set sail for Karachi, Pakistan. There, Ricky had wheeled and dealed a half kilo of high-grade heroin from a dissipated, and very rich, fan of Poison Pig and stashed it aboard the boat. Then they had sailed around Cape Comorin at the southern tip of India and called in at Madras. But the Indian authorities had proved to be less than tolerant of the rich Americans and only a large and well-placed bribe had allowed them to escape with their cargo intact. Rather than retrace their steps, they had decided to sail into the South Pacific and consume their hoard of drugs in the idyllic solitude of a blue lagoon. Now they were becalmed in the Andaman Sea between India and Malaysia.

"Come on, Spencer," she urged, impatient at the long delay in his return. The corners of her lips pulled down and she smothered her irritation. Instead, Heather Courtland contrived ways to make Troy Spencer more attuned to her desires. It was a lesson she had learned from her father. "Dear old father," she said as a mental image of Senator William Douglas Courtland in a full rage played in front of her. Her soft lips pulled into a dark frown and she forced the image away. She never wanted to experience the reality of that rage again. Heather had learned discretion.

Her father had driven that lesson home to her from that very first time when she was eleven and later when she was a teenager. He had made it most clear that discretion was a key to survival, especially in the political jungle he prowled. Rebelling and determined to be free of him, Heather tried to do as she pleased. He had been most gentle and kind trying to persuade her to follow his rules. Unfortunately, she made the mistake of continuing to go against his wishes and ran headlong into the impenetrable wall of resistance her father built around her. Overnight, her privileges and pampered way of life started to disappear. The more she rebelled, the more things disappeared. Then she found herself in an all-girls school in Colorado that operated on the principle that good conduct had rewards of many kinds. Heather Courtland soon learned how to change her behavior to get what she wanted. Her education was complete.

Loud voices echoed up from the cabin and she could hear Mark Livingston's loud bellow. "Heather! Get your ass down here!"

"What now?" she mumbled as she pulled herself up.

Mark's wife, DC, short for Dana Claridge, was standing in the galley as she climbed down the ladder. "For God's sake,

Heather," DC snapped, "put something on." She threw Heather one of the T-shirts from Ricky and Nikki's band. Heather threw the shirt onto the settee and ignored DC. The hired help would not tell her what to do. She deliberately rubbed past Mark as she moved forward to where Troy and Nikki were standing. Heather admired Nikki because she was living proof that a girl could never be too skinny or too rich. Unlike Heather, Nikki Anderson was wearing clothes—the bottom of a bikini. Nikki's small breasts were firm and pointed. A fine gold chain was strung between the gold rings that pierced each nipple.

"I got this off Troy," Mark said, his voice low and full of anger. He was holding one of the plastic bags that contained three "bullets" and a vial of cocaine. "You are the stupidest collection of dumb shits I have ever met."

"Not your fuckin' worry," Ricky Martel said. He was sitting at the table eating the breakfast DC had cooked, seemingly unconcerned about Mark's anger. Ricky and Troy were mutual clones and both were highly ranked in the heavy-metal hierarchy with masses of teased hair, tattoos, and a hard-core drug habit. Like Troy, Ricky was skinny but his arms and legs were sticklike with no muscular development. The other noticeable difference was their hair. While Troy's was a natural blond, Ricky's was dyed jet black and had a hairpiece woven in to give it the fullness required by his rank.

Heather had never seen Mark Livingston so angry and she felt a tingle in the area below her navel as she watched the heavy chest muscles of the former football player from the University of Miami contract and expand. She liked Mark's well-conditioned body and her eyes dropped, studying his cutoff shorts. She wondered what he was like in bed.

"Look," Mark growled, now in control, "we're low on water, food, fuel, and just about everything else except this goddamn shit." He waved the plastic bag. "I told you we're going to Penang in Malaysia and you promised me the boat was clean."

"Like I said, dude," Ricky replied, "it's not your worry."

"I guarantee you it won't be after we reach Penang," DC said from the galley. Mark's wife was the image of the all-American college girl, athletic with an eye-catching figure, pretty face, and light brown hair pulled back into a pony tail.

"You thinkin' of jumping ship?" Troy asked.

"For-get-it," Ricky snarled. "No way I'll pay you. What you gonna do without bread in shit-ass Malaysia?" He had kept Mark and DC from leaving earlier by threatening not to pay them. He was confident the threat would work again.

"Watch," Mark said. He threw the plastic bag to DC, who threw it out the hatch and overboard.

"What the fuck you think you're doing?" Ricky roared. He and Troy ran up the ladder and dove overboard to save the bag. Heather and Nikki raced after them. Once the two couples were out of the cabin, Mark banged the hatch shut and dogged it down, sealing them in. "Hey, you assholes!" Troy yelled when he climbed back on board, "Open the fuckin' door."

"No way," Mark yelled back. "Come on," he told DC, "let's shake the boat down." They made sure the other hatches were secure and started a methodical search for the rest of the drugs.

DC found a small sealed plastic bag with white powder and threw it out a porthole. They heard a splash as someone dived in after it. "We'll have to scatter it," she said, pouring another bag of cocaine out of the same porthole. They went about their work with a vengeance and ignored the threats coming from the deck.

On deck, Heather kept looking from Troy to the first plastic bag he had saved from sinking. "Come on," she begged.

"Okay," he said and opened the bag. He fished out a "bullet," a small transparent plastic capsule about an inch long. It was shaped like a Mercury space capsule, big at one end and then tapering to a small neck at the top. Heather turned a valve on the side that released a charge of cocaine inside and sniffed sharply at the neck. Troy snatched the bullet out of her hand and dropped it back into the bag. Heather relaxed as the cocaine did its work.

Troy looked over the side and froze when he saw a cloud of white powder pour out of a porthole. "I'll kill those sons of bitches," he promised.

"What with?" Nikki asked as she touched his tattoo. She knew what the spider web meant—he had killed somebody, somewhere. The thought of seeing a murder thrilled her.

"Hey, man!" Ricky shouted. "Help's on the way." He pointed to the east. The smudge that Heather had first seen on the horizon had turned into a ramshackle wooden fishing boat that was bearing down on them. He moved over to the hatch and yelled, "We're gonna nail you assholes now. There's a boat coming our way." They moved aside as Mark opened the hatch and climbed out. Troy pushed past him and hurried down to his cabin. Heather followed him, now eager to get out of the hot sun.

DC climbed on deck and studied the boat. "What do you think?" she asked.

"Don't know," Mark answered. "They could be pirates." He walked aft to the steering post and flipped open the panel to the engine controls. He hit the ventilation fan switch to purge the engine compartment and bilge of any fumes.

"Pirates, my ass," Ricky said. "They hung the last pirates two hundred years ago."

"Wrongo," Mark replied. "There were some pretty gruesome stories about Thai pirates a few years back. They preyed on the Vietnamese boat people."

"Yeah, sure," Ricky said, interrupting him. He never read newspapers or listened to news on TV. His world was what he made it and he tuned out anything that had to do with reality.

"I remember that," DC said. "But didn't that happen off the coast of Vietnam?" She snatched up the binoculars hanging from the compass and studied the fishing boat. It looked like all the other Asian fishing boats they had seen.

"We're at least seven hundred miles from there and in a different sea," Mark told her. He took the binoculars from DC and studied the boat. "No need to take any chances. I'll start the auxiliary and we'll move out of their way." His fingers stabbed at the switches to start the small diesel engine that could push them at a speed of five knots. The engine coughed to life and he engaged the propeller.

"Why didn't you do that sooner?" Nikki asked. "We could have been to Penang by now."

"Because I was saving what fuel we had left for an emergency," Mark replied. "I never had a chance to refuel at Madras. Remember?"

"Because you can't do your fuckin' job," Ricky snarled.

"I do my job, you fuckin' hair farmer," he shot back, "when I'm not bribing the authorities to keep our asses out of jail and your boat from being confiscated."

Troy Spencer came rushing up the ladder out of the cabin. He had pulled on a pair of ripped jeans and was shaking with fury. Heather was right behind him, still naked. "You fuckin' assholes!" he shouted. "You dumped it all overboard!"

"Right," Mark shouted back. "You know what they do in Malaysia to drug smugglers?" He waited for an answer. There wasn't one. "They hang them."

"You believe that shit?" Troy spit at him. His hand reached

behind his back and he pulled a .357 Magnum out of his waist band.

"Yes," Nikki breathed. She was shaking with anticipation as Troy jabbed the muzzle of the handgun into Mark's midsection. She could feel the chain swinging between her breasts jiggle.

"You are one dead mutha—"

"The fishing boat!" DC shouted, creating a diversion. Troy glanced in the direction of the fishing boat and was surprised to see it so close. He blinked. But Mark had never taken his eyes off Troy and the distraction was enough to allow his hands to flash in a well-coordinated movement. Mark's right hand grabbed Troy's wrist, while with his left hand he swept the gun out of Troy's grasp in a cross-movement. Mark held the gun by its barrel and swung it back into the side of Troy's head. Then he dropped Troy's wrist and grabbed a hand full of hair and jerked. Troy simply obeyed one of the laws of physical anatomy and his body followed his head, which was down to the deck.

"The boat!" DC screamed, terror in her voice.

"Holy shit!" Ricky shouted. "One of 'em's got a gun." The fishing boat was bearing down on a collision course and they could see three men on the forward deck. They were short, dark, and wiry. All were stripped to the waist and wearing cloth headbands. One of them was holding a shotgun.

"DC," Mark shouted as he spun the wheel to break out of their path. "Get on the radio and send an SOS. Get 'em all below." A shot rang out from the fishing boat and a hole appeared in the flapping mainsail. Heather, Nikki, and Ricky disappeared down the ladder after DC. But Troy shook his head, still groggy from the blow, and crawled toward Mark who was crouched low in the cockpit well.

"We gotta do this together," he told Mark. "Gimme the gun, man." Unlike Ricky, Troy Spencer did not suffer from the same drug-induced mental burnout. He had deliberately turned his back on the wealthy and privileged world offered by his parents and sought out the dangerous, seamy side of life. There, he found a natural outlet for his violent nature. But he had learned his lessons well, and knew they were now fighting for their lives.

"No way," Mark growled. "You steer if you want to help." Troy nodded and took over the wheel. "You got more ammo for this?" Mark asked.

"In my cabin," Troy said. "Heather knows where it is."

Mark bobbed his head up to check on the fishing boat. It was getting closer. He scrambled forward and dropped down the companionway. DC was sitting at the radio. "I'm in contact with Thai customs authorities," she shouted.

"Stay in contact and tell them everything that's happening," Mark said. "Heather, get the extra bullets for the Magnum. And put something on." The girl nodded dumbly and went into her and Troy's stateroom. She came back out with a box of ammunition and wearing a T-shirt. Mark grabbed the shells and ran for the ladder. "Everyone stay below," he yelled, disappearing out the hatch.

"They're getting closer," Troy yelled at him. Mark chanced a quick look and dropped back onto the deck. Then he bobbed back up and emptied the .357's chamber at the fishing boat. A series of barked commands in a language they did not recognize were followed by two shotgun blasts. "They're getting closer!" Troy shouted.

Mark reloaded and fired. He gauged the fishing boat was less than fifty yards away. "Turn!" he shouted. Troy spun the wheel and the sailboat heeled over. But it gained them nothing as the fishing boat was slightly faster and could turn more sharply. The distance separating them was now less than twenty-five yards. Mark worked his way back to Troy and handed him the gun. "It looks like they're going to ram us," he said. "Fall off at the last moment and start shooting to keep their heads down. I'll try to push them off with a boat hook. Got it."

"Let's do it, man," Troy said. Mark worked his way forward and crawled along the protected side to the cabin to unlash the boat hook. Now they could hear a series of yelps from the fishing boat as it closed on them. Mark crawled back to the cockpit and waited.

"Here they come!" Troy shouted. The high bow of the fishing boat loomed over them. Troy spun the wheel and cut loose with a wild barrage. Splinters flew off the fishing boat as the shells tore into it. They could hear more shouting but didn't see anyone. Mark stood up to push the fishing boat away and the shotgun roared. Mark fell back into the cockpit, his face and chest a bloody, pulpy mass. Troy fumbled as he reloaded and a man jumped off the fishing boat and clubbed him to the deck.

Heather had heard the gunshots and shouting and had cowered in a tight ball on the cabin's settee. When the fishing boat crashed into them she had shut her eyes while Nikki and Ricky ran forward to hide in their stateroom. DC had stayed at the radio, still transmitting. Then a dark figure appeared over Heather, grabbed her hair and jerked her off the settee. Heather's anger momentarily flared as she struggled to her feet, glaring at the hard, wiry little man who was shorter than her. He slapped her hard across the face. Then a harder slap followed, knocking her back to the deck. Heather lay there, stunned. She had never been hit that hard, not even at the girls school in Colorado. Such pure physical violence was new in her life, something that only happened to other people or in the movies. The pirate's brown face split into a nasty grin, showing his yellowed, snaggled teeth. He barked commands in a language she had never heard before.

Another pirate pushed Ricky and Nikki into the cabin from their stateroom. Tears streamed down Nikki's face and she was shaking from fear. A third man had twisted DC's arm behind her and was holding her head down on the table in front of the radio. The men pushed the four Americans together onto the settee and exchanged a few words. It sounded like a babbling gibberish to Heather. She noticed that none of them had a gun but all were carrying wicked-looking knives. One man went back on deck while the remaining two jabbered at each other, ignoring them.

"What are they going to do to us?" Nikki asked, her voice barely audible and quaking.

"I don't know," DC answered, fear in every word, her hands shaking.

"Did they hurt Troy or Mark?" Heather asked. DC only gave her a worried look in reply. They heard laughter and a loud splash that sounded like someone falling overboard. Then more laughter echoed from outside and they could hear Troy shouting. Suddenly, he was propelled down the companionway, stripped naked. His face was blotched with red marks and his lower lip was bleeding. The two men followed him down.

"They killed Mark," he gasped. The three girls stared at him, fully understanding what the splash had been. The oldest of the pirates, who was plainly in charge, grabbed Ricky by his long hair, pulled him over to the dinette table and jammed his face down with a gnarled hand onto the hard surface. He held him there by the hair while he cut his clothes away with a knife. The three other men searched the boat.

"Are there only four?" Heather asked. She was bitterly aware that she was only wearing the flimsy T-shirt.

"Yeah," Troy said. The old man guarding them shouted something and slammed Ricky's head on the tabletop. He clearly wanted them to be silent.

Now the three men started to ransack the boat while the old man guarded them. Two men threw everything they could onto the deck while the third ripped out the radios, navigation equipment, and radar set. Their guard let go of Ricky but kept him bent over the table.

After what seemed an eternity, they were finished in the cabin and three men went up on deck. Then they heard a winch start to creak. It was twilight before the pirates had ripped out the yacht's auxiliary engine. Finally, they were finished and the three men came back down the companionway ladder and started eating as they talked. The old man gestured at Ricky, who was still bent over the table, and kicked his legs apart. With the blade of his knife, he scraped the open sores that were festering on the inside of Ricky's thighs. "What's the matter with Ricky's legs?" Heather whispered to Nikki. Nikki didn't answer. The pirates continued to discuss Ricky's sores. A decision made, they grabbed him, tied his hands behind his back and pushed him up on deck. The Americans could hear him being loaded onto the fishing boat. Then the men came back.

One of the younger men dropped his trousers and grabbed Troy's hair. He held a knife at his throat, bent him over the table in the same position as Ricky had been and hunched over him. "You bastard," Troy groaned. The man slammed his face down onto the table, hard, making his nose bleed. "I'll fuckin' kill you." Again, the man slammed Troy's face onto the table as he entered him.

The three girls tried to turn away, not wanting to watch the rape. But the other men kept slapping their faces, making them watch until it was over. Troy bucked when they tied his hands. Two men punched at his face until he quit struggling. They shoved him into a corner, laughing at his impotent rage.

The old man's right hand flashed out and ripped the T-shirt off Heather. He grabbed her by the hair and bent her over the table. "Do you know who I am?" Heather shouted. The men laughed as the old man shed his pants. "My father is a United States senator!" There was no sign that they understood a word she said. "Senator William Douglas Courtland!" she shouted. Again, no sign of comprehension. And then in a low, pleading moan, "He's going to be President of the United States."

The old man paused. "I speak English." He grinned at the

other men and buried a hand in her hair, holding her over the table, while his other hand stroked her bare back. Then he felt lower and spread the cheeks of her rear end. He barked in amazement when he saw Heather's tattoo and called the other men over to examine it. They were fascinated by the small snake that had been tattooed on the inside of her cheeks, coiled around her anus. The old man raped her while Troy, Nikki, and DC were dragged to the forward staterooms. Heather clenched the far edge of the table, making herself endure the violation. She forced herself to think about surviving and tried to shut out the sounds of the other three being raped. I know how to survive, she kept repeating to herself. I know how to survive. . . .

Tears streamed down her face. Then the men switched.

An hour later, the three girls and Troy were thrown naked into the fishing boat next to Ricky. They watched as the beautiful sloop was torched, a beacon lighting the night. A small plane flew over and circled before heading back to land. One of the pirates started the engine and pointed the fishing boat in the same direction.

ONE

The White House, Washington, D.C.

It was the woman's first solo shift as the night duty officer in the Office of the President and the communications section had hummed with its normal nighttime routine, lulling her into a sense of complacency. The phone call from her counterpart in the State Department had jolted her fully awake. "Sally," the veteran bureaucrat said, his voice coming through scratchy on the secure line, "a hot one just came in. The Bangkok embassy reports that Senator Courtland's daughter has been kidnapped."

The woman's fingers flew over the computer keyboard at her desk as she recorded the details of the phone call for future correlation and reference. When the caller had hung up, she replayed the tape, making sure she had all the details correct. Then she told a technician to transcribe the tape immediately into hard copy. Her lips compressed into a narrow line as she stared at the clock: 3:32 A.M. Then she made her decision—they should wake the President of the United States with the news. But she first had to check with her boss, the President's chief of staff. Leo Cox answered his phone on the second ring, listened without comment and gave her the okay. Her hand was steady when she jabbed at the buttons on her communications panel to call the President's valet.

Matthew Zachary Pontowski opened the door that led to the small office off the President's bedroom and walked in. A simple dark blue robe covered his lanky six feet and he was carrying his glasses. His blue eyes were clear and his full head of silver-gray hair was only slightly ruffled. As usual, he walked with a slight hunch to his shoulders and a definite limp, a legacy from World War II. His prominent, aquiline nose reminded the woman of a hawk but his face was not harsh. The laugh lines at the corners of his eyes promised warmth and understanding. He looked and acted ten years younger than seventy-six years of age.

"Well, Sally," he began. "Charles says you have something important."

She could hear friendliness in his voice and relaxed. "Yes, sir, I think so." She handed him a transcript of the phone call from the State Department. He sat down at his desk and adjusted his glasses. Zack Pontowski could read at over twelve hundred words a minute, faster than a person could talk. He preferred to read and to ask questions later. It was a well-established routine in the White House.

"Charles," he said through the still-open door, "would you please get some coffee." He reread the transcript and thought about the young woman still standing in front of him. "Please sit down," he told her, motioning to a comfortable armchair next to him. "What do you think Leo will say when he learns you woke me up so early?" He glanced at a small carriage clock on the desk. Leo Cox, a former general in the United States Air Force, ran a relaxed but well-controlled office for the President.

"He's already said it, Mr. President. I called him before I called Charles to wake you. General Cox should be here in fifteen minutes." On cue, Charles walked in with a fresh pot of coffee.

"Was he the only other person you woke?"

"Yes, sir," she answered, now certain she had done the right thing. The gentle warmth in his voice was very reassuring.

Pontowski smiled, pleased with her. Cox does pick the right people, he thought. She keyed on the political sensitivity of this immediately and wasn't afraid to get the ball rolling. How much further can she carry it? "What do you recommend I should do first?" he asked, his voice serious.

"Make a personal phone call to Senator Courtland with the

news," she answered immediately, "and arrange a meeting with him at the first opportunity."

Pontowski picked up the phone and spoke to the operator. "Please put me in contact with Senator Courtland immediately." He hung up. "How do you think the good senator will respond?" he asked.

"He'll try to crucify you with it, sir."

William Douglas Courtland stretched an arm over the sleeping girl to pick up the telephone. The first insistent ring had woken him and he was fully alert. "Yes," he said, not letting the touch of hostility he felt at being disturbed show in his voice. "Of course, I'll take the call."

The girl stirred as he sat upright and pulled the covers away. "Oh...what...?" she mumbled. The dewiness of sleep gave her the look of a twelve-year-old nymph.

Courtland placed a hand over the mouthpiece of the receiver. "It's Pontowski," he told her. "I need to take this in private." She nodded and slipped out of bed. He smiled at her as she disappeared naked into the bathroom. She's younger-looking than most of them, he thought, but a hell of a lot smarter. "Yes, Mr. President," he said, his voice now smooth and rich. He listened silently, making the appropriate responses. Then: "Yes, thank you for calling and I'll be there." He hung up and sank into the pillows.

"Can you make some coffee?" he called.

"Coming right up," the girl answered and appeared in the bathroom's doorway, still not dressed. "Trouble?"

Courtland grunted an answer and watched her walk across the room, dragging a towel. She is beautiful, he thought, and the same age as Heather. He worked through the contradictory emotions he felt for his daughter. Heather in trouble again, this time serious. Goddamn! Why couldn't she stay low-profile? Out of trouble. And who in the hell has kidnapped her? I never did think much of her going on that trip anyway, not that telling her would have made a difference. Probably just made her more determined to do it.

The senator thumbed through his small black notebook, finding the telephone number he wanted. He quickly dialed the number, calling Troy Spencer's parents. "Hello, Keenan? Bill Courtland here. I'm afraid our kids are in some trouble." He went smoothly through the motions of telling the Spencers what he knew about the kidnapping and reassuring them that everything possible was being done. "I've already contacted the President and he's agreed to see me first thing," he told them. "Yes, I'm quite sure he will be responsive to this. I'll make sure of that. I'll call you right after I see him."

Courtland hung up and smiled when he thought what a good political ally the Spencers would be in his ongoing battle with Pontowski. I'm going to get you, you dumb Polack son of a bitch. It was an old promise that burned deep inside of him and one that he had been making to himself for years. "Coffee yet?" he called.

"Not quite ready," the girl answered and walked back into the bedroom. "You want something else first?" she smiled and held up one of her small and immature breasts for his inspection. He threw the covers back for her, momentarily forgetting about his troublesome daughter.

The Malaysian Jungle

Mackay crouched motionless in the underbrush, his legs aching. Insects buzzed around his head and he fought down the urge to slap at them. Out of the question, he reasoned. Any unusual noise in the jungle would be a dead giveaway, blowing the ambush. Sweat poured down his face and for a moment, he wondered if his ancestors in Africa had had to cope with the same problem. Probably not, he decided; they had to be smarter than me. He concentrated on watching the spot where Carlin, the sergeant carrying the Racal SatCom, satellite communications radio, had disappeared. He moved his muscular six-foot-four-inch frame into a more comfortable position. His foot made a soft squishing sound in the wet earth as he shifted.

The foliage in front of him moved and Sergeant Carlin's face appeared, his eyes hard and full of reproach. The grim set of his lips told Mackay that his movement had been heard. How can those British bastards move so quietly? he wondered. He knew the answer. Practice. Now they had to wait.

Lieutenant Colonel John Author Mackay, United States Army, forced his restless mind to split and work in two modes. One part of his mind would work on the training problem at hand, the laying of an ambush deep in the jungles of Malaysia, while another part would roam elsewhere. Between the mental gymnastics, he could forget about the insects buzzing around him. Remember to check for leeches the first chance you get, he added to his checklist of things to be accomplished. Mackay had a very well-organized and disciplined mind. Much like his body.

At thirty-seven years of age, Mackay was still a young lieutenant colonel. He knew there was little chance of his being promoted to colonel in the near future, at least not in the peacetime army. He suspected that he would eventually be promoted and that it was just a matter of time. He had been told many times that he was an outstanding officer with unlimited potential. Never mind that as a lieutenant he had chalked it all up to his being black and a patronizing attitude by the white establishment in the U.S. Army.

But when a white colonel with a deep southern accent drove home a series of lessons to Mackay, he realized what the Army was telling him was true. The colonel didn't care about the color of Mackay's skin as long as he could do the job better than anyone else. A good thing that, Mackay often thought, considering the fact that I'm so damn ugly. The harsh reality was that his high forehead, jug-handle ears, misshapen nose, receding chin, and bad case of pseudofolliculitis barbae terrified children on sight. Smiling only made the overall effect worse.

To compensate for his harsh scarred looks, Mackay had taken to sports as a teenager and learned that along with his large size, he was extremely well-coordinated. And much more important, he had discovered that he was smart. It had come as a shock when he realized he could outthink his teachers and all the bloods who terrorized his high school. When a cousin had come home on leave from the Army, Mackay had listened to him and seen a way to escape from his home in Washington's black ghetto. He had immediately transferred to another high school, worked on his grades, and excelled in sports. During the eleventh grade he had applied to the military academy at West Point and was accepted during his senior year.

West Point had opened up a new world to Mackay and he thrived on the competition and challenges. He graduated number two in his class. The newly commissioned infantry second lieutenant was five years too late for Vietnam and went through a series of assignments as the U.S. Army rebuilt, trying to recover from the damages it had suffered in the Far East while re-forming into an all-volunteer service. Mackay had played a small role in that transformation as he pursued a career centering on the infantry, Rangers, and Special Forces—the Green Berets. The war in the Persian Gulf had almost passed him by and he was lucky to have gotten in on one small operation. It amused him that his only contribution in that war had been to accept the surrender of twelve hundred Iraqis who acted as if he were their savior.

His current assignment as an exchange officer with the British Special Air Service regiment, the SAS, was a logical step in his career. But he had not been prepared for the reality of the SAS. His first lesson had to do with military dress and courtesies. The "Sass" as the SAS called itself, had little time, or respect, for the conventions of normal military units and was totally committed to battle discipline. They demonstrated that while he passed through the four-week selection course that all volunteers underwent before being chosen for SAS training. One man drowned during a swimming exercise and most dropped out before the halfway point. Only three men emerged at the end of the four weeks and Mackay was one of them. After that, he wore the regiment's beige beret and winged-dagger badge with pride. As he trained with the SAS, he came to appreciate their motto, Who dares wins. And he learned what was important.

A slight movement in the jungle foliage off to his right side brought the two halves of Mackay's mind together and he tensed, ready for action. Captain Peter Woodward stepped into the clearing and motioned his patrol forward, abandoning the ambush site. Silently, six men emerged from the underbrush and shadows. Woodward glanced at Mackay and motioned him to fall in as number three, an indication that he was being punished for his clumsy noise. It could be worse, Mackay thought. Woodward had thrown one man fully clothed and equipped into a stream when the trooper had made too much noise during a river crossing. The line of eight men disappeared into the jungle, making their way westward along the Thai-Malay border.

That evening, the patrol made camp. No fires were lit and they ate a cold meal. The blocklike shape of Woodward emerged out of the shadows and hunkered down beside Mackay. As usual, the thirty-three-year-old British captain was all business. "Not bad out there today," he said. "Other than your mucking around behind that tree." He cracked a smile. "I suppose all that brawn and muscle you carry around is an inconvenience at times." Mackay didn't respond. His entire body ached and he wondered how many others were feeling as tired as he was. "We did make good time today," Woodward said. It was as close to a compliment as the Englishman would come. "Interesting message came in on the SatCom," Woodward continued, getting to the reason for the one-sided conversation. "We may have to send you back."

"Why?" was all Mackay asked. He knew it had nothing to do with his performance on this training exercise. He was holding his own.

"There might be some trouble in front of us." Woodward looked at Mackay. "A small group of terrorists, really nothing but a bunch of thieves and murderers left over from the MRLA, is operating in the area. We've been asked to drop in on them."

Mackay grunted, thinking about what Woodward had said. The MRLA, or Malayan Races Liberation Army, had not been heard from since the early 1980s. Something was up. "Cut out the crap," Mackay said. Woodward only looked at him. "Was this ever meant to be a training exercise?" He didn't wait for an answer. "I've come this far. I'll go the rest of the way."

Woodward nodded. "Get some rest. We've got a long way to go tomorrow."

The American lieutenant colonel was up and ready to move out before the first trooper stirred the next morning. Woodward was surprised to see him sitting against a tree, his Heckler and Koch MP5 submachine gun resting in his lap. The MP5 was the personal weapon of choice in the Sass. "Bloody hell," Woodward mumbled, impressed underneath his hard exterior. "I suppose you want to lead?"

"Rangers lead the way," Mackay said, his face impassive. "Now what's going down."

Woodward rolled out of his hammock. "Realistic training." Mackay waited for the captain to continue as the men went about the routine of breaking camp. The SAS was divided into four Sabre squadrons and Woodward's specialized in cross-country mobility and long-range patrols, which was also Mackay's specialty. "The Sass has an informal arrangement with the Malaysian government to train in their jungle," Woodward said. "If we should 'happen' to stumble on any suspicious characters, well, we can also train on them. All left over from the Emergency in the 1950s."

Mackay suspected that the Englishman was glossing over a security agreement the Malaysians had with their former colonial ruler. It was the way the Brits worked, he thought. He regretted that the United States didn't train the same way for he had some definite ideas about what the Rangers or Special Forces could do in the Philippines or Latin America. "And according to the

SatCom," Mackay said, "there are some 'suspicious characters' out there."

"Apparently," Woodward allowed. He opened a meal pack and started to eat. The patrol was almost ready to move out. "Some fishermen," the captain explained, "who fancy themselves pirates in their spare moments, captured an American yacht. The crew got a message out and a Thai customs plane overflew them. The bastards took six Americans hostage, burnt the yacht and are heading toward the coast. They should land not too far from us." He dug out a map. "Probably here." He pointed to an abandoned Gurkha camp that the British had used during the Emergency in the 1950s. Mackay noticed that an airstrip was next to the camp.

Mackay asked, "When do they make landfall and how far?"

"This afternoon. Eight miles away," Woodward answered.

"I suppose calling for a helicopter for insertion is out of the question."

The captain grinned. "This is a training exercise." It was his way of telling Mackay that they were strictly on their own and could not ask for such obvious support.

The lieutenant colonel stood up and looked around. There was enough light to travel. One of the first lessons he had learned was that it was too dangerous to move at night in a jungle. Better to rest and travel more rapidly during daylight. He punched at the buttons on the hand-held Magellan NAV1000M he carried to fix their position. The Magellan was a monitor that linked them into the Global Positioning System, or GPS. It weighed less than a pound and could fix their position to within twenty-five meters, eighty-one feet, anywhere in the world. It took all the guesswork out of navigating through the jungle and no one had an excuse for getting lost. Mackay oriented his map and took a compass bearing. "I'll lead," he said, putting the map away. "Have Carlin follow with the SatCom. We've got to move fast."

Both men knew that eight miles was a long trek through a jungle. "Wish we knew what the bloody clock was," Woodward grumbled. The SAS ran every exercise or operation on a precise time schedule and trained to "beat the clock." It was part of their formula for success.

The long range-patrol fell to and moved out, leaving no trace of where they had spent the night.

For the first few miles they moved fast because the jungle floor was relatively free of underbrush and open under the shade of the rain forest. Mackay hunched forward under the weight of his ninety-five-pound pack and set a relentless pace. Again, he split his attention. But this time, one part of his restless mind concentrated on land navigation while the other evaluated the situation and planned ahead.

What's the threat? he asked himself. Their eight versus a small number of fishermen. Bound to be more, he thought. Why was the boat heading for the old Gurkha camp? Was it the closest landfall or was it because of the airstrip? Has Woodward told me everything? Probably not. What was the best course of action? Get the patrol there with time to reconnoiter and plan an attack. The attack would be Woodward's responsibility. Would Woodward let him be part of it? Probably not. We'll see about that, Mackay thought. He increased the pace.

A nagging question kept hovering over him, refusing to go away. Why wasn't the Malaysian or Thai government responding? They certainly had plenty of time to move a police detachment or a conventional military unit into place. He didn't like the answer—they didn't want to get involved.

No longer did the patrol stop to practice the immediate action drills that had been a constant part of their routine. They just slogged on. Sweat streamed down Mackay's face and his back ached from carrying his heavy pack. He ignored the pain. Every fifty-five minutes, he would break and take a five-minute rest before resuming the march, not wasting a second more.

They had covered over six miles, fortunate to be able to follow jungle ridges and ravines rather than having to cross them, before they hit the coastal swamp. "Can we break, sir?" Carlin, the SatCom operator asked, fatigue and respect in his voice. Mackay halted and the men moved into cover.

Woodward came up and checked their position on the Magellan GPS monitor with Carlin. "Good navigation," he said. Carlin told the captain that Mackay had only double-checked their position once during the trek. Woodward lifted an eyebrow. "I'll be damned," he allowed, beckoning Mackay over. The two men hunched over a map, plotting a way through the swamp. "A mile and a half, direct," Woodward said.

"We can make faster time by making an end run around the swamp and coming down from the north," Mackay said, tracing a route on the map. For the next few minutes they discussed the tactical problem in front of them. Finally, it was decided to split their small force. Mackay would lead one team to the north and move into a blocking position on the coast while Woodward would penetrate the swamp, following what looked like a low ridgeline.

When Woodward asked the men who would like to go with Mackay, Carlin said that he would go just to see if Mackay could maintain the same pace, which he doubted. Each of the other men responded in the same vein and Mackay knew that he had been accepted as one of them without reservation. There would be no question about his taking part in the action. A look crossed Mackay's face that none of them recognized. "My God," Woodward muttered, "I hope that's a smile." It was.

Mackay continued the punishing pace when he led out the three men. The route Mackay had picked led them across a series of gentle hummocks and through shallow streams and pools and they made good time as they skirted the swamp. They reached the coast and moved down onto the northern side of the Gurkha camp, arriving thirty minutes ahead of the scheduled time Woodward had set for them. Mackay sent two of his team, John and Trevor, forward to scout while Carlin contacted Woodward on the small hand-held radio each member of the patrol carried.

The reply was not reassuring; Woodward could not penetrate the swamp and had retraced his steps. He was following Mackay's route and was at least two hours behind him. "This one's yours," he told the American, "until we join you."

An hour later, John, the younger of the two men Mackay had sent forward, came back. The twenty-two-year-old man had been hardened in the rough and impoverished working-class section of Manchester and then found a home in the SAS. His youthful looks gave no indication that he was a deadly, professional killer. "The place is crawling with little brown buggers," John told them. "All armed . . . mostly AK-Forty-sevens. . . . Two of them have Uzis. One boat at the dock—not a fishing boat. I counted seven down there and six more at the airstrip. Looks like they're expecting someone to drop in for a visit. Trevor's working his way around to the southern side. Should be there by now." Mackay did not approve of a man operating alone but made no comment.

John drew a map of the compound on the back of Carlin's map and they discussed possible ways to enter the camp. Mackay was hoping Woodward would catch up with them before the fishing boat arrived. His personal radio crackled and the fourth member of their team, Trevor, checked in. The southern side of the camp was deserted and his head count agreed with John's. Mackay was fairly certain that there were thirteen men in the camp. "I hope they're only carrying small arms and nothing big."

"If they've got anything else," Carlin said, "it's probably on the boat. We'll have to neutralize it first." They all knew what he meant. "Trevor's got his Hilton."

Mackay grunted. The Hilton was a multipurpose single-shot gun that could quickly convert from an extremely accurate twelve-gauge shell to a forty-millimeter grenade launcher. Trevor had a particular fondness for the weapon because it was light, rugged, and multipurpose. Since the men carried everything on their backs while on patrol, it was the logical choice over weapons like the much heavier Hawk multiple-round grenade launcher. Mackay had seen how Trevor could lob ten rounds a minute at maximum range with extreme accuracy and provide fire support much like that of a small mortar. "Find out if he's in range of the dock," Mackay said. Carlin keyed the radio and relayed the question.

"Four hundred meters," came the answer.

Mackay thought for a moment. That was the maximum range for the Hilton. Could Trevor do it from his present location? He knew the answer. The SAS trooper would have told them if he was out of range. Mackay admonished himself to keep up with his men. "Your recommendations," he said.

"Wait for the captain," Carlin said. "If it goes down before he gets here, neutralize the boats and anything on the airstrip. Then withdraw." John nodded in agreement. "They won't be going anyplace and we go in at night." Again, John agreed.

The radio came alive and Trevor told them he could see an approaching boat and that he was moving closer to the dock. John moved down to the water's edge and scanned the horizon with his binoculars. Then they heard the drone of an approaching aircraft. "Good timing," Mackay said, now fully aware that he was confronting a well-organized group and that caution was called for. John reported back that the approaching vessel was the fishing boat. Things were moving fast.

"Okay," the lieutenant colonel said, his decision made. "Here's the drill. The idea is to trap our 'freedom fighters' here with the hostages in the camp. I'm betting they'll move the Americans from the fishing boat to the airstrip the moment they dock. You"—he pointed at Carlin—"stay here and act as Trevor's spotter. You call in fire when the prisoners are clear of the dock and moving. Destroy the boats and then you withdraw to here." He pointed to a place on the map. "Rendezvous with Woodward and bring him up to date. Trevor retreats into the swamp.

"John and me will cover the airstrip. We key on your barrage, nail the plane, or make sure it can't land. We move on and join up with Trevor. Now we've got two teams flanking the camp and they ain't going anywhere. We pick it up from there and go in at night. Right now it's a containment action only." The two Englishmen listened to Mackay's plan and did not argue. Mackay and John disappeared into the brush as the fishing boat came around the headland and sailed toward the dock.

John moved fast, leading Mackay to the airstrip. They could hear the circling airplane but couldn't see it yet. "Twin-engine," John said, his voice low but not a whisper. His head jerked up. The airstrip was deserted. He looked at Mackay.

"They don't need it," Mackay said, reaching for his radio. "Carlin, what's happening?" he transmitted.

"Bloody fucking seaplane," came the answer. "The boat's at the dock but they haven't moved the Americans. The plane's circling to land in the bay."

"Can you make them abandon the boats?" Mackay asked.

Trevor answered, "Can do." They heard the muffled pop of what sounded like a shotgun followed by an explosion. Mackay and John retraced their steps, taking care to stay in the underbrush, hearing more explosions from the dock.

Carlin spoke quietly into his radio, directing Trevor's fire. The first round was far out to sea. He moved the second one in closer to the boats as if he was getting the range. The third one was closer still. The men on the dock got the idea and started shouting. Carlin told Trevor to halt the barrage as he watched the men drag the Americans out of the fishing boat. His lips compressed into a grim line when he saw the three girls and two young men, all naked, being pushed onto the dock. The blond-haired male pushed and shoved back at the small dark man behind him. "You fuckin' bastard!" the American yelled, his voice reaching across the clearing. The guard jabbed the butt of his shotgun into the American's back and sent him sprawling on the dock. A swift kick drove him to his feet and hurried him after the others. Carlin focused his binoculars on the girls and could see blood on the inner thighs of one.

"Are the hostages clear of the boat?" Mackay asked as he rejoined Carlin.

"There's only five, not six," the radio operator answered. "The boats look completely abandoned. I think that's all of them."

Mackay nodded. "Tell Trevor to hit the boats," he said. Carlin relayed the order and the fantail of the fishing boat disappeared in the bright flash of an explosion. The three men watched in satisfaction as the lone trooper on the south side of the camp poured six more rounds into the boats and dock, setting all on fire. "Cease fire," Carlin said and the barrage stopped.

"Tell Trevor to beat feet into the swamp," Mackay ordered. "They'll probably go looking for him."

A wicked grin split John's youthful face. "That would be a terrible mistake," he said. He pulled a telescopic sight out of his pack and fitted it to the 7.62-millimeter Enfield sniper rifle he carried. "Sir," he said, pointing to the seaplane that had landed but was motionless in the water, not moving shoreward.

"Discourage him," Mackay said.

"And be good about it," Woodward's voice said from behind them. Mackay twisted around, glad to see the captain but worried that he had found them so easily. He had thought they were better concealed than that. Woodward sank to the ground, his face haggard from exhaustion. "Homing device on the Magellan," he explained. "Good to within a few meters." He motioned for the rest of his team to come in.

Mackay watched in amazement as the three men staggered in. They were exhausted from the forced march. But he could tell from the looks on their faces that they would be ready to fight after a few minutes' rest. What kind of men are these? the American thought. He calculated that Woodward had moved around the edge of the swamp twice as fast as he had.

"You Yanks don't have a monopoly on marching," Woodward said, "when the bloody clock is ticking." The pleasantries over, he turned to business. "John, go." He pointed to the seaplane. The young trooper did not move. "Cover him," the captain said. Carlin and one of the exhausted men stood up and followed John into the underbrush. "He's the best sniper we have," Woodward said.

A few minutes later, they heard the crack of the rifle. Mackay studied the seaplane through binoculars as it moved farther offshore and then halted. The rifle cracked again from a different location. John was moving between shots. This time the seaplane did not move. "He's probably out of range," Mackay said. Again, the rifle sounded and the plane moved farther offshore. Mackay nodded his head in approval at John's marksmanship.

"Trouble," Woodward said. "They've got an inflatable." Mackay joined the captain and focused his binoculars onto the five Americans. They were dragging an inflatable motorboat with an outboard motor from between two buildings down to the water, obeying shouted orders coming from the buildings. Two of the girls lay down on the rubber pontoons, shielding it with their bodies while the other girl and two boys hurried back to the building. Now they came back out forming a human shield for two of the men off the fishing boat. One was an old man and both were carrying Uzis. "Damn," Woodward said. "Get John back here."

"Not too much we can do," Mackay said, bitterness in every word, a coppery taste in his mouth. He watched in frustration as the two armed men lay in the bottom of the boat and made the five Americans launch them into the water. Then the five sat on the pontoons as the motor started and the boat moved toward the seaplane.

John rejoined them and sighted the boat through his telescopic lens. His youthful face was calm and innocent as he studied the boat. A man's head appeared above the pontoons at the bow, guiding on the seaplane. John squeezed off a shot and the top of the man's head disappeared in a bloody mist. The expression on John's face was unchanged. "Got one, sir," he said.

A hand reached up out of the boat and grabbed the blond hair of one of the girls and dragged her head down to the muzzle of an Uzi. For a moment, the men froze, certain they were about to witness an execution. "Hold your fire," Woodward said. The girl's head did not move as the boat approached the plane.

"Shit!" Mackay said. The rare outburst surprised him; he had not used profanity since he was a teenager. It didn't help. They watched in silence as the boat bumped against the seaplane and the five Americans were pulled into the rear hatch. They were followed by the old man lying in the bottom of the boat. The seaplane turned into the wind and they heard the engines run up as it started a takeoff run. Finally, it lifted clear of the water and curved out to sea, heading north.

Woodward motioned for them to move out and the patrol shifted its position away from the camp.

Thirty minutes later, Trevor rejoined them. "Thirteen left in camp," he said holding up two fingers, indicating he had taken out two men who had been trying to hunt him down. Mackay wondered who had been doing the hunting.

A hard look crossed Woodward's face. "I don't think they'll be going anywhere, do you?" It wasn't a question. "I would like to know who they are. Should we drop in on them tonight for a chat?" It also was not a question or open to discussion.

"They are being very cautious," Woodward said. "Look at the way they still maintain cover." It was night and he was studying the camp with one of the two Pocketscope passive viewers the patrol carried. The fat, four-inch-long night vision scope weighed less than two pounds and could be fitted onto the MP5s they carried as a sight. Woodward handed the scope to Mackay.

Mackay said nothing and focused the scope on the old Gurkha camp. A greenish figure materialized out of the heavy undergrowth and moved toward them. Mackay handed the scope back to Woodward, pointed out the figure and moved away from the captain, drawing his knife. The figure could be either Trevor or John returning from planting surveillance microphones on the outside walls of the buildings. The small, but very sensitive mikes could pick up movement and voices from inside the buildings and were invaluable for pinpointing the opposition.

"Blackpool," Mackay whispered from under cover. It was the challenge part of the recognition code.

"Rock," Trevor responded, completing the code. He emerged out of the dark. "They're pretty good," the young SAS trooper said, telling Mackay and Woodward what he had learned. "Trained by Cubans, I'd say." They paused when movement in the underbrush caught their attention. Mackay whispered the recognition code and John joined them.

"Count?" Woodward asked.

"I still count thirteen," Trevor answered.

"Twelve," John said. "One stumbled into me." He made a cutting motion with his hand. "They won't find him until it's light."

"Are the mikes picking up anything?" Woodward asked, staring into the night.

Carlin cupped his hands over his earphones, trying to identify the different voices coming through on his headset. "I've got eight identified in the old headquarters building." He paused, concentrating. "Chinese. Two of 'em are speaking Chinese." He handed the headset to Woodward who had studied both Mandarin and Thai. Each member of the patrol had studied at least two foreign languages and Mackay alone spoke only English.

"Mandarin," Woodward said, identifying the language. He listened intently. "They know we are out here and have posted five men outside as guards. Hold on, one came back in. He says it's quiet." Again, Woodward paused. "They think we may have left."

Woodward moved the headset clear of his ears. "Here's the drill. Three of 'em are unaccounted for, presumably on guard duty outside. We send three pairs in to take them out." He called in the first two men and told them to search the southern side of the compound for sentries. "For God's sake," he warned them, "don't stray outside your area. The other chaps will be out looking and I don't need you 'practicing' on each other in the dark." The two men moved out and Woodward called in another pair. He outlined their area and sent them off with the same warning.

Finally, he called Carlin and John over to him. "You sweep the area on this side of the camp," he told them.

"Let me take this one," Mackay said. "Keep Carlin here on the radios with you." Woodward thought about it for a moment then nodded. Mackay and the baby-faced sniper, John, disappeared into the night.

The two men moved silently through the underbrush until they were against the back of a building. Mackay could barely see John's silhouette in the dark. With deliberate and slow motions, John pointed at Mackay and then pointed at a spot in the dark, the forefinger of his right hand extended and his thumb pointed down—the hand sign for 'enemy.' Mackay understood that John was telling him to take the man out.

Mackay slung his MP5 submachine gun onto his back and drew his knife. He crouched and moved toward the spot John had pointed at. When he reached the spot, he gently moved some heavy foliage aside with his left hand and found himself staring into the face of a man. For a split second, both were too surprised to move and they looked at each other for what seemed an eternity. Without thinking, Mackay's right hand slashed out, rattlesnake quick, driving the point of his knife into the man's throat. He felt cartilage surrounding the trachea give and he jerked the blade sideways. The man collapsed to the ground and Mackay jerked his knife free.

The harsh, gurgling, rasping sounds of the dying man trying to breathe filled the night but Mackay could only stand there, unable to move. He had seen corpses before, but this was the first time he had to watch a man die because of his action. He sucked in his breath and stared at his handiwork, a coppery taste in his mouth. His stomach twisted and he could feel his own throat move and his gorge rise.

John materialized out of the darkness and dropped beside the dying man. He grabbed the man's hair and twisted, shoving his face into the soft ground, burying the gurgling sounds. "Noisy bugger," the young SAS trooper said. "Sounds just like a busy coffee pot." He looked up at Mackay, still holding the man's face down. "First time?" Mackay nodded. "You are fuckin' quick." There was respect in his voice. "Next time muffle him, though." The man twitched and then lay still. John slowly moved his hand away and searched the body, handing Mackay a small radio, much like the ones they carried. He rolled the corpse into the under-brush and stood up. "Press on," he said and pointed to the building.

Twelve minutes later, Mackay and John had completed their sweep and were back with Woodward. The other two teams had returned, each reporting a kill. "Nine inside," Woodward said, "and all accounted for." He then detailed how they would take the building and assigned specific tasks and timing to each man. "You stay with me," he told Mackay. This time, he got no argument. "It's on," he said, "for God's sake, I want at least two of the bastards alive. The clock's running. Go."

Mackay watched the six men disappear and tried to split his attention, falling into his waiting routine. But this time it didn't work and the face of the man he had killed, his eyes filled with surprise, kept breaking in, demanding the lieutenant colonel's attention. "It will pass," Woodward said, reading his thoughts. "It was you or him out there. Better him." The British captain understood.

The sound of breaking glass followed by the sharp explosions of four stun grenades shattered the stillness. Woodward was counting aloud, "And one and two and . . . " The crack of breaking wood and the rattle of submachine gun fire echoed across the camp. Then silence. Two more shots, this time from a pistol. "That's it," Woodward said as he checked his watch. "Did it by the clock." His words were matter-of-fact but Mackay could hear satisfaction and the pride of a professional soldier when things are done right. The radio crackled and Carlin's voice told them to come in. They had taken three prisoners.

Once inside the building, Woodward surprised Mackay by barking out a series of orders while his men jumped about like puppets driven by fear. A back room was cleared and Mackay watched as Carlin placed two of the small microphones, bugging it. Then the three bound prisoners were pushed inside and the door slammed. Woodward nodded at his men and Mackay realized it was all an act to establish Woodward as a leader deeply feared by his own men. The men cleared the dead out of the room while Woodward listened on the headset, monitoring the three prisoners.

"I've got it," Woodward told them. "The one closest to the door is the leader." He stood up and walked to the door, motioning for Mackay to follow him. "Smile at the bastard I'm talking to." He slammed into the room and walked to the man at the far end. He snapped out a series of questions in Chinese, asking for detailed information on where the Americans had been taken and who was behind the kidnapping. Mackay put on what he hoped was a sincere smile. The man being interrogated couldn't take his eyes off Mackay's face and he shook with fright. Woodward was getting the reaction he wanted. Then the frightened man glanced at the group's leader who glared back at him. The man started pleading that he didn't know. Woodward drew his pistol and shot him in the head, splattering brains and blood over the other two prisoners.

"And just how bloody thick are you?" he yelled at the next man in English. Mackay, shocked by the brutal execution, forgot to smile. It wasn't necessary. The man was blabbering, his eyes darting between Woodward and Mackay. The group's leader shouted something in Chinese and the man hesitated for a second. Woodward drew his pistol and the man couldn't talk fast enough as he kept repeating a name.

Woodward turned to the leader and said in English, "Where did they take the Americans?" The man challenged him with a hard look and Woodward repeated the question. "I know you speak English," Woodward said, his voice now soft and cajoling.

The man snarled his answer. "Ask General Chiang Tse-kuan when you beg for your life." He spit in the British captain's face. Woodward casually raised his pistol and shot him in the head.

"What in the hell are you doing?" Mackay shouted. The numbness of the emotional shock that had bound him was wearing off and he was returning to reality.

"Smile at the bastard," Woodward said, ignoring the outburst and pointing at the one man still alive. Mackay did as he was told and Woodward repeated his last question, demanding to know where the Americans had been taken. A torrent of words gushed from the man, but he was obviously repeating himself. "That's all we're going to get," the British captain said. Then he shot him in the head.

"You're a fucking butcher!" Mackay yelled.

"Really?" Woodward answered. "You have no idea, do you?" He walked out of the room and told Carlin to call in a helicopter to airlift them out. "We've got to get out of here tonight." Then he turned to Mackay. "Do you know who General Chiang Tse-kuan is? This changes everything."

Mackay was speechless. Moments ago this man had summarily executed three men and he was now acting like a perfectly sane and rational teacher explaining a difficult problem to a student. Mackay shouldered past him and stomped out of the building, into the night.

The White House, Washington, D.C.

General Leo Cox, the President's tall and cadaverous chief of staff, escorted the senator into the Oval Office. President Pontowski stood up and walked around his desk to greet his most formidable and unrelenting political opponent, Senator William Douglas Courtland. Cox stood back and watched the two men meet. The tall and angular, slightly potbellied Pontowski looked like a statesman, his gray hair, blue eyes, hawklike nose perfect for the role. But Cox, more than any other man, had experienced the searing intelligence and implacable will that lay underneath the man's surface. Cox was certain that history would have nice things to say about Pontowski and his stewardship as President.

And history, Cox thought, will deal properly with William Douglas Courtland, that smooth and calculating son of a bitch. For a moment, Cox wondered if Courtland might be illegitimate. That might help explain the devious bastard, he thought; not that Pontowski would ever use such a fact for political gain. Cox had seen how Pontowski could crucify any member of his staff or political party who crossed the bounds of ethical conduct.

The contrast between the two men struck at Cox. Courtland stood exactly five feet six inches tall and was built like a fire plug. The senator's immaculately tailored suit shouted East Coast establishment while his voice carried conviction and warmth with every word. Cox had long ago pegged Courtland as a demagogue who would do anything to win the presidency of the United States.

"Bill," Pontowski said, shaking Courtland's hand, "so far we don't have much to go on." He ushered the senator to a couch and the two sat down. "We should have something more concrete within a few hours." Pontowski spoke in his slow way and captivating way, recapping all he knew.

Courtland clasped his hands and interlaced his fingers together in his lap, a worried look on his face, his high forehead wrinkled with concern under a full head of dark hair. "I thought that you would have more information by now," he said. Both Pontowski and Cox caught the veiled implication that the United States government was not doing all it could. Or was it only the deep worry of a parent they heard?

"Leo," Pontowski said, "would you please check with the Situation Room and find out if anything more has come in?" He looked at the door and Cox understood that Pontowski wanted to be alone with Courtland. "We've set up a Crisis Action Team to stay on top of this," he explained as Cox closed the door behind him.

"Really?" Courtland questioned, more skepticism in his voice now that they were alone.

"Bill, I *am* concerned," Pontowski said, trying to convey his own worry. "I've ordered the CIA and NSA to give it top priority. The Navy is moving the *Taos* into the Gulf of Siam and the Fifty-first Strategic Reconnaissance Wing has an RC-One-thirty-five on station now." Both the RC-135 and the *Taos*, the U.S. Navy's most sophisticated spy ship, carried state-of-the-art communications monitoring equipment.

"And what will all that accomplish?" Courtland asked.

Pontowski masked his irritation. Courtland was the chairman of the Senate Armed Services Committee and had been instrumental in getting the *Taos* for the Navy. He should have some idea of its capability. "With the *Taos* and one RC-One-thirty-five on station," he explained, "we can monitor every form of electronic communications in the area. We've got them wired for sound and sooner or later, someone is going to start talking."

"And how can we monitor that amount of communications traffic—all in foreign languages?" Courtland's questioning aggression was more obvious.

"Rapid, high-volume scanners linked with computers programmed to pick up key words to alert the translators on the *Taos*. We will flush out whoever is behind this, just like we did in Beirut."

"A lot of good that did," Courtland said. Pontowski said nothing, not willing to reveal how once the identification and location of the terrorists holding the American hostages had been established, the supersecret Intelligence Support Agency had convinced the parties involved that it was in the interest of their own health to release the hostages.

Pontowski's sixth sense started bonging, warning him of danger. For all its irrationality, long experience had taught him not to ignore it. "Bill, if we work together, we can get your daughter back. But going public at this point won't help."

"I seem to remember us being a 'government of the people, by the people,' or have I missed something?" Courtland said. Pontowski could hear the oratory behind the words. "I noticed," Courtland continued, "that you didn't mention the DEA being part of your Crisis Action Team." The senator was on a roll now and the old animosities were surfacing. He hated being in the Oval Office, on the turf of his oldest political enemy, acting like a supplicant. "Did it ever occur to you, or any of your staff, that what happened to my daughter is a reaction to your antidrug operations in Southeast Asia?"

"The Drug Enforcement Administration has a representative on the team," Pontowski told him.

Courtland's heavy dark eyebrows shot up—the gauntlet had been thrown. The senator had constantly criticized Pontowski about his antidrug policies. Courtland had struck some deep seed of fear and discontent in his attacks on the DEA and had made political hay by calling it the Double ICC, "an inept collection of clowns being led by an incompetent cluster of clods." It was one of the clubs Courtland was using to beat his way to the presidency.

"I'm doing all I can to rescue your daughter and her friends from these terrorists," Pontowski reassured the senator, hiding his exasperation.

A knock at the door interrupted him and Cox appeared. "More communications traffic, Mr. President," he said. Pontowski nodded for him to come in. "We've a report that three young women and two men were transferred from a fishing boat here," he unfolded a map and pointed to the old Gurkha camp on the Malaysian coast. "They were loaded on a seaplane and flown to near Bangkok. The plane landed on the water, just west of the resort at Pattya Beach and transferred to a power boat that was last seen headed for Bangkok."

"Was my daughter one of them?"

"The descriptions of the three women matched that of the girls on the yacht," Cox told him.

"What about the young men?" Pontowski asked, concerned about all five.

"They matched the descriptions of Richard Martel and Troy Spencer," Cox said. "Mark Livingston is unaccounted for."

"Were they okay? Were they harmed?" Courtland asked.

Cox looked at Pontowski, indicating there was some bad news. Pontowski nodded. "The women showed signs of possibly being raped."

Courtland stood up, his face flushed with anger, fists clenched. With a visible effort, he fought for control. "And so far you've done nothing."

"I'm doing what I can, Bill." Pontowski reassured him.

The look on Courtland's face changed and he sat back down, not about to apologize for his breach of etiquette. "What are the sources of your intelligence?" he asked.

Again, Cox looked at Pontowski who nodded. "The British . . . "

"The British?" Courtland interrupted. It was not a question. "What happened to the CIA?"

"Sir," Cox continued, apparently unruffled by the senator's outburst, "a British Special Air Service squadron was training in the area and observed the transfer. They did attack the camp and try to save the hostages. Unfortunately, the transfer was made offshore and they had no way to stop it. They did manage to interrogate one of the terrorists left behind."

"Special Air Service?" Courtland asked. "Isn't that the SAS? What did they discover?"

"Yes, sir," Cox answered, "it is. They reported the terrorist identified General Chiang Tse-kuan as being involved in some way. We do not have any specifics."

"Chiang!" the senator shouted. He fought for his self-control. "I told you this had to do with your antidrug campaign. There's your proof. If Chiang has Heather—" He cut the thought off, his point made.

"We don't know that for sure," Pontowski said. "But it does help us in our search. Leo, can we get custody of the terrorist?"

"I'm afraid not, Mr. President. He died from his wounds."

A heavy silence came down in the room. "Mr. President," Courtland finally said, his voice flat and mechanical, "I appreciate your concern and everything you're doing. I haven't told my wife yet because I wanted something more positive, more hopeful. But I can't wait any longer. I'll have to tell her something. Our only daughter ... being held captive by one of the most vicious drug lords in the world. . . . My God!"

"Bill, you know how these things develop. We need time to work the problem. At this point, we are not sure that Chiang has your daughter."

"For everyone's sake," Courtland said in a low voice, "I hope you do this one right." Pontowski and Cox heard the threat in his words.

"At this point, we need time," Pontowski repeated.

"The one thing my daughter doesn't have," Courtland interrupted.

Pontowski's mind raced as he sought a way to bring Courtland around but every political instinct he possessed told him they had reached a standoff. Courtland simply wasn't going to be understanding. Nothing productive would come from this meeting. "Would you like to talk to the team? They're in the Situation Room."

"Thank you. Perhaps later," Courtland answered. There was no emotion in his voice. "If you'll excuse me, Mr. President, I need to get back to my wife." The two men rose and went through the ritual of departure. Pontowski walked with him to his waiting car, still trying to show his concern. Finally, the senator was gone.

"What do you think?" Pontowski asked Cox as they descended the stairs to the Situation Room in the basement.

"The good senator from California," Cox answered, the implied contempt in his words not lost on Pontowski, "is going to make political hay out of this if he can."

A Marine guard held open the door to the Situation Room for them to enter. Inside, four men and a woman were clustered around one end of the table while another young staffer tacked up the last of a series of eighteen- by twenty-four-inch sheets of paper on one wall that outlined the current situation. "Mazie," Pontowski said to the young woman, "sometimes I think you live here."

Mazie Kamigami smiled at him, her round oriental face full of warmth. "Mr. Cagliari does let me go home occasionally," she replied. The rumpled, professorial-looking man sitting next to her was Michael Cagliari, the national security adviser. He only shook his head and muttered in his beard. Mazie Kamigami was the most aggressive and brightest member of the National Security Council staff and cut a swath across the highly compartmentalized NSC. Whenever a crisis broke, she always appeared in the center of things, working eighty and ninety hours a week, limitless energy flowing out of her squat, round body. She was Cagliari's most valuable assistant.

"We were just told," Michael Cagliari said, "that a U.S. Army exchange officer was with the SAS team. No name yet."

"Find out who he is and get him here," Pontowski said. "Also keep Senator Courtland posted on all new developments." Mazie shot a worried glance at her boss, Cagliari. Pontowski caught it. "I know," the President said, "that could be a problem. But we've got to work with the senator on this one."

"Sir," Mazie said, not afraid to voice an opinion, "Senator Courtland chases reporters down the street throwing classified and sensitive information at them. He's more like a geyser than a leak. Reporters call him Old Faithful—good for an outburst every hour."

"The stakes are different this time," Cagliari said.

"I hope so," Pontowski said as he left, Cox in tow.

Senator William Douglas Courtland was buoyant with anticipation when he entered his offices and called for his two most trusted assistants, George Rivera and Tina Stanley, to join him. The man and woman who entered his private office could have blended with the thousands of other men and women who prowled the halls of the Capitol in search of power and status. However, this pair were credited as being the most skilled and unscrupulous operators in Washington, D.C. Courtland paced the floor in his eagerness. "I've got that dumb Polack in the White House backed into a corner," he told them. The senator recounted the situation and laid out his strategy.

The man and woman sat impassively, waiting for Courtland to issue their marching orders. "George, I want you to wring every contact you've got in the CIA dry. Call in every marker that's owed you. I want the raw stuff and I don't give a damn about verification or authenticity. Dig it out. Tina, suck whatever cock you have to in the NSC and do the same." Neither said a word. "I want this to be the screwup of the century," Courtland said, his face stone hard.

The two exchanged glances. "We can make that happen," George Rivera assured him. Tina Stanley nodded in agreement.

"The press conference has been set up for two o'clock this afternoon," Leo Cox told Pontowski. The two men were sitting in the Oval Office going over the day's revised schedule with the press secretary.

"We expect most of the questions will be about the kidnapping," Henry Gilman, the press secretary said.

"Any feel for the mood of the press corps?" Cox asked.

"Still digging for angles," Gilman said. "Right now they are neutral and waiting to see what develops."

"Good," Pontowski said. "Leo, have the Vice President cover the luncheon with the delegates from the American Bankers Association for me. I'll have lunch with Tosh and join you both in the Oval Office for a final review before the press conference. Have all the players there." The two men rose and left the room.

Outside, Press Secretary Gilman said, "He always talks to Tosh before a press conference."

"She's still his best adviser," Cox told him.

Pontowski walked upstairs to his wife's bedroom. He knocked gently at her door and waited until the nurse answered. It was one of the small things he did to keep his wife's morale up; she always wanted him to find her looking her best. The way the nurse smiled at him as she held the door open signaled that Tosh Pontowski was having a good day. A smile spread across his face when he saw her sitting at the small table near the windows. He walked across the room and joined her.

Tosh Pontowski smiled at him. "The wolf is losing today," she said. As always, her lilting accent captivated him and touched the love he held for her, a love made stronger by her courage in coming to terms with and fighting the disease that ravaged her—systemic lupus erythematosus (lupus—the wolf). The disease was well named for the way it came and went unexpectedly, suddenly leaping out to rip and tear at human flesh and then sneaking away, only to return without warning to attack another part of the body. At first, it had only been a mild skin rash and Tosh had not been overly worried by the flare-ups that continued for a number of years. But then lupus had attacked her joints, and then had returned as kidney paralysis. But that had disappeared and then the wolf had returned again, this time attacking her heart.

He reached across the table and took her hand, hoping that she was in remission again. But his inner alarm warned him otherwise. How much longer? he wondered. He knew he could go on without her but life would lose most of its luster.

As usual, Tosh Pontowski refused to give in to her disease.

"Press conference today?" He nodded a yes. "L'affaire Courtland no doubt."

"Can't hide much from you, can we?" Pontowski observed. Charles, his valet, entered with a tray holding his lunch.

"Courtland will turn this against you," she said, watching him eat. "He knows he must discredit you if he is to defeat the candidate you endorse in the next presidential election."

"I know," he answered. "No matter what we do, he'll claim it isn't enough. He'll work the sympathy angle for all it's worth."

"Then you must defuse it," she counseled. "Recall your own escape."

"But I was never in captivity."

"No, but you were wounded, frightened, and pursued. It was a near thing. Build on that."

Matthew Zachary Pontowski leaned back in his chair and recalled when he had indeed been a terrified, desperately wounded fugitive.

1943

RAF Church Fenton, England

The battered Austin ground to a stop in front of the mat-black Beaufighter. "Right, sir," the driver said, "here you are." Zack Pontowski and Andrew Ruffum clambered out, dragging their flight gear with them. "Good luck," she added before crunching the gears and driving off. Zack drew himself to his full six feet and sniffed the cold January night, waiting to feel any strange tingling sensations that might warn him about this particular aircraft they were going to fly tonight. Nothing unusual assaulted his senses and he relaxed.

Sergeant Newman was waiting for them with two other aircraftsmen of his ground crew. "She's in tip-top," he told them. Both men could hear a sadness in his voice.

"Not happy about the conversion?" Zack asked. The first of the squadron's new Mosquito aircraft and their crews would arrive at Church Fenton the next day and the Beaufighters and their aircrews would depart. But the ground crews would remain. Zack and Ruffy had the dubious distinction of flying 25 Squadron's last mission in Beaufighters before the conversion. The sergeant gave a shrug that could have meant anything and took Zack's parachute to load it in the cockpit for him. He passed it up the open forward escape hatch in the belly of the Beau. Ruffy was already scrambling up the entry ladder in the hatch behind his position. Zack lit a cigarette, knowing they had some time before engine start. Newman rejoined him and also lit up.

"Think you'll like the new kites?" Zack asked.

"They say the Mosquito is bloody fast with those big Merlins," Newman answered. The Rolls-Royce Merlin engine that powered the new Mosquito fighter-bomber was already a legend among the ground crews.

"I'd like a shot at flying one of them," Zack allowed.

"The Beau's an honest lady," Newman said, loyal to the very last.

The American pilot had to agree with him. The Beaufighter was a sturdy, aggressive, and reliable aircraft and the blunt nose reminded him of a crouching bulldog as it sat on its conventional landing gear. But you had to be strong to fly it, since the mechanical flight controls were heavy and unassisted. The plane was like the British, Zack thought, as he studied it in the dark, his eyes moving down the fuselage and stopping at the shapely tail fin. Well, I always have liked pretty behinds, he thought.

He stubbed out his cigarette and climbed in after Ruffy, working his way past Ruffy and up the catwalk of the dark, tunnellike fuselage. His flashlight reflected off the breeches of the four 20-millimeter cannons mounted below floor level. They were each loaded with a sixty-round drum of ammunition, which Ruffy could replace in flight. He climbed through the pair of armor-plated doors that led into the pilot's compartment. He always left the doors open, hoping it would make Ruffy feel not so alone in the bowels of the fuselage. Then he settled into the center mounted seat and went through the cockpit check that would lead to engine start, taxi, and takeoff. He was very methodical in his approach to flying.

Ten minutes later they were holding short of the runway and waiting for the green light that would clear them for takeoff. The light blinked at them from the tower and he eased the throttles forward. He was careful on the lineup for the Beau had a tendency to swing on takeoff. He rolled forward to straighten out the tail wheel and slowly eased in the power. By using coarse rudder, he kept the tail straight. Then it lifted and he eased in full power. The main gear came unstuck and they lifted skyward, reaching into the clear dark night.

The two men settled into the normal and very predictable routine that had marked every flight since their first patrol when they had downed the Junkers. Zack and Ruffy had taken more than a fair amount of good-natured kidding about how gravity had done their job for them. But their sector had been quiet since then and they were itching for action to prove everyone wrong. But again, it was a quiet night. "Looks like another bust," Zack said, wiggling his cold toes. The heating system on the Beau was not up to the job and his feet were always numb from the cold at altitude.

"Woodbine Twenty-four"—the radio/telephone came alive as the GCI controller detected an intruder on his radar set—"this is Falcon, bandit for you. Turn to zero-eight-five and climb to Angels one-eight. Buster."

"About time," Zack grunted over the intercom as he hauled the Beau around to its new heading and shoved the throttles forward.

"That heading's going to take us to the extreme eastern side of our area," Ruffy said, warning him that they would be far out over the North Sea.

"Pull out all the stops on that magic box of yours," Zack answered.

They were climbing through sixteen thousand feet when Ruffy called out, "I've got him on the nose, range six miles, a little above us. Level off." The navigator had performed a small miracle on the Mark IV radar set by getting a contact at that range.

"Contact," Zack called over the radio, telling the GCI controller that they were painting the bandit on their radar. He switched the guns to "fire" and selected the machine guns.

"He's flying level," Ruffy said, "but weaving back and forth through about sixty degrees. Off to your port side, should be coming back now. Range two miles." They were in a tail chase and closing.

"No joy," Zack said, straining to get a visual sighting through the windscreen. He caught a flicker of an exhaust at his eleven o'clock. "Tallyho! Got him!" He eased the throttles back a notch and slowly closed from the right, working into a position directly astern the bandit. In the darkness, he could make out the distinctive profile of a Junkers 88: twin-engine, cigar-shaped fuselage, blunt nose, and big distinctive glasshouse canopy. Despite his previous engagement with a Junkers, Zack had a healthy respect for the aircraft and knew that in the hands of a skilled pilot, it was a worthy adversary. He closed, matching the Junkers's turns, fully intending to gun the unsuspecting fighter-bomber out of the moonlit sky before the German knew he was there. There was nothing glamorous or chivalrous in what he was doing.

Suddenly, the Junkers rolled up onto its right wing and turned hard to the right. Then the nose of the German aircraft started to swing around directly onto the Beau. There was no doubt that the crew had seen them. Zack hauled back on the yoke and zoomed as he slammed the throttles full forward. He gained a slight advantage in altitude and then turned hard into the Junkers as the German pilot reversed his turn and broke back to the left. "Gotcha!" Zack shouted. The German was turning his tail to them and had to be a green and inexperienced pilot to turn away like that, solving Zack's problem.

"Oh, shit!" Zack grunted as the Junkers rolled violently back to the right as Zack tried to follow him. It had been a deliberate feint and the German pilot was proving himself to be anything but inexperienced as he aerobatted the Junkers, rolling back to the left and crossing behind Zack's tail. He had spit the Beau out in front of him.

"Hard left!" Ruffy shouted over the intercom. Zack wrenched the Beau around to the left as hard as he could, laboring at the heavy controls, not able to hold his altitude. Sweat was running down his face in the cold cockpit. A stream of tracers reached by them on the left and slightly above. Only Ruffy's command had saved them. Zack hardened up his turn as he descended and pulled back into the fight. The Beau could outturn the Junkers if he was strong enough. Now they were in a descending, turning engagement, each on the opposite side of the circle, canopy to canopy. "We need to get away from this bugger," Ruffy shouted over the intercom, acknowledging what Zack was thinking. They might be in a faster and better-turning aircraft, but there was no doubt the German was the better pilot.

Zack continued to descend and turn, coming more and more to the Junkers's tail with each full circle. He planned to take the fight down to the deck, just above the choppy surface of the North Sea, and then take a snap shot at the German as he broke out of the turn. He would outclimb the Junkers and hide in the night.

Again, the German pilot surprised Zack by rolling out and flying straight ahead, still in a shallow dive, pushing the Junkers for all it was worth. "You son of a bitch!" Zack roared with exaltation as he fell in behind the German. "He's lost sight of us," Zack told Ruffy.

"Not bloody likely," Ruffy shot back. "Let's get the hell out of here."

But Zack ignored him and he triggered a long burst from the six .303 Browning machine guns in the wings. He watched in amazement as the line of tracers passed harmlessly to the left side of the Junkers. "What the..." The German was skidding his Junkers slightly to the right in the dive, destroying any tracking solution for his pursuer. Zack was learning how to dogfight the hard way.

"We're a long way from home," Ruffy said. He wanted Zack to turn away and let the Junkers escape. But again Zack ignored him and the sudden tingling sensation of approaching danger that shot through him. He wanted to nail the coffin shut on the German in front of him. He sent another burst of machine gun fire toward his adversary.

A line of flaming golf balls reached up from the surface of the North Sea toward the Beaufighter. "Oh, Jesus!" Zack yelled as he hauled back on the control column and pumped the rudder pedals.

"Flak trap!" Ruffy shouted. Both men could see the source of the tracers: a long low shadow in the water. An E-boat. The Beau rocked violently from two hits.

"Ruffy! You okay." There was only silence from the rear of the plane. Zack shouted it again. Silence. "God damn you to hell," he gritted as he caught a glimpse of the Junkers off his left wing. He had lost sight of the E-boat in the dark, but he knew roughly where it was and he could avoid it. He was positive that the Junkers and the E-boat were working as a team and had led them into a trap. Zack tested his flight controls and the sturdy Beau responded. A killing rage he did not know he possessed took hold of him and he flew straight at the Junkers and selected cannons. His right thumb came down hard on the firing button and he felt the plane shudder as the twenty-millimeter cannons fired. The German pilot saw the tracers coming at him and broke into Zack, but it was too late. The Junkers came apart as Zack held the button and emptied the four cannons into the dying aircraft.

"My God!" came from behind his right shoulder. Zack twisted around to see Ruffy standing in the well behind the pilot's seat.

Relief flooded through him. "Sorry, mate," Ruffy said. "Took a bit of damage in the back. Should be okay but don't get too enthusiastic on the controls."

"How come you didn't answer my call?" Zack asked.

"Intercom panel shot to hell and I was busy with a fire."

"You okay? Not hurt?"

"Should be okay." It was Ruffy's way of saying he was slightly wounded.

"I want to nail that fuckin' E-boat," Zack said.

"Always love to return favors," Ruffy agreed. "Give me a moment to reload and strap in. By the way, we are a bloody long way from home."

"Any idea where we are."

"Over the North Sea."

"I was hoping you could be a little more specific," Zack said.

"A vector of two-six-five for one hundred thirty-five miles should get us back to Church Fenton," Ruffy told him and disappeared through the pair of open armor-plated doors behind the cockpit. Zack could feel him move around through the controls as he reloaded the sixty-pound ammo drums on each of the four cannons. Then Ruffy was back, standing behind him.

"When you want me to reload, fly straight and level and wiggle the tail a bit for a signal." He disappeared again and this time closed the armor-plated doors.

Zack turned back in the direction of the E-boat, scanning his engine instruments and playing with the throttles and pitch control. All responded as normal. He carefully moved the flight controls and, again, all felt okay. They may have taken battle damage but the Beaufighter was living up to its reputation as a flying tank. He set up an expanding-square search pattern, still determined to find the E-boat before low fuel forced him to return to base.

On the third leg, he found it. The boat was moving fast through the water, heading to the southeast. "Your turn," he muttered to himself and dropped down onto the deck for a strafing run. He bore down onto the E-boat's four o'clock position, jinking back and forth in short, sharp turns. Tracers erupted from the stern of the boat when a gunner momentarily caught sight of him. The rounds passed harmlessly to the left, wide of the mark. Then he stabilized and walked a burst of the twenties across the E-boat. Then he was off, jinking as hard as he dared, worried about the damage they had taken from the first engagement. A line of tracers passed harmlessly behind them.

As he came around for a second run, he could see a fire spreading behind the wheelhouse. "You are going to buy the farm," he promised the E-boat as he rolled in. This time, two batteries opened up at him and he broke off. "You are one tough son of a bitch," he said to himself. He checked his fuel gauges and calculated he could make one more run. He climbed to five hundred feet and circled to the bow of the E-boat, hoping the fire amidships might mask him from the aft battery.

He rolled in for the last time, determined to destroy the E-boat. He was pressing, thumb over the trigger, almost in range of the lethal twenties when a barrage of tracers from the E-boat reached out to him. There were now three batteries firing at him. Where had the extra guns come from? he thought. He mashed the button, emptying the four cannons into the E-boat. He was pulling off when the Beau rocked from a series of hits. Zack was vaguely aware that pieces of his right wing were shredding and the always heavy controls were suddenly lighter, but they were still flying.

Now pain ripped through his right leg, more intense than anything he had ever felt. "Oh my God," he said weakly, and for a moment he was certain he was going to die. Then a granite-hard determination chased any fear of death away. He wasn't going to die until he had Ruffy safe on the ground. "Ruffy!" he shouted, knowing there was no way the young Englishman could hear him over the noise in the Beau. But he felt better for trying. No answer. Automatically, he transmitted, "Mayday! Mayday!" over the radio. But it was dead.

"Fly the airplane," he told himself, forcing his attention onto the controls and instruments. The control column felt sloppy and loose in his hand but the rudder pedals felt normal. The Beaufighter was flying but was not responsive. At the same time, he glanced at the instrument panel. The lamps used for illuminating the panel were out and he couldn't read the instruments. "Hell of a time for power failure." He fumbled for the flashlight he carried in the left leg pocket of his flying overalls. "Engines sound good, must have cut the wiring." He was vaguely aware of loud wind noises. He directed the beam of his flashlight onto the instrument panel. Only the engine gauges were still alive. All his flying instruments were dead.

No, wait, he cautioned himself, you've still got an altimeter. "Jesus Christ!" he exploded. They were at sea level and he had almost inadvertently crashed into the sea. He eased back on the yoke. Nothing. A sudden dizziness swept over him. Was he going to pass out? The pain was still with him, drawing his attention away from his primary duty, flying the Beau. "Am I bleeding?" he asked himself aloud. He forced the beam onto his right leg and almost passed out. His lower leg was drenched in blood. How long have I been bleeding? he thought.

With a massive force of will, he drove away the dizziness that threatened to engulf him and he fumbled for the first aid pouch that was under his seat. His fingers searched for it but couldn't find it. He bent his head to look and almost passed out. Dumb, he thought. Now his fingers felt the kit and he grabbed it, shaking it out in his lap, fumbling with his left hand until he found a large compress bandage. He tore it open with his teeth and bent over, holding the control column against his shoulder and shoving the bandage into the open wound. Then he tied another bandage around it, slowing the bleeding to an ooze.

"Now fly the damn airplane," he told himself. "Ruffy!" he shouted. Still no answer. "Altitude, go for altitude." Again, he tested the yoke but the Beau didn't climb. He reached for the elevator trimming tab wheel on his right and rolled it back, feeding in nose-up trim. He eased the throttles forward and the plane climbed.

"Where's home?" He knew he was talking to himself but it seemed to help. Again, he used his flashlight to check the instrument panel. The turn and slip indicator was also good. Concentrate, he warned himself; you're missing things. He checked the reliable AM Mark II compass on the right console that he used to set the gyro-stabilized direction indicator. They were headed to the southeast—toward the continent. "Wrong way," he muttered. He pressed on the left rudder pedal, favoring his wounded right leg, and turned the wheel to the left. The Beau responded slowly and the turn and slip indicator told him it was an uncoordinated turn. "Must have lost the ailerons."

The Beau started to shudder and he eased off the turn, again flying straight and level. He checked the compass. They had turned less than six degrees and were still headed for the German-held coast. He reached for the rudder tab control forward of compass and fed in trim, calculating that if it had worked with the elevator to climb, he could turn the same way. Nothing happened. "Damn!"

A blast of air and wind noise behind him caught his attention and for a split second, he was certain that the Beaufighter was coming apart, disintegrating from the battle damage it had taken. He turned his head slowly, not wanting to bring the dizziness back on. A feeling of relief swept over him when he saw Ruffy crawling through the opened armor-plated doors. A heavy bandage was wrapped around his head and he was moving slowly. "Not bloody much left back there," he yelled at Zack. His voice was strained and labored. "The fin's all but shot away, right wing looks like a sieve."

"Left wing?" Zack shouted over the noise.

"Ailerons are in bits and pieces."

The control problems now made sense to Zack. They were lucky to still be flying. "We're going to have to ditch." He explained the situation to his radar nav. "I can climb and probably descend, but I'm afraid if I jockey with the power too much or try to turn, I'll lose control."

"Plenty of open spaces in the back to crawl out through," Ruffy told him. The nose-heavy Beau had a reputation for turning into a death trap on ditchings. "The Jerry worked us over good. New tactic, using E-boats as a flak trap like that."

"Think it was Young Ernst?" Zack asked.

"Most likely," Ruffy answered. "The Intel types need to know about it. Maybe you got the bastard."

"Worry about that later," Zack said. He checked the compass again. "We're on a heading of one-four-zero degrees. Not good."

Ruffy pulled a map out of his leg pocket. "Need your torch," he said. Zack handed him the flashlight over his right shoulder. Ruffy studied the map for a moment. "If we don't get turned around, we'll hit the coast of Holland. Really not the tourist season, this time of year." Ruffy was unflappable and never changed.

"Hold on. I'll see what I can do." Zack inched in the power on the right engine, experimenting with differential power and turning into his good wing. Again, the Beau started to shudder and he eased the throttle back. "She only wants to go straight ahead," he told Ruffy.

"Bloody cow," Ruffy swore.

"Where do you think we should ditch?" Zack asked. "Here or closer to shore?"

"Any chance of being picked up?"

"The R/T is dead," Zack answered.

"It does tend to get a bit cold in the water. We won't last long even in a dinghy."

"Okay, we go for the coast, put her down in shallow water, might not sink. Maybe we can make contact with the Dutch underground."

"More likely with the Gestapo," Ruffy predicted.

"Better destroy your box," Zack said, not wanting their radar to fall into the hands of the Germans.

"Don't have to," Ruffy told him. "The Jerries took care of that." A shell had hit the radar set and it had blown up. Luckily, Ruffy had been looking to the side and the fragments had cut into the side of his head, missing his face.

Silence came down as they droned into the night. Neither was overly optimistic about their chances of avoiding capture but it seemed better to take their chances on land than in the frigid waters of the North Sea. Zack wracked his brain thinking of ways to make the Beau turn, but every attempted maneuver started a vicious shaking and forced him to keep the aircraft straight and level.

Ruffy saw the coast first. "There," he said, "straight ahead." Zack could barely make out the dim line on the horizon that marked the low sand dunes of the Dutch coastline.

"Strap in," Zack told him as he eased the Beaufighter down to the water's surface. He tried to estimate how far out they were but gave up. He watched the altimeter unwind down to zero as he fed in nose-up trim and retarded the throttles. They settled into the water tail first and he cut the engines.

The Beaufighter came down with a hard slap, leaped back into the air and bellied back down only to bounce into the air again. On the fourth bounce the Beau dug its nose into a low swell and Zack was certain they were going to pitch-pole onto their back. But the Beau flopped back onto its belly and skidded to a halt. Then it nosed over and started to sink.

For a stunned moment, Zack sat in the cockpit, not moving. He was vaguely aware that his face was bleeding. "Ruffy!" he yelled, releasing his safety harness and twisting in his seat to see if his friend was okay. But the armor-plated doors had slammed closed. His fingers tore at the buckles on his parachute harness. He had to shed it if he was to get out through the big easy-out window on the right side of the cockpit that had been designed for ditching. He pulled himself up and released the latches to the hatch and pushed it open. Then he reached behind the seat and pulled on the dinghy but it wouldn't move. In a panic he remembered that he had to unstrap it but water was gushing through the hatch and the cockpit was under water. The Beau was going down fast. Panic drove him and he fought to pull himself through the hatch.

Somehow, he pushed free of the sinking aircraft and clawed his way to the surface. He twisted around, inflating his life jacket and looking for his navigator. "Ruffy! Where the hell are you?" No answer. He swam furiously around the spot where the aircraft had sunk. He stopped flailing and pulled the flashlight out of his leg pocket. He mashed the button but no light came on and he let it slip out of his fingers as a deep despair for his missing friend rolled through him.

He lay in the water and for a moment welcomed the thought of death. But suddenly, a much stronger emotion washed over him—revenge. He twisted in the water trying to get his bearings and determine where the shore was. He was completely disoriented. A low sound caught his attention. "Surf?" the pilot mumbled. Now he could hear a barking dog. "Chrisamighty! Please, not sentries." With measured strokes, he swam toward the sound, dragging his legs behind him. The sound of the crashing surf grew louder.

"Keep moving," he told himself as the biting cold numbed his body. "Keep moving." Now he could see flakes of white in the surf in front of him and low sand dunes. "Where's that damn dog?" The dark shadow of a small boat emerged out of the dark directly in front of him and Zack could see the distinctive silhouette of a man looking at him. A hand reached out and grabbed the harness of his life jacket. He tried to resist and push away, but the hand pulled him back and he hit his head against the side of the boat, stunning him. Another set of strong hands helped drag him into the boat.

The hunger for revenge that had driven him to shore drowned in a tidal wave of helplessness and fear.

TWO

Bangkok, Thailand

The first tremors of fear brushed past Samkit when the gates leading into the villa grounds rolled back and two white Range Rovers rolled into the courtyard. A gleaming pearlescent-white Rolls-Royce followed, crunching across the carefully raked gravel and sending yet a stronger shock wave rippling through the villa. Two more heavily armed Land Rovers brought up the rear of the convoy. The gates rolled closed and a foreboding silence ruled, punctuated by the heavy slamming of car doors. Samkit faced into the epicenter of the disturbance and made a *wai,* her hands together as if in prayer, a nod of the head, eyes closed and her face alight with a beautiful smile when General Chiang Tse-kuan walked past.

Two of the general's secretaries scurried after him, one a short dumpy man, the other a stylishly dressed middle-aged English-woman. "They should be here in six minutes," the woman told the general.

"I'll meet them on the veranda," the general said, his voice carrying the accent and inflection of an English public school education. He was a slender and dignified Eurasian in his mid-fifties, dressed in an expensive Savile Row linen suit. His cos-

74

mopolitan bearing made the unsuspecting think of a wealthy and sophisticated Hong Kong businessman. The male secretary spoke briefly to Samkit, telling her to make sure the veranda was clean and in good order.

Samkit gathered two of the other servant girls and ran across the lush garden, past the swimming pool and to the veranda. Samkit's legs snapped against her tight pasin, the traditional saronglike tubular skirt that reached to her ankles. Still, the slender forty-two-year-old woman never lost the graceful bearing that pleased the general. Her practiced eye inspected the veranda and she set the two girls to work while she arranged the table and chairs the way the general preferred. When she was satisfied that all was in order, she and the girls withdrew into an alcove to await their master and be available for whatever service he might require. They would return to their normal routine after the seismic shocks upsetting the villa subsided. She used the time to make sure her jet-black hair was still in place, drawn back into a tight bun, her blouse tucked neatly into her pasin, and that her face was composed and serene. Samkit Katchikitikorn was a lithe and charming Thai who was careful to appear the loyal servant. She feared Chiang and what he would do if the truth was discovered. But her loathing of the man and all that he represented drove her on. Samkit accepted the future and her fate since both were beyond her control.

The two young girls stopped their nervous chatter when Chiang's bodyguards walked out of the main house. Samkit could feel the girls stiffen with apprehension when Chiang appeared. But her attention was captured by the six people being escorted by four armed guards across the garden. "The old man looks like a fisherman," one of the girls whispered.

"He is," Samkit answered.

"Are those Americans?" the other girl asked. The three girls and two young men were a scraggly group, all wrapped in saronglike thin towels. Four of them stood quietly with their arms folded in front of them. Only the blond-haired man was handcuffed and agitated.

"Hush, child," Samkit said. She watched as the old man went through the ritual of greeting Chiang and begging his attention.

"Why should these Americans be of any interest to me?" Chiang asked, speaking fluent Thai.

"This one," the old man said, smiling through his yellowed teeth, "is the daughter of a U.S. senator. Very important." He pulled Heather Courtland to the front for Chiang's inspection. "She is very pretty."

"There are a hundred senators in America and pretty girls are cheap in Bangkok," Chiang said, disinterest in every word.

"But her father is the Senator Courtland who will be the next President," the old man protested.

"You know little of American politics, old man," Chiang answered. "Every senator believes he alone should be President."

Samkit scrutinized the one called Heather and half-listened as the two men fell into a contest of wills, bargaining for the sale of the hostages. Yes, she decided, the general would like this one, once she is washed and properly dressed. Samkit had seen the general buy women before. It was only a matter of establishing the price.

But the old man knew the value of his goods and was a relentless bargainer. Finally, he pounded his chest, insisting that the price Chiang was offering would never compensate him for the loss of his son who was killed by a sniper bullet during the transfer of the hostages. "What price is my family?" he wailed. But Chiang would go no higher. The old man ripped Heather's wrap away and stood back, letting them all see the naked girl. Then he stripped the other girls. "They are all worth much more," he insisted.

Chiang rose from his chair and circled Heather. "Are you truly Senator Courtland's daughter?" he asked in English. Surprise crossed Heather's face when she heard Chiang's English accent. She nodded dumbly.

The old man's face was impassive, but he could sense Chiang's interest. He stroked her arms and made her skin ripple. "She has the most beautiful skin," he said, "Very smooth and tight, without a blemish." Besides being a shrewd broker, the old man was a gambler. He knew the price would tumble if Chiang spread Heather's buttocks and saw the tattoo. But it was a chance he was willing to take. He lifted one of her breasts and let it fall. "Very firm. She is a rare beauty." He touched the nipple that had held the diamond earring and pushed it in. It popped back out.

Chiang ran a hand over Heather's body feeling her skin tone for himself. "Please open your mouth," he told her. She did as she was told and he held her chin, smelled her breath and examined her teeth and tongue. Then he circled DC and repeated the examination. He gently wiped away the tears that were streaming down her face. "I'm not going to hurt you," he promised. He gave Nikki Anderson a quick inspection. Heather saw his face stiffen when he touched the two gold rings that were still dangling from her breasts. For the first time since she had been taken captive, Heather started to think.

"This one is of little value," Chiang said and the hard bargaining started. The old man kept referring to his dead son. Finally, Chiang said, "You have other sons, but in his honor, I will make one last offer." The old man knew Chiang had reached the limit he would pay before cutting his throat and taking the hostages by force. The deal was quickly done and Chiang agreed to pay him 7 million baht in gold—$280,000—for the five Americans.

While the old fisherman waited for payment, Chiang beckoned to the three servants in the alcove. "Samkit, take them to their rooms and have those two dress for dinner." He pointed at Heather and DC. Then he spoke to the guards, who led Troy and Ricky away to a different part of the compound. Samkit picked up Heather's wrap and handed it to her. Then she led the three American girls into the villa.

"Is your name Samkit?" Heather asked. "Do you speak English?" Samkit nodded in reply. "Who is that man?" Heather asked when they were well away from the men.

"General Chiang Tse-kuan," Samkit answered.

"What were they doing back there?" DC asked. "I felt like a piece of beef at a cattle auction."

"General buy you," Samkit told her.

"No way," DC protested.

"He buy all of you," Samkit repeated. "You do what he says now." She led them through a set of beautiful rooms in the house and into a huge and airy bedroom with a canopied bed. She motioned to a large and modern bathroom where they could hear the sound of running water. "Two hours," she said and pointed at Heather and DC. "You be ready."

"Ready for what?" Heather asked.

"To do what general says." Samkit could not credit how dense the Americans were. She walked into a huge closet and selected two cheongsams made of Thai silk. She carried them back into the room and laid them out on the bed. One of the high-neck Chinese dresses was bright blue and the other an equally vivid green. Both were split dangerously high up one side.

"Well," Nikki said as she stroked the dresses, "we know what the General has in mind. What do I do?"

"You stay here and take bath," Samkit told her. "Wash hair and take gold rings off."

Nikki threw herself onto the large bed. "That's fine with me," she announced. "No way I'm going to fuck a chink." Samkit did not try to correct her and explain that she would do whatever the general wanted. "I need a blast," Nikki said.

"What is 'blast'?" Samkit asked. Being a good servant, she would provide whatever she could.

"You know, blow . . . nose candy."

Samkit looked confused. "She means cocaine," DC explained.

A terrified look swept across Samkit's face. "No, missy. You no do that. Samkit no do. No drugs near general." She bit her words off and made a violent slashing motion across her neck.

Both Heather and DC could see the woman tremble and the terrified look on her face. "I think she means it," Heather said. "I'm going to get ready." She dropped her wrap and walked into the bathroom.

"Ready to do what?" Nikki called.

"Whatever the general wants," Heather answered. "Which, I think, roughly translates as 'ready to perform.' "

Ipoh Barracks, near Kuala Lumpur, Malaysia

Captain Peter Woodward crossed the compound at Ipoh Barracks with his usual rolling gait and half-ran up the stairs into the officers mess of the Malaysian Rangers. He found Mackay hunched over a table in the lounge, a white-coated steward hovering in the background and ready to replenish the lieutenant colonel's drink. "Gin and tonic," Woodward told the steward who promptly disappeared with a look of relief. Mackay was deliberately working at getting drunk.

"Interesting message just came in," Woodward said. "We have to send you back." He sat down.

Mackay looked up from his fourth drink in less than an hour, showing few signs of reaching his intended goal. "That sounds familiar," he said, recalling when Woodward had used the same words before the patrol went charging off to the Gurkha camp. "Who wants me out of here?" A cynical bitterness etched his words.

"Actually, your people," Woodward told him. "We need to get you to Kuala Lumpur to catch a flight to Guam. Should be a plane there laid on to take you to the States."

"All very organized," Mackay observed. "You must be anxious to get rid of me." He was slurring some of his words.

"Whatever are you talking about?" Woodward asked.

"Your interrogation techniques leave something to be desired."

"I see," Woodward replied. "That was all very necessary, you know. We were pressed for time. Actually, I'm sorry to see you go but we would appreciate a few words for the after-action report before you leave. Must tidy up all the loose ends."

"Really," Mackay said. "And what trash can will it end up in?"

Woodward was losing patience with the lieutenant colonel. "You Yanks can be so bloody thick at times that I wonder how you ever . . ." His words trailed off and he stared at the big black man sitting opposite him. "Look, we don't, as you Yanks say, get 'wrapped around the axle' about the wrong things. We were dealing with some not very 'nice' men out there who have absolutely no idea of what the rules are or would even play by them if they did. In order to stay alive, the Sass does have rules. We go in as quickly as we can, do what we have to do, then get out. Our superiors understand that and we don't have to muck around with legal niceties. More importantly, we do not have to cover up what we do because our politicos don't hang us out to dry afterwards."

"Right," Mackay snarled. "The end justifies the means."

"On operations, quite right."

"I don't work that way," Mackay said, motioning for another drink.

"At the present moment," Woodward said, "you and, I believe, the hostages are still alive." The captain stared at Mackay, who missed the point. "Well, we are pressed for time."

"Who really wants me out of here?" Mackay asked.

Woodward shook his head. "Not us. The message came from your National Security Council. I believe they are the chaps who talk directly to your President." He stood up to leave.

Mackay jerked to his feet, pushing his chair over. "You are a cold-blooded bastard," he said, carefully pronouncing each word.

"Probably," Woodward replied. He turned and walked out of the room. Mackay followed him.

Bangkok, Thailand

"Must I?" DC asked, appraising the bright blue cheongsam Samkit held out for her to wear as she emerged from the bathroom. She shot a glance at Heather, who was sitting at a dressing table carefully combing and arranging her hair. "How can you be so calm?" Panic worked at the edges of her voice.

"Don't think about it, DC," Heather answered.

"I can't do this." Tears rolled down DC's cheeks. "I'm not a whore or slave," she whimpered, trying desperately to beat back the fear that was conquering her. "This whole thing is so bizarre . . ." She collapsed to the floor as sobs wracked her body.

Heather came over and knelt beside her, putting her arms around her. "Don't think about it," she repeated, trying to console the young woman, searching for the right words. "They wouldn't be going to all this trouble if they were going to hurt us. Think of getting out of here and this as a jail sentence. We'll do what it takes to survive." DC trembled as the tears flowed and Heather saw the despair that had become her master. Then worry and fear of the unknown started to gnaw at her own self-confidence. "We can do this," she said, trying to convince herself. Then it came to her; DC couldn't help and she would have to do it alone. She turned to Samkit and pointed at DC. "My friend is very sick."

"She is not sick," Samkit said. "She is afraid because she understands what is happening. It is our fate because we are women."

Heather stared at the woman, surprised at how good her English had suddenly become. "What's going to happen to us?"

"You working girl now"—Samkit's English reverted back to the singsong pidgin English she had been speaking—"like me during war in Vietnam. Many GIs come to Thailand and I go work in bar at Ubon where Americans build big air base. Many GIs like me and say they are working on railroad, lay a Thai a day. I make much money but bar manager owns me. I only seventeen then and very pretty. I think GI marry me. When GIs leave I have baby but no husband."

"How old are you?" Heather asked.

"I forty-two. Not pretty now." She pointed at the Americans, pain in her voice, "You, me, same now." She hurried across the floor when DC started to throw up, a greenish bile puddling on the oriental carpet. "You clean up," she told Nikki.

"Get lost," Nikki snapped.

Samkit walked over to the bed, grabbed Nikki's dark hair and dragged her off the bed. Nikki tried to resist but Samkit slapped her. Nikki pulled back and Samkit slapped her three more times.

She dropped the girl beside DC, walked into the bathroom, returned with a towel and dropped it on her. "You clean when I say," she ordered. Nikki did as she was told.

"You get ready now," Samkit told Heather. "No waste time." She pointed to her watch and helped DC into the bathroom to care for her. "Hurry," she called.

Nikki cleaned up the mess as best she could while Heather sat back down at the dressing table. She poked at her hair briefly, applied mascara, a green eyeliner, and a subdued lipstick, before selecting a set of diamond stud earrings. She stood, dropped her towel, and slipped into the bright green cheongsam. She appraised her image in a full-length mirror. The dress fitted like a glove and only the split up the side allowed her to walk normally. She turned to examine just how high the split reached. "Damn," she moaned when she saw her exposed panties. She slipped them off and kicked them into a corner. She smoothed the dress with her hands and studied herself in the mirror. "Flashy," she said, half-aloud to herself.

"But definitely not cheap," a clipped British voice said from the doorway. Heather turned, wondering how long Chiang had been standing there, watching her. He was leaning against the door jamb holding a martini, one hand was in the pocket of his white dinner jacket and his left foot crossed the right at the ankles. He frowned at Nikki and gestured her out of the room.

What sort of games are we playing here? Heather thought. "Are you Cary Grant or Noël Coward?" she asked.

"Neither." He smiled at her. "Would you care to join me for cocktails before dinner?" He stepped aside and motioned with his martini glass down the hall. Heather followed him, fully aware how right DC had been when she called the situation bizarre.

"This is like a bad movie from the thirties," Heather mumbled under her breath.

"Not really, Miss Courtland. I just happen to be an admirer of things English." He moved with a confident grace that matched the tone of his voice. "I find it gives a sense of permanence to a rapidly changing world, don't you."

"I had never thought of it that way," she answered.

"But then that isn't the American way, is it? Seeking permanence." He held a door open for her and they walked into a large and comfortably furnished room that could have been lifted directly from an English country home. "Please." He motioned her to the couches in front of a large fire.

In the background, Heather could hear the soft whir of an air conditioner keeping the room cool. She gazed at her strange host and estimated that he was in his early fifties and about five feet ten inches tall, but couldn't decide if his angular features could be considered handsome. She sat down and crossed her legs, letting the dress fall away and showing off her well-shaped legs. "I don't believe this," she said, taking in the surroundings.

"Ah," the man said, "but you must, for it is very real."

Heather rose and prowled around the room, inspecting its contents. She paused in front of a bookshelf filled with video cassettes, surprised to find everything that Humphrey Bogart had played in and an entire shelf filled with nothing but old English movies. The only modern film was *White Mischief,* a movie about English planters in Kenya in the late 1930s. This guy thinks he's an English gentleman or colonial planter, Heather decided.

"Miss Courtland," he said. She turned to face him and he motioned her into a dining room where four servants were waiting. The meal proved to be exquisite and she found herself captivated by the man's witty conversation and charming manner. It wasn't what she had expected.

"I love French cuisine," she said over coffee. "You have an excellent chef."

"I am most fortunate in that regard." He smiled. "He's one of the foremost chefs in the world. Of course, he is at your disposal while you are here. Perhaps there is something else I can provide?"

Heather's mind raced through the various requests that might lead to something else. "I would like to know what to call you. General sounds so . . . well, so . . . old." She was careful to smile helplessly.

Chiang looked into his cup as if he was trying to read some hidden meaning. Then he raised his dark eyes and smiled at her, his white even teeth and smile charming. "I did have an English nanny who took to calling me 'Bertie.' "

"Bertie!" Heather was surprised at the genuine amusement in her voice and warned herself to keep up her guard, not be drawn in by this strange man.

"Yes, it seems the British upper class had the habit of giving their children an interminably long list of names and then insisted on using a nickname that had nothing to do with any of their other names. She called me Bertie and always insisted that I was a Bertie."

He rose and led her back into the lounge where she noticed that a set of French doors leading into a bedroom were open. She could see a large bed with the covers pulled back revealing satin sheets. She remembered Samkit's words about her being a "working girl." "Do you still see your English nanny?" Heather asked, unconsciously seeking a way to postpone the inevitable.

"She was killed in a bombing raid during the Vietnam War." His voice was still smooth but Heather was certain she heard a different tone. His face had gone rigid and hard.

"Oh, I'm sorry," she said quickly, too automatically. It sounded false to her. "I shouldn't have asked."

"It's quite all right." He poured them each a snifter of cognac. "She was the only person who cared for me in my childhood. It's a debt I'll repay someday." She heard resolve in his voice. "My mother was French and my father half-Chinese and Japanese . . . a product of the Japanese occupation of Manchuria. Neither of them had any time for me. You have no idea what it means to be of mixed blood in Asia." Beneath the British accent and cool exterior, Heather could hear the agony of a lonely childhood. "Fortunately, my father was quite rich . . . a planter in Laos . . . the Plaine des Jarres." Now his voice hardened. "Quite rich, that is, until the CIA came with their Air America. My home was destroyed in the monstrosity of the Vietnam War."

"But wasn't the Plaine des Jarres one of the world's richest opium poppy growing regions in the world?" Heather asked.

"Yes, it was. But that had nothing to do with your war in Vietnam. For some reason, your CIA turned its attention to us. I can still remember the night the planes came . . . the bombs." He stared into his glass. "My nanny, the only woman who ever loved me, died that night." He looked at her, the pain still evident. "She was quite old, and of course no longer my nanny, but I swore that I would avenge her death. Like I said, it's a personal debt still outstanding."

Understanding flashed through Heather and a feeling of compassion for the man fluttered deep inside. So much made sense and she wanted to tell him, shout at him, that none of them had anything to do with his nanny's death. Then another thought froze her emotions. Her father had been one of the foremost "hawks" in the United States Senate and had pushed hard for a vigorous military solution to the Vietnam War. Instinctively, she knew that she had to change the subject and break the spell of the past that bound him. It was a question of survival.

Heather set her drink down and came gracefully to her feet.
She turned, gave him a lingering look and walked to the French
doors that opened into the bedroom. She held out her hand to
him and he came across the room, joining her. "Unzip me," she
whispered, turning her back to him. She felt his fingers work the
zipper and then gently caress her waist before pulling away. She
pulled the dress over her head and let it fall to the floor before
turning back to him. Slowly, Heather extended her hand to the
man who called himself Bertie and led him into the bedroom.

Samkit was waiting in the one-room bungalow built on stilts
when the monk entered. His saffron-orange robe was slightly dirty
and stained. She rose and gave a deep bow, saying nothing as
she gave him a clean robe and motioned to a basin of water in
the corner. She withdrew while the monk bathed and changed
robes. Even though there was food on the table, he did not eat
since Theravada Buddhist monks never ate after eleven-thirty in
the morning. When he was ready, he sat on the floor and composed himself. Samkit reappeared and sat to one side, not looking
directly at him.

"Have you been well, mother?" he asked.

"Most well," Samkit answered.

"And what has happened in the demon's household?"

Samkit recounted all the events that had transpired in Chiang's
villa since they had last met. She finished her report with "It is
rumored that Chiang is returning to his Burma stronghold."

"It is becoming very dangerous for you," the monk said. "I
do not think you should go to Burma. Plead ill health. Chiang
will leave you here."

Samkit did not contradict him. That would have been disre-
spectful and contrary to the great deference accorded to monks.
"Our Lord Buddha will not release me from this moral dilemma,"
she said. "I must do what I can to defeat this demon who poisons
the world with his drugs and our lives with his influence."

"Mother," the monk said in exasperation, "we have been over
this before. It is not a simple moral issue, but also an economic
and political problem."

"And it continues to corrupt all life," Samkit reminded him.
"Are you going to turn away from this evil?"

"No, of course not." The monk had dedicated his life to destroying the drug culture that would consume his religion.

"Then neither can I."

The monk knew that he could not dissuade his mother and pulled what looked like a Walkman radio from a bag. "Then I will go to Burma and become a village monk," he said. "But it will be too dangerous for us to meet. Use this instead." He punched at the radio's buttons, showing her its hidden features.

The Executive Office Building, Washington, D.C.

The elevator doors swooshed open and the unlikely, mismatched pair stepped into the wide black-and-white marble corridor of the third floor of the Executive Office Building across the street from the White House. "Who's your friend?" one of the bureaucrats who inhabited the staff offices of the President of the United States asked. Mazie Kamigami ignored the question and glanced up at the tall army officer. He was not what she had expected and the file folder on Lieutenant Colonel John Author Mackay had not prepared her for the sheer physical presence of the man. It wasn't often that she felt intimidated, but Mackay seemed to be doing it and he had barely said five words to her.

"You have an unusual middle name," she said, making a try at small talk and perhaps gaining some insight into the personality of the man.

Mackay looked down at her, aware that they were drawing stares. The men and women who worked in the executive offices of the President had never seen a warrior before. They were used to dealing with the smooth and businesslike staff officers from across the river in the Pentagon, not someone who looked like his business was killing and was very good at it. His massive bulk towered over the short and dumpy Mazie and he walked with an easy, confident gait. His uniform fit his muscular body perfectly and his tailor had wisely not used shoulder pads. The carefully knotted tie looked like it would rupture if he flexed his neck muscles. "My mother misspelled 'Arthur' on my birth certificate," he told her.

"And you didn't change it?" she asked.

Mackay didn't answer her. He had no intention of explaining that his mother was almost illiterate and that he would never hurt her by changing the name she had given him.

"Here we are," Mazie said uncomfortably as she pushed through the door into her cluttered office. Mackay looked around, the messy office grating on his sense of order. "Find a seat and make yourself comfortable. You can hang your coat over there."

She gestured at a coat stand. "Coffee or tea?"

"Tea would be fine," Mackay answered.

When he took off his coat, Mazie realized there was not an ounce of fat on the man. She buzzed her secretary to bring tea in. "Well, we've got some work to do," she told him.

"Miss Kamigami, I assume that the reason for my being here and talking to you has to do with the five Americans that were kidnapped." She nodded an answer. "And because I was involved in nailing a few of the bastards that did it." Again, she nodded. "And you think I can help appease Senator Courtland and keep him off your back."

"You've read the newspapers," she said, quickly reevaluating the man. Although he was dog-tired and suffering from jet lag, he had correctly analyzed the situation and why he had been summoned. A few of her fellow staffers on the National Security Council were going to make a serious mistake in underestimating him.

One of Mazie's strengths was her ability to size up a person in short order, and every instinct she possessed told her that Mackay could be trusted. It was an intuition that had never failed her. She made a decision; she would bring him in. "I've got people around here fooled into thinking I'm the local expert on the Far East so I get involved anytime there's a flap." She stopped, appalled at the look spreading across Mackay's face.

"Miss Kamigami, when someone belittles themselves, I go into a deep defensive crouch and immediately cover my wallet." His voice was warm and friendly.

Mazie stared at him, struck by the look on his face that was at odds with the friendliness in his words. "Is that a smile?" she asked. He nodded an answer. "Please call me Mazie. Okay, you're here because this kidnapping has the potential to be a political time bomb for President Pontowski and we need all the information we can get."

"Your specific role in all this?" he asked.

"I'm the National Security Council's special assistant on the Far East and working on the NSC's Crisis Action Team that Mr. Cagliari, he's the national security adviser—"

"I know who Mr. Cagliari is," Mackay interrupted her. "And how the NSC works."

"Sorry," Mazie replied, thinking that she too had underestimated Mackay. "The team's job," she continued, "is to make sense out of this mess and come up with some concrete proposals for the National Security Planning Group. They and the President will call the shots. We give them the options."

"Sounds complicated," Mackay said. "Who's in charge?"

"Believe me, the President is firmly in charge. And it's not really so complicated. The National Security Planning Group, NSPG for short, are his chief advisers in situations like this. The Crisis Action Team, we call it the CAT, is the staff that does the legwork." She waved a hand at the mess in her office. "Do you have any idea how much raw intelligence comes in here every day? It's overwhelming and much is contradictory. For example, who is really behind all this? So far we're not sure."

"Chiang Tse-kuan," Mackay told her.

"So we've heard. But you're the only source for that information. We have no secondary confirmation. There are too many competing groups in that region that could do something like this. If we focus on the wrong one, the whole thing blows up in our face. I have to come up with an answer to the hard question—who is behind this?"

"I wasn't aware of other competing groups," he told her.

"Well, for one, the Colombian-Germans are trying to move into the Golden Triangle and there is a definite Japanese connection."

"Start with Chiang," he said, "but keep looking for others."

"Once this thing starts rolling it is possible that some people are going to be killed. We cannot afford to kill the wrong ones. We've got to be sure."

"Chiang," he repeated.

"Why are you so sure?"

"Because I was there when we interrogated the bastards."

"How reliable is a wounded man?" she asked.

"*They*"—Mackay stressed the word—"weren't 'wounded' until after the interrogation. They were telling the truth."

"We were told that only one person was interrogated."

Mackay shook his head. "Three."

"Okay, that helps. Still, just being there won't hack it. It would help if we had custody of . . . " Another thought came to her. "What did happen to them and why are you so certain that Chiang was behind it?"

"You don't want to know," Mackay said.

"Damn it, Colonel, I do need to know." In a few well-chosen words, Mackay told her exactly what had happened and how Woodward had interrogated and shot the three men. "My God," Mazie whispered when he was finished. She looked at him, not able to credit that such a sane and rational-sounding man could be part of what she had just heard. "I can't take that upstairs."

"Is that all, Miss Kamigami?" Mackay stood up and pulled his coat on.

"I can't believe—"

"Can't believe what? That the only rule out there is survival? You've lived in the civilized world too long, Miss Kamigami." He was moving toward the door.

"Not so damn fast, Colonel." Her voice was shaking. It was the first time she had been exposed to the reality of covert operations. "The CAT is meeting with Mr. Cagliari in twenty minutes. You need to be there." Mackay sat down and watched her poke through the mass of paperwork, quickly extracting the summaries, source reports, and intercepts she wanted to take to the meeting. Mackay was impressed that she knew exactly where everything was. Her organizational approach may have been totally different from Mackay's but she was just as efficient.

"Let's go," Mazie said and led him down into the basement and through a tunnel underneath West Executive Avenue to the Situation Room in the basement of the White House. The national security adviser and the rest of the CAT, the Crisis Action Team, were there.

"Okay," Cagliari said, not waiting for introductions, "we've got an hour to get our act together."

"But I thought the NSPG wasn't meeting until this afternoon," Mazie protested.

"It still is," Cagliari told her. "But this is taking on some heavy political dimensions and a general from Special Operations Command is joining the CAT. Let's get to work."

Mackay sat in a corner and watched the team hash through the mass of information they were deluged with, trying to paint a coherent picture of the kidnapping. Finally, the critical question was before them—who was responsible? "Chiang Tse-kuan," Mazie stated, hard conviction in her voice. When the protests that they could not be sure became too heavy, she had Mackay tell them about the interrogation. When he was finished, stunned silence came down in the room.

"What was your role in all this?" Cagliari demanded.

Mackay leaned across the table, remembering Woodward's words about being hung out to dry by politicos. "I just smiled at whoever Captain Woodward was interrogating," he said, deciding to smile at the national security adviser.

"And that made them tell the truth, I suppose," Cagliari shot at him.

Mazie Kamigami was not above rattling her boss. "He's smiling at you now," she said.

"My God," Cagliari said. A green light came on over the door, drawing his attention away from Mackay. "President's coming . . . not expected . . . be cool." Everyone stood up.

"The President likes to do this," Mazie told Mackay, "drop in unannounced on his staff when we're working and talking." Mackay could sense the tension in the room. A few moments later, the door opened and Pontowski walked in. He was followed by three men: Cox, his chief of staff; General Charles J. Leachmeyer, the Army's Chief of Staff; and an Air Force three-star general.

"I think you all know General Leachmeyer," Pontowski said. He liked making introductions. "And this is Lieutenant General Simon Mado from Special Operations Command. General Mado has flown in from Florida to join you." Everyone in the room knew that the United States Special Operations Command, US-SOCOM, was headquartered at MacDill Air Force Base outside Tampa, Florida, and that by making Mado part of the CAT, the President was seriously considering military action to free the five Americans. Mado certainly looked the part: tall, athletic build, dark blond hair with touches of gray, stern jaw and clear blue eyes.

"Mr. President," Cagliari said, "this is Lieutenant Colonel John Mackay, the exchange officer with the SAS."

Pontowski walked around the table to shake hands with Mackay. "I understand things got a little exciting for you," the President said.

"Yes, sir," Mackay replied.

"I believe Chiang Tse-kuan could be involved in this," Pontowski said as he sat down. He looked at Mackay expectantly, waiting for a response. No one else answered.

Mackay was impressed. The President had done his homework, drawn his own conclusions, and got right down to business. "Sir, I'm certain that he's behind it," Mackay answered.

Pontowski looked at his national security adviser. "Mike, what do you think?"

"It all fits," Cagliari said. "Although we cannot be absolutely sure at this point. I think we should proceed on the assumption that Chiang is behind it but keep looking for other players."

"Please show me what you have," Pontowski said.

Cagliari nodded at Mazie, who stood up. She walked over to a wall map and quickly summarized the situation to date, using selected intelligence to support her interpretation of events. She was cogent, persuasive, and well-organized. Mackay made a mental note to avoid arguing with the dumpy woman. When she was finished, Pontowski nodded and stood up. "Mazie," he said, "I want you at the NSPG meeting this afternoon to tell them the same thing." He stopped on his way out of the room. "Why don't you all get acquainted with General Mado"—he grinned—"while I wander through the Office Building and shake up a few of your colleagues." Then he was gone.

Cagliari had Mazie brief Mado on what the CAT was doing and how the team was organized. Different members would add details when she touched on their areas of expertise. It was a smooth and productive introduction.

"I think," General Simon Mado said when she was finished, "that it is obvious why I'm here. The President is seriously considering using military force to rescue the hostages. As you know, that is my area of expertise. Perhaps you recall Operation Warlord when I commanded Task Force Alpha and successfully rescued two hundred and eighty POWs out of Iran."

Cagliari bit his tongue and said nothing. He had been in the National Military Command Center when the rescue went down and Mado had been little more than a passenger aboard the orbiting AC-130 gunship that had provided fire suppression to the rescue force. Others on the ground had been responsible for the success of the rescue but owing to the nature of the military, Mado had gotten the lion's share of the credit. The then Chief of Staff of the Air Force, General Lawrence "Get the Hell out of Here by Sundown" Cunningham, had tried to set the matter straight, but a heart attack had killed the crusty old general before he could nail Mado. Cagliari was convinced that the Air Force had been going downhill ever since Cunningham had died.

"I take it then," Cagliari said, "that USSOCOM has a plan in the works to rescue the hostages."

"We have a plan for a scenario such as this," Mado said. "But we need to thoroughly evaluate the situation, coordinate with other agencies, and revise the plan before we implement it."

Mazie keyed on what Mado was saying. I need to check this guy out, she thought. And why is he staring at Mackay?

After the meeting broke up, Mackay headed for the underground tunnel that led back to the Executive Office Building. "Colonel Mackay," General Mado called, stopping him. "I need to speak to you for a moment." Mackay walked back and joined Mado outside the door of the now darkened room. "I know you will be shortly returning to your normal duties. Please keep me apprised as to your whereabouts so I can contact you in case I need more information."

"Yes, sir," Mackay said, careful to keep his face impassive, wondering why Mado would be concerned with so small a matter. He certainly wanted to get out of Washington, D.C., at the earliest opportunity and away from the shaky ground of politics.

"Also," Mado said, "I don't want any misunderstandings about this. But after listening to what happened at the Gurkha camp and your failure to effect a rescue, I'm not impressed."

Mackay thought about that for a moment before he decided that the general didn't have a clue about special operations. The general gave a sharp jerk of his head and quick-stepped up the stairs.

Now what was that all about? Mackay thought as he watched Mado disappear. Michael Cagliari stepped out of the darkened room, surprising Mackay. "He's a piece of work," the national security adviser told Mackay. "This lovely part of his personality has been coming out ever since Operation Warlord."

"I don't understand," Mackay said.

"Mado is trying to stake out special operations as his private preserve and doesn't want any competition on the scene."

"I'm only a lieutenant colonel," Mackay reminded him.

"Rank doesn't hold much water in special operations. During Operation Warlord," Cagliari said, "a captain, James 'Thunder' Bryant, made him look like a fool."

"Bryant was black?" Mackay knew the answer even as he asked the question and a deep anger flared in him.

"Right," Cagliari said. "But not to worry." He walked down the hall, leaving Mackay wondering just what games were being played in the corridors of power of the nation's capital. Whatever the games are, he decided, they have nothing to do with combat and I'm not going to get involved.

Within twenty-four hours, three events took place that were to prove him wrong.

Mazie Kamigami walked calmly to her car, no sign of the frustration she felt visible on her bland and smooth face. She did

slam the car door of her beloved 1969 bright yellow Beetle convertible harder than normal, but she immediately apologized.
"I'm sorry, Humphrey," she told the car. She sat in the car thinking about the problem of Simon Mado. She had checked him out
and three sources had confirmed her suspicions that he was a
political general—not one of the doers. If the President did want
a rescue mission mounted, the CAT would need someone with
the necessary military expertise to drive a decision, not play politics. She had a recommendation in mind who she would mention
to National Security Adviser Cagliari.

It was clear that Mado would not agree to any plan until it had
been coordinated with just about every intelligence agency in the
government and received their "chop," meaning their agreement.
In Mazie's experience that was a sure formula for paralysis. The
way to solve that problem was to present Mado with a clear-cut
situation and force him into agreement. That way, they could
bypass the intelligence community, where fights over turf were
much more important than getting the job done.

What Mazie needed was a source of intelligence that was unimpeachable. And that required an operative on the inside, which
the CIA would not, or could not, provide. To get an intelligence
collection operation started, she would have to send a Clandestine
Intelligence Operations Proposal up through the bureaucracy to
the CIA's Policy Coordinating Staff, who, given their past record,
would most likely staff it to death, taking anywhere from six to
eighteen months to give it their stamp of approval. She needed
to get a spy inside Chiang's operations and bypass the CIA. Fortunately, she had access to System 4, the highly classified computer system that the NSC used to monitor all covert intelligence
operations and she knew how to read between the lines.

She wheeled out of the parking structure and headed for Fort
Belvoir, calling ahead on her car phone for an appointment. Her
ID got her past a sharp MP at the gate and she headed for the
Special Activities Center on the northern part of the post. The
Special Activities Center was the Air Force organization respon-
sible for HUMINT—human intelligence—bureaucratese for old-
fashioned spying. Once inside, she was ushered into the office of
Brigadier General William G. Carroll, an old friend.

"Mazie," he beamed at her, standing up, "it is good to see you
again. Who've you been terrorizing lately?"

"How's the boy wonder of military intelligence?" she replied.
"Don't you ever get old?" At forty-one years of age, Carroll

looked ten years younger and was the youngest brigadier general
in the Air Force. Other officers, unfamiliar with his career, would
sarcastically speculate how a nonpilot, a ground pounder, could
rise so fast through the ranks until they saw the medals on his
chest. The dark and slender general was one of the most decorated
officers on active duty and wore the Air Force Cross on top of a
heap of medals. He had earned them all the hard way, by duty
in the field. The general was a fluent linguist and had been instrumental in rescuing 280 POWs out of Iran before that country
realized the United States was not the enemy. Then he had played
a key role in keeping the latest round in the Arab-Israeli war
from jumping the firebreak and flaring into an exchange of chem-
ical and nuclear weapons.

"Compliments now!" Carroll laughed. "You must want some
big favor." He waved Mazie to a seat and sat down next to her.
"No doubt, something to do with the abduction of Senator Courtland's daughter," he added.

"Am I too late?" she asked, "or do I have to get in line with
all the rest?" He gave her a noncommittal smile. "You do play
your cards close to the chest," she told him.

"You know I'll help if I can," Carroll told her. He listened
impassively as she recapped the situation. When she was finished,
he turned and looked at a group picture on the wall labeled "Task
Force Alpha." "That's Simon Mado," he told her, pointing to a
man seated in the middle. "He's one of the most competent
managers in the service and, without a doubt, the biggest asshole
in the Air Force. Be careful how you handle him." He looked at
her, his decision made. "We've got agents in the area and can
help you." He stared at her. "That's close-hold information not
to go outside this office."

"Does the CIA know?" Mazie asked.

"You've got to be kidding. It was pure luck and a spinoff from
another, very much approved operation, that got our operatives
in place. We have no intention of losing these sources because
of bureaucratic infighting over who controls them." The CIA and
many of the other intelligence-gathering agencies of the United
States were experts at high-tech reconnaissance and monitoring
communications. While they could count the tiles on the roof of
buildings and tell when the lawns were watered or how many
times the toilets were flushed, they knew little about what went
on inside. The Air Force Special Activities Center under Carroll
had a different philosophy of operations. "I'll set you up with a

contact," Carroll said as he buzzed for his assistant.

Michael Cagliari, the assistant to the President for national security, took pains to corner General Leachmeyer, the Army Chief of Staff, alone during a cocktail party at the elegant George-town townhouse of one of the power brokers of Washington, D.C., society. The men spoke quietly and three minutes later, Leachmeyer had agreed to let the National Security Council use the services of one Lieutenant Colonel John Author Mackay, United States Army.

Tosh Pontowski was sitting up in bed when her husband walked in to share a morning cup of coffee. They exchanged looks and he knew immediately that the wolf was back. "It's too soon to tell," she said. Lupus, the disease that ravaged her body, came and went with frightening unpredictability and intensity. "I suppose 'l'affaire Courtland' still has top billing," she said, changing the subject.

"Along with the balance of trade, a health care system that is crumbling, and a Congress that doesn't understand the meaning of compromise or fiscal responsibility." He made himself comfortable in a chair next to her bed.

"All can be dealt with."

"In time, love, in time." He smiled at her, as always, amazed at her unfailing optimism. "Unfortunately, time is the one commodity in short supply with Courtland. We are dealing with too many unknowns—"

"And given the uncertainty," she interrupted, "who to rely on."

"Yes," he replied, "and when to act."

"You've had to live with those uncertainties before."

"Yes, I have," he said, remembering.

1943

Off the Coast of Holland, near Zandvoort

Zack Pontowski lay in the bottom of the small boat in two inches of water listening to the urgent whispers of the two men who had pulled him out of the frigid waters of the North Sea off the Dutch coast. Why are they whispering? he thought. In the distance, he could hear the dog barking again. Zack strained to hear what they were saying, surprised that he was having trouble understanding them. Because his mother was German, he was fluent in that language and had been mistaken for a native German many times.

One of the men bent over him and examined the wound on his face while the other started to row. The pilot flinched as the man's fingers explored the cuts on his face. Zack understood him to say, "He's bleeding badly from two cuts. Probably smashed his face into the windscreen."

The rower muttered something like "The patrol has moved south."

Then it came to Zack—they were speaking Dutch, not German. "I'm an American and speak German," he said in German. It was a mistake. The rower lifted his oar out of the oarlock and brought it down hard, knocking him out.

Dust filtered down through the cracks in the boards three feet over Zack's head and he sneezed, waking himself up. His head pounded and he tried to see in the darkness. He could feel a thick bandage wrapped over his head and under his chin. His right leg ached. Slowly he became aware of his surroundings. He was lying on a hard pallet in a crawl space between floors and could hear voices above and below him. He was thankful for the thick down comforter that covered him since he was naked. "What the hell . . ." he muttered in English.

A hatch near him popped open and the head of a teenage girl appeared. "Are you feeling better?" she asked, her voice marked with the harsh guttural consonants of the Dutch language.

"Yes," Zack answered. "I think so. I'm hungry . . ." The hatch dropped closed and he could hear the girl asking her mother for food. Then she was back, passing him a large bowl of soup and a spoon. "*Danke schon,*" he said in German.

"It is better if you say, 'Dank u,'" she said in passable English. "Speaking German almost got you killed." She pulled herself into the hatchway and sat on the edge of the opening, an obvious interest in her eyes.

"What happened? Where am I?"

"You're far from the sea," she explained. "They brought you here to avoid the search." She paused, studying him in the faint light. "You were lucky . . . two young men were trying to escape to England in a small boat and saw you crash in the sea. . . . They got to you before the Germans. . . . When you spoke German, they almost threw you back into the water. Then you started speaking English, mumbling a name. You were in a daze. They were going to drown you but thought twice and came back to shore."

"Ruffy," Zack said. "I was asking about Flight Officer Andrew Ruffum. Have they found him?"

The girl shook her head. The news drove a wedge of unbearable sadness into Zack, his face clouded and he took three quick breaths. Another, more positive emotion eased the pain in his chest as he refused to believe that Ruffy was dead—his best friend was missing in action, much better than being a known casualty. The girl watched him as he struggled with his inner turmoil. Then she said, "Finish your food. A man will come to talk to you tonight. I'll get your uniform."

"What's your name?"

"Never ask names," she said. "It is better that way."

The girl was back in moments with his freshly laundered and mended uniform. He almost passed out when he sat up. "I can't believe I'm so weak," he muttered. The girl scooted across to him and helped him dress, now very interested in his body. "How long was I out?" he asked.

"You've been delirious with fever for four days. You are very badly hurt. Rest for now." She disappeared down the crawl hatch and left him in darkness.

The 'man' that came to see him that night was a stout woman in her fifties. She quickly explained that she was from the Dutch underground and they had to move him. "An informer . . . the Germans know you are around here . . . hurry." She helped him out of the crawl space and into the kitchen below. A man was there to catch him when he fell through.

"Where is the doctor?" the woman demanded. Zack could hear a hardness in her voice and she almost spat when she said "doctor."

"She's waiting in the car," the man answered. They helped Zack change into civilian clothes, don a heavy topcoat, and then walk outside to enter the backseat of a large black Mercedes. They made no attempt to hide him and covered his legs with a blanket.

The man slipped behind the wheel to drive and the older woman was beside him in the rear seat. "Your name is Jan van Duren. You're my son and were attacked and beaten by Dutch bullies.

You suffered head injuries and we're taking you to a specialist clinic for treatment. When we get stopped by a patrol or come to a checkpoint, say nothing and let her do the talking." Zack could only see the dark silhouette of the doctor's head in the front seat.

They drove in silence through the night until they reached a well-lighted and permanently constructed roadblock. An officious-looking German sergeant approached the car as the doctor stepped out with their papers. In the light, Zack could see she was wearing a heavy cape. The sergeant jerked the papers out of her hand as she explained their business. She spoke with a distinct French accent. The sergeant scanned their papers and he suddenly became courteous and respectful. "A moment, please, Frau Doktor," he said and disappeared into the guard shack. The woman stood patiently and another guard came up and offered her a cigarette, which she declined. The guard was not offended and stood there, shifting from one foot to another. Then she turned and Zack saw her face in the light for the first time.

She was beautiful. Her dark hair was pulled severely back in the manner of nurses and accentuated her high cheekbones and finely arched eyebrows. Her mouth was set in a grim line but held the promise of a beautiful smile. With a rush of emotion, he realized what made the guard so uncomfortable. "She's the flame unto the moth," he said in German.

The older woman glanced at him. "Men," she fumed. "You speak excellent German. Remember, you have a serious head wound so slur your words and act dazed."

The sergeant hurried out of the guard shack and handed their papers to the woman. He gave a short bow and held the car door open for her. She settled into the seat and from the look on the sergeant's face, Zack was certain she had given him a smile. He stood back at attention to let them pass. "Everything is in order," the woman said over her shoulder, her voice soft and lyrical with its heavy French accent. Zack wanted to talk to her, to hear her voice, and look at her while she answered.

"Of course," the older woman snapped. "The only thing false is the patient. Drive on," she ordered as the barrier in front of them lifted. As it came up, Zack could see the distinctive plaque announcing "Zoll" mounted on the bar. They were crossing a border.

"What country are we in now?" he asked.

"Germany," the woman answered.

"This is crazy," Zack protested. "I want to escape from the Germans, not jump into their arms."

The woman started talking in a low voice. "The manhunt for you in the Netherlands is closing in and this is the quickest way to get you to safety." There was pain in her words. "My husband is working with the Nazis . . ."

"Madeline!" the driver barked, "that is enough. No more." The woman nodded. She would not tell the American that her husband was fiercely loyal to the House of Orange and was using his position in the headquarters of Reichskommisar Arthur Seyss-Inquart to pass information to the Dutch underground.

"Our son was brutally beaten by Dutch students because of my husband's activities. He suffered head injuries and it was arranged to transport him to a special clinic in Baden-Baden, Germany, for treatment . . ." It was becoming harder for the woman to continue, "But we are moving you in his place. . . . It has all been arranged."

"But what's going to happen to your son?" Zack asked.

"He was murdered yesterday as he slept in his room. That's when it was decided for you to take his place."

"I'm sorry," Zack murmured. Then more strongly, "Who killed him?"

"Her," the woman said and jutted her chin in the direction of the woman in the front seat.

Confusion swirled through Zack's head as he tried to tie all the loose ends together. Supposedly, he was in the hands of the Dutch underground but he was now in Germany traveling in the guise of a Dutch traitor's son who had been murdered by a beautiful French doctor sitting less than three feet from him. His head ached with it all.

A sign announced they were entering Monchen-Gladbach. "You board a train here," the older woman said, "for the rest of the journey. We have to return to The Hague." Zack said nothing as he was helped into a wheelchair that had been strapped to the back of the Mercedes. The older woman pushed him into the train station while the young doctor walked briskly ahead. The driver followed carrying two suitcases. As they entered the main concourse, the doctor asked two young German soldiers for directions and they willingly escorted the small group to the correct platform. The soldiers gave the group an appearance of authority and the conductor ushered them to an empty compartment on the waiting train.

The woman and driver left and Zack found himself alone with the doctor as the train started to move. She raised her chin and turned her gaze onto Zack, studying him. Her pale blue eyes were incredibly bright and drew him in. "You are Jan van Duren," she reminded him. "I am your attending doctor. Please remember you have a serious head wound." For the next twenty minutes she filled him in on the real Jan van Duren. Occasionally, she would pause and have him repeat back all she had told him.

The conductor knocked on their door and entered to examine their tickets and travel papers. "We'll be stopping at Düsseldorf in a few minutes before continuing to Cologne," he explained. "You need to change trains at Cologne for Mannheim. Change trains again at Mannheim for Karlsruhe. From there, you can transfer to a train to Baden-Baden. So far it is quiet and the British are staying home tonight." The train slowed as they pulled into Düsseldorf. "I must go," the conductor said. "I'll try to ensure your privacy."

"What's your name?" Zack asked his traveling companion when they were alone. He was captivated by her accent and wanted to hear her talk. She ignored him and stood up, lowering the window to their compartment as the warning shriek of an air raid siren started to build. A sense of utter helplessness and fear cut through Zack as the wail filled the small compartment. All the lights in the train went out and the woman sat down and huddled in a corner.

He stood at the side of the window so he could see forward. "We're pulling into the station," he said. "We'll be okay." He was surprised at how calm and assured his voice sounded. Then he realized that the sixth sense that warned him of danger was quiet, sending no signals.

"How can you be so sure?" the woman asked, her voice betraying how young she was.

"Inbound bombers are usually detected and tracked while still over the North Sea," he explained. "We've got plenty of time before they reach here—if they're even headed our way." The first bomb exploded, making a liar out of him.

"Get away from the window!" she shouted.

But Zack stood there, drawn by the sight of the building inferno around them. A geyser of flame erupted in front of them as the train continued to pull into the station. The exploding bombs pounded at his senses and he could feel the concussions in his bones. Now the entire train station was a wall of flames and still the train kept moving. He felt the train cross a switching point and pick up speed. "He's not going to stop," Zack yelled, doubting if she could hear him.

Ahead, he could see a platform off to their right and people running out of the flames across the tracks and toward the moving train, desperate to escape. "My God" was all he could say as another stick of bombs rained down on the station, rocking the train with their concussion and momentarily blinding him. When he could see again, the tracks were littered with bodies. The train was still moving.

"Get away from the window!" she shouted again and pulled at his coat.

He pushed her away, vaguely aware that the glass in the window had blown out, somehow missing him. "I've got to see this," he said, not understanding what was driving him to witness the hell they were passing through. More people were running for the train now. He watched in horror as a burning man emerged from the flames holding a child at arms length in front of him. He stumbled crossing the tracks and went sprawling, throwing the child clear of him. A woman scooped up the child and kept running for the train, which was now picking up speed. She reached the train and disappeared from his view. "She made it!" he shouted, only to see her fall back away from the train without the child.

"My God" was all he could manage. "I didn't know . . . " The horror of saturation bombing had come home to Matthew Zachary Pontowski and he would live with this, his personal version of hell, for the rest of his life.

Now they were pulling free of the station and picking up speed. Shouts in the corridor broke the iron bands of the horror that still held him. The compartment door slid open and the conductor yelled, "Doktor, we need you . . . the goddamn British . . . " The woman hurried from the compartment and Zack sat down, wondering if the conductor had noticed he was standing by the window.

Time had no meaning for Zack as the train moved southward toward Cologne. The engineer saved us by not stopping, he thought. But how many people did he condemn to a sure death? What if he could have stopped long enough to . . . No, he decided, that wouldn't have worked. We'd have been a sitting duck.

Then it came to him—no man should have to make decisions like the one the train engineer had just made.

The lights came back on and Zack pulled the curtains over the open window. But the wind kept blowing the curtains back, so he turned the lights off, blacking the compartment out. The conductor came through and grunted something unintelligible. "Hans, here," he shouted down the corridor before moving on. A maintenance man appeared carrying a precut board and fit it into the window. He turned the lights back on and swept up the broken glass. It was a well-practiced after-action drill.

The train was slowing when the woman came back. Her clothes were spotted with blood and she was visibly shaken. "Are you okay?" he asked. She said nothing and sat down.

"There are many injured," she finally told him as the train drew to a halt in the Cologne Hauptbahnhof.

The conductor opened their door. "Frau Doktor, may I thank you? I will report what you did to the authorities. We are very grateful for such allies like yourself. The newspapers carry such terrible reports about the French."

"My father is a loyal Nazi," the girl said, "and I am working in the Netherlands. We all do what we must."

The conductor shouted and two men came to help them off the train. Zack was certain his fever was coming back and was grateful for the help and the waiting wheelchair. The conductor ushered them into a large waiting room and found her a seat at a crowded table and made room for Zack's wheelchair. "I will tell the stationmaster to get you on the next train for Mannheim," he said. Then he turned to the people sitting at the table and told them they had the privilege of sitting with a loyal French ally who had saved many German lives when the train had been bombed. A wave of friendly nods and comments went around the table as the conductor left.

A feeling of relief swept over Zack when he realized the waiting Germans had readily accepted them into their midst. So much like the English, he thought, remembering the time he and Ruffy had waited in the train station at Leeds when they were on their way to their first assignment at RAF Church Fenton.

The loudspeaker announced an arriving train bound for Berlin and the room cleared, leaving them alone in a sea of empty tables and chairs. He almost twisted out of his wheelchair when he heard an English voice behind him say in a distinct cockney accent, "In here, mate. I think they want us to wait inside."

"Right," another British voice said. "Too bloody cold out here." Then the same voice added, "Not much warmer in here."

Zack forced himself not to turn and look. He could hear the scraping of chairs behind him as the group sat down. "Who are they?" he mumbled to the woman.

"Three British prisoners, air force," she answered. "Two sergeants and a flight lieutenant, I think. Four guards." She touched his forehead and examined the bandage on his head. "Your fever is back," she said. A woman attendant directed her to a private office where she could tend to Zack. She pushed him out of the room as it started to fill with more passengers from the newly arrived train. When the door closed behind them and they were alone, she quickly examined his leg wound. "It's septic," she told him and replaced the bandage. She shoved the old bandage into his coat pocket. "We must hide this. Your travel papers say you only have a head wound. If I take you to a hospital with a leg injury, someone will become suspicious and turn us in. We've got to hurry and find help."

"Where will you find help in Germany?" he asked.

She shook her head. "We're going to France."

"How can we do that?" The woman ignored him and packed up her medical bag. "Then at least tell me your name," Zack protested.

"So like the English," she said. "You must have proper introductions." Zack heard a new tone in her voice. Was it amusement?

The little break in her reserved attitude drew him in and he looked up at her face, smiling. "But I'm not English. I'm an uncouth Yank."

A slight smile played across her face and he thought how pretty her mouth was. "Mijnheer Jan van Duren"—she gestured gracefully at him with her right hand, reverting back to his cover—"may I present Mademoiselle Chantal Dubois," and she turned her hand toward herself.

"Ah, Miss Dubois," he answered, wanting to keep the moment going, "I have broken through your proper French reserve. Perhaps we can now enjoy the rest of our journey?"

Chantal Dubois's face turned sober and the rigid facade she maintained flashed back into place. "There is nothing to enjoy." She opened the door and pushed him back to the waiting room as a group of soldiers entered. A man at their table had held their places and Chantal adjusted Zack's wheelchair so he could see the English prisoners and watch the new arrivals.

The soldiers that had entered stood inside the door looking for seats as more soldiers poured in. Zack estimated there were at least sixty of them and from the way they wore their uniforms and carried their weapons, they were hardened combat veterans. "From the eastern front," a woman at the table said in a low voice, "Many of them are wearing the Iron Cross." A nine-year-old boy at their table scurried across the room to talk to the soldiers. One of the soldiers smiled, squatted, and talked to the boy. Carefully, he showed the youngster his submachine gun and then stood up, playfully rubbing his head and sending him back to his mother.

"They were at Stalingrad," the boy told them breathlessly. "They fought their way out and wouldn't surrender." The table went silent in admiration. "They are being reassigned to France."

Zack could sense Chantal stiffen at the news.

The soldiers came to attention when a major entered. It was not the disciplined posturing of the Prussian military but rather the mark of respect willingly given by soldiers to their leader. The German major reminded Zack of his high school chemistry teacher; middle-aged, close-cropped thinning brown hair, ordinary-looking in the extreme. He took time to speak to most of the men individually. "Well, Rudi, still studying French?" A mumbled answer and the major moved on. "Erich, have you heard from home yet? I will send you on leave if you want." The man shook his head and the officer turned to another man. "Manifred, are you better? You should be in a hospital and thinking about going home with such a wound."

Manifred grinned. "Others have been hurt worse and they are still here."

"Crazy," the major said, "you are all crazy." He shook his head. "The bombing at Düsseldorf was bad, *ja?*"

"Why do they bomb civilians?" another soldier asked.

"It is the way the English and Americans make war," the major answered. "Not our way." Then he saw the three English prisoners sitting at the table next to Zack's. The major walked across to the English and the four guards jumped to their feet. "May I sit down?"

"Of course, Major," one of the guards said and held a chair for him.

The major stared at the three prisoners. "RAF?" he asked.

"What do the bloody uniforms bloody well look like?" the sergeant with the cockney accent answered.

"Do you fly bombers?" the major asked, his English heavily accented.

"That's enough, Jimmy," the flight lieutenant ordered.

"Perhaps you were on the Düsseldorf raid and shot down?" the major asked. "I was there when your bombs fell. It is a nice way to fight a war when you never have to see your enemy and confront him man to man." His voice was polite but hard. "Tell me, how does it feel to look your enemy in the eye now?" The three Englishmen said nothing and looked away. "Please have the courage to look at me," the major continued. All three did as he ordered. "No doubt you choose not to answer because I am armed, with my men and you are prisoners. That is wise."

The hostility in the room was a hard presence and Zack could see the hate-filled glares of the civilians. The Englishmen in their midst were the men who had destroyed their homes and killed their loved ones with seeming impunity.

"Me mum," the cockney sergeant said, "granddad and sisters were all killed in the blitz when Hermann 'Look the Blighters in the eye' Goering leveled the East End of London."

Hushed words went around the room as the conversation was translated into German and tension crackled like a high-voltage power line with the passing. Now the room was absolutely silent.

"Sergeant Groscurth," the major said casually, "order the men not to interfere." The wounded man whom the major had earlier addressed as Manifred barked an acknowledgment and Zack saw that every soldier had his gun at the ready. A clicking of safety catches and slapping of leather were the only sounds in the room.

Slowly and deliberately, the major drew his pistol and pulled the slide back to charge the chamber with a round. The snap of the slide closing and ramming the nine-millimeter shell home was a thunderclap. Then he laid the automatic on the table exactly halfway between him and the cockney sergeant. "I assure you, all is equal now." He nudged the pistol a little closer to the Englishman. The two men stared at each other.

The loudspeaker came alive and announced the train for Mannheim as the stationmaster hurried across the room. He gasped at the scenario in front of him. "Frau Doktor, the train. . . . I have a compartment for you." He couldn't take his eyes off the pistol lying on the table between the two men.

"Thank you," Chantal said and stood up. She pushed Zack out of the silent room, leaving the two men frozen in time.

Zack's fever was raging and he shivered in the cold train compartment they shared with three men. "We're almost to Mannheim," the oldest of the men said. "You should be taken to a hospital." Zack shook his head and mumbled that he would be fine. His slurred German words did not arouse suspicion.

"I was hoping we could make it to Baden-Baden," Chantal said. "It has been arranged for him to enter a hospital there."

Another man in a black leather trench coat stared at them with the coldest blue eyes Zack had ever seen. "Perhaps I can be of service," he began, his voice carrying a warmth totally lost in his eyes. "The trains are very irregular and Baden-Baden is not that far, perhaps a hundred and twenty kilometers. I can arrange for a car." Zack tried to work through the fog in his brain and convert 120 kilometers to miles, but couldn't do it. Chantal thanked the man for his kindness and it was soon arranged.

A man in a sheepskin coat was waiting with a car outside the *Bahnhof* at Mannheim and ran up to take their suitcases when he saw the man in the leather trench coat. Zack was settled in the rear seat and they drove off without a word. It seemed strange to Zack that the driver was not given directions but he kept spinning off into the fever-induced fog that was claiming him. He was vaguely aware when they turned into the courtyard of a large mansion and stopped.

The man in the black leather trench coat jumped out of the car and barked a command at two men waiting inside the entrance. Then he turned to Chantal. "Gestapo headquarters," he announced, opening the rear door and motioning to the entrance.

Don't sleep or pass out, Zack kept telling himself. He willed himself to fight the drowsiness that kept flooding back. He dug his fingernails into his palm, anything to keep awake. You'll talk in your sleep, he warned himself. He forced his mind to note the details of the room he was locked in, to listen for any sound. A woman's muffled scream reached down the busy corridor outside the heavy door and then was abruptly cut off. Where was Chantal? What had they done with her? Footsteps passed, not the heavy tread the movies delighted in stereotyping the Gestapo with, but the measured, purposeful walk of people going about their business. The activity outside the door indicated he was in the main part of the building.

A bolt in the door slid back and Zack closed his eyes, feigning sleep. Someone entered the room and he was aware of a presence leaning over him. A sharp slap stung his face and his eyes blinked open. A man in a dark suit and carefully knotted tie was looking at him. "Mueller," he announced, introducing himself as his expert fingers probed the bandage on his head and examined the marks on his face. "Yes," the man said to someone behind him, "he has received a head injury. But that does not account for such a high fever."

"Then what is causing it, Doktor," an unseen voice said. Zack recognized the owner—the trench coated man from the train—a Gestapo agent. Instinctively, Zack realized that truth was his best defense and pointed to his right leg. The doctor produced a pair of scissors from his case and cut up the seam of Zack's pant leg, laying open the bandage.

"Ah," the doctor said, much more interested now.

"His papers say he has a head wound," the Gestapo agent said. "There is no mention of his leg being hurt."

The terror that gripped Zack drove away the last of the fog. Falling into the hands of the Gestapo was his worst fear. Again, the woman's scream reached down the corridor, much louder now that the door was open. Was it Chantal? What had she told them? "Düsseldorf," he muttered, thinking of the only logical reason for him to have another injury. Would the fresh bandage convince them? What about the old bandage in his coat pocket? "An air raid, I was wounded on the train." He let his mouth go slack and his gaze drift away.

"His accent is not German," the doctor said.

"Yes, I know," the Gestapo agent said, "that's what made me suspicious. His papers identify him as being Dutch." He turned and walked out of the room.

The doctor clucked his tongue and cut the bandage away. "Ah yes, sepsis. You are fortunate, my young Dutch friend, that the Gestapo provides its doctors with the best in medical supplies." He cleansed the wound and examined it. "You need surgery, there are serious complications here." He gave Zack a box of pills. "Sulfa" was all he said.

The Gestapo agent was back. "Bring him. The Frenchwoman confirms he was wounded during the bombing and the station-master at Cologne reported that she treated many of our injured."

There was the sound of disappointment in his voice. The doctor hastily bandaged Zack's leg and helped him to his feet. Another man was waiting in the corridor and helped support Zack as he hobbled to another room.

Chantal was sitting in the room and looked up with relief when she saw Zack. Then she glared at the Gestapo agent. "Do you know who my father is?" she demanded.

"Yes, mademoiselle," the agent said, "I know who you say you are. We are checking on that now." He stomped out of the room, leaving them alone. Chantal gave a slight shake of her head, warning him to be quiet. It wasn't necessary as every warning bell Zack possessed was in full alarm. The agent came back and dropped their passports, IDs, and travel papers on the floor. "All is in order," he snapped.

"Since we have missed our train," Chantal said, ice in every word as she picked them up, "perhaps you will provide the car you promised."

"But of course, mademoiselle," he said, giving her a withering look and holding the door open.

A few minutes later, the car dropped them back at the train station. Zack's wheelchair was still where they had left it on the platform. Chantal helped him into it. "No one would touch it after seeing the Gestapo take us away," she said.

"They're first-class bastards," Zack said. He saw her shudder.

"I saw a woman they were questioning," she said. "You must have heard her scream. They made sure I saw her when they dragged her outside. She was naked and covered with burn spots. . . . She had piano wire tied around her neck." She stopped, unable to talk. Then she forced herself to continue. "I think they were going to hang her." There were tears in her eyes.

For a moment, Zack could see Chantal twisting naked, strangling at the end of a piano wire noose. The thought cut through him like a knife. "And they wonder why we bomb them."

They waited in silence as another train drew into the station and stopped. Fresh-faced young soldiers clamored down, full of life and humor. Zack recalled the major and his veteran soldiers they had seen at Cologne. "They are not all the same," he said.

"No, they are not," Chantal said and wheeled him toward the train.

Chantal was kneeling on the floor of the train compartment in front of Zack stitching the leg of his pants that the doctor had cut open. An elderly woman traveling in the same compartment had lent her a needle and thread and watched in approval as Chantal finished the job, not waking the sleeping Zack. Chantal checked his temperature and was worried that it had not gone down. The sulfa drugs the doctor at the Gestapo headquarters had given Zack hadn't taken effect yet. "His fever is worse," she said.

"You are a good seamstress," the old woman clucked, "as well as a good doctor. But this delay is not good. He needs to be in hospital." Now there was stern disapproval in her voice. The train had been sitting on a siding for over four hours and the conductor would not let anyone off. "Surely, we can't be too far from Baden-Baden," the old woman said. She dropped her knitting into her traveling bag and stood up, determined to do something for the injured man. "Your trouble is you are too polite," she told Chantal. "Your parents raised you correctly. I will find the conductor and resolve this." The old woman marched purposefully out of the compartment.

"Where are we?" Zack said. He had been drifting in and out of sleep for a few minutes.

"I'm not sure," Chantal said. "Somewhere near Baden-Baden."

The name of their destination jolted Zack fully awake. His inner alarms were clanging furiously. "I don't think we should go to Baden-Baden," he said.

"I had never intended to," she said. "My contacts are in France and it would be very difficult to get you out of the clinic once admitted."

The elderly woman came back with the conductor in tow. "It is necessary to take proper care of this man," she told the conductor. "You have delayed us too long."

"I assure you," the conductor said, "I have nothing to do with this delay."

Chantal sensed that the conductor was wilting under the old woman's onslaughts. "Where are we?" she asked.

"At Rastatt, ten kilometers from Baden-Baden. We will be moving soon. Please be patient." He dug a map out of the small black notebook he carried jammed with schedules and tickets. "Here." He pointed to a small town north of Baden-Baden that Chantal estimated was less than seven kilometers from the Rhine River and the French border. She made her decision.

"Herr von Duren's fever is returning," she announced, changing his cover name to 'von' and implying that he was a member of the old German aristocracy. "I must get him to a surgery immediately."

The conductor looked at Zack. "Surely he can wait until we reach Baden-Baden?" He had taken the bait and worry was in his voice.

The old woman turned into a fury and blitzed the conductor with a torrent of German that made Zack want to smile. The conductor beat a hasty retreat out of the compartment. He returned in less than fifteen minutes. "It is arranged," he said, "for you to leave the train. You will be taken to a small clinic in Rastatt." He helped Zack down the corridor and off the train where a small enclosed one-horse carriage was waiting for them. The old woman watched Zack settle in and when she was certain all was correct, she shook hands with Chantal in the formal German manner and wished them well. She gave the conductor a sharp look of reproof and climbed back on board, her work done.

The horse pulling the carriage was as old and as decrepit as the driver and the sour smell of beer and dried sweat surrounded them both like a fog. The old man demanded they pay an outrageous fare before he would move. "It's not far," he said, leering at her. "The clinic is in a doctor's house on the edge of town." Without a word, Chantal paid him half, saying she would pay the rest when they reached their destination. She decided not to squeeze into the small cab and be subject to the driver's foul odor. Instead, she walked beside the carriage as the old man headed the horse through the small town.

She shuddered from the cold and drew her cape around her, shutting out a sharp wind that blew harder as the evening darkened. "How much farther?"

"French," he spat, not liking her accent. He tugged a flask out of his pocket and took a long pull at it. The horse plodded on and the old man emptied the small bottle. "*Scheisse,*" he muttered, cursing the French. "Too damn cold tonight to be hauling Froggies around." He stopped in front of a *Gasthaus,* covered the old horse with a smelly blanket, and disappeared inside without a word. When he didn't come out, Chantal went after him. She saw him sitting at a table buying drinks for two other men. The money she had just paid him was laying on the table.

Her frustration flared but she sensed that she would have to drag the old man out and that would cause a scene, drawing attention she did not want. She went outside and checked on

Zack. His fever was getting worse. She snatched the blanket off the horse and wrapped it around them both, using her body heat to keep them warm. She hoped the driver would soon come out of his own accord.

When Zack started to shiver, she grabbed her purse and went back inside the gasthaus. The driver and his two mates were now visibly drunker. She marched up to the table and flung a handful of Reichsmarks down. "The rest of what I owe you," she said and walked out of the smoke-filled room.

"*Leck mich doch am schwanz!*" he yelled after her.

Chantal blushed at the crude reference to fellatio as she rushed out the door. She heard someone sharply reprimand the driver and say he was a worthless drunk. She climbed into the driver's seat and unwound the reins. Before she could prod the horse into moving, the driver staggered out the door of the *Gasthaus* carrying a bottle. He jerked the carriage door open and yelled at her while he pulled himself into the seat. After pushing her aside, he dropped a full bottle of schnapps into her lap and grabbed the reins.

"*Strichmadchen,*" he muttered, calling her a whore, "you shamed me in front of my friends." He whipped the old horse and they jolted down the street and crossed over a bridge that marked the end of the town. He hauled the horse to a halt and started to turn around. "*Polizei,*" he muttered, "maybe they should check your papers . . ."

Chantal grabbed the heavy bottle in her lap and swung, hitting him in the right temple. He slumped forward and the horse stopped moving. She hit him again in the same spot, feeling a reassuring crunch. She pushed the inert body out of the door.

Zack watched her through feverish eyes, slow to realize what was happening. "What are you doing?" he asked in English.

"Speak German," she commanded as she dragged the unconscious man under the bridge. Zack staggered down to the ground and leaned over the rail in time to see her hold the driver's head under the water. After what seemed an eternity, she let go and uncorked the bottle and poured most of it into the stream. "Maybe they'll think this was an accident," she said. "A drunk slipping and falling into the water."

She scrambled back up the bank and helped Zack back into the seat. "Where are we going?" he mumbled, still speaking in English. His fever was getting worse.

She slapped him hard. "Speak German," she ordered. He nodded and forced himself to think in German, not sure if he was mumbling or not. She started the horse down the road. "We're very close to the border," she explained, "and this may be our only chance to cross over." His head nodded as he drifted into sleep and only the sounds of the horse's plodding hoofs broke the silence of the night.

Zack awoke and a sudden panic gripped him. He didn't know where he was. "I'm here," Chantal said. "You're safe." Her words calmed him as he tried to push through the fever that bound him. Slowly, he became aware that they were bundled up on a hard seat, sharing a smelly horse blanket and body heat. But he couldn't recall her name. Then he remembered she had killed an old man. Why had she done that? Then he remembered, they were escaping from the Germans.

Through the trees he could see a wide river in the morning mist. "Where are we?" he asked, remembering to speak in German. "Your name is . . . "

"Chantal," she answered, not worried about what he said as long as he did not speak English in his feverish state.

Zack forced himself to concentrate. "Dubois," he said, completing her name.

"Can you remember you're Jan van Duren?"

His panic came back as pieces of his memory came into focus. "Didn't you kill him, too?"

"Yes."

The simple answer stunned him back to rationality. "Why?"

"It was a mistake," she said and turned away, looking across the Rhine and into France.

THREE

Navarre Sound, near Hurlburt Field, Florida

A gentle breeze drifted down Navarre Sound, touching the smooth surface of the Inland Waterway. It reached the causeway that crossed the sound and ruffled the palm fronds that marked the roof of the Pagoda, the tropical outdoor bar that was nestled on the sand next to the bridge. Underneath the branches, S. Gerald Gillespie found a seat at the bar among the other Wednesday night regulars who gathered for the volleyball league. Mike the bartender automatically drew a draft beer, dropped a wedge of lime in, and shoved it toward Gillespie. "Yo, Gill, playing tonight?" he asked.

"Not unless someone needs a fourth," Gillespie answered. He wasn't much of a volleyball player but was always available as a substitute. With a little luck, he thought, Allison's team might be one player short and need a fourth. What a sacrifice, he thought, playing on Allison's team, laughing at his own ineptness as the only male on the team of four. The league rules dictated that the teams had to be mixed with at least one female member and all the teams but one were made up of three males and one female. Allison, in her own contrary way insisted on doing exactly the opposite.

The first two teams were warming up on the sandy court next to the beached catamarans and Gillespie moved over to the railing to watch. He liked the good-natured crowd that played at the Pagoda and they had readily accepted him into their midst, even though he was a klutz at volleyball. Everyone had a good time at the beach bar—it was Mike the bartender's number one and most rigidly enforced rule.

Behind the volleyball players, the setting sun cast a golden shadow down the sound, creating a gentle glow. "Best sunsets in northern Florida," the man leaning over the rail next to him said. Two F-15 fighters from nearby Eglin Air Force Base arced across the sky in tight formation and the old frustration caught in Gillespie's throat. I should be flying those, he said to himself.

Gillespie was still coddling his beer when the first match ended. He could see Allison's team had its full complement of four and he secretly envied the lone male player who was surrounded by three of the best-looking women at Navarre Beach. Damn, he muttered to himself, why can't I be that lucky. Unfortunately, women thought of S. Gerald Gillespie as "cute" and since he had bright green eyes, freckles, and red hair on top of his skinny five-foot four-inch body, he understood why they tended to pat him on top of his head. "Yo, Gill," Mike the bartender called, "Donna's Dynamos need a fourth. You up?" Gillespie gave an inward moan and joined the team led by Donna Bertino, a pixieish seventh-grade teacher who reminded Gillespie of her students. He lined up directly opposite Allison at the net, not exactly what he wanted.

On the fourth rotation, he found himself back at the net with Allison, totally distracted by the image towering over him. She was straight out of any issue of *Playboy* and what she did for her thong bikini was criminal. He had visions of his face buried between her large breasts. Donna, his team captain, served and the return was set up for Allison to spike. She jumped and reached high above her head, smashing the ball down onto Gillespie. The ball caromed off his head and bounced into the water over twenty feet away. Everyone laughed as Gillespie staggered about, claiming he had been taken advantage of. It was going to be a long game.

The game turned into an upset and the tough and wiry Donna spurred her team on, defeating Allison's Amazons. Afterward, the winners, per Mike the bartender's second rule, set a round of beers. Donna stood beside him on the sand and talked about the game, professionally dissecting his play. "Actually, you're pretty good," she told him. "You anticipate well and move faster than hell. But, you're intimidated by the other players. Don't let their height get to you." She looked over his shoulder. "Oh, oh. Bimbo alert." He turned and looked up into Allison's beautiful face.

"Hope I didn't hurt you out there, Carrot Top," Allison said, giving his hair a playful scrub as she walked by.

"No problem," Gillespie called to her back, wanting to stroke her perfect buttocks. He turned back to Donna. "Got to go. Early-morning flight at oh-dark-early. Thanks for the game." He glanced in the direction of Allison before he made his way along the path to the parking lot, feeling very much like the defeated male. He was hopelessly in love.

Donna watched him go. "Men are so stupid," she grumbled to herself.

The ungainly shadow came to life in the early-morning dark that enveloped Hurlburt Field. Slowly, and then with increasing speed, the six-bladed, seventy-two-foot diameter rotor of the MH-53J Pave Low helicopter beat at the air and became a blur as it picked up rpm. Then the shadow moved across the ramp into a takeoff position. In the cockpit, Captain S. Gerald Gillespie sat in the left seat, reading the before-takeoff checklist. As the instructor pilot for this mission, he also had to play copilot. "Checklist complete," he told the lieutenant sitting in the right seat, the aircraft commander's position. He called the control tower for a release and they were cleared for takeoff. The lieutenant gave the command and Gillespie reached for the throttles on the overhead panel and moved them forward. Because the aircraft was well below its maximum gross takeoff weight of forty-two thousand pounds, the Pave Low helicopter lifted easily into the air and flew across the incredibly even treetops of the pines that covered the terrain north of Hurlburt Field.

Gillespie monitored the instruments and the FLIR scope, forward-looking infrared, under his night vision goggles as they flew through the dark. He glanced over at the lieutenant who was also wearing a bulky pair of ANVIS-6 goggles. Although the NVGs, night vision goggles, were designed to enable the pilot to see outside visual references in the dark and still be able to look under them to see the instruments, it was difficult to constantly transition between the two. So Gillespie read the instruments out for the lieutenant, making things much easier. "Piece of cake," Gillespie said over the intercom, trying to reassure the young pilot. Engine noise from the two 4,330-horsepower turbo shaft engines and the whirling seventy-two-foot rotor reduced normal conversations to screaming matches without the intercom.

"Easy for you to say," the lieutenant replied, tension straining his voice.

The flight engineer sitting between and slightly aft of the two pilots glanced at Gillespie and shook his head. The sergeant had flown with the lieutenant before and didn't trust him. Gillespie knew what the sergeant was thinking—the kid flew by the numbers, relied heavily on instruments, and couldn't fly by the seat of his pants. He was low on PT, pilot technique. Not good, Gillespie thought; in this squadron, you've got to be able to do it all.

The 20th Special Operations Squadron, better known as the Green Hornets, in the 1st SOW, 1st Special Operations Wing, flew the Air Force's most sophisticated helicopter and ruthlessly trained to "conduct day or night low-level penetration into hostile or enemy territory to accomplish clandestine infiltration/exfiltration, aerial gunnery support, and reinforcement throughout the world." At least that's what the official paperwork said. For the generals and colonels, that meant the crews had to be carefully selected and trained, every mission deliberately planned on the ground, and above all, flying safety had to be paramount. Gillespie and the sergeant agreed with all that, as far as it went. But training and experience had added two other factors to their personal equations for success that caused the same generals and colonels to grind their teeth in their sleep and fear for their jobs. Gillespie and the sergeant knew that for a slow-moving, noisy helicopter to survive in modern combat, the pilot had to have an instinctive feel for flying the machine and every one of the six crewmen had to have balls that required specially designed skivvies to support.

In spite of his desire to fly high-performance fighters, his frustration at being a complete idiot on the volleyball court, and his unrequited lust for the tall and beautiful Allison, every inch of S. Gerald Gillespie's small frame was packed with what it took to live up to the motto of the 1st SOW—Any time, any place. He didn't know it, but the sergeant sitting next to him did.

Gillespie cross-checked their position on the inertial navigation set by map reading through the FLIR. They were on course and close to the small clearing they had picked as their first LZ, or landing zone. "You should have the LZ on the nose, in sight," he told the lieutenant.

"Tallyho," he replied. "Jesus Christ! It's too fucking small for a night landing!"

"Don't panic," Gillespie said. "It would be a helluva lot smaller without NVGs. You've done it before during the day and it hasn't changed size just because you're wearing night vision goggles. I'll talk you through it." With deliberate casualness, he kept his eyes on the FLIR, instrument panel, and outside references as he talked the pilot down. They touched down with a hard bump in the center of the clearing. "As advertised," he told the lieutenant, "a piece of cake." Even in the dim yellow glow of the instrument lights, he could see the kid was drenched in sweat. The sergeant only shook his head. "You want me to do the next one?" Gillespie said.

The lieutenant let out a heavy breath, ripped off the heavy NVGs, and leaned back in his seat. "Yeah," he said, relief flooding over him.

They switched places, Gillespie waited a few moments for him to settle down. He should have never removed his NVGs. It was a bad sign and Gillespie used the time to think about what it meant. By squadron standards, the landing was routine and should have been a "piece of cake." The lieutenant just didn't have what it took to fly Pave Lows. He knew what he had to do and once they were back on the ground at Hurlburt, he would tell the young pilot, as gently as he could, that he should go fly somewhere else. If the lieutenant didn't listen to him, he would drop a word into the shell-like ear of Standardization and Evaluation and they would rip him a new one. Standardization and Evaluation, better known as Stand Evil, was the group of officers and NCOs responsible for testing and grading all aircrew members in the wing. Their job was to make sure everyone could hack the mission and to have any poor performer reassigned to a less demanding outfit. They planned on having Gillespie join their ranks when he had a bit more experience as an instructor.

"Time to boogie," Gillespie said, now certain that the best way to keep the lieutenant alive was to get him transferred out of the 1st SOW. "Comin' up. Clear left? Clear right. Overhead?" The

MH-53 seemed to take on a new life as it lifted smoothly into the air, pivoted 135 degrees to a new heading, rose out of the clearing, and headed for their next landing zone. For the first time since they had left Hurlburt, the sergeant relaxed into his seat. Gillespie had "the touch."

The officers sitting around the table in the conference room at the headquarters of the 1st Special Operations Wing, located a few blocks away from the flight line at Hurlburt Field, could sense the anger and frustration boiling beneath the surface of Colonel Paul "Duck" Mallard, the commander of the 1st SOW. Mallard had just returned from a meeting with his boss, the commander of Air Force Special Operations Command, known simply as AFSOC. AFSOC was one of the Air Force's new commands, just over four years old, and was the air arm of United States Special Operations Command, or USSOCOM. They were worried, for Colonel Mallard was normally a cool and reserved gentleman, courteous to a fault, but always sure of what he wanted. Now something was wrong.

"Gentlemen," Mallard said, his voice in tight control, "my boss at AFCOM just received a phone call from General Mado on the STU-Three." The STU-III was a key-controlled, plug-in-anywhere, secure telephone that could carry top-secret conversations. Mallard paused to stare at his hands, composing his thoughts. No one had to explain who Lieutenant General Simon Mado was; they all knew he was the vice commander of US-SOCOM, United States Special Operations Command, the unified command of the Department of Defense responsible for all special operations conducted by the United States military. They were all equally aware that AFSOC, Air Force Special Operations Command, which meant them, fell under the OPCON, or operational control, of USSOCOM.

To the average civilian it was all alphabet soup, but to the men around the table it was a vital question of command and control. The 1st SOW could only go to war when United States Special Operations Command (USSOCOM) ordered them to do so. And USSOCOM was commanded by an Army general who had definite ideas about special operations that did not include the Air Force. And even though his vice commander, Lieutenant General Simon Mado, was an Air Force general, Mado would not cross the Army general.

"No doubt," Mallard continued, "you have all been following, with some interest no doubt, the recent kidnapping of Senator Courtland's daughter. Apparently, the President is considering a rescue using special forces." He let the news sink in.

"The only problem," the colonel said, biting his words into clean little bullets, "is that we are not part of it." He stood up and slapped his hands down hard onto the table. "It's wrong to have a war without us!" He sat back down, once again in firm control. "Unfortunately, you can be sure no one at USSOCOM will press for our involvement." The "no one" he meant was Mado. That was as close as Mallard would come to openly criticizing a superior. "However," Mallard continued, "AFCOM has talked to Operations Training at USSOCOM and they have agreed to let us conduct intensive training at a forward location in Thailand."

Four hours later, Gillespie found himself standing in a line with his crew and baggage waiting to be manifested onto an MC-130E. Major Eric "E-Squared" Eberhard, a pilot from the 8th Special Operations Squadron that flew the MC-130E "Combat Talon," was harassing the clerks to "get the lead out" so he could load his passengers and take off. E-Squared Eberhard, who had absolutely no respect for duly constituted authority unless they could outfly him, grinned at Gillespie. "Got to keep the ground pounders on their toes."

"Where the hell we goin' this time?" Gillespie asked. They had only been told to take their tropical gear and pack for a thirty-day TDY, temporary duty.

"You ever been to the Windsor Hotel in Bangkok?" E-Squared asked Gillespie. Gillespie shook his head. "You'll like it," the boyish-looking major assured him. "It's party time." Eric "E-Squared" Eberhard was infamous for his wild and, at times, very wicked ways. He was also the best aircraft commander in the wing and could employ his MC-130E with a skill, courage, and determination that was the textbook example of what a Combat Talon could do. "We got some serious flying to do. The Beezer has already taken off and will start the party without us." Hal "the Beezer" Beasely was a craggy lieutenant colonel who flew AC-130 gunships called SPECTRE and shared E-Squared's penchant for wild parties.

"At least we got a clue now," Gillespie told his crew. This was shaping up to be a major training exercise.

Fort Benning, Georgia

Command Sergeant Major Victor Kamigami ran down the dirt road, his size-twelve combat boots pounding the hard dirt. He was running alone, much to the relief of the other platoons also doing their early-morning physical training. They all had a healthy respect for the CSM, command sergeant major, a huge Japanese-Hawaiian who stood six feet four and weighed 260 pounds, and hated it when he ran with them. Invariably, Kamigami would set a bruising pace and wear them out. As usual, he wore combat boots, fatigue pants, and a T-shirt, refusing to go along with Army regulations that required shorts and running shoes for physical training. Kamigami claimed that he intended to fight in fatigues and combat boots and would train that way. No one bothered to contradict him. He ran past a platoon moving more slowly down the road and ignored them, deep in thought. "Thank you, Lord, for big favors," the lieutenant leading the platoon mumbled aloud, meaning every word.

On this particular morning, Kamigami was thinking about his last assignment before retiring. He knew it was time to leave the Army, for he was wearing out and slowing down. At first, he had ignored the occasional morning stiffness and the times he could no longer catch a fly between his thumb and index finger on the first try. Then he had accepted it all with philosophical calm. He had no idea what he would do in civilian life, since he had been in the Army since he was seventeen. It had been his life. He thought about his only child, Mazie, who had a good job in Washington, D.C. She had always been the smart one in the family and she might have some good suggestions. Maybe he should take the assignment to the Pentagon that had been offered him. At least, he would be near his only child. He probed his feelings about that offer—Command Sergeant Major of the Army. What a final act, he mused. Then he rejected it.

Back in his office at Division, showered and dressed in a class B uniform, Kamigami was ready to go to work. He glanced at his watch and decided that an old buddy in charge of senior NCO assignments in PERSCOM, Personnel Command in the Pentagon, should be at work. He grabbed the phone, his massive hand engulfing the receiver, and poked at the buttons. "Brew," he said, his soft voice totally at odds with his size, "I don't want it.

I'd go crazy in the Pentagon. Nothing but fumble artists and pigeonholers puzzling their way to a promotion there." He listened to the protests from the other end for a few moments, his round face impassive. "The rumor mill has it that Delta Force is going to need a new CSM." He listened as the man told him it was out of the question. "Brew, when was the last time you had your attitude adjusted?" he asked. Then he hung up, confident that the skids would be greased and the orders assigning him to Delta Force at Fort Bragg, North Carolina, as command sergeant major would be in the mail that day.

Bangkok, Thailand

Samkit zipped Heather's dress up and stepped back to inspect her. "Very pretty, missy," she said. Heather studied herself in the big mirror in her bedroom and smoothed the sides of the very short, skin-tight, black cocktail dress. Heather had discovered that Chiang preferred her to dress on the flashy side when they were alone and much more conservatively when they went out in public. She was his constant companion now and he was introducing her to the power brokers of Thai society. But they would be alone tonight and she plotted how to entertain him. Chiang was very pleased with her performance in the bedroom but, increasingly, she had to rely on DC for coaching on more intellectual matters. Chiang was proving to be very sophisticated and cultured and Heather sensed that if she was to survive as his consort, she would have to be his match.

"I hope DC knows what she's talking about," Heather said as she walked out the door.

The testing started after dinner when they were sitting on the veranda enjoying a cool breeze and the soft fragrances of the garden. "You seem to be enjoying yourself lately," Chiang said.

The truth of his simple statement surprised Heather. "Yes, I am."

"Unfortunately, I must return to Burma. My home there does not offer the same amenities as Bangkok. I was hoping that you would accompany me." Then he offered her the choice. "Or you may return to the States, if you wish."

"Oh, I would rather go with you," she said without hesitating, passing the test. "Would it be possible for DC to come? She and I are good friends."

Chiang nodded, pleased with her answer. He had no intention

of releasing any of his hostages but he did prefer Heather to be a willing captive. It made things so much easier. "Of course," he agreed. "Perhaps I can do something else for you before we leave?"

Heather considered his offer. As before, she considered what she could do that would draw her closer to him. "I still have nightmares about what happened on the boat. I wish they would end. If that old fisherman—"

Chiang finished the thought for her, "—would receive the justice he deserves?"

"Yes," Heather answered. "Exactly."

"That is a simple matter," Chiang assured her. "Is there anything else?"

"I want my father to know about it."

Chiang nodded and sipped his cognac. She was his.

The anger that had been brewing inside Nikki Anderson was nearing the boiling point, and with each visible step Heather made in improving her status with Chiang, the more her anger steamed. It spewed into the open when she saw Heather get out of the white Rolls-Royce with Chiang and board the waiting Gulfstream III executive jet at Don Muang airport. "Look at that bitch." She spat. "She's fucking her way out of this mess." The guard motioned for her and DC to get out of the Land Rover and follow them on board. Ricky and Troy followed, both handcuffed.

"We got to get out of this place," Troy grumbled.

"You got any ideas?" Nikki asked.

"Yeah. We start by beating the shit out of a few of these muthafucking goons." A guard pushed him on board the Gulfstream.

A saffron-robed Buddhist monk watched as the Gulfstream taxied out to the main runway. He checked the jet's flight plan, saw that the destination was listed as Chiang Mai in northern Thailand, and went outside to hitch a ride.

The Gulfstream landed at Chiang Mai fifty-five minutes after taking off and taxied to a parking spot on the ramp near the main terminal. Four white Range Rovers were waiting for the passengers and the transfer was quickly made. Inside the terminal, a stout German watched with seeming disinterest before he detached himself from a group of German tourists waiting for their baggage and hurried outside to his car.

The Range Rovers were sandwiched between two trucks, form-

ing a small convoy as they moved down the road. Troy Spencer
and Nikki Anderson were in the last Range Rover with a guard
and the driver. From his seat in the back, Troy kept looking out,
trying to determine where they were headed. "Where we goin'?"
he asked a guard. The man snapped a command at him in a
language he didn't understand.

"I think that means 'shut up,' " Nikki said from the middle
seat. The driver shouted the same command and she fell silent.
Not able to talk, she concentrated on the odometer and mentally
calculated how many kilometers they had traveled since leaving
the airport at Chiang Mai. They had covered seventy-five kilometers when they turned off the two-lane highway onto a dirt
road. The cars in front of them kicked up a cloud of reddish dust
and they had to roll up the windows, stifling in the heat. After
an hour of sweating, Nikki said, "Please turn the air conditioner
on." To her surprise, the driver did as she asked and cool air
flooded into the car. The driver gave her a toothy smile as the
convoy ground to a halt. The driver climbed out of the Range
Rover to check on the delay. "Now what?" Nikki grumbled. Four
men spilled out of the rear truck and talked to their guard. Then
the guard jumped out and disappeared into the bushes to relieve
himself. The rest of the men clustered around the open hood of
the lead truck.

"Breakdown," Nikki said. She turned around to face Troy.
"The keys are still in the ignition."

Troy moved fast and dove into the middle seat and rolled into
the floor next to her. "Did they see me?" he asked.

"No," Nikki answered. "They're all moving over to the far
side of the truck. I can't see our guard."

"Now or never," Troy grunted and he rolled into the front
seat. He lay in the seat and fumbled at the key ring until he found
the key to the handcuffs. Once free, he started the engine, still
lying in the seat. "What's happening?"

"Nothing," Nikki told him. Troy moved behind the wheel,
slipped the Rover into gear, and released the parking brake.
He turned to the left, away from the side where their guard
had disappeared into the bushes, careful not to race the engine.
Nikki held her breath as Troy idled the Rover through the turn.
Then they were around and on the shoulder, still moving, still
undetected. Now they were past the truck and in the clear.
"Go!" Nikki shouted, not able to stand it any longer. Troy
gunned the engine and raced back down the road. It was a

mistake. Their guard heard the engine rev and ran out of the bushes to investigate. He managed to get off a short burst from his submachine gun before the Rover disappeared around a bend. "He missed!" Nikki shouted triumphantly. "They'll never catch us now."

"Yeah," Troy agreed. "This is one sweet machine and can move. And they've still got to get turned around. No way they'll catch us."

He was wrong. A bullet had ricocheted off the road into the gas tank and fuel was streaming out behind them. They had not reached the main highway before the engine died from fuel starvation. Troy swore and slammed the door open, running into the jungle that lined the road. Nikki was close behind him. Another mistake. They should have gone back up the road, toward their pursuers, and entered the jungle at a point away from the abandoned vehicle. Their pursuers would have searched for them in the opposite direction. As it was, they left a clearly marked trail behind them. Twenty-five minutes later, they heard one of the guards crash through the underbrush, only a few meters behind them. Troy pulled Nikki into a dense clump of undergrowth and waited. When the guard walked past them, he jumped on the man and tried to strangle him, finally able to give action to the fury that had been growing in him like a cancer. Nikki joined in the fight and wrenched his submachine gun out of his grasp. She jammed the muzzle into his stomach and the man collapsed in pain.

Troy grabbed the weapon and was methodically beating the man's head in when three other guards surrounded them. One shot him in the leg. One man threw Nikki to the ground and kicked her in the side while the others examined their dead comrade. They talked and reached an immediate agreement. One of the men tied a rope around Troy's wrists, threw the line over a tree branch, and hoisted him up, his feet barely off the ground. Another guard unsheathed his machete and walked over to the American. Troy twisted and shouted from the end of the rope, his eyes wide with fear. He kicked at the guard who only sneered and swung the machete, almost cutting Troy's foot off. Then he methodically worked his way up, hacking at Troy's thighs before slamming one vicious cut into his stomach, making a dull thumping sound. He continued to hack.

Nikki screamed until a guard pounded her into unconsciousness.

                              *   *   *

The men had left, leaving the grisly remains of Troy Spencer hanging in the tree and dragging Nikki Anderson behind them. A man stepped out of the underbrush—the German from the airport terminal. His face was granite hard as he pulled a small camera from his shirt pocket and snapped three photos. Then he disappeared back into the underbrush.

Fort Bragg, North Carolina

"Have you ever been to Wally World?" the driver of the U.S. Army staff car asked. No answer. He wheeled the car onto the side road. "This is Chicken Road," the driver said, "and that big white stucco building with the red tile roof and chain-link fence is Delta's compound." Still no answer. "It was built in the eighties . . . " His voice trailed off since he had relayed all he knew about Delta Force, which was considerably more than most people knew.

Kamigami sat in silence as they drew up in front of the compound. Four NCOs were drawn up waiting for his arrival: the command sergeant major he was replacing and the sergeant majors from each of Delta's three squadrons. They were wearing dress greens with bloused trouser cuffs and green berets. All came to attention when he got out of the car and walked up the steps. "Welcome to Delta," the retiring CSM said.

"Who you trying to impress, Caz?" Kamigami asked. They were old friends. "I thought Delta was allergic to drill and ceremonies?" The men of Delta were an extremely focused group and their professionalism was so great that they paid little attention to the formal trappings of the military.

"Jesus H. Christ," the retiring sergeant, Caz, said. "I'd never ask them to march. They'd only embarrass themselves."

"You can take them out," Kamigami deadpanned, "but you can't dress them up."

"Absolutely right," Caz replied. "Nothing's changed. Come on, let's take care of the paperwork so you can get down to business. The CO, Colonel Robert Trimler, is at headquarters USSOCOM. He should be back by the weekend. That'll give you a chance to get acquainted with the troops."

After Kamigami had signed the paperwork that took him off Army rolls and put him on the Directed Assignment Roster, he asked for a training schedule and saw that a team from A Squadron was scheduled for a fifteen-mile cross-country march. "I don't have a rucksack with me," he told Caz, "but maybe someone will lend me one." Caz told him that he would get the word to A Squadron.

When Kamigami walked out to meet the team, he sensed the conspiratorial mood and sighed inwardly, resigning himself to what was coming. It was the good-natured get-the-CSM type of attitude he had experienced before. He looked around to see whose rucksack had been loaded down with rocks and would magically appear in front of him when he asked to borrow one for the march. He decided to play the game. "Can I borrow someone's rucksack?" he asked. On cue, a rucksack was produced and he was puzzled for it looked normal and had no unusual bulges indicating it had been packed with rocks. Then he picked it up and estimated it weighed close to 150 pounds. They had raided the physical conditioning room and packed it with weights. They are resourceful buggers, he decided. The CSM easily shouldered the rucksack and moved out, the team from A Squadron following.

The first five miles went at the usual pace and Kamigami moved among the men, asking about their backgrounds and what operations they had been on. About half had been on Special Operations in the Persian Gulf War and he detected a certain smug confidence among that group that worried him. Then he changed into a higher gear and picked up the pace. Two miles later, the first complaint was heard but the voice was quickly smothered. Now the men started to spread out and only the most determined kept pace behind Kamigami. He heard someone ask, "Did he get the right rucksack?" The answer was obscene.

Kamigami again picked up the pace. "What the hell's goin' on," one of the trailers moaned. "He's an old man." Again, the answer was unprintable.

Green headbands, commonly called drive-on rags, started to appear and the march began in earnest. "Look at him," a voice said, now full of awe, "he's hydroplaning the earth." The stragglers started to encourage each other, determined not to be left behind, and most of the men were able to follow their new CSM into the compound in more or less good order. Half of them sank to the ground, thankful the ordeal was over.

"What asshole said he was an old man?" came from ankle level. "He smoked us."

"Normal rules don't apply to CSMs," a sergeant, still able to stand, said.

Kamigami handed the rucksack to its owner, careful to keep his face impassive and not show the pain he felt. "Enjoyable," he said. "We'll do better tomorrow." He left the men in stunned silence and headed for his office. Once inside, he closed the door behind him and sank into a chair. You are getting old, he thought. That hurt more than it should have. It is time to retire. But not until I fix what's wrong.

Then he allowed a smile, certain that he had found the perfect assignment to end his career, pulled the local phone book out of a drawer, and searched the yellow pages until he found the section he wanted: livestock dealers.

The White House, Washington, D.C.

The President was silent as he slipped the three photos back into the folder. The director of central intelligence, Bobby Burke, cast a furtive glance at Leo Cox, taking his cues from the President's chief of staff. Cox gave a slight shake of his head, warning Burke not to talk. Pontowski stared at the painting of Theodore Roosevelt, his favorite President, hanging over the fireplace. It was so much different in your time, he thought. Or was it? Perhaps the moral choices were easier to see. He tried not to think about the grisly photos of Troy Spencer, mute testimony to his savage and brutal execution. He let the light and airy atmosphere of the Oval Office work its magic and calm his racing emotions. He focused on the seal of the United States in the center of the rich royal-blue carpet that covered the floor.

"How reliable is the source?" Pontowski finally asked, tapping the folder, once again the master of his emotions. "Is this really Troy Spencer?"

"We cannot get a positive ID from these photos," Burke replied. "And we have no secondary sources for confirmation."

"Is the source good enough to act on?" Pontowski probed.

Burke dropped his head and took a deep breath. Acting on one source of intelligence grated on every conservative instinct in his bones. "I can only tell you that this source has been absolutely reliable in the past," he said, hedging his answer.

"What other resources does the CIA have in place?" Cox asked. Burke only shook his head in answer.

"Do you have the resources to mount a covert rescue operation?" Cox was like a pit bull worrying its dinner.

"Yes, we do," Burke answered, brightening. "But to employ

them, we'd have to get approval from the Senate Select Committee on Intelligence. They take their watchdog responsibilities over our covert operations very seriously. They'll approve it—eventually—after they've covered their political behinds."

"How long to get approval?" Cox asked.

"Two, maybe three weeks, to get their blessing," Burke answered, glancing at Pontowski, trying to gauge his reaction.

Pontowski touched the folder. "I want this report sanitized for dissemination to the key players. Just say that we have an unconfirmed report from a highly reliable source that Mr. Spencer was killed by his guards while attempting to escape and that we are trying to confirm through second sources. Bobby, I don't want these photos to go beyond this office." He shoved the folder with its grisly contents across his desk. "Get with your people and come up with a rescue plan to get them out. Start putting it together but keep it strictly in-house. Don't go to the committee looking for approval yet." Burke nodded and left, eager to get to work.

After the door had closed, Pontowski studied TR's portrait, wondering what he would have done. "I don't think the CIA can do this," he said. "I'm thinking of using Delta Force."

"It's tailor-made for them," Cox agreed. "But we have to solve the basic problem first." Pontowski's heavy eyebrows arched at this. "We don't know," Cox continued, "where the hostages are. Once we do, everyone's going to want a piece of the action. You know the military, always looking for a way to justify their existence. Too many cooks, et cetera."

"And this from an old warhorse," Pontowski said, a sardonic grin splitting his face, recalling Cox's career in the Air Force.

"Fact of life, sir."

"This is one of those times I worry about our intelligence services," Pontowski said. "Why can't we match the Israelis or the standards set by Allied intelligence during World War Two?"

1943

The Rhine River, near Rastatt, Germany

Chantal found a small rowboat behind a shed less than fifty feet from the Rhine River. She concealed Zack in the shed while she guided the old horse and carriage deep into the dense woods a half mile back from the river. She unhitched the horse and hobbled him so he couldn't wander away. Then she ran back to where she had left Zack, relieved to find his fever going down, and dragged the rowboat down to the water. She deposited Zack in the bow and used a narrow six-foot-long plank to scull them out into the current. The early-morning mist provided a welcome cover and she let the current do most of the work. They bumped against French soil near the small town of Seltz, three miles downstream from where they had put in. There, Chantal simply made a phone call and established contact with the French Resistance. Two hours later, they were hidden in a safe house miles from the Rhine.

"Mademoiselle," the woman who lived in the house said, "I wish we could get him to a hospital—" she gave an expressive shrug—"but this is the Alsace and loyalties are not always what they seem. We are too close to Germany." Chantal told her that she understood. "Also," the woman continued, "we should move him before the Boche start a search."

"What did she say?" Zack asked in German, not understanding French.

"Don't speak German in my house," the woman rasped at Chantal.

Chantal nodded. She recognized the deep and total hatred that many of her countrymen carried for the Germans and everything German. She also appreciated how the same hatred was mother's milk to the resistance movement, nourishing it, keeping it alive in the dark winter of early 1943 when only a fierce hatred could motivate ordinary people to rise above themselves and willingly take risks they would never contemplate in normal life. In quiet moments she had come to terms with her own feelings and had totally committed her life to the liberation of her country, partially out of personal dedication, but also to erase the stain of her father's treason when he had thrown in with the Nazis. But she had a problem: German was the only common language she and Zack shared. They had to leave. "The Germans will be searching for us by tomorrow. We must move on tonight." The woman jerked her head in agreement and left to arrange it.

"Don't speak German," Chantal told Zack in German.

"I hope you speak English then," Zack said.

"I'll learn," Chantal replied. She had a flair for languages and had always wanted to learn English. That was the beginning of the English lessons that would fill the long hours of hiding during the next weeks.

Zack touched her hand. "Hand," Chantal said. He pointed to her eyes. "The—"

"Don't say 'the,' " Zack corrected.

"Eyes," Chantal said. They were bundled up in a hay loft on a remote farm in the Dordonne. The French Underground had conveyed them across France, hiding them in a series of houses and moving them in broad daylight when the roads were clear. Chantal had given him geography lessons about her country while they traveled and estimated they were about halfway between Limoges and Toulouse. Now they were south of the Dordonne River, well inside Vichy France and passing time with English lessons. Zack touched his elbow. "Elbow," Chantal said. He pointed at her breasts, merriment in his eyes. "Tits," Chantal said, catching the glint in his eyes and correctly interpreting it. "You're making fun of me," she scolded in German. Zack laughed and burrowed into the straw. "Tell me the correct word. This is important." She bombarded him with straw.

He gave up. "Okay, okay. It's 'breasts.' " He crawled out of the straw and gave a little wince. He had used the last of the sulfa and his leg was bothering him again. He wiggled a finger, extended it toward her and barely touched her stomach.

"Belly," she intoned. Then it came to her. "Tell me the correct word," she demanded in German.

"Stomach," he said. She repeated the word a few times and then looked expectantly at him, now well into the game. He pointed to her rear end.

"Tosh," she said.

"Tush," he corrected.

"Now what is the correct word?" she demanded, her features alive with amusement. A playful mood swept over her and he was enchanted by the young girl who flitted out from behind the reserved mask.

"Buttocks."

She rolled the word around in her mind, forming her lips to pronounce it; then she scowled, the sound an assault on her French sensibilities. "I like 'tosh' better," she announced.

Zack laughed. "So do I."

That night his fever came back.

*   *   *

The small delivery van pulled into the courtyard between the house and the barn shortly after first light. A thin, nondescript man got out and spoke quietly to the farmer before they walked into the barn. Chantal heard their voices and sat up in the straw shivering, chilled by the cold air. She did not want the newcomer to think she was driven by fear and huddled in her cape.

"It's time to go," the newcomer said as he pulled himself up into the loft.

"I'm very worried. His fever is back and the infection in his leg . . ." Chantal's voice trailed off.

"Yes, it is a worry. But we must go now. The police are looking for someone, but the Germans are not involved yet. Must be small cheese." He helped Zack down the ladder. "Easy there, lad," he said in English.

"You are not French," Chantal said.

"No," he replied, "just helping out." He gave her a hard look. "Please be careful when you ask questions in this game." He relented when he saw the look on her face. "My job is to get you into Andorra, where you'll be passed over to a 'friend.' He'll move you into Spain. There, you'll be put in contact with the right people and we should be able to get Mr. van Duren here to hospital."

Now Chantal was certain she was dealing with a British agent. The farmer had told her the Underground was in contact with the British. "What is your name?" she asked in English.

"Call me Leonard," he answered.

"Damn," the man called Leonard swore. "Too many road-blocks, too many patrols, and too bloody many Vichy." They were hidden in a bedroom in the small town of L'Hospitalet in the Pyre-nees Mountains, four kilometers short of the Andorran border.

"Can we cross at another place?" Chantal asked.

He shook his head. "This is the best place. The Andorrans have specialized in smuggling for centuries and are experts at outwitting the authorities. Our friend there"—he gestured at Zack, who was lying on the bed smothered in blankets—"is just another commodity to be smuggled for the right price." He fell silent, thinking. "The Germans are pressing the Vichy to find someone and I think it's you and our friend here they are looking for. We can't wait any longer. I'm going to try to arrange it for tonight." He slipped out the door.

Chantal sat on the bed next to Zack and laid her hand on his forehead and then gently caressed his cheek. She held it there, concern on her face, and estimated his fever to be about 39 degrees, slightly over 102 degrees Fahrenheit. Zack's eyes opened and he touched her hand, gently pressing it to his face. "I heard," he said. "You'd better go on without me, escape while you can." He dropped his hand away from hers.

A look came into her eyes that he did not recognize and she did not move her hand away. "No" was all she said.

"Why?"

"I can't run away from you."

Zack thought he heard more than just a professional concern in her words and cursed the language barrier that separated them. A strong emotion urged him to envelop her in his arms, hold her, to feel her body next to his. But more than language separated them. "Chantal, I've got to know about the real Jan van Duren. ... You said you killed him." Now it was out in the open. Slowly, she pulled her hand away and turned away from him, still sitting on the edge of the bed, clasping her arms about her.

Tears rolled down her cheeks. "My father is a fascist and a Frenchman and I'm not sure who he hates more, the socialists or the English. I cannot tell you how many times before the war he said, 'Better Hitler than Blum.' The thought of a socialist prime minister of France drove him crazy. I was away at school, finishing my last year of medical studies, and did not know how much he meant it. When the Nazis marched into Paris, he actually rejoiced and immediately threw in with them. He was proud of what he was doing." She looked at Zack, letting him see her tears. "But I was ashamed and joined the Resistance.

"My father did prove himself useful to our Nazi masters. So useful that two attempts were made on his life. The second one killed my mother but he escaped unharmed. Then it was decided to make him the French ambassador to the Netherlands to save his worthless life." In spite of her tears, her words were hard and measured. There was no weakness, no plea for pity or forgiveness in her voice. "The leader of my cell saw it as a chance to establish contact with the Dutch Underground and an attempt on my life was staged. The reaction of the Nazis was predictable. Two innocent men were picked up off the streets and shot. I was sent to join my father in the Netherlands.

"I could not bear to live with him but I could not escape him. So I threw myself into my practice. It was a perfect cover to establish contact with the Dutch Underground and I treated many who were only sick of the German occupation of their country. But I tended mostly Dutch Nazis. I was someone who could be trusted. When Madeline van Duren approached me to care for her son Jan, I thought she and her husband were like my father. Herr van Duren is the Dutch minister of education under the Nazis and very well connected. A faction of the Dutch Underground not with the House of Orange had decided to punish the van Durens by assassinating their son. They tried to beat Jan's brains in but they failed and he survived. That's when the van Durens sought me out to be his doctor. I was someone they could trust. Jan was scheduled to be moved to the clinic in Baden-Baden for treatment when I was asked by the Underground—I don't know which group—to finish what they had started." Her voice trailed off. Then, almost inaudibly: "He was very weak."

Zack stared at her, trying to take it all in through the fog of his fever. "But Mrs. van Duren knew . . . She was with us."

"I didn't know at the time that the van Durens were working with the Dutch Underground."

"Then Jan van Duren was totally innocent," Zack interrupted.

"Yes, like all the victims of this war. The Underground told the van Durens their son was dead and asked if you could be substituted in his place. They said it was a matter of taking advantage of an opportunity."

"Did the Underground tell them who killed Jan?" Zack asked. Chantal nodded an answer. "And the van Durens still cooperated." This last from Zack was not a question but a statement filled with awe. Then it came to him: "Was Jan deliberately killed so I could take his place?" Chantal looked away and didn't answer. Zack pulled himself upright on one elbow and grabbed her arm, hurting her. "Answer me," he demanded.

Before she could answer, voices echoed from downstairs, not loud but persistent. Chantal pulled free from his grasp and listened. "I only hear French, no German accents," she said, biting her lower lip.

"Police?" Zack asked, collapsing back in bed, too weak to move.

"Yes," she answered. Now they could hear footsteps move through the house below them. "There may be a way," she said, thinking about the men who were searching the house. For a Frenchman, there was only one logical explanation for finding a young man and woman together in a bedroom. "Get undressed."

Zack stared at her as she quickly pulled her own clothes off. "Hurry," she urged. He pulled his shirt off and was unbuckling his belt when she stepped out of the last of her clothes. He lay there, not able to take his eyes off her. Like many young unmarried men of his generation, Zack had never seen a naked woman before. The sight of her small and firm breasts, flawless back and well-shaped buttocks, narrow waist that flared into smooth hips, perfect legs and thighs that led his eyes naturally upward to the black triangle of hair overpowered him. "Please," she whispered, "don't look at me." And he knew that she was a virgin.

"My God," he whispered. "You're beautiful." She ignored him and threw their clothes around the room in wild abandon. Then she moved to the door and unlocked it, opening it a crack. Measured footsteps were climbing the stairs. She hurried to the bed and pulled his shorts off, careful not to disturb the bandage on his leg. She could see signs of the fresh ooze of blood. She threw his shorts to the floor and mounted him, adjusting the blankets to cover the lower halves of their bodies. "Please," she whispered again, "don't look at me." She made a rocking motion back and forth as if they were coupled and bent over him, her small breasts rubbing against his chest, her long dark hair hanging down, caressing his shoulders and face.

The door flew open and a man in the dark uniform of a French constable, a gendarme, stood there. "Raymond, Paul," he shouted, laughing. "I have found what we are looking for." Two other men appeared behind him and pushed him into the room. Chantal collapsed onto Zack's body and pulled the blankets up after they had all gotten a good look.

"Please," she cried, "go away. My father, if he finds out . . ."

The three men shook their heads and laughed, delighted at their unexpected find. "Ah, mademoiselle," the older of the three said, "we must examine your papers." He said it in a mock-serious tone, enjoying the break in the search they had been detailed to conduct. Chantal rolled out of bed, careful to leave Zack's legs covered and scrambled for her clothes. She held them in front of her, trying to shield her body from their stares. The same man stepped up to her and pulled one of the garments away from her, pretending to carefully search it. Then he dropped it to the floor. "No identification papers there," he said and pulled her skirt from her grasp. Again, he made a show of searching it, before dropping it to the floor and pulling the next garment out of her hands. Now Chantal was standing naked in the center of the room, the three French policemen surrounding her.

"Perhaps you have not searched her carefully enough," the youngest said, running his hand down her side and across her pubic hair.

"Do you wish to search for my papers?" Zack said from the bed in perfect German. His voice was loud and commanding and he was propped up on one elbow, trying to act in control. The heads of the three men jerked around in unison and the one who had stroked Chantal stepped back. "Perhaps you would like to explain to your superiors how you embarrassed an officer of the Schutzstaffel who was traveling incognito? Yes?"

Only the oldest of the men spoke German but the two younger ones caught the word "Schutzstaffel" and they stood back and came to attention. The reputation of the SS was one they appreciated. Fear was plainly written across their faces. "Sir," the oldest said, "we did not know. We are searching for two British pilots who are reported in the area."

The relief Zack felt at this news shot through him like a warm tonic, reviving him and giving him hope. Perhaps, he thought, the vaunted German reputation for efficiency was overblown as the Vichy French were not searching for them. He had no way of knowing that the Germans were not even looking for them and their cover had held while they were in Germany. The authorities had not connected what looked like the accidental death of a drunken cabdriver with the nonarrival of one Jan van Duren and his attending doctor at the clinic in Baden-Baden. Cracks caused by the stress of wartime were spreading through the German bureaucracy. Their only danger was of being picked up in a routine sweep by the police.

"Do we look like British pilots?" he asked, trying to put the right inflection in his words, the right combination of boredom, disgust, and superiority.

"No, of course not," the policeman said, now searching for a way to escape. Then his basic nature pushed through the fear that was clouding his judgment and demanded that he remember he was French and not a lackey to the Germans, especially a young arrogant bastard like the one in front of him. "If we could see your papers," he spread his hands in an elegant gesture. "Surely you understand, a mere formality."

Zack's mind raced as he fought the fever and tried to find a way to give Chantal time to escape. He motioned for Chantal to return to the bed and the movement of the naked girl momentarily distracted the men. Zack was about to say that his official papers were in a nearby hotel and that they would go there when he was finished here. It was all he could think of. A loud, "Chantal!" came from the doorway and everyone turned. Leonard was standing there with another man. "Oh, no," Leonard whispered sotto voce. "Colonel von Duren, I had no idea." He had heard the entire conversation and keyed on Zack's story. He drew himself up in righteous indignation. "Chantal, get dressed. Wait for me downstairs." He turned to the three Frenchmen. "My daughter ... a foolish girl infatuated with a gallant officer. Please, you must understand . . . " He beckoned the three Frenchmen into the hall and they followed him out. "That's Colonel von Duren," he told the policemen, "the Butcher of Beauvais. You've heard of him and what he did there." He dropped the thought as if it were a hot potato. "He is traveling incognito as a Dutchman, a Jan van Duren."

"I've never heard of this Butcher of Beauvais," the oldest of the three said, still trying to act in charge.

"Then you may handle him any way you wish but please let me and my daughter withdraw. The man can be very dangerous."

"Wait," the policeman ordered and walked back into the room, surprised to see Chantal back in bed in the same position as when they had first discovered them. Zack pointed at his coat on the floor and the Frenchman rifled through the pockets. The Germans are so damn arrogant, he thought, ordering our women about, degrading them, not caring what we think. His Gaulish anger flared and he wanted to shoot the German. But it was out of the question. As a gendarme in Vichy France, he was identified with the Germans and knew that his own well-being was linked to that of the Germans. Then he did what any self-respecting Frenchman would have done: He focused his anger on the girl and one single word formed in his mind—collaborator. He pulled out Zack's Dutch passport. The name and picture tracked with what he had just been told. He glanced at Zack and froze. Chantal was rocking back and forth on top and Zack was staring at him with the coldest look he had ever seen. "All is in order," he blurted, now determined to escape from this situation. "Please forgive the intrusion. . . . We were only doing our duty . . . surely you understand?"

"Not if I'm disturbed again," Zack growled. "I hope you understand."

The Frenchman came to attention and saluted, almost knocking his cap off. He assured Zack that he understood perfectly and beat a hasty retreat out of the room and down the stairs, taking the other two with him. Outside, he paused for breath and tried to think of a way to make contact with the Resistance. He had to cover his own involvement with the fascists. One day the Germans would be gone. . . .

Leonard and the stranger walked back into the room and waited until the sounds of the three departing men had faded away. Chantal rolled off Zack and Leonard passed her clothes to her as she dressed under the covers. "Good acting, old chap," Leonard said. "I don't think we'll be bothered by them again."

"Don't be so sure of that," the newcomer said. He was a dark, massive man, dressed in a dirty dark suit with an old-fashioned collarless shirt that was equally dirty. He wore a greasy beret and hadn't shaved in three or four days. The stubble on his face was streaked with gray and he needed a bath.

"This is one of the men I told you about," Leonard explained. "He can get us across the Pyrenees into Spain."

The smuggler examined Zack and shot a hard look first at Leonard, then at Chantal. He paused, evaluating the girl as she crawled out of the bed and stood up. "He is much worse than you told me and he needs to be in a hospital. This will be difficult."

FOUR

The Executive Office Building, Washington, D.C.

Mackay's first three days on the staff of the National Security Council had been marked by confusion as he settled into his office, a windowless walk-in vault down the hall from Mazie. Wave after wave of intelligence inundated his office but no one would tell him what he was supposed to do with it. So he decided to get organized. He used the big table inside the vault to sort the masses of documents, reports, and reconnaissance imagery into ordered stacks. Then he spent the weekend wading through the various piles and made voluminous notes. Satisfied that he was at least treading water and no longer caught in a rip tide, he sat down at his desk and leaned back, making connections. Then he walked over to the table and worked through the pile labeled "Top Secret Ruff," which contained the latest Keyhole 14 satellite imagery and analysis of Chiang's Burmese compound. Mackay did not like what he was seeing.

"Oh, no!" Mazie said when she walked in. "I'll never find anything now."

"But I will," Mackay replied.

"Have you seen this?" Mazie asked. She handed him a report with photographs from the CIA's chief of station in the Bangkok embassy. The report detailed how a body had been thrown over the wall of the embassy. The dead man had been gutted, his head cut off and wrapped in his intestines. Included among the photographs was a picture of the diamond pendant earrings that had been stuck in the man's earlobes.

Mackay reread the doctor's description of the man and studied the photos. "This guy could be one of the pirates," he said. "Heather Courtland was wearing a diamond earring like that one."

"I hadn't seen anything on that," Mazie replied. "How did you know about it?"

"Something very bright was dangling from one of her breasts when they were transferred to the seaplane at the Gurkha camp. I saw it through binoculars and thought at the time that it might have been an earring."

"We can check that out," Mazie said. "But if it's true, that raises even more questions." Mackay gave her a probing look. "Why would Chiang kill the man and then make sure we knew he was Heather's kidnapper? Is he trying to send us a message?"

"This is getting weird," Mackay said.

"It's always weird," Mazie replied, thumbing through the stack of Keyhole reports Mackay had been working on. "Find anything here?"

"Yeah," he grunted. "Chiang has some pretty stiff defenses around his compound. He's got a regiment-sized army, maybe two thousand men, all well-armed and trained by Israeli mercenaries."

Mazie raised an eyebrow at this. "Source?" she asked.

"That comes from the Mossad," Mackay answered. "And his air defense net is eye-watering. He has a Soviet-built Long Track radar for target acquisition that feeds a central command post in his compound. For engagement, he has four SA-Six Gainful surface-to-air batteries. Who knows where he got those. To back them up, there are concentric rings of ground observers armed with SA-Fourteen Gremlins." Mazie looked confused. "The SA-Fourteen is an improved version of the Soviet SA-Seven Grail," he explained. "It's a shoulder-held surface-to-air missile that can engage an aircraft pulling eight g's, head-on, and out to four thousand meters. The Soviets call it the Igla, the Needle. And it can put it to some pretty fancy aircraft. A slow-flying helicopter would be dead meat. The bottom line is that an aircraft can't get within fifteen miles of that compound without being engaged and that it will take a major assault on the compound to free the hostages."

"Isn't this what Delta Force is for?" she asked.

"Nope," he replied. "This calls for battalion-sized units complete with air strikes to soften them up."

"An attack on that scale would destabilize the current Burmese government," Mazie told him, "and that's not on the political agenda. Is there any way our Special Forces can go in?"

"They can go in," Mackay replied. "Getting them out is the trick. The sad fact is that the U.S. does not have a good record at bringing off small, surgical-type rescues. Sure, we do great at the big stuff, like Grenada when we went in after the medical students or Operation Warlord when the Rangers brought the POWs out of Iran. But those were big operations."

She changed the subject. "What's the latest on the hostages?"

"We're still not sure where they are. I did see a report on Troy Spencer collected by Willowbranch, whatever that is." He showed her the report.

"Willowbranch," Mazie mused as she spun the combination of a heavy safe. She rooted around until she found what looked like a car key that gave her access to the System 4 computer terminal in the vault. After inserting the key, she typed in her personal access code. When the code was recognized and she had given the correct responses, she turned the key to the last detent, activating the program that the NSC used to monitor all covert intelligence operations. "Willowbranch is a CIA operation and produces good stuff" was all she said as she read the complete, unedited report. Mackay did not have the "need to know" that Willowbranch was the code name of a German national operating under cover as an anthropologist on an archaeological dig sponsored by the Burmese government.

"Too bad Willowbranch doesn't know what happened to Anderson," Mackay replied.

"I know where she is," Mazie told him, her round face impassive.

"Then perhaps you should tell someone else besides me."

The Capitol, Washington, D.C.

Senator William Douglas Courtland's two aides were waiting for him to return to his ornate offices in the north wing of the Capitol. George Rivera was much more excited than Tina Stanley and kept telling her, "Wait until he sees them." Tina wished he would calm down. Finally, the senator arrived and motioned for them to follow him into his private office.

"These are grisly, but I think you should see them," George said as he handed an envelope to his employer. The senator fingered the envelope, knowing what was inside but hesitant to look at the contents. George sat down, trying to be calm, but he was enjoying the senator's obvious discomfort. Like so many of the power brokers in Washington, D.C., Courtland tried to avoid facing the down side of their environment. Environment, George Rivera thought, that's a good word to describe the arena they contended in—the brutish world of politics, money, rule, and, in its final congealed form, raw power. It did have its ugly side.

"How did you get them?" Courtland asked as he slipped the three photos out of the envelope.

"A contact in the CIA," George told him. "Pontowski told Burke to bury them." The aide allowed a slight smile, the smile of the insider who knows how to make the system work. "There's always some asshole who thinks he can manipulate the system—just another virgin eager to become a slut. They play a game when they don't know the rules and we win."

Courtland cleared his throat and looked at the photos. George successfully masked his smile as Courtland gasped for air. "My God," he managed, struggling for control. Courtland was a gutter fighter who consistently played on the foul line of politics. His feet may have been covered with chalk dust, but he knew where the line was and, more important, the penalties for crossing it. "We can't leak these to the press—too gruesome. Reporters will start investigating, digging for the story behind the story. They'll reveal my office was the source and that would mean a showdown with Pontowski. I can't take that kind of heat. Look, you don't know that Polack bastard like I do. He'd stab me in the back thirty ways from Sunday over this."

"I know a middle man," Tina Stanley ventured.

Fort Bragg, North Carolina

The heavily built, sandy-haired colonel walked briskly through the compound, glad to be away from the paper shufflers at head-quarters USSOCOM and back with his command, Delta Force. As usual, Colonel Robert Trimler felt better when he was with his men. It was six-fifty in the morning and most of them were in "the rough," dressed in civilian clothes or wearing beige shorts, T-shirts, and tennis shoes for physical training. The shorts were Navy UDT issue, which had been relieved from Navy-Seal ownership during a joint exercise. Trimler took it all in as he walked through the building, satisfied with the fanatical concern his men gave to physical conditioning.

When he entered the command section, Sergeant Dolores Villaneuva stood up. "Welcome back, sir," she said, her voice a low contralto. The statuesque brunette had been at work an hour and had his desk ready. "The usual paperwork," she told him. "No critical fires that need to be put out. And the new CSM, Sergeant Major Kamigami, is on board."

"No doubt," Trimler said, his southern accent remarkably strong, "he's impressing the troops in his own inimitable way." He gave her his misshapen grin. "I knew the CSM while in the Rangers. We were on Operation Warlord together." The secretary was impressed. She, like most connected with special operations, had read the after-action reports on that operation and had heard the unofficial accounts that told much of the true story. "Staff meeting in twenty minutes," he told her as he disappeared into his office.

The eight men who made up Delta's command section were standing when Trimler entered the room. He shook hands with Kamigami and then asked them to sit down. He came right to the point. "Delta has been ordered to start planning and training for the rescue of the five American hostages being held by Chiang. At this time we can only assume they are in Chiang's compound in Burma." He was pleased that no one was surprised by his announcement. Every person in Delta was highly tuned to world events and they were always looking for trouble spots where they might be involved. From the discussion that went around the room, Trimler knew that they had anticipated the mission and had given it an enormous amount of thought. The men of Delta could take bad news but they hated surprises. In this case, they were unanimous that it was bad news.

After the meeting broke up, Trimler motioned for Kamigami to join him. The sergeant headed them down the corridor toward the Shooting House as they walked and talked. "Well, Sergeant Major," Trimler asked, "what are your first impressions?"

Kamigami didn't answer him at first and kept pace beside his commanding officer. "Much as I expected," he finally said. Trimler waited for more. Kamigami was a man of few words and those he did use were carefully budgeted. "There is one problem."

Trimler's right eyebrow shot up. He had assumed command of Delta after the Persian Gulf War and had found it highly motivated and with high morale after the clandestine missions they had carried out against the Iraqis. He was satisfied that he had not inherited a barrel of problems bequeathed to him by the former commander. In fact, his impression had been just the opposite. But he knew from personal experience that he had best listen to what Kamigami had to say. "Lay it out, Sergeant Major. I can't take a basket case into combat."

"They're not a basket case," Kamigami said. "Morale is sky-high and they are well-trained." Kamigami gave an inward sigh. This was going to be a long speech for him and he hoped the colonel would understand his point. "What I see are three hundred shooters who live up to the image of Delta. They all wear nice watches, a Rolex or Seiko, are absolutely fanatical about staying in shape, every one of them is field-oriented, and I doubt if one has his hair or mustache within Army standards. You don't see a single tattoo and most of them have a Skoal ring on the hip pocket of their jeans." Kamigami nodded toward a sergeant wearing blue jeans and Trimler could see the white circular outline of a snuff can etched on his right hip pocket.

"I hadn't noticed the watches or the tobacco chewing," Trimler said.

Again, Kamigami said nothing for a few moments. "I'm not surprised, sir. What you saw was what you expected."

"I don't see any of this as being a problem, Sergeant Major."

"It's how the watches and Skoal rings got there that's the problem. Sir, I've talked to the old heads about what they did in the Persian Gulf. It was too easy."

Trimler said, "You've lost me."

"Sir, the Iraqis were too easy. Delta went in, did its job, helped dispatch a bunch of Iraqis to paradise, mostly by laying a laser designator on a target, and only lost three men. Those three were killed when the helicopter extracting them ran into a sand dune. The Skoal rings and watches tell me they are full of self-confidence. That's good. But it's a self-confidence gained by taking on a bunch of clowns. Chiang has a small army of highly motivated and trained soldiers. They are not Iraqis."

"And that's a problem?"

"Yes, sir, it is. Especially if we have to go into Chiang's back-yard. Every one of these eccentrics has got to believe that he's taking on a new and much better opponent."

Trimler was beginning to understand Kamigami's concern. It was a very finely drawn point that many of his fellow officers would consider a fit subject for a chat with a psychiatrist, not worthy of long discussion between a commander and his CSM. But that was what gave a unit like Delta a razor-sharp cutting edge—the very edge that could make all the difference when they were up against a fanatical enemy. "So what do we concentrate on?" the colonel asked.

"Killing," Kamigami answered.

"Any idea which of our men aren't up to it?"

"As of now, I don't know. But I know how to find out." Trimler didn't answer and only looked at his CSM. "We assume everybody needs to be refocused," Kamigami said. "And we start with you and me." He pushed the door to the Shooting House open and called for the NCO in charge.

The sergeant in charge of the Delta's Shooting House was detailing the exercise Kamigami had laid on. "This is a routine part of our training," the NCO said, more concerned with impressing the CSM than Trimler. He sketched a diagram of the exercise room, explaining the setup. "The three dummies standing around the room holding weapons are terrorists. The dummy tied to the chair is the hostage. A four-man team will clear the room, killing the terrorists and releasing the hostage. A cut-and-dried operation."

"Then anyone in Delta can do it?" Kamigami asked.

"Affirmative," the NCO answered, putting all the confidence he could into that single word.

"Good," Kamigami continued. "Select four men who are virgins and tell them they're on in fifteen minutes. Live ammunition, hostage seated, terrorists standing but location in the room unknown. I'll place the dummies." The NCO nodded, thinking that it would be a walk-through, even for four men who had never been in combat. The telephone rang and interrupted them with a message for Kamigami; a delivery truck was outside with the goods he had ordered. "I'll fix the room and take care of the delivery. Start without me if I'm not back in time," the CSM said as he disappeared into the exercise room.

The four men the NCO had selected for the exercise were relaxed and confident, ready to enter the corridor that led to the room with the dummy hostage and terrorists. They were hatless and dressed in the old-style jungle fatigues and boots. Each was wearing a lightweight flak jacket and carrying a Heckler and Koch MP5, nine-millimeter submachine gun with a silencer and thirty-round clip. They valued the MP5 because of its incredibly smooth roller-locking bolt system and equally efficient silencer. The NCO glanced at his watch. "No CSM," he said.

"He said to start without him," Trimler said. The two stepped into an observation booth and peered out the small bulletproof window. The NCO dimmed the hall lights and gave the four men the high sign. They entered the hall and moved down the corridor, not making a sound. The fourth man in moved backward, covering their rear and relying on the third man to warn him of obstacles. He stopped so he could cover the entrance and discourage any unwanted visitors while keeping their escape route open. The first three men moved to the closed door. One crossed in front to the other side while one crouched and readied a stun grenade they called a flash-bang. With his free hand he tested the doorknob and, finding it unlocked, cracked the door open, tossed in the grenade, and closed the door. A bright light flashed through the cracks around the door outlining it and a loud bang echoed from inside.

The crouched man threw the door open and the man on the other side rushed in at an angle. The third man followed the first shooter through the door at a cross angle. Both were firing as they went, aiming high to hit the standing dummies but to miss the dummy tied to the chair. There was no deafening clatter of sub-machine-gun fire but only the sound of popping, bolt actions, and spent cartridges clattering to the floor. The flash-bang had blown out the light bulbs so they were firing in almost total darkness. Then it was silent and the man crouched at the door directed the beam of his flashlight into the room, making sure he was not in the line of any fire that a wounded terrorist might send his way.

In the observation booth, the NCO and Trimler heard a loud "Goddamn!" followed by total silence. They rushed out of the booth and into the hall. Both men felt an empty void in their guts and a coppery-bitter taste flooded Trimler's mouth. Something had gone terribly wrong. The NCO turned up the lights and stood in the open doorway, staring into the room.

Trimler pushed his way past the NCO, fully expecting to see one of the shooters lying on the floor in a pool of blood, ripped apart by his partner's gunfire. The MP5 was horribly efficient at close quarters. But only three dummies were lying on the floor, their upper torsos shattered by gunfire.

But instead of the dummy in the chair, Kamigami was sitting there, a rope looped around his body, making him look like the hostage. He glanced at the stunned men. "Good shooting," he allowed. His voice unchanged from its usual soft and gentle tone.

"Goddamn it, Sergeant Major!" the NCO roared. "You could've been killed. This was a live-fire exercise."

"You told me they were good," Kamigami said.

"Yeah, but Jesus Christ," the NCO sputtered, "we don't take chances like that."

The first shooter who had charged into the room sank to the floor on one knee, shaking slightly, staring at his weapon. "I didn't expect to find a real person in here," he muttered.

"What did you expect to find in here?" Kamigami asked. There was no immediate answer.

Finally the second shooter blurted an answer, the standard answer expected from Delta: "We expected to find three terrorists who we were to service."

"You mean kill them?" Kamigami's words were barely audible.

The first shooter stood up, now fully in control of his emotions and ashamed of the momentary show of weakness. "That's the idea," he said, his words much stronger. "Two bullets in each head."

"Have any of you ever killed anyone? Personally?" Kamigami asked. Only Trimler did not shake his head. "Okay," Kamigami continued, "let's end this. How would you get out of here now?" The four men were galvanized into action and they cleared the hall and moved Kamigami, now the freed hostage, out of the Shooting House. "What would you do if you stumbled onto a terrorist who was blocking your escape route but didn't see you?" the CSM asked.

The first shooter pulled out his Gerber survival knife. He was anxious to prove that what they had seen in the Shooting House was not a sign of weakness. "I'd proceed to debilitate my opponent."

"Does that mean kill him?" Kamigami asked. The shooter jerked his head yes.

Kamigami pointed to the corner of the building. "Good. Do it."

It was a command and the four men responded to it. The first shooter worked his way to the corner of the building and bobbed his head around the edge in the approved fashion. "Shitfuckhate," he groaned and stepped around the corner. The other three men looked around the building and followed him.

"Going around a corner like that could get a dumb shit wasted," the Shooting House NCO grumbled. He followed the team around the corner.

Trimler and Kamigami were right behind and found the men clustered around four spring lambs frisking at the end of their tethers. "Goats," Kamigami groaned. "I'd ordered goats, not lambs." One of the lambs was full of life and jumping straight up and down, its legs little springs.

"Well?" Trimler asked.

The team looked at their CSM. "There's the opponent you're going to debilitate," Kamigami told them.

"Oh shitski," the first shooter moaned. He rolled his knife in his hand and took a half step toward the lamb closest to him, the one jumping up and down and bleating lustily. He hesitated. With a blinding speed Trimler could not credit, Kamigami disarmed the shooter, threw him to the ground, scooped up his knife, and grabbed the back of the lamb's head. With a quick motion he cut the lamb's throat and dropped the lifeless carcass to the ground.

"That's what debilitating your opponent means," Kamigami told them. "Now finish it."

Trimler watched as the three lambs were dispatched, none as efficiently as the first. "What now, Sergeant Major?"

Kamigami shrugged his shoulders. "Barbecue tonight. I'll probably have to show them how to gut and skin 'em," he said.

"You've made your point," Trimler said, walking back to his office, deep in thought.

The Executive Office Building, Washington, D.C.

Mazie Kamigami picked up the phone on the first ring. The message was a crisp "He's out and about." She hung up and surveyed the wreckage in her office. It looked no more cluttered than normal and she knew where everything was. Besides, the President had seen it before. She chuckled to herself, not worried about impressing Zack Pontowski during one of his so-called walkabouts.

"Klutzes," she mumbled to herself. "They haven't figured it out." She found it a never-ending source of amusement that so many of the White House staffers would screw themselves into

the ceiling whenever Pontowski chose to go on one of his unscheduled visits through the White House executive offices. It was
obvious to her that the President used these informal visits to
boost morale and keep people on their toes. Nothing focused the
mind like knowing the most powerful man in the world might
drop in unexpectedly and ask a simple question like "What are
you working on?" and then sit and listen to your answer. It gave
him a source of unfiltered information totally free of the spins
and twists that bureaucrats put on information and intelligence
as it passed through their clutches. Mazie understood how the
man worked.

She glanced at her desk, not bothering to sit down, picked up
the letter from her father, and stuffed it into one of the cavernous
pockets of her skirt. Every skirt, dress, or pair of pants she owned
had pockets that served as part of her filing system. She didn't
care that a full pocket only made her look more rotund and
dumpy. A typical letter from Pop, she thought, clearly recalling
every word:

Dear Mazie,

I just got a new assignment. Not coming to Washington after all.
This will be my last tour and then I'll retire. Hope to see you soon.

Love,
Dad

She pulled out the letter and glanced at its postmark: Fort
Bragg, North Carolina. You must have gotten Delta Force, she
decided. Why else would you turn down Command Sergeant Major of the Army? Mazie also understood her father. She was still
standing in the middle of her office and holding the letter when
the President of the United States walked through the door with
her boss, National Security Adviser Cagliari.

Cagliari came right to the point. "What's the latest on the
hostages?"

"Perhaps," Mazie said, "we had better go down to the vault
and talk with Colonel Mackay."

Pontowski listened without comment while Mackay went over
their latest information. "So, you're telling me," he finally said,
"that Miss Anderson has been separated from the other three
hostages, who, we assume, are now in Chiang's compound, and
that we need a much larger force than Delta to neutralize Chiang's
defenses." He paused, thinking. "Do we know where Miss An-

derson is?" Mackay shot a questioning look at Mazie and did not answer. He knew when he was in over his head.

"Officially, sir," Mazie began, choosing her words carefully, "we don't know."

"And unofficially?" Pontowski replied.

"She's with the three guards who killed Troy Spencer. They got worried about what Chiang would do to them for killing Spencer and took off with their own hostage—Nikki Anderson. They're hiding in a village in Thailand just south of the Burma border, Ban Muang Dok."

Pontowski chewed on this latest intelligence.

"When and where did this information come from?" Cagliari asked. He was upset because this was news to him.

"I received it over the weekend," Mazie answered.

"Why wasn't it included in the PDB?" Cagliari asked. The PDB, President's Daily Brief, was a glossy, slickly printed intelligence summary that appeared every morning on the President's desk. It was assembled by a committee of bureaucrats in the CIA and given limited distribution. Supposedly, it contained the best intelligence available to the United States.

"It was backdoored to me."

Silence. Mackay studied them, trying to fathom what was going on. To him it was a simple matter of command and there should be no reason for all this pussyfooting around. Either they had good intelligence or they didn't.

"I see," Cagliari finally said. "Your source has an informant that he doesn't want to pass over to the CIA." Mazie only nodded in reply. She gave a silent prayer that he would not upset the apple cart and tell the CIA. "Which," Cagliari continued, "makes sense considering the recent leak about Troy Spencer." Mazie gave a very visible sigh of relief, which contrasted with the perplexed look on Mackay's face. He hadn't heard of any leaks.

"Who is your source?" Pontowski asked.

Mazie did not hesitate. "An Air Force general, William Carroll. He recruited a Buddhist monk who has set up a network of monks throughout Thailand and Burma. The village monk at Ban Muang Dok saw Anderson and the three guards."

"I know Bill," Pontowski said. "I thought he was a Middle East expert. How did he get involved in the Far East?"

"He's in command of the Special Activities Center now, handling HUMINT for the Air Force."

"We need to get this into the system . . . officially," Pontowski said. "Let Carroll keep his source."

"It can be passed through Mossad to the CIA," Mazie suggested.

"The Israeli connection is always helpful to a Middle East specialist like Carroll," Pontowski said. He looked over his glasses at Mackay. "Welcome to the wonderful world of the bureaucracy." Then he rose and was out the door.

"What was that all about?" Mackay asked.

"Turf battles," Mazie told him. "Every intelligence agency wants to control its own sources. But it's more efficient if a single office manages it all. In this case, the CIA."

"I thought that was the way the system was set up."

"It is," Mazie explained. "But what happened to Troy Spencer was leaked to the press. With the CIA resembling a sieve, the smart players are running for cover until the leak is plugged." Without thinking, Mazie pulled her father's letter out of her pocket and stroked it. Oh, Pop, she thought, I may have put you back into it.

"I've got to get out of here," Mackay said.

The three men who made up Pontowski's inner core of advisers relaxed into the couches and comfortable chairs clustered in front of the President's big desk in the Oval Office. Leo Cox, his chief of staff, sat farthest from the desk at one end of a couch sipping coffee. Michael Cagliari, his national security adviser, thumbed through the notes carefully arranged in the folder on the couch beside him. Bobby Burke, the director of central intelligence, fidgeted in the big overstuffed chair, his restless hands darting from the arm of the chair to the folder in his lap. They were an unlikely trio who would have never have struck up a friendship on their own. But they had been individually captured by the magnetism of Matthew Zachary Pontowski and had been pulled into his orbit, becoming a powerful constellation that guided United States policy.

The tall and skinny, cadaverous Cox had reached the rank of brigadier general in the Air Force by kicking the intelligence structure until it became responsive to operations and plans. It had been a painful but productive experience for many intel officers. Like most professional officers in the military, Cox had an innate distrust of intellectuals like Michael Cagliari, a former

Princeton professor who specialized in national security and foreign affairs. Cagliari, a former student of Henry Kissinger, looked like an Ivy League professor, always wearing a rumpled Harris tweed sport coat with leather elbow patches and sporting a well-developed beard. Behind his bland brown eyes and hidden somewhere in his flabby body beat the heart of a tiger and one of the most devious souls in the United States. Bobby Burke, the director of central intelligence, and consequently in charge of all intelligence agencies in the United States government, was a professional bureaucrat who had worked his way up from the lowest ranks of the CIA. When asked by strangers what he did, he would fidget, shifting his weight from one foot to the other, and tell them that he was a bureaucrat. And like many bureaucrats, he spoke in a pompous voice, obviously impressed with his power and position. Most people instantaneously dubbed him an "asshole," and never suspected that the chunky and slightly balding fifty-two-year-old man was in tip-top physical condition, had a record as an outstanding agent in the field, spoke six foreign languages, and had personally killed four people in the line of work. He was a bureaucrat whose specialty was intelligence and covert operations. And like most high-ranking bureaucrats in the government, he was very good in his field of expertise.

While the three men waited for Pontowski to enter the Oval Office, Burke seriously pondered the feasibility of eliminating two men: Courtland's aide George Rivera, and the CIA staffer who had leaked the photos of Troy Spencer. Burke wondered if he could bring it off. Pontowski would crucify him or any government official caught engaging in "wet operations." Burke suspected that Pontowski would enjoy the task, relishing the opportunity to give an object lesson to other power brokers in ethics, civics, and personal responsibility.

"Good morning," Pontowski said when he entered the office. Only Cox stood up, his old habits from years in the Air Force overriding Pontowski's wish to keep things informal. Pontowski sat down and picked up the PDB, the President's Daily Brief. "Mossad seems to have expanded its operations into the Far East," he said. "Good work, Bobby, keeping the Israeli connection open."

Burke accepted the compliment. "Well, sir," he explained, "this one was pure luck. The Mossad didn't tell us how they learned about Nikki Anderson but you can be sure the intelligence is reliable or they wouldn't have passed it on. Besides, this couldn't have come at a better time. Courtland is using the press to put the heat on and force us into a precipitous action to rescue the hostages. If a rescue attempt fails, he could use it to his advantage in the upcoming election. It has happened before." Both Cagliari and Cox nodded in agreement.

"I think," National Security Adviser Cagliari interrupted, "that Bobby and I are thinking along the same lines." He immediately relinquished the floor to Burke, not wanting to steal his thunder.

"Ah, yes," Burke continued, aware that Cagliari had given his words added support with the President, "we can act on this and preempt any of Courtland's attempts to embarrass us."

"So what do you suggest we do?" Pontowski asked.

"Rescue Nikki Anderson," Burke replied. Again, the other two men supported the DCI.

"There's another problem," Cagliari said. "Whoever gave Courtland those photos might tell him about a planned rescue of Anderson. He won't like us going after Anderson and not his daughter."

Burke stopped squirming and looked directly at Pontowski. The tone in his voice was calm and his words carefully measured. "I've solved that problem. One of my people was the leak." Cagliari almost asked the DCI how he could be sure but stopped himself in time. With a flash of the intuition that amplified his prodigious mental skills, he knew that Burke had spoken the truth and that no one in the room needed to know the details. Plausible denial had to be a reality at their policy level when Burke went about the dark business of disciplining rogue intelligence officers. Cagliari filed a mental note to watch for any unusual incidents among CIA personnel. "Also," Burke continued, now squirming again, his voice pompous, "I would rather the CIA did not affect the rescue. We would have to clear the operation through the Senate Intelligence Committee and that would invite delay and the possibility of another leak."

"Delta Force should be able to handle this one," Cagliari said, thinking about what Mackay had told him and the President.

Pontowski leaned back in his chair, his decision made. "Order Delta Force to rescue Miss Anderson as soon as possible. Start looking at ways to get the hostages remaining out. Dry up Courtland's sources as best you can."

Fort Bragg, North Carolina

When the order came down from USSOCOM tasking Delta to deploy to Thailand and effect the rescue of Nikki Anderson from the village of Ban Muang Dok, the men started a well-rehearsed routine. Ammunition and explosives were checked and packed in special containers. Radios were carefully tested and fresh batteries installed. Personal weapons were gone over with a fanatical care before being carefully stowed. Uniforms and personal equipment were stuffed into the rucksacks known affectionately as Alice the Wart.

The staff fell into a flurry of activity as they reviewed the basic plans they had developed and trained to implement. They studied the intelligence available to them and selected their course of action. Then fourteen men received a special briefing, were issued tickets and money, and sent on their way as tourists.

The fourteen men were careful to travel in pairs or alone and to ignore each other. For the most part they looked liked civilians, except that most of them sported mustaches that only approximated Army regulations, wore an expensive Rolex or Seiko watch, and all were in exceptionally good physical shape that no casual clothes could hide. Kamigami inspected each man before he left the compound and made sure that no traces of Skoal rings were present on the hip pockets of their jeans. The sergeant major seriously doubted they could slip by a watchful observer. But he was certain they would know if they were "made" and could avoid being followed.

Fresh intelligence came in and the staff started to modify their plan. It was a process that would go on until they actually launched the mission and they would have no end of help and inputs from higher headquarters.

"I think we should take fifty shooters," the lieutenant colonel in command of A Squadron told Trimler and the rest of the staff after seeing the latest high-resolution reconnaissance photographs of the Thai village where Nikki Anderson was being held.

"Too damn many unknowns," Trimler finally said. "We don't know the exact location in the village where Anderson is being held, what the defenses are. . . . Hell, we're not even sure how many gua ⌐s there are. We could be walking into a meat grinder."

Kamigami used a magnifying glass to study the photos. Then he fished through a stack of older photos and pulled one out that was twenty-four hours older. "Here." He pointed to a small compound on the western edge of the village. "In the older photo, you can see a Range Rover in the compound. That's too expensive a car for a village like Ban Muang Dok. Now look at the latest photo. No Range Rover. But there are a single set of fresh tracks leading into a shed." He passed the two photos around. "I'm willing to bet the tread of those tracks is the same as a Range Rover."

"Sergeant Major, are you saying that the location of the Range Rover is the key to Anderson's whereabouts?" Trimler asked. The big NCO only gave a short nod in reply.

"We still don't know the size of the opposing force," the lieutenant colonel said.

Kamigami gave him an inscrutable look, hiding his thoughts. "The number of vehicles is the clue," he said.

"But we can't be sure," the lieutenant colonel protested, a hard doubt about the wisdom of the mission behind every word. "We need better intelligence."

"Then we go in with maximum surprise," Trimler said, "and maximum violence." He had brought the mission down to the basic way Delta worked.

Udorn, Thailand

Nearly twenty years of neglect had extracted a heavy price and the air base was a shabby image of what it had been. Captain S. Gerald Gillespie wandered down the long-abandoned flight line and tried to see the base as it had been in its prime. But the former American base at Udorn, Thailand, had changed and the captain could not visualize the ramp when it had been packed with a wing of F-4s, the premier fighter aircraft of its day, and over four thousand American servicemen. "So this was the home of the Triple Nickel, the MiG killers," he mumbled to himself and again, he looked down the ramp, now only seeing a vast empty expanse of concrete with grass growing between the cracks. He was looking at an abandoned parking lot.

He looked back in time and called up images of a World War II movie with B-17s taxiing out to takeoff for a bombing mission over the Third Reich. Then he changed the scene to Udorn, with images of F-4s taxiing out of revetments to marshal up for a MiG sweep over the skies of North Vietnam. It worked, and for a brief moment, he was there, launching with both the Eighth Air Force in World War II and the 555th Squadron in Vietnam as the nerve-shattering roar of F-4s blended with the howl of radial engines from an even more distant past. "Damn," he muttered, "and I'm only a rotorhead."

A shout brought him back to the present. "Gill! We need your body." The captain turned to see E-Squared sitting in a pickup truck with Hal "the Beezer" Beasely, the AC-130 aircraft commander. Gillespie gave a last look down the flight line as he crawled into his seat. "We got a hot one," E-Squared told him.

"More training?" Gillespie asked.

"Not this time," E-Squared answered. He drove rapidly to the Air America compound at the far end of the base that was in much better shape and still occupied by Americans.

"I wonder what in the hell the CIA's still doing here?" Gillespie wondered.

"Don't ask," E-Squared told him. The veteran C-130 driver had been in special operations most of his career in the Air Force and knew that wherever they went, the CIA was sure to be there. But it wasn't something they talked about. The exterior of the building they entered was as shabby as the rest of the base. But once inside, things changed. The interior was modern, clean, and plush. "Whoever works here likes their creature comforts," E-Squared observed. They were escorted into a briefing room.

"What's the Old Man doing here?" Gillespie whispered when they entered. Their commander, Colonel "Duck" Mallard was sitting in the room with a few members of his staff.

"This ain't a training exercise anymore," E-Squared told him.

Mallard waited until they had all found seats. "Gentlemen," he said, "we have been asked to go in after one of the hostages. Now don't you all go wetting your pants over this," he cautioned them. "Our job is to insert a team from Delta Force, maintain cover with an AC-One-thirty gunship, and provide an MC-One-thirty as an airborne command ship. Not much in it for us. But we can start to work and select potential landing zones around the target area and find equivalent training sites. A contingent from Delta Force will arrive tomorrow and we'll start training immediately." He turned the meeting over to his chief of intelligence, Lieutenant Colonel Leanne Vokel, who went over the details.

Near the end of the meeting, E-Squared raised his hand. "What's the threat in the target area?" he asked.

"The only reported threat is small arms fire," came the answer.

"Intel is always wrong," E-Squared said, sotto voce.

1943

Zaragoza, Spain

The man called Leonard stomped across the small room and focused his gaze out the dirty window. The Andorran smuggler called Felipe who had helped them cross the Pyrenees Mountains into Spain had been gone for over forty-eight hours and he did not want Chantal to see his worry. "Waiting is the hardest part," he said. The tone of his voice told more than he intended. The wind hammered at the window and a swirl of dust scurried across the floor toward the bed where Zack lay wrapped in blankets. Chantal rose from the edge of the bed and joined the British agent at the window. Her frustration matched Leonard's worry, for there was nothing she could do for the wounded pilot.

"He's dying," she said. The words ripped through her and tears ran down her cheeks. "We must get him to a hospital soon. I don't know what's wrong with his leg and can't tell without an operation. His blood circulation is not correct." The dome of Zaragoza's cathedral on the banks of the Ebro River caught her attention and, for a moment, she wondered if prayer would help. "How dependable is he?" she continued. The Andorran had safely gotten them as far as Zaragoza, but the dirty, foul-smelling man did not inspire confidence in her.

"These things always take longer than we want." He wouldn't tell her the truth about the Andorran.

Chantal conceded the point by falling silent. She turned back to the feverish pilot. "Not much longer," she whispered.

Three hours later, they heard the familiar heavy tread of the Andorran as he climbed the rickety stairs outside their room. He shuffled into the room carrying a small suitcase and collapsed into a chair. "It's arranged. We take him to hospital. A doctor and an army officer will be waiting."

"Why an army officer?" Chantal shot at him, worry driving her words.

Felipe shook his head in resignation. "This is Franco's Spain. Nothing out of the ordinary happens without the army knowing. It is quicker this way."

"The fascist bastards," Leonard growled.

"I don't understand," Chantal said.

"Spain is controlled by fascists," Felipe told her. "Franco won the civil war in 1939 with the help of Mussolini and Hitler. Now they call Franco the Caudillo, the Leader. He rules the country with an iron, and very bloody, fist."

"But I thought Spain was neutral," Chantal said.

"Switzerland is neutral," Leonard replied. "Not Franco."

"Things change," Felipe said. The two men glanced at each other. "Fortunately, everything has a price in Spain." The Andorran picked up the suitcase and opened it. He fished out a Dutch passport and handed it to Chantal. "You are now Chantal van Duren, the sister of Jan van Duren." He nodded toward the unconscious Zack. "You will take him to the hospital and explain how you and your brother were traveling to Portugal to visit relatives when he was hurt in a bombing raid. Since the wound appeared to be healing you continued on your way but now complications have set in. It has all been arranged." He handed over a small bundle of travel papers, exit permits, and official clearances to go along with the fake Dutch passport. "The Spanish authorities will think you are like so many others trying to escape the war. Keep your story simple." He passed over a small bundle of pesetas. "If you have to, offer small bribes as necessary 'fees' you are willing to pay." Then he handed Chantal the suitcase. "Take a bath and change into these."

Chantal examined the contents of the suitcase. "These are very nice traveling clothes," she told him. A blush crept across her cheeks. "I've never worn underthings like these."

"Use the bath on the bottom floor," the Andorran said. "It's been arranged." Chantal closed the suitcase and hurried out of the room.

"Why the clothes?" Leonard asked in English.

"She's the bait to make it all happen," Felipe answered. His voice had lost its rough edge.

"I think you mean she's the bloody 'price,' " Leonard swore.

With an effort he did not know he was capable of, Zack pushed through the fog of his fever and concentrated on Chantal. Speak German, he told himself, and remember who you are—Jan van Duren. He could not take his eyes off Chantal as a nun guided his wheelchair into the hospital. The new clothes that Felipe had produced had transformed her into a sophisticated, dark-haired beauty and the fashionable trench coat accentuated her trim figure. She moved with an assured charm and grace that mesmerized the young American and he wanted to tell her that he loved her. He fought that impulse down but resolved to mention it at the first opportunity.

A crisp-looking Spanish army officer met them and gave their passports a cursory inspection. He seemed much more interested in Chantal than their travel papers and spoke in Spanish to the waiting doctor. The doctor then spoke to the nuns who wheeled Zack into an examination room. Zack twisted to say something, he didn't know what, to Chantal but the door had closed behind him. Two orderlies lifted Zack onto the examination table and cut his trouser leg up the seam. The doctor then peeled the bandages back and gently probed Zack's wound while keeping up a constant flow of Spanish. The soft modulated tones of that language were reassuring. Then he was transferred to a gurney and pushed back into the hall. He twisted to see Chantal but only caught a glimpse of her back as she disappeared down the long hall with the army officer. Then he was moved into an operating room.

"Señorita," the army officer said as he opened the door into the ornate chambers that served as the province commander's personal offices, "you are being afforded a rare honor. General Alfonse de Larida y Goya seldom speaks to civilians. It is a matter of pride with him." They entered a large, marble-floored room that was richly decorated with antiques and paintings. Chantal recognized two Goyas and wondered if there was any connection with the general's last name. A tall and lean, silver-haired man stood up from behind his desk. The younger officer clicked his heels and gave a short bow from the waist. "General Goya, may I present Mlle. Chantal Dubois, the daughter of the French ambassador to the Netherlands."

Chantal was stunned and she fought for her breath. Slowly, she turned and looked at the young officer, fighting for time to think. The calm and urbane way he had cut through her cover and the nonreaction of the general were ample warning that she had been betrayed. For a moment she could not think clearly as her mind was overwhelmed with the implications of that betrayal. It had to be Felipe. All her doubts about the man were confirmed. She forced her panic to bend to her will and nodded graciously. "In these times it is often best to travel incognito," she announced. She was going to say more, improvise a story, but decided against it. Simple and understated was better. It was now up to her to save Zack—and herself.

"Indeed?" the officer said.

The general focused his cold brown eyes on Chantal and said nothing. His face was a rigid stone mask as he studied her. Then he gave a sharp jerk of his head and the army officer escorted her into a sitting room next to the general's office. He motioned for Chantal to sit down and snapped his fingers. A steward in a white coat pushed a tea trolley between them and automatically poured the officer a cup of coffee. "Tea or coffee?" the officer asked.

"Tea," she answered. The silence was heavy as the steward poured her a cup. "How did you find out?" she finally asked, her voice amazingly calm and controlled. She was looking for a key to her problem. How much had Felipe told the Spanish?

"The Andorran told us," the officer answered companionably. "We also know about your other two friends. The wounded pilot"—he paused and looked at her over his cup of coffee as if she was expected to take special note of what he was saying—"is being operated on and will be released as soon as he is strong enough to travel. He and the other Englishman are of no concern to us as long as they do not break our laws. After all, Spain is a neutral."

To this, Chantal raised an eyebrow and said, "Indeed?" giving the word the same inflection as the officer had used only moments before.

He smiled, seeming to enjoy the exchange. "I do hope you appreciate the, ah, situation."

"I believe I do," Chantal said.

"That is good," the man continued, "for certain 'accommodations' still need to be made. That is why we are talking here—in private."

"And these 'accommodations'?" Chantal asked. She expected to hear a large sum of money, probably in gold, mentioned.

"The general, as you can see, is an old man who requires certain comforts to sustain him in his arduous duties as the province governor. We have found that when these comforts are provided, the province is more smoothly regulated." The man set down his cup and crossed his legs, his immaculately polished riding boots reflecting the afternoon light. He folded his delicate hands together in his lap. "The general prefers to share his bed with young, shall we say, inexperienced maidens." Chantal visibly stiffened as a pure, intense loathing for the man sitting opposite her flared. She reined in her feelings, determined to maintain her dignity. She would not lower herself to the level of this charming, ever so civilized, degenerate. He may wear a uniform, she thought, but he does not compare with the others. A strong image of the German major in the Hauptbahnhof at Cologne and his battle-hardened eastern front veterans flashed in front of her. They may have been the enemy, she decided, but they were soldiers. She had this man's measure and feared him. "We are told," he continued, "that you are such and the general obviously approves of you. We have a doctor waiting to confirm your, ah, condition." He let the full implication of what he was saying sink in. "Of course, your cooperation would make it possible for your traveling companions to be ignored and permitted to continue on their journey."

Chantal reached out and sat her tea cup on the coffee table. Her hand was shaking. "If you need some time to think about it . . . " The officer rose to leave. "Of course, we must ask that you remain here."

She gave a slight shake of her head. "No, that's not necessary. I've made my decision." She also stood up. "The doctor?"

"Ah, mademoiselle, a most wise decision. Of course, it is not necessary for you to say anything to the general. In fact, it is preferred."

"Easy lad," Leonard said, waking Zack from his nightmare. "You're safe." Panic raced through the American until his surroundings made sense. They were traveling again. This part of their journey had started when Leonard and Felipe had checked him out of the hospital in Zaragoza the third day after the operation on his leg, bundled him into a car, and driven four hundred miles to the west. His breathing slowed. They were far from Nazi-occupied Europe and safe inside the neutral, but friendly country of Portugal.

Felipe, the Andorran smuggler, was standing by the door. "*Zut,*" he said, "you do talk in your sleep. But no one hears you, I think. God only knows why not. What is this 'tosh' you shout?"

Zack was still groggy and confused. "It's a word, that's all." That triggered another thought. "When is Chantal going to get here?"

"Soon," Felipe answered.

"You said that at the hospital," Zack shot at him. He was

angry at her prolonged absence and now that they had reached Portugal, was certain that the Andorran was lying to him. He tried to stand up, determined to confront Felipe and, if necessary, beat an answer out of him. But he was too weak and sank back onto the bed.

Leonard felt his forehead and was relieved to find no trace of fever. The Spanish doctors had done their work well and straightened out the jangled mess of arteries and veins in his leg, restoring proper circulation to the limb. He glanced up at Felipe and then back to Zack. "She won't be joining us for the rest of the journey," he said.

"But you told me . . . " Zack stammered. A sense of betrayal mingled with a taste of bitter loss as he stared at the two men.

"This is a hard business we're about," Leonard explained. "She stayed behind to give us time to escape."

Now anger washed over the American and engulfed his other emotions. "And just how in the hell could she do that?" he shouted.

"You don't need to know," Felipe said.

"Look," Zack tried to shout, but he was too weak to sustain the effort, "I'm not worth that type of sacrifice." He fell back against his pillow, exhausted.

"You're right, lad," Leonard said. "You're not. But he is." He nodded toward the Andorran. A hard silence came down in the room. "You're here only because he wants to take you along with him." The look on Zack's face was ample indication that he was totally confused.

"Explain it to him," Felipe grumbled. He picked up a suitcase and left the room. The perpetual sour odor that followed him like a cloud evaporated once he had left.

Leonard took a deep breath and started speaking in a low voice. "I could have never moved you out of France without Felipe . . . he's my control. The situation is rapidly changing in both Spain and Vichy France and he is instrumental in making those changes happen. You couldn't have heard, but Franco is pulling his Blue Division of forty thousand men from the eastern front."

"I didn't know the Spanish were fighting with the Nazis in Russia," Zack said.

"Few people do," Leonard grumbled. "Now Franco is convinced the Nazis are going to lose the war and he wants to be more 'neutral.' Even the Vichy are getting twitchy and looking for a way to approach the Allies. That's why Felipe has to get to

England . . . to help 'arrange' that rapprochement." He gave a cynical French pronunciation to the last word, letting Zack hear his contempt for the Vichy French. "They should hang all those bastards. I hope de Gaulle will." Then almost as an afterthought: "I don't know why Felipe decided to take you along with him. You'll have to ask him."

"But you said he was an Andorran smuggler," Zack said.

"He uses many covers." They fell silent as Zack tried to make sense of it all.

Twenty minutes later, the door opened and a man in a well-tailored dark gray suit walked in. At first, Zack didn't recognize the immaculately groomed and dignified-looking man. It was Felipe. "It is time to leave," he announced. Even his accent had changed with his appearance and now he spoke English in the carefully modulated tones of a professional diplomat. He and Leonard helped Zack to his feet. "We will be picked up tonight."

"Felipe," Zack began, "why have you bothered with me?"

Felipe gave an expressive French shrug. "Because you can fly airplanes and bomb the Boche. I can't do that."

A smile cracked Leonard's grim look. "He does hate the Germans."

Felipe drove fast, leaving the sleepy town of Braga behind them. Zack shifted his attention out the window as they drove through the night. A lousy night for flying, he thought, studying the low clouds scudding across the sky. When they had passed through the town of Barcelos, Felipe stopped and a man crawled into the backseat next to Zack. The stranger spoke with a harsh accent that was matched by a change in Felipe's tone. Then they were driving again, the stranger giving directions. A small van fell in behind them as they entered the vineyards that filled the coastal plain. Then the man directed them down a side road until they reached a long stretch clear of trees and buildings. The van parked at one end while they parked at the other end. The pilot in Zack recognized a makeshift landing strip when he saw one. They waited and, within minutes, they heard the low drone of an aircraft above the clouds. Both vehicles switched on their headlights and the silhouette of a small, single-engine, high-wing monoplane dropped through the clouds.

"The Lizzie's right on time," Leonard said. "Damn good navigating."

Zack watched the plane fly a short final to landing, touching down just as it cleared the van. It was a Westland Lysander, the small and ungainly aircraft that served the British well, dropping off supplies and agents in Nazi-occupied Europe and then ferrying out special passengers. A ladder dropped down from the high cockpit and two men scrambled down. Four bundles were passed down, followed by six small suitcases. "Radios," Leonard said in a low voice. "Worth their weight in gold." Then the pilot climbed down.

"Who's for homebound?" he asked. The man was no older than Zack and carried himself with a cool confidence. "Could use a bit of petrol." Felipe motioned at the van, which was moving toward them. "Very good," the pilot said. "We might have been swimming the last hundred miles or so."

While the men refueled the Lysander, Felipe and Leonard helped Zack to the ladder. "Sorry, mate," the pilot said, "only had orders to bring one back. Not you."

"My friend," Felipe said, "we must speak alone." He pulled the pilot to one side and spoke in a low voice.

"I thought you were going," Zack said to Leonard.

"Not possible."

"What are you going to do now?"

Leonard didn't answer at first. Should he tell the young pilot that he was returning to Zaragoza to find Chantal? "That doesn't concern you," he mumbled.

Felipe and the pilot rejoined them. "It's been arranged," the pilot said. He scrambled up the ladder and settled into the high cockpit.

"What did you tell him?" Zack asked Felipe.

"I merely explained the situation to him and suggested that three returning to England was much better than none."

"Would you have done that?" Zack was incredulous.

"No," Felipe said. "One sacrifice was enough to get you this far."

A sick feeling stabbed at the bottom of Zack's stomach. There was no doubt that the sacrifice was Chantal.

FIVE

Udorn, Thailand

"The home folks are getting serious about this one," E-Squared told Gillespie as they found seats in the crowded operations room in the Air America building.

Gillespie looked the new arrivals over and saw nothing that distinguished the men of Delta Force from other Army troops he had worked with in the past. "Because General Mado is here?" he asked.

"Nope. Because there is some real talent in this room. See that Army colonel and the big sergeant?" E-Squared pointed to Trimler and Kamigami, who were standing near the front.

"The sergeant is hard to miss."

"The colonel is Bob Trimler, the commander of Delta Force, and the sergeant is Victor Kamigami, his command sergeant major. I met them on Operation Warlord. Kamigami can crunch rocks with his teeth and Trimler is one tough hombre whose got his sierra stacked in neat piles. He led the rescue team that went into the prison to free the POWs. He was a captain then."

Gillespie looked at E-Squared with a new respect. "I didn't know you were on Warlord."

"Yeah. So was the Beezer—and Mado. Mado probably made

his third star because of Warlord." E-Squared stared at his hands recalling that operation. "I suppose that's why he's the vice commander of USSOCOM. He's the world's ranking asshole. Makes a puke like me wonder about life."

"Whose line is it about 'life not being fair'?" Gillespie asked.

The rear door swung open and a lieutenant colonel stepped into the room. "Room!" he barked. "Ten-hut!" The men sprang to their feet as Lieutenant General Simon Mado entered. Colonel Paul "Duck" Mallard followed him.

"Let's get started," Mado said as he stepped onto the low stage. He kept the men standing at attention. "As you all know, we are here on a special operation which I have named Operation Dragon Noire." He gave the name a French pronunciation. "I have overall command as the joint task force commander, Colonel Mallard is the airborne mission commander, and Colonel Trimler is the ground commander." Satisfied that the command arrangements were carefully spelled out, he turned the meeting over to Mallard.

"Seats, please," Mallard said. Mado was visibly annoyed by Mallard's allowing the men to sit. Gillespie labeled the general as a raging egoist.

"Way to go, Duck," E-Squared muttered.

Mallard quickly recapped the situation and called on the 1st SOW's Intel officer, Lieutenant Colonel Leanne Vokel, for an intelligence update. Vokel took the low stage as the lights dimmed and a slide projector flashed on. She covered the latest reconnaissance imagery and then told the group that only three men were holding the hostage, Nikki Anderson.

"Colonel Vokel," Mado interrupted, "what are your sources for that last information?"

"I can't answer your question, sir," she replied. "Everything we receive has been sanitized as to source." Mado grunted in dissatisfaction. "But my experience," she hurried to explain, "indicates that what we're getting is good. It correlates with other sources and is validated by photo reconnaissance. And we are operating in a friendly environment with the full cooperation of the Thai government."

"I think I love you," E-Squared mouthed, pleased with the way the woman stood up to Mado.

The look on Mado's face indicated he was not convinced. "Put this one on a back burner for now," he said. "Colonel Trimler, what does Delta require to execute Dragon Noire?"

"Now it starts," E-Squared groaned to Gillespie.

Trimler stood up and moved to a chart that had been pinned to the wall and quickly covered what Delta needed. "We want the First SOW to insert a landing zone team near the village where the hostage is being held. Further, we would like to conduct at least one mission rehearsal. I recommend we use the training site the First SOW has been using. It meets all our requirements."

"Who selected that training site and why?" Mado interrupted.

Gillespie wondered why the general should be concerned with such a minor point. He should be more concerned with the security measures that were in place to protect the training exercise from compromise.

"Sir," Mallard answered, "the First SOW has been conducting a training exercise here for over three weeks. We selected that training site in cooperation with the Thai authorities. It will be an easy matter for Delta to blend in without arousing suspicion. That gives us the cover we needed to prevent a security compromise while we practice."

"Too good to be true," Mado spat. "And when something is too good to be true, it usually is." He turned and stared at Mallard. "It looks like you were anticipating this mission, Mallard. By jumping the gun and starting training prematurely, you may have tipped our hand and compromised this mission. You should have cleared your exercise through USSOCOM first."

"He's doing it," E-Squared mumbled.

"Doing what?" Gillespie whispered.

"Doing an 'off me, on you.' By finding problems he has to correct, he can delay making any decisions. That shifts the monkey onto someone else's back."

"General Mado," Mallard replied calmly with no sign of stress in his voice, "I did not act unilaterally. This training exercise is consistent with the training we conduct in many parts of the world. For once, we were in a position to capitalize on training currently in progress. Further, this exercise was approved by USSOCOM."

"Go get him, Duck," E-Squared mumbled.

Gillespie looked around the room, trying to gauge the reaction of the others. He suspected that the First SOW was training for this mission because Mallard had anticipated the need. Wasn't that what colonels were paid to do? Why are they playing games with each other? He glanced at the huge Army command sergeant major. Kamigami's gaze was totally focused on Mado and his face was expressionless. For reasons that escaped him, Gillespie sensed that he was looking at an extremely dangerous man.

In the silence that followed, Trimler brought his briefing to an end. "Sir, we have selected this landing zone near Ban Muang Dok as our primary LZ." He handed Mado an aerial photograph of the landing zone that was on the edge of the village. "One practice run and we are ready to go, sir."

"Who approved this landing zone?" Mado asked.

"I did, sir," Trimler answered.

"You approved the LZ?" Mado shot at him. "In my book, the First SOW should have picked the landing zone since they have to do the insertion."

"I assure you, sir," Trimler replied, "it was not a unilateral decision on my part and the First SOW was part of the process."

Mado stood up. "It seems the wrong people are making the critical decisions on this operation," he said. "And I don't like it."

"Excuse me, sir," E-Squared said, "but the ground team always selects the LZ in an operation like this one. We tell them if we can do it and what the risk is. The LZ that was selected looks like a good one, close to the objective where Miss Anderson is being held and there is no threat."

"Major"—Mado turned a cold, fish-eyed stare onto the MC-130 pilot—"your input was not asked for. Let's get one thing straight, I will not order men under my command into a poorly planned operation like this one. Back to the drawing boards, gentlemen."

Mado slapped his hands down on the table and leaned forward, his arms stiff. "If you people in this room are not reading my lips, this mission is on hold until the planning and training are up to my standards. Mallard, Trimler, I want you in my office so I can sort this mess out." He stalked out of the room with the two colonels in tow.

The men sat in stunned silence. "Ah," E-Squared finally said, "it's good to know there are certain constants in the world and that General Mado is one of them." He stood up. "Let's go get a cool one. Dragon Noire is dead in the water."

"What the hell is going on?" Gillespie asked.

"Mado in action," E-Squared explained, his cynicism not lost on Gillespie. "He will never make a decision that can be pinned on him in case this all turns to shit. I saw it before during Warlord. So did the two colonels and Kamigami." Gillespie looked confused. "Hell," E-Squared continued, "he's a high roller. What did you expect?"

"Colonel Mallard doesn't work that way," Gillespie protested.

The Golden Triangle, Burma

Heather Courtland was lying by the large swimming pool in Chiang's Burma compound. The pool had been carefully designed to resemble a natural lagoon and a waterfall hid the entrance to a small grotto perfect for lovemaking. Chiang had taught her all about it. DC and Ricky were treading water under the waterfall and talking. He is looking better, Heather decided. Ricky's long hair had been unceremoniously sheared, a doctor had shot him full of antibiotics and vitamins, put him on a healthy diet, and the guards had dried up his supply of drugs, forcing him to go cold turkey. DC had nursed him through his withdrawal and now he was dependent on her. The two of them became closer and turned away from Heather. I wonder if they're screwing? Heather thought. Then it came to her—they were enduring their captivity by holding on to each other.

Heather languidly stretched a leg out to examine her tan. Perfect. "What a life," she murmured to herself, feeling remarkably contented. Heather was not an introspective person, so it amazed her that she could feel so good trapped deep in the Burmese highlands. She liked what was happening to her. "Samkit," she called. The woman immediately appeared out of the shadows to attend her mistress. "I'd like fruit and ice tea for lunch. And bring me the wraparound skirt that goes with this bikini." Samkit hurried to carry out her instructions. Heather was not a patient person and had become more imperious over the last few weeks.

"DC," she called. "What do you know about Dostoevski?"

The young woman detached herself from Ricky and swam across the pool. "Actually, not too much. I did read *Crime and Punishment.*"

"You'd best tell me what you remember. Bertie asked me to read it."

"Well, it's about guilt," DC began. She was going over the plot when Samkit came back with the wraparound skirt.

"Missy Heather," she said, a worried look on her face. "General asks for you." Heather stood up and stepped into high-heeled sandals and wrapped the expensive skirt around her waist. She shook her hair out and adjusted her top, making sure her breasts had maximum exposure. "General in bunker," Samkit told her.

"We'll talk later," Heather said to DC, "without Ricky. Samkit, come with me." She led the way into the tunnel that led to Chiang's underground command post. "Have you ever been here before?" she asked Samkit as they went through a heavy blast door and descended a concrete staircase into a labyrinth of corridors. They were in a heavily fortified military-style command bunker.

"No, missy," Samkit said, carefully noting everything she saw. They had to wait in a control room with a bank of TV screens. "What that?" she asked.

Heather was amused at how backward Samkit could be. "TV monitors," she said and stepped around to the control panel. She played with the controls and a screen flashed, changing to a panorama of the service gate at the rear of the compound. Heather played with the controls, changing the camera's height. Samkit decided that the camera was on a telescopic arm that retracted into a hidden niche. She fixed its location. Heather called up a camera at the pool where they had been moments before. DC and Ricky were gone. Then she switched to a camera in the grotto behind the waterfall. They were inside, talking quietly, not touching. Heather turned a dial until she could hear their voices.

"I've bribed one of the guards," Ricky said. "I promised him a quarter million in gold if he'll help us escape."

"When?" DC's voice was barely audible.

"He's not sure. Maybe in a week or two. Don't worry, he'll get us out of here."

"I still think we should tell Heather."

"No fuckin' way," Ricky growled.

Heather's face was impassive as she switched the monitor back to the outside pool. The inner blast door swung open and Heather told Samkit to follow her into Chiang's command post. She liked having an entourage, however small, at her beck and call. But Samkit hesitated. "I wait here," she said, fear in her voice. Heather shrugged and walked inside.

Chiang was sitting at the central console surrounded by four aides. "We have received some interesting news," Chiang said. "We know where Nikki is and you should be enjoying her company in a few days."

Heather nodded, a slight smile on her face. "Yes, I would like that. Besides, it sends a clear message that you're in complete control. By the way, DC and Ricky have bribed a guard." She recounted the conversation she had overheard on the monitor.

"That will not present a problem," Chiang assured her. The guard had already told him about the attempted bribe. "You"—

he smiled at Heather—"do indeed make a royal consort."

The compliment pleased Heather.

Later that same evening, Samkit climbed the eight steps into the small hooch she called home. She was tired from the long day spent running after Heather and attending to her every whim. Soon, she thought, it will be over. She had seen a succession of young women who had shared Chiang's bed and then later disappeared into the brothels of Bangkok. This one is no different, she reasoned. She frowned, remembering the time long ago when Chiang had called her his "royal consort." She had learned much from her brief visit to the bunker.

Samkit lit a lantern and started a small charcoal fire to cook her dinner. While the coals caught fire, she reached under her bed and eased up a loose floor board. She pulled out the small radio that resembled a Walkman. But this one was different. She pushed at the on/off button until it gave a hard click. The radio was now in a record/store mode. She spoke into the speaker, which was also a microphone, relating the day's events and all she had seen in the bunker. It was a much longer message than normal. When she was finished, she hit the button again and returned the radio to its hiding place. She fell into her nightly routine, thinking about her son and how proud she was of him. She did not worry about what tomorrow would bring.

Early the next morning, a saffron-robed monk walked past Samkit's hooch as he begged for a meal. He reached inside the plastic bag he was carrying and keyed what looked like a cellular phone. A short-range signal activated the transmit feature on Samkit's radio and it broadcast a high-speed playback of the stored message. Anyone in range and able to monitor the transmission would have only heard a short burst of garbled noise. The monk's phone recorded the message and Samkit's radio automatically erased its storage disk. He would play it back when he was alone. The monk was proud of his mother and would pray for her safety.

Washington, D.C.

Mazie never chewed her fingernails, but now she was chomping on her right thumbnail as she jockeyed through Washington, D.C.'s evening rush hour traffic. She worried the nail harder as she tried to decode the phone call she had received from Bill

Carroll. "Damn it, Humphrey," she told her beloved Bug convertible, "Why did he call me and not use our normal arrangement? This must be important. Have I missed something?"

The traffic light blinked green in front of her and a honk brought her back to the moment. Roll with it, she thought, this one is breaking fast.

Eighteen minutes later, she was sitting in a coffee shop in Chevy Chase, Maryland, when Bill Carroll sat down beside her. He was dressed in civilian clothes and looked more like a young high school teacher than a brigadier general in command of the Air Force Special Activities Center. His message was short. "Chiang knows where Nikki Anderson is. He's going after her."

"How long do we have?" Mazie asked.

"Who knows. Twenty-four hours at the most."

The National Security Council's Crisis Action Team was gathered around the table in Mackay's office and going over every scrap of information they had on Nikki Anderson. Like an amoeba, the CAT would gather in clumps to look at one aspect and then re-form when another subject was broached. The team kept referring to an exquisite large-scale topographic chart displayed on a large video monitor. The Defense Mapping Agency had computerized its map base and the team could call up whatever map they needed from a set of twelve-inch video disks. The computerized system allowed them to place the village of Ban Muang Dok at the exact center of the screen and not be plagued by the old military axiom that battles are fought on the edge of a map.

"If this latest information is correct," Cagliari told the small group, "time is not on our side. We've got to move fast."

Mackay kept referring to a thin paperbound volume labeled "OPPLAN Dragon Noire." "I don't see any problem," he told them. "All the pieces are here and the players are ready to go. This is a chance to finally bring off a hostage rescue without it falling apart on us."

"I know you don't think much of our ability to execute this type of mission," Cagliari said. "Why are you pushing this one so hard?"

"Sir, our track record does suck," Mackay replied. "But here's a chance to do it right. In special operations if you snooze, you lose."

"I suppose that is your quaint way of saying timeliness is a factor," Mazie said.

"It's everything in this business," Mackay assured her.

"Okay," Cagliari said, "enough. I'm going to see the President in a few minutes and recommend that we execute the rescue tonight. That still doesn't solve the problem of the remaining three hostages. By freeing Miss Anderson, we lose any element of surprise in rescuing the others. Chiang's going to be expecting us now. Now how do we get around that problem? Start working it."

Start working it, Mackay thought. The man's amazing the way he keeps pushing ahead. Okay, what's the key? Speed and surprise. No wonder the SAS keep insisting that they've got to "beat the clock." An image of Peter Woodward materialized in his mind while an idea tickled just below the surface.

Cagliari stood up to leave. "One other thing," he said, "Tosh is very ill. It's her heart this time." He didn't have to say that the wolf, lupus, had again returned to ravage the wife of the President.

"Mazie," Mackay said after the national security adviser had left, "can you tap into System Four and do a little digging?"

Leo Cox focused his full attention on every word that Cagliari was telling the President. He was sitting in the Oval Office along with the director of central intelligence, Bobby Burke, who also was very interested in what Cagliari was saying. But not for the same reasons. While Burke agreed with Cagliari's recommendation that Delta Force be sent in to rescue Nikki Anderson, he was wondering where Cagliari had gotten his information. It had not come from his source, Willowbranch.

"I agree that this is an opportune time to act," Burke said. "But you did say the joint task force commander, General Mado, wants more time to prepare."

"This," Cagliari said, "is one of those cases where we've got to build a fire under the military."

"I can sympathize with General Mado," Pontowski allowed. "During World War Two my job was to fly and carry out orders. Oh, it was dangerous, but it was a very simple, uncomplicated life. Simple but dangerous. I only had to keep two people alive, my navigator and myself. I was the cutting edge. Now I have to act on Mado's recommendations and make the decisions that drive the cutting edge. What I say determines who lives or dies. And

I don't like being rushed into action when other people's lives are on the line."

He paused to let what he was saying register with his three advisers. "Only an egomaniac willingly shoulders such a burden."

"Mr. President," Cagliari finally said, "you are not an egomaniac."

"I hope not," Pontowski said. "Thank God I'm much older than you three and won't have to live with the consequences too much longer." His decision was made. "Order Delta to go in tonight."

Burke pulled Cagliari aside when they were outside in the hall. "Don't you think," Burke said, "that it's time we pooled our resources?" Cagliari didn't reply. "Come on," Burke insisted. "You've got a source inside other than Willowbranch. It's just a matter of time until I find out who."

"Plug some of your leaks," Cagliari told him, "then maybe we can do business."

"They've been plugged," Burke assured him.

"Really?" Cagliari answered. "Was the leak plugged when that boat on Chesapeake Bay blew up and sank?"

Burke humphed in his bureaucratic way. "You mustn't believe what you read in the newspapers," he said as he walked away. Heads-on-heads intelligence was not a game for the squeamish. Especially, the way Burke played it. The truth of the matter would die with him.

Udorn, Thailand

The Combat Talon MC-130E taxied into its parking slot on the ramp at Udorn next to the Beezer's AC-130 gunship. The dark paint schemes on both aircraft glistened from the rain that had doused the air base moments before. A startling sunset was in the making as the clouds peeled back in multihued layers. E-Squared had just returned from a short hop to Bangkok's Don Muang airport and the pilot played a tune with the throttles, varying the power to different props and moving one prop in and out of reverse. "You can always tell when the major is happy," the crew chief told Gillespie. "He must have a load of beer." The two waited for the big four-bladed props to spin down.

When E-Squared stepped out of the crew entrance hatch, Gillespie grabbed him and rushed him to the waiting pickup truck.

"Come on," he urged, "the heavies are wetting their knickers and want us in Ops ASAPist."

"We must have got a go for the mission," E-Squared allowed.

"What makes you think that?" Gillespie asked.

"The signs are right and if we don't go in soon, the well will be dry when we get there."

The operations section in Air America's headquarters building was crowded with officers and NCOs, all talking in hushed tones. E-Squared led the way through the crowd and found a seat at the back next to the Beezer. "Watch Mado run for cover," he told the two men. He settled down to wait.

He was disappointed when only Mallard and Trimler walked into the room. "Gentlemen," Mallard announced, "we have been ordered to execute Dragon Noire tonight. General Mado is talking to the National Military Command Center in the Pentagon via SatCom as we speak." He did not mention that Mado was speaking out of both sides of his mouth, telling his superiors in the NMCC that they were ready to go but that he would like a few more days of training to ensure success. "Further," Mallard continued, "they're asking us for a recommended execute time." A hush fell over the room.

"Holy shit," E-Squared said, his stage whisper carrying across the room, "someone with a clue at Fort Fumble asking the working troops how to do it."

"Hey," the Beezer chimed in, "the Pentagon is like a stopped clock—right twice a day."

"Unfortunately," Mallard snapped, "this is not a humorous matter. Colonel Vokel," he turned to the First SOW's intelligence officer, "tell them the bad news."

"Yes, sir," Vokel said as she stood up. "We received a report that an unidentified convoy of four trucks is moving down this road." She pointed to an unimproved dirt road leading from Burma into Ban Muang Dok. "We don't know what the convoy is, but suspect it could be hostile. At their rate of movement, the convoy should reach Ban Muang Dok no later than twenty-two hundred hours tonight." The room was silent.

"Do the heavies in the Pentagon know about this?" E-Squared asked.

"Yes, they do," Mallard answered. "No doubt the rescue team has been ordered to move into place."

"Where did that team come from?" Gillespie asked E-Squared in a low voice.

"Don't ask," the C-130 pilot whispered. "The details of the rescue itself are not our business. We only have to know how they expect us to support them."

"When would we have learned the details?" Gillespie asked. "That can be critical." He was confused and wondered how wise it was to keep half the players in the dark about what was really going on.

"About this time. You should have read the signs. Didn't you notice during training how the team you were inserting only secured the LZ and then rapidly pulled in? Obviously, someone was coming to you."

"We still need an execute time," Mallard said. "The original plan called for a three A.M. rescue. I think we need to be in and out before those trucks arrive."

"Colonel," the Beezer called out, "killing trucks is what Spectre was made for."

"Unfortunately," Mallard replied, "we don't know for certain if those trucks are hostile. General Mado ruled out attacking any trucks unless they commit a hostile act." The Beezer conceded that Mado had a point.

A variety of suggestions erupted from the group. Finally, Gillespie spoke. "I'd recommend going in right at the end of evening twilight." Everyone looked at the young pilot. Embarrassed by the sudden attention, he reddened. "Well," he stammered, "I know our infrared systems are degraded because it's right at crossover when land and air temperatures equalize and our systems are degraded. But that's the time when the Thais are all inside watching TV. At least they were in the village where we've been training. And every TV set is at full throttle." Nods went around the room. They had all experienced it. The wail of Thai TV at full volume had to be heard to be believed. "That should help mask our noise. If we go in earlier, someone will be outside and see us. Later on, after things quiet down, they'll hear us coming." More nods.

"Captain Gillespie," said Mallard, "can you find the LZ with a degraded FLIR?"

"Yes, sir. I can." It was a statement of fact. The Pave Low helicopter had other, equally sophisticated, systems.

"Colonel Trimler, does that give you any heartburn?" Mallard asked.

Trimler glanced at his second-in-command, the lieutenant colonel in command of A Squadron, and then at Kamigami. They both gave short nods. "We can do that," Trimler answered.

Mallard considered it for a moment. "I agree. I'll pass the time to General Mado. Mission brief in ten minutes." He left the room.

"Well, I'll be damned," E-Squared said. He heaved himself to his feet and ambled over to Lieutenant Colonel Leanne Vokel.

"Without a doubt," Gillespie told E-Squared's back.

Twelve minutes later, a very unhappy General Mado marched into the room. The men all sprang to attention. "We have a go," Mado announced. "There have been some changes in the operational lineup. Colonels Mallard and Trimler will be aboard the MC-One-thirty to monitor the accomplishment of mission objectives. I will be in the command post here and maintain radio contact with the airborne command element and the NMCC via SatCom." He turned the briefing over to the operations staff and the men sat down.

A weatherman gave them the latest forecast for that evening. Then the classified mission booklets were passed out. Each booklet consisted of a small bundle of five-by-eight inch plastic-sheathed pages held together by a two-pronged page fastener. The booklets carried the vital information they would need to carry out the mission. No one had to remind them that if one of the booklets fell into the wrong hands, the operation would be fatally compromised.

"Here's the lineup and times," a lieutenant colonel said. "Ready to copy?" The men flipped open their mission booklets to the second page and pulled out grease pencils to fill in the blanks with the latest information. He read off the details. "The rescue team is in two elements, call signs Pogo One and Pogo Two. They will go in at nineteen-forty-three hours local. Our LZ time is twenty hundred hours local. Helicopter call signs are Rascal One, Two, and Three. Captain Gillespie in Rascal One will launch at seventeen-forty hours local with the LZ team. Rascal Two is the airborne backup and will launch with Captain Gillespie. Rascal Three will hold on the ramp here as the ground backup. Major Eberhard's MC-One-thirty, call sign Hammer, will be airborne command and control and will launch at eighteen-thirty. Lieutenant Colonel Beasely's gunship, call sign Spectre, will launch at the same time." He turned the briefing over to Trimler.

"You've heard the latest intelligence that indicates we should encounter only token resistance in the target area." A wicked gleam lit the colonel's face. "Now how many of you are ready to proceed on that assumption?" A chorus of grunts and guffaws mixed with a very definite "No way!" greeted him. "I thought so," Trimler said. "Remember how we do it: Maximum surprise—maximum violence." Then they were finished and the room rapidly emptied.

Gillespie shoved the mission booklet into the leg pocket of his flight suit and zipped it closed. "This one should be a piece of cake," he said.

"You seem pretty sure about that," E-Squared said.

"Hell," Gillespie replied, "you heard the same intelligence briefing that I did."

"Intelligence is always wrong," E-Squared intoned.

The Capitol, Washington, D.C.

The Army colonel was leaving Courtland's offices as Tina Stanley, the senator's aide, entered. She was visibly upset and near tears. "Close the door," Courtland said. He motioned her to be seated and paced his office. "What did the Coast Guard say?"

"They claim it was a fuel tank explosion. I had to identify the body." A shudder ran through her slender frame. "It was George."

"And the other body?"

"No positive identification—yet. But I'm certain it was George's contact in the CIA. Senator, I think it was a hit."

"Did their blood test positive for drugs?" Courtland asked. She nodded. "If it was a hit," the senator said, disappointment in his voice, "then it was drug-related. Pontowski doesn't work that way."

"This has been a terrible day," Tina moaned.

"That colonel had some good news," Courtland told her. "The Polack is sending Delta Force in to rescue Anderson." He recounted what the Army colonel had told him. He paced faster. "With a little luck, Operation Dragon Noire will be a bust. Even if he does get Anderson out, it will be a warning to Chiang to get his guard up." He was swinging his arms like he was holding a baseball bat. "Do you know what that does to the chances for rescuing Heather?" The woman did not know exactly how to answer that question.

"It shoots 'em all to hell," the senator said. He swung at an imaginary pitch. "Home run!"

The White House, Washington, D.C.

Zack Pontowski walked beside the wheelchair as the nurse pushed his wife to the helicopter that was waiting to fly her to Bethesda Naval Hospital. "Is this really necessary?" she protested.

He smiled at her. "You know how doctors are." Her old fighting spirit was back and for a moment he remembered the time in Zaragoza when he had been on a gurney being taken away. They reached the helicopter and, for one of those rare times at the White House, the press corps did not yell questions but held back out of respect for her privacy.

"They are being good today," Tosh said as she waved at the reporters. For a brief moment, Pontowski convinced himself that she would recover like she had in the past. How many times had the doctors expressed amazement at how she fought off the ravages of lupus with sheer willpower. But an inner voice warned him that it was not to be. Not this time.

The staff and support units that surrounded the President moved with their usual efficiency during the short flight to Bethesda. Airspace was cleared and secured, Secret Service agents, some obvious but most totally submerged into the background, moved into place and cast a net of protection around the presidential couple. Radios crackled with coded commands and backup units moved into position. The Vice President was notified that the President was airborne and stayed on the ground. When the helicopter touched down on the pad at the hospital, the staff was prepared and waiting and Tosh was quickly moved into a suite. Pontowski stayed by her side during the entire time and saw how exhausted she was after the short move. He sat down beside her bed and placed his hand gently over hers.

"You are a worrywart," she told him. "I'll be all right. Now what do you think Courtland is up to?" As usual, the political animal in Tosh was coming out and, again, she was his most trusted and valued counselor. For a few minutes, they discussed the difficult senator's latest moves. "I really believe," she said, "that he would sacrifice his own daughter."

"He wants the presidency," Zack said. "He's got to discredit my administration . . ."

"If he wants to defeat the candidate you back in the next

election," Tosh said, completing the thought for him.

"Men do strange things when they want the presidency."

"Yes, they do," Tosh whispered. But Pontowski wasn't thinking about Courtland. He was wishing for a time of healing, much like he had in the spring of 1943. "Go on back," she told him, "and let me take a nap."

"I'll be back," he told her. He gently kissed her and left, taking the first steps of another hard journey while his wife renewed her battle with an old enemy—the wolf.

1943

Sherston Hall, Suffolk, England

The old duke stomped up and down the south terrace of the huge country house, impatient and caustic as usual, ignoring the nurses and officers taking the afternoon sun. He kept eyeing the path that led to the stables and checking his watch. "Impertinent pup," he grumbled. He occupied his time by surveying the grounds that surrounded Sherston Hall, his eighty-eight-room ancestral home that had been built in the 1650s. He glanced at the crowd on the terrace and snorted.

It had been hard for the old man to adjust to the hodgepodge of medical staff, orderlies, and wounded officers who filled his country house with chatter. He regretted allowing his wife to open up Sherston Hall as a convalescent home for officers wounded in the war. The noise and commotion that went with fifty to sixty young officers on the mend in the company of a bevy of young nurses and female orderlies had shattered his peaceful way of life. "Damn magpies" he called them with gruff impatience. He would never admit that he actually liked his "guests," at least not to himself. He was anxious for the war to end so he could settle back into his old tyrannical ways.

Still, he had made it his duty to get to know each of the officers while they were under his roof by inviting them to share afternoon tea with him. When, from time to time, one would die or later be killed in action, he always wrote to the parents or wife expressing his and Lady Crafton's condolences. He had been delivered a severe shock at one of those teas when a newly arrived RAF officer had spoken with an American accent. He had uttered, "A damn colonial" without thinking and had immediately received a smiling "Oh, I hope so, sir. But it's only a small imperfection."

The duke was startled by the reply. Not many were willing to brave his crusty reputation. "Humph," he snorted. "Never met a colonial who knew damned-all about horses."

"That's the worst thing Charles can say about a person," the duchess said, trying to smooth things over. "Don't pay any attention to him."

"I know a bit about horses . . . for a colonial," the American had said. The duke had proceeded to bombard him with questions and discovered that he knew more than just "a bit about horses." They became instantaneous friends.

A gust of wind whipped at the duke's open coat, revealing a well-tailored mustard yellow waistcoat stretched tight across his big stomach. Perhaps because of his age and rotund body, the old-fashioned plus-four trousers that belted below his knees suited him. He pulled at his handlebar mustache when he saw the tall figure he had been waiting for walk around the far bend of the path leading from the stables.

"The boy's been giving the nags their exercise," he said to no one in particular. A nurse smiled at him. She, like almost everyone else at the country estate, had come to like the young American and was glad when he was around to divert the duke's attention at afternoon tea. Somehow, the American had tamed the old man while he recovered from a nasty leg wound and life in the big house had become more pleasant. They would all miss him when he returned to operations. After that, the duke would then turn his full attention to what he called "maintaining civilized behavior under my roof." She remembered only too well the torrent of abuse he had unleashed on her and a most appealing young RAF flight officer when he had discovered them locked in a passionate embrace in the maze. "Ask Flight Lieutenant Pontowski to join me for tea," he commanded, again speaking to no specific person. The nurse and two others made a mental promise to get the word to Zack. "Damn nags," he groused. "Damn magpies." He stomped down to the far end of the terrace to wait.

Fifteen minutes later, Zack walked through the tall French doors opening out from the drawing room. He had washed and changed out of the rough clothes he wore when exercising the duke's horses and was wearing his RAF uniform. The duke studied his gait, much as he would a piece of prized horse flesh. "Humph," he grunted, gesturing at the chair opposite him. "You look fit enough. Time you stopped wreacking havoc in my stable and abused the king's property instead."

Zack ignored his comments and sat down. "I'm expecting a posting anytime," he said. "The quack said I'm no longer u/s."

"U/s?" the duke grumbled. "Isn't that the gibberish you use around those confounded airplanes?"

"It means unserviceable," Zack told him. "Seems to fit."

The duke looked genuinely distressed. "Soon?"

"They say the orders will probably come down next week."

"Then you'll be here over the weekend. Good. I'd like you to meet my granddaughter . . . Wilhelmina . . . headstrong young filly . . . needs taming." He stirred his tea and took a sip. "Infatuated with the wrong chap . . . Roger Bertram . . . absolutely worthless."

"I take it that means he can't ride and doesn't like horses," Zack said. He stifled a grin.

"Quite the contrary. Bertram's mad about them. Rides like a demon. But that's about all he can mount. Breeding all wrong. Good chest development, short in the withers but weak in the head. All wrong for the girl."

"If your granddaughter is true to her lineage," Zack said, "nothing is going to change her mind." He suspected that Wilhelmina would be built like the duke, horse-faced, and spoiled rotten.

The duke of Crafton humphed at the American and decided not to answer. Underneath his eccentric personality beat the heart of a shrewd and capable breeder.

"Is that the duke's granddaughter?" Zack asked the orderly, who doubled as the bartender in the evening. He was standing at the bar table in the far end of the reception lounge that had been turned into a common room.

The man looked in the direction of the big double doors opening onto the main hall and studied the young, short dumpy blonde who had just entered. "Sorry, sir. Never seen 'er ladyship before. But this one does match the lot." The young woman was talking with the marked accent that went with the English upper class.

"I was afraid of that," Zack said, thinking of ways to escape without the duke seeing him. But he was too late; the old man came in and motioned for him to come over. "Where are those orders," he moaned, walking across the room. "I need to get out of here."

The duke said, "I want you to meet my granddaughter, Wilhelmina."

Zack turned to the woman. "Hello, pleased to meet you."

"I'm Willi's cousin, silly." She looked behind Zack and nodded. "This is Willi."

He turned and felt his mouth go dry. Standing in the doorway was a slender blonde. Her naturally curly hair fell in a heavy cloud down to her shoulders and in high heels, she matched his height. Her hair framed a beautiful face, a classic peaches-and-cream complexion, and the most profound blue eyes he had ever seen. He was speechless.

"Lieutenant Pontowski," she said, extending her hand. Her voice was a cool contralto that matched her face. "Grandfather has been singing your praises." He shook her hand dumbly, not sure what to say.

"Very quiet for a Yank," a voice said beside her. For the first time, Zack noticed the tall British Navy officer standing with her. "Could we have a polite American in our midst?" His laughter made Zack think of a horse trying to imitate a goose's honk.

Zack could sense the hostility behind the officer's words and his combative instincts flared. Be careful, he warned himself. If this is the guy the duke told me about, Roger Bertram, he is only protecting his territory—Wilhelmina. "Perhaps," Zack said. "There must be at least one of us over here by now."

"How refreshing," the Englishman replied.

"Please, Roger," Willi said. "They are our guests. Behave yourself." She gave Zack a perfunctory smile and dismissed him. "So nice to have met you," she said and swept past him into the lounge with Roger Bertram in tow.

"Overpaid, oversexed, and over here," Roger said in a loud voice.

"Not overpaid in the RAF," Zack said in a loud stage whisper. From the way their backs stiffened he knew he had hit home.

Willi turned and shot him a cold look. "A drink, please," she said, walking away.

"Damned wrong," the duke said, capturing Zack's attention. "I did that all wrong. Told her you were a decent chap. Should have called you a scoundrel, worthless. Then she'd have been interested."

* * *

Zack was up early the next morning. He dressed quickly in the old comfortable clothes the head coachman had lent him for riding and stole down to the kitchen, careful not to wake his roommate. As usual, the two cooks let him eat breakfast in the kitchen. After he had gulped down a last cup of tea, he thanked them and headed for the stables. "He's the only decent one here," one of the cooks said. "I hear he's leaving shortly. I'll miss him." The other cook agreed.

At the stables, he was surprised to see all the horses but one gone. "Sorry, sir," the old coachman who had come out of retirement to care for the duke's horses said. "Miss Wilhelmina and her friends went for an early-morning ride."

Zack shrugged and went to work helping the old man muck out the stalls and pitch fresh hay down from the loft. The smell of the hay brought back a vivid image of Chantal and he paused, resting on his pitchfork, thinking. An ache boomed through his chest as he visualized her curled up in the hay, waking from a night's sleep. And then other images played across his memory, her kneeling in the hay, a playful look on her face as he taught her English, the first brief sight of her totally nude, and then the last glimpse of her standing in the hospital corridor as he was wheeled into the operating room. For a moment, he could again feel her body pressed against his, her heart racing, as the heavy footsteps of the gendarme stomped down the hall toward their room. Will I ever see you again? he wondered. He forced his mind to think of the present and forget the past. "The past is gone and best forgotten," he told himself.

The one horse left behind in the stables was a mare, too old to ride and kept in graceful retirement by the duke. Zack forced his attention onto her and was carefully grooming the horse when the duke walked past on his early-morning inspection. The old mare had been his favorite mount when he had still been able to ride. But a stiff hip, the result of an artillery barrage in the Boer War, had finally put an end to his equestrian endeavors. "There, there Nancy," he said, feeding the horse a handful of carrots. Zack leaned against the stall wall cleaning the curry comb while the duke examined his handiwork. "Well done, lad. Who taught you?"

"An old cowboy who worked on the stud farm where I spent my summers."

"Ah, yes. So you've said. You must have enjoyed your vacations."

"It wasn't a vacation," Zack answered. "I worked like a dog."

"What did they breed?" the duke asked, now very interested. "Thoroughbreds?"

"Nope, polo ponies."

"Ever play?"

"Occasionally, during a practice chukker when they needed a fourth," Zack answered. The duke wandered away, deep in thought.

That evening, the duke sent him word to please join him in the family's quarters. He was unfamiliar with that wing of the palatial house and a maid had to show him the way. He was not surprised to find Willi and Roger Bertram with the duke. The duke came right to the point. "They tell me the nags are in excellent condition," he said. "Your doing. An interesting group getting together at Moncton Hall tomorrow. All very keen on horses. Care to join us." This last was not a question and was only the duke's way of being polite.

"Hopefully," Roger said, "we might be able to arrange some entertainment." He smiled at Zack's confusion. "Polo, you know. Haven't done it in years. Just not on during the war. The duke tells me you understand the game."

"A little." Zack smiled.

"They'll be riding over," the duke interrupted. "I'll take the carriage. You come with me."

Zack said that he would like to go and, from the quiet that followed, sensed that he was dismissed. He made his way back to the big lounge. Now what the hell is that all about, he thought.

The ride the next morning with the duke was not what he had expected. The old man insisted on driving himself and had to be helped onto the seat. But once he had the reins in hand, he was formidable. He drove the matched pair at a brisk trot and had no trouble wheeling the carriage down the lane and through the narrow gate leading to Moncton Hall. Once there, and since the duke was oblivious to most social niceties, he abandoned Zack.

Zack went with the flow of people who meandered in the general direction of a big marquee set up on the lawn. He was grateful that his RAF uniform blended in with the hodgepodge of uniforms and clothes the other guests were wearing. From overheard scraps of conversation, he learned that an important conference was being held at Moncton Hall and that Lord Moncton had used the occasion to schedule a garden party for the participants to break the monotony and drudgery of a war that seemed to have no end.

Once, he caught a glimpse of Willi and felt a sudden urge in the lower regions of his body. She was dressed in a riding coat and breeches that accentuated her figure and had attracted her own small following of admirers.

Can't say I blame them, Zack thought, wondering where the ever-present Roger had disappeared to. He turned away and bumped into a tall, dark-haired man who was dressed for a polo match. "Sorry, sir," he apologized instantly.

"Ah, our polite American cousin," Roger said as he emerged from behind the newcomer. He was also dressed in riding breeches, boots, and a polo shirt the same color as that of the man Zack had almost bowled over. "Admiral Mountbatten," Roger said, relishing the moment, "may I present Pilot Officer Pontowski, currently on the mend at Sherston Hall."

Mountbatten extended his hand and Zack was struck by the firm handshake. "I see it's Flight Officer Pontowski," Mountbatten said. "Roger's not too keen on rank in the RAF." His voice was warm and friendly.

The old duke came waddling up. "Dickie," he said to Mountbatten. "Rotten luck about the match. Can't find a fourth for the other side."

"All understandable," Mountbatten said, obviously disappointed. "It was a spur of the moment idea anyway. Too bad, the prime minister would have loved it."

"Winston Churchill is here?" Zack blurted.

The duke nodded. "The old boy loves a good chukker," he said, chin on his chest. "It's been—what?—three years since we last had a match. Damn war. Would have been good for us and the nags. All need a break." Then his round face shot up, a wicked gleam in his eyes. "I say, Pontowski. Didn't you ride on a team?"

Before Zack could protest that he had only been an exercise boy, he was shanghaied into the match, Willi was called over to find him some riding clothes and to get him to the paddock while the others left to warm up the ponies. "What the hell," Zack mumbled, "I haven't played in years."

"Neither have they," she said, coldly eyeing him. "Whatever did Grandfather have in mind?"

Willi proved very efficient in her duties and had him at the paddock within fifteen minutes to meet the other three members of his team. "There," she said. "That should do." Then she left.

"Don't take any notice of the Ice Queen," his teammate James said. "She hates Yanks on principle." James was the number three man on the team and would play as the team's quarterback, feeding balls to the one and two man.

Zack grinned and shook hands with his team. Then he mounted the pony he was to ride in the first chukker. "Go easy," James warned him. "The ponies aren't up to scratch." Zack cut a few figure eights, swinging his mallet. "I do believe he's done this before," James said to the other two members of his team as he watched Zack and the pony blend into one. "I think we should put him in as two." The number two man on a polo team is the hustler whose job is to always be scrapping for the ball.

The crowd were clustered around different players when Zack trotted onto the field. He caught a glimpse of Mountbatten and Roger standing beside their horses talking to Willi and Winston Churchill. The prime minister was the shortest of the group and Zack touched the bill of his helmet when Churchill looked his way. No response.

From the first bowl-in when the referee rolled the ball between the two teams, it was obvious that Roger and Mountbatten were skilled players and had played together before. Zack wasn't even in the same league. But he was a good horseman and aggressive. At the end of the first chukker, seven and a half minutes of play, his team was down three to zero and they gathered together to plot some new tactics while they changed mounts. "Roger seems to be tiring," James said. "Press him a bit." Zack nodded, thankful that they were only going to be playing four chukkers and not the normal six. Polo takes a great deal of upper body strength and even though he was well-developed from the years he had spent in amateur boxing and muscling the heavy Beaufighter through the sky, he was tired.

During the second chukker, Mountbatten's team scored early on. Then Mountbatten made a fantastic under-the-neck shot to Bertram, who charged the goal, driving the ball in front of him. Zack thundered after Bertram. In polo, the ball creates its own right-of-way when it is hit and the player who hit it is entitled to hit it again unless another player drives his pony's shoulder in front of the horse's shoulder of the first player. Zack's pony instinctively responded and rode Bertram's mount off the ball, giving Zack a shot. He fed it back upfield to James, who made an easy goal.

Zack was surprised at the applause and admitted to himself that it was more the doing of his pony than a result of his own skill. Mountbatten granted him a "Well done" when he rode past.

When they lined up for the bowl-in, James, his team captain, said that he had heard Churchill asking about him. Now Zack, encouraged by his pony, pressed Roger hard and broke up a series of plays, keeping the other team scoreless through the rest of the period and all of the third chukker. Finally, they were into the last period and Zack was delighted to discover that his last pony still had lots of steam left.

"Good boy," he told his mount, patting the side of the horse's neck. "Time for a little razzle-dazzle." He charged after Roger when he saw Mountbatten setting up a pass and intercepted the ball, swinging his mallet and tapping the ball to pass behind Roger. They both swung around together and charged the ball, riding shoulder to shoulder and bumping each other. It was a classic ride-off, each pony bumping into the other as the men fought for the ball, mallets raised and then swinging. Zack muffed a shot and the ball dribbled to Roger's off side. But they had overridden the ball and they cut back together, the ball now between them. Roger had a clear shot and cocked his mallet back. But Zack inadvertently hooked the head of Roger's mallet with his own. Instinctively, he jerked and much to his surprise, almost pulled Roger out of the saddle. His shoulder crashed against Roger's chest as they caromed off each other. He had a vague impression of Roger fighting for his balance, barely able to stay mounted as he charged after the ball. Now Zack had a clear shot and swung, feeling the satisfying "thunk" as he smashed the ball through the goal posts for his team's second goal just as the bell sounded, ending the match.

He turned and trotted up field, surprised to see Roger lying on the ground. Willi was running toward the inert figure. He urged his pony forward and reached them moments after Willi had fallen to her knees beside the unconscious man. She looked up at Zack, fury written across her face. "He was wounded, you know," she spat at him. "You Americans don't care who you hurt as long as you win."

Zack wanted to protest that his team had lost. Instead, he snapped, "He shouldn't have been playing if he wasn't up to it."

"Bastards. You're all bastards."

He wheeled his pony and cantered off the field.

The following Tuesday morning Zack's orders arrived posting him back to his old unit, 25 Squadron at Church Fenton. He spent his last day in the stables, helping the old coachman who was showing signs of his age. The duke sent word that he would like Zack to join him for tea that afternoon and Zack dutifully presented himself at exactly four o'clock. But this time, rainy weather had driven them all inside and he was escorted into the library where the old duke waved him to a couch.

"Sorry about Sunday," the duke said. His wife's right eyebrow shot up. In all the years they had been married, she had only heard the crusty old man apologize once before. "Didn't happen as I had planned. The girl is stubborn, like her mother."

Zack sipped at his tea. "She does seem to have a built-in aversion to Yanks," he observed. "Don't know what I did to make her so hostile."

"She works with Americans," the duchess said. "It's some very hush-hush job, intelligence I think. She claims that Americans are all a pack of Bolsheviks at heart, very rude and have no breeding. Wilhelmina doesn't like them at all."

"So I've heard," Zack replied, recalling James's comments at the polo match. "But she does seem to like Roger."

"She likes the company Bertram keeps," the duke grumbled, his chin on his chest.

"Roger," the duchess explained, "served under Mountbatten on destroyers. Quite valiant."

"Until they were sunk," the duke groused.

The duchess shot him a withering look. "Later on," she continued, "Roger was given command of his own destroyer and was badly wounded in the raid on Dieppe. He almost died. Now he's on Mountbatten's staff at Combined Operations." She held her hand to her mouth. "Oh, I shouldn't have said that. All very secret you know."

"The secret is safe with me," Zack said, smiling at the old lady. He changed the subject. "I take it you've heard that I've been posted back to my old squadron. I'll be leaving tomorrow morning."

"Ah," the duke said. "The call to duty."

Zack smiled. "It's either that or going to jail."

The duke bit off his reply. So like the Americans, he thought. Always hiding their idealism behind a flippant manner. "Confounded machines you fly," he groused. "Sorry to see you go." Again, his wife's eyebrow raised. It was obvious her husband had become very attached to the young American.

"Twenty-five Squadron is flying a new aircraft called the Mosquito," Zack told them. "Very fast and maneuverable."

"Be careful," the old man said. "Come see us when you can."

Zack said his good-byes that evening and packed. When he came down the stairs early the next morning, the two cooks and the old coachmen were waiting for him. "Had to say good-bye, proper like," the old man said, shaking his hand. The cooks had packed him a lunch large enough to feed four people and had tears in their eyes when he kissed them on the cheek. They walked with him to the door and stood back. Outside, drawn up in fine array, was a four-in-hand coach. Sitting on the box was the old duke, wearing a top hat and greatcoat. A polished boot rested on the brake and he looked very pleased with himself. "I'll drive you to the station, lad," he shouted.

"Bloody great fool," the coachman grumbled. "He can't handle four horses."

Zack threw his bag on top and pulled the door open. "Come on then," he said to the two cooks and coachman, motioning them inside. The three climbed on board with a great deal of embarrassment and Zack followed them as the duke looked on, saying nothing. Then he cracked the whip and drove smartly down the drive.

The train to York was crowded and dirty and Zack shared a compartment with a group of young British soldiers headed for an antiaircraft unit in the Orkney Islands. He broke open the large lunch the cooks had given him and passed it around. "Wherever did you get this?" the sergeant in charge of the group asked. "Black market?"

Zack laughed. "A going-away gift from the cooks in the hospital. Knowing those two old gals, it might be." They all laughed and made short work of the lunch. Later on, the sergeant told him that was the best food they had had in months. "Things getting pretty tight?" Zack asked.

The sergeant nodded. "We've had almost four years of this bloody war and there's no end in sight. Maybe now that you Yanks are in, things will change." He was looking at a village they were passing through. "This could be my village," he said, "seedy, run-down." Then he straightened up and changed the subject. "Why the RAF uniform?"

"It's the way I started," Zack told him. "Back in the States I thought this was our war. But in 1941, it looked like we were going to stay out of it. I didn't like that so I joined the RAF and got involved. The Japanese changed all that at Pearl Harbor but by then I was in the RAF. I could transfer to the U.S. Army now, but why change horses in midstream?"

The answer seemed to sit well with the sergeant. "I suppose it's best to meet problems head-on and not hide from them, hoping they will go away—like we did with Hitler in 1936 when he marched into the Rhineland. We should have had done with him then and avoided all this. Only Churchill saw him for what he was. But we didn't listen to him. Stupid bloody fools, all of us. We can't let this happen again."

The compartment fell silent as the men settled in for the night. He's right, Zack thought, we can't let this happen again. But why did Churchill see it when no one else did?

It was a question he wanted answered.

Early the next day, he reached the gate at Church Fenton. The guard told him to wait while he called for a car to pick him up and take him to his squadron. Three Mosquitoes captured his attention as they took off and climbed into the darkening sky. The speed of the machines surprised him and he was still watching them when a car drove up. "It's about time you quit playing silly buggers and came back to work," a familiar voice said. It was his navigator, Andrew Ruffum.

"Ruffy!" Zack shouted. "What . . . how . . . " Suddenly, he was at a complete loss for words.

"Had the devil of a time getting out of the Beau," Ruffy deadpanned, lighting his big pipe. "Half-drowned you know. Chaps from the Dutch underground found me when I waded ashore. They were kind enough to provide temporary accommodations until a rendezvous with a submarine was arranged. Quite routine."

"Right," Zack deadpanned back.

SIX

Chiang Mai, Thailand

The young and lean American ambled across the lush grass of the hotel until he reached the path that led to the pool of Thailand's best and newest mecca for tourists at Chiang Mai. He was at ease in the posh surroundings yet seemed out of place among the wealthy Japanese and Europeans. He and his friends were the only Americans staying there, much younger than the other guests, and tight jeans and loose shirts could not hide their well-conditioned and muscular bodies. The older men among the rich and pampered hotel guests had tried to ignore the young Americans with their quasi-military haircuts and drooping mustaches, but it was difficult because the women were definitely attracted to the Americans. And since the Americans all seemed dedicated to their favorite game of "getting drawers," many fruitful relationships had been established. The female players of the game would have been horrified, thrilled, or perhaps a mixture of both, if they knew their young and energetic partners in the game were dedicated and remarkably proficient commandos.

When he reached the pool, he threaded his way among the glistening and well-oiled bodies until he found his friend. He sat down on a sun lounge and pulled a Skoal can out of his hip pocket for a quick dip. "Where's Joey?"

"In his room."

"Alone?"

"No way."

"Who this time? The German blonde?"

"And her sister."

"You'd better go get him before he screws himself silly. It's a good thing Kamigami isn't here."

"Is it that time?"

"Yeah. I'll get the others. Meet in twenty minutes." He picked himself up and returned the smile of a well-preserved forty-six-year-old Frenchwoman who had demonstrated her favorite perversion to him the night before. "Shit, my tongue still hurts," he mumbled to himself, wondering if there was an exercise that developed tongue muscles.

Within twenty minutes, the fourteen Americans had all gathered in a truck garage on the outskirts of town. The casual way they had slouched through the door in twos or threes disappeared once they were inside. The German who spent most of his time working as an anthropologist was also there. He came right to the point. "No change in the status of your target. She is still in the same location with the same three men. No change in their routine." That was all to the good, but there was more. He produced a map. "There are four trucks from Chiang's Burma compound moving down this road." He traced the route that led to the village that was also their objective. "We've lost contact with the trucks but estimate their time of arrival around ten this evening." He left the map and disappeared out the door.

"There's been a change in plans," the group's leader said. "We go in at nineteen forty-three tonight, rendezvous at twenty hundred with the helicopter at the primary LZ, and get the hell out of Dodge City quickest. The backup team repositions here." He pointed to a spot on the road three miles north of the village. "Those trucks have to come down this road. Set up a roadblock to stop them if they show up before we go in." Like any competent leader, the American tailored his words to the personalities of the men who would carry out his orders. "You're a road watch team. Don't go shooting the shit out of anyone. Your job is to stop those trucks and give us a heads-up if they're a factor. We don't want to go causing some international incident and get our asses in a crack."

Joey studied the map. "Why don't we blow this bridge? It's perfect."

"Except it's too close to the village."

Joey looked disappointed. "Give me a break. A few well-placed charges . . . blow the shit out of the bridge . . . with them included. God, I love demo." Like most demolition men, Joey enjoyed his work and had a world of confidence in what he could do with C4 explosive. There was no doubt in his mind that he could solve the problem of any hostile trucks foolish enough to drive down that road.

The leader smiled and shook his head. "Forget the bridge. Block the road and report. Withdraw into the jungle at the first sign of trouble. Simple enough, okay?"

The men broke up into two groups and the team of six who would set up the roadblock left first. They had six hours to move into position. "I don't like these last-minute changes," Joey's leader said.

"Hey," Joey replied, "flexibility, man, flexibility. Got to be like Gumby."

The team of eight shooters who would do the actual rescue left fifteen minutes later.

Udorn, Thailand

Gillespie settled into the right seat of the MH-53 Pave Low helicopter. His hands flew over the switches and controls as he ran the Before Starting Engines checklist. Then he wound and set the correct time on the eight-day clock and waited. He glanced over at his copilot and then back into the cargo compartment. In the rear, he could see the looming bulk of Kamigami strap in with the team that would secure the landing zone. "Loading the sergeant major creates a definite weight and balance problem." He grinned at the copilot, trying to ease the snowballing tension. He got a grunt for an answer. Gillespie stared out the windscreen and took a deep breath. The waiting was the hardest part and the tension was becoming an avalanche as the time for engine start neared. Gillespie's mind roamed back in time and he could visualize an F-4 crew sitting on the same ramp a generation earlier waiting for an engine start that would launch them over North Vietnam and into one of the most heavily defended pieces of airspace ever recorded in history. *Has it always been this way?* he wondered.

The minute hand on the clock moved with maddening slowness, dragging its way around the clock's face. Now the second hand started its last sweep. "Starting two," Gillespie said as it finally touched the twelve.

The tension was broken.

"Hammer," the Have Quick radio squawked, "Rascal Two returning to base at this time." The strain in the backup helicopter pilot's voice was unmistakable over the Have Quick radio as he told the two colonels on the MC-130 that he was aborting. Because the Have Quick relied on rapid frequency hopping to defeat any monitoring or jamming of its transmissions, the men could speak freely without fear of monitoring or jamming. It was also re-markably clear and free of noise and static.

"Rascal Two, this is Hammer, say problem," Mallard replied from aboard the MC-130.

"Hydraulics," came the answer.

Damn! Gillespie raged to himself after hearing the exchange. "The goat" strikes again. Like all helicopters, the MH-53 was a flying contradiction of ten thousand parts all trying to go in sep-arate directions. He glanced at his flight engineer sitting between him and the copilot, just aft of the center console. The sergeant scanned the engine instruments and gave him a thumbs-up signal.

"Hammer," Gillespie radioed. "Rascal One is healthy. Enter-ing holding at this time." The pilot turned onto a racetrack pattern to lose eight minutes so he would be inbound to the landing zone when the ground team went in to rescue Nikki Anderson. They did not want the early arrival of the big helicopter to send any warning signals to her captors.

"Roger," Mallard replied. "Rascal Two," he continued, "re-turn to base. Repeat, RTB. Rascal One, I'm scrambling Rascal Three now." While still in contact with Gillespie on the Have Quick, Mallard keyed the SatCom radio to relay the situation to General Mado in the command post at Udorn. The general de-manded to know all the details before he would scramble the backup helicopter. When he was satisfied that Mallard had made the right decision allowing Rascal Two to RTB, he ordered Rascal Three to scramble. But the MH-53 still on the ground could not bring a generator on line and that was all the general needed to abort the mission. He ordered Hammer to send the abort message terminating Dragon Noire.

"That doesn't make sense," Trimler told Mallard. "We're only using the helicopters for rapid extraction. There's no current threat on the ground and we can leave the same way we went in. We're trained and ready to do that. No big deal."

"Mado won't buy that unless we give him a damn good reason," Mallard said.

Trimler gave it to him. "General Mado," he radioed. "Be advised that the ground teams have already reached their initial positions. Given the situation on the ground, there is a good chance of discovery if they withdraw at this time. That would put the hostage at risk. I recommend we continue with option three of the plan."

"Stand by," Mado replied.

Trimler looked at his watch. "If I know Mado," he told Mallard, "he's looking at the plan right now to see what option three is. By the time he figures it out, we'll be going in."

"Rascal One departing holding now," Gillespie radioed.

"Continue," Mallard answered. Lacking firm direction from Mado, he had no choice but to allow the mission to continue.

Gillespie eased down the collective stick on his left, applied slight forward pressure on the cyclic stick between his legs, squeezed in a little right pedal for trim, and made an easy, co-ordinated, descending turn onto his run-in heading. With an innate skill and finesse that few pilots possess, the captain made all ten thousand cantankerous parts bend to his will as he kept the aircraft within the tight control parameters that coaxed the MH-53 to perform as its designers dreamed of on good nights. In reality, it was a balancing act much like trying to make love in a hammock.

The captain sitting in the left seat as copilot and the flight engineer exchanged glances. The captain gave a reassuring nod for Gillespie had "the touch." Now they were skimming along the treetops, rushing toward their LZ at two and a half miles a minute, on time, on course, but very much alone.

Near Ban Muang Dok, Thailand

Joey and his partner were the first of the six-man road team to move into position. Both men were puffing from the long run from where the team's four-wheel-drive truck had broken down. They had pushed the vehicle past its limits on the last forty-five miles of dirt road and it had overheated. The engine had finally frozen as they approached the bridge, still two miles from the site of the intended roadblock. The men had quickly stripped their arms and equipment out of the useless truck, crossed the bridge, and run down the road, fully aware the clock was running out on them.

The spot they were making for was perfect for a roadblock. The road made a sharp bend around a large outcropping of rock and then narrowed, making a tight S curve through a heavy stand of trees on the side of a steep slope. Joey could hear a truck laboring up to the rocks when he reached the spot. He dumped his heavy rucksack and ripped it open, pulling out a ribbon charge of C4 explosive. He quickly wrapped it around the base of a tree and attached a fuse. Now he could hear the truck slowing to work its way past the rock outcropping. He pulled the igniter, grabbed his rucksack and MP5 submachine gun and dove into a small fold in the terrain. He wished the underbrush had been thicker to give him more cover, but the heavy stand of trees had shaded out much of the jungle foliage. A sharp crack rewarded his efforts and the tree fell across the road. His partner gave him a thumbs-up and pointed to a second tree. Joey popped his head up and dropped right back to the ground. The tree had fallen across the road but could be easily pushed aside by a truck.

He had to do it again. But judging by the sound, the truck was less than a hundred meters and one bend away. He didn't hesitate and ran to the tree that he calculated would do the job. One part of his mind registered that the truck had stopped and he could hear shouted commands, not in English, as he set the charge. He pulled the igniter and ran for cover. A burst of machine-gun fire chased him into the thickest part of the trees and he felt a sting across his left buttock. He ignored the pain as his team returned fire, giving him the cover he needed to reach safety.

The Americans quickly pulled farther back into the trees and re-formed, moving into defensive positions where they could now see two trucks backed up behind the trees blocking the road. Men were jumping out of the trucks and running for cover while an officer tried to get them working on pulling the two trees aside.

The man leading the Americans motioned two shooters to a forward flanking position on his right and pointed at the other pair to pull back and to his left. While the men were moving into position, he keyed his radio and transmitted in the blind, telling Hammer the trucks were early and hostile. Then he and his partner opened fire on the trucks, exploiting the confusion. His partner's M-249 SAW, Squad Automatic Weapon, sent a hail of 5.56-

millimeter bullets into the trucks while he raked the soldiers with his MP5 submachine gun.

The nose of another truck appeared around the outcropping of rocks and stopped. Between bursts, they could hear shouted commands and see more men in the trees now moving directly toward them. The team leader's partner jammed a fresh "assault pack" of two hundred rounds into his M-249 and squeezed off a short burst to drive the opposition to cover. The two men quickly fell back, leapfrogging into a position behind the other shooters. The two forward shooters waited until the soldiers started chasing the first pair and then opened fire. They cut down six of the attackers from the flank before they withdrew, again exploiting the confusion to leapfrog to a position behind the others. The Americans rapidly gave ground, moving out from under the heavy growth of trees and into the heavier jungle but still paralleling the road that led to the village. The leader radioed for help. "Hammer, this is Pogo Two," he transmitted. Now he could hear the sounds of a helicopter. Whose was it?

"Pogo Two, this is Hammer," Trimler replied, his transmission weak and scratchy, "read you two-by." As ground commander, Trimler controlled the teams on the ground.

"We're in contact, withdrawing toward the primary objective. I hear a helicopter in the area, can it give us cover?"

"Helicopter is unknown, not ours. Spectre is on the way. Say position."

"A hundred meters west of the road, moving south, away from trucks currently blocked on road."

Another voice came on the radio. It was the Beezer in the AC-130 gunship. "Roger, Pogo Two. Spectre copies all. Will be over your position in six minutes. Stay up this frequency."

Joey materialized out of the heavy underbrush and silently dropped beside his leader. He rolled over onto his back and jammed a fresh clip into his MP5. "We're in deep shit." He pointed in the direction they were moving. "A deep ravine."

"Can we get across?"

"Negatory, not with these bastards breathing down our tails. Got to cross at the bridge." Pogo Two's leader grunted and started his team moving toward the bridge, hoping they would cross and blow it down before the soldiers moving down the road reached them. That would solve their problems. The Americans could hear crashing sounds behind them and realized they were being deliberately herded, driven up against the ravine. "Those fuckers are good," Joey grudgingly conceded. "Real good."

"Yeah," the leader conceded. "We should have blown the fucking bridge to begin with and none of this fancy stuff." He mashed his radio transmit button. "Spectre, Pogo Two," he radioed, "moving towards road bridge. Will attempt to cross. The opposition needs some discouragement."

The sounds of the helicopter grew louder as the Americans neared the road. They were a hundred meters short of the bridge when they saw the helicopter touch down on the bridge's approach and three men jump out and run for cover. Before the team could move into position and fire, the helicopter lifted off and flew right over them. They could see a gunner in the door and started firing at the helicopter. A short burst of machine-gun fire from the helicopter cut into Joey and he collapsed as the helicopter passed over. One of the Americans ran for his fallen buddy as the helicopter disappeared. The sounds of trucks moving on the road echoed over the five men.

Simon Mado's face numbed as the reports filtered in over the radio. He closed the operations plan he had been consulting and stared at the title. His jaw moved, grinding his teeth. Events had overtaken him and he was no longer in control. He calculated what other options were now open to him.

The leader of Pogo One in the village heard faint explosions and gunfire coming from the north. "Trouble," he said to the three men crouched in the shadows behind him. He dropped to the ground and inched his head around the corner of the dilapidated storage shed they had parked behind. Through the deepening shadows, he could clearly see the raised bungalow on stilts and the low wall that surrounded it. The loud wail of a TV set reached out and blended with four or five others in the village, masking the distant gunfire that was growing in intensity. He crawled back into the shadows. "As advertised," he told the men. Then he keyed his radio. "Lee, you in position?"

"Affirmative," came the answer from the other half of his team.

"Going in now," the leader said.

"Roger."

The leader raised a clenched fist, snapped his hand open, fingers rigidly extended, counted to three, made a fist, and jerked his hand down—the signal to "go." The four men moved silently out from behind the shed and spread out, running for the low wall that surrounded their objective. They drifted over the wall like ghosts and kept moving for the raised bungalow. A lone pig grunted and moved out of the way. Now they were among the stilts that raised the bungalow off the ground. The sound man stood up and attached a small microphone to the overhead. He moved to a second position and attached another microphone. He repeated the drill two more times. Then they waited while he listened, monitoring the movement in the rooms above him.

The team's leader riveted his eyes on his wristwatch, counting down the seconds. After an agonizing wait of less than a minute, the sound man held up two fingers and pointed toward the back room, his thumb down—two enemy. Then he pointed with one finger to the front room and held his hand open, palm up—one unknown. He pointed to an area halfway between the two rooms and repeated the gesture—another unknown. The team leader raised a clenched fist and repeated the go sign. The two inside men went up the steps, silent and dark phantoms, while the outside man moved under an open window. The sound man moved under the back room, readied his MP5 and concentrated on the sounds coming through his headset. When he heard a tap followed by two quick raps, he hit the off switch of his headset, mashed the trigger on his MP5, and sprayed the ceiling above him, aiming for the center of the sounds he had last heard.

At the same time, the outside man threw a flash-bang grenade through the open window. Then the two inside men on the steps were through the door while the outside man moved into a covering position at the front steps. Two shots rang out. Now silence. The sound man heard a "We got her" and gave the high sign to the outside man. Then he keyed the radio clipped to his belt and spoke into the whisper mike on his shoulder. "Lee, we're coming out." Instantly, he heard the low rev of an engine and a car drove into the compound as the two inside men came down the steps, carrying an inert body between them.

"As advertised," Pogo One's leader said. Nikki Anderson was pushed into the backseat and the car drove off, heading for the LZ. The four men sprinted for their car.

"Pogo Two," the Beezer transmitted from his AC-130. "Say position." He was on the same radio frequency as the two colonels and the trapped team.

The voice that answered was low and filled with strain. "On the edge of the ravine, one hundred meters to the east of the road bridge and moving east, away from the bridge."

"Say number," the Beezer said as he wrapped his gunship into a firing orbit.

"Five," came the answer. "One KIA."

"I've got 'em," the sensor operator in the booth on the gun deck said.

"All others are hostile," the Beezer told his crew. "Time to rock and roll." The fourteen men aboard the gunship went through a well-rehearsed routine.

"TV and IR have targets," the sensor operator called.

"Take IR guidance," the fire control operator answered.

"Give me twenties," the Beezer ordered. The two 20-millimeter Vulcan cannons the AC-130 sported could each fire twenty-five hundred rounds per minute. The six-barreled gatling gun was the best weapon he had for discouraging the soldiers advancing on Pogo Two.

"Guns ready," came from the gun deck.

The Beezer looked through the Head-Up gunsight mounted to his left and saw at least a dozen soldiers inside the lighted diamond symbol—the targets the sensor operator had found using the infrared detection system. He jockeyed the AC-130 and moved the circle that showed where any round he fired would impact the ground over the target diamond and mashed the trigger button. The two Vulcan cannons spewed a torrent of fire at the men and he could see targets fall to the ground. He would never be sure, but he was relatively certain that he had killed at least half of the men he had hosed down. He slid the big plane into another orbit to the north and selected another target. Again, he mashed the trigger and the Vulcans gave out with their loud buzzing sound, not the sharp staccato normally associated with a machine gun.

Now the Beezer could see the lead truck moving through the roadblock. "Give me the forty," he ordered. The crew repeated their deadly routine and this time the forty-millimeter Bofors cannon that could fire up to a hundred rounds a minute gave out a heavy thumping sound as Beasely worked the trucks over.

"Break right!" The illuminator operator at the rear of the cargo ramp shouted. "Flares! Flares!" He had just seen the flash of what looked like a shoulder-held surface-to-air missile. It was a Soviet-made SA-7 Grail and only his early warning call saved them. The Beezer honored the threat and skidded the big plane into a hard right turn as decoy flares popped out behind them in a long string. Then he nosed over, unloading and accelerating before he reversed his turn and pulled up, loading them with almost two g's. The maneuver worked and the missile's seeker head was captured by one of the flares. But another missile was coming at them. Again, Spectre outmaneuvered the missile.

They never saw the third Grail that hit their number four engine. But Spectre had been built to take battle damage and survive. The Beezer headed south as they sorted out the emergency. After feathering the engine and hitting the fire extinguisher, he ran a controllability check. Not good. "Hammer," he transmitted, "Spectre disengaging with battle damage. Looks like we took a hit on the right outboard wing. Number four feathered. Some control problems. Best guess is a Grail missile got us. Say the word and we'll go back in."

Now the monkey was on Mallard's back. Would he risk the AC-130 and its fourteen crewmembers to support Pogo Two on the ground? Experience had taught him what the AC-130 crew was up against. He talked to his ground commander, Bob Trimler. "Can Pogo Two get clear for an extraction?"

Trimler keyed his radio and spoke briefly to Pogo Two's leader. Then he turned to Mallard. "Can do. Spectre worked the Gomers over good and Pogo Two is clear and withdrawing to the east."

The decision was made. "Spectre," Mallard radioed, "Return to holding. Repeat, return to holding."

"Roger," the Beezer answered. They could hear the disappointment in his voice.

Gillespie had the LZ in sight through his night vision goggles when Spectre reported in with battle damage. He filed the information away for later use and concentrated on the problem at hand. He slowed the helicopter and it shuddered through the translational lift as his forward airspeed decreased to the point where the rotor blades lost the extra lift generated by the helicopter's forward motion. Gillespie adjusted automatically to the change in lift and brought the big MH-53 in. Since he was looking outside and his copilot was reading out the instruments, it was a masterful combination of seat of the pants and instrument flying. For a moment, the helicopter hung gently in the air. Then it touched down.

The landing zone team exploded into action and ran down the rear ramp. "My God!" one of the gunners said over the intercom, "you oughta see that big guy move!" The gunner was watching Victor Kamigami lead the way and he could not credit the speed of the man.

The Army lieutenant colonel in command of the LZ team stayed on board the helicopter and moved forward to monitor the radios with Gillespie. "Nice landing," he told the pilot when he was on headset.

"Thanks, Colonel," Gillespie said. "Just goes with the territory."

The copilot smiled. "Being humble when you don't have to is very becoming in junior captains. But it was one shit hot approach and landing." The flight engineer nodded in agreement.

Gillespie did not take off his night vision goggles and kept looking outside to maintain his night vision. He watched as the landing zone team established a perimeter in a well-rehearsed routine. Then he saw the headlights of two cars approach. He turned his head away so the sensitive night vision goggles would not pick up the headlights and momentarily blind him. "Looks like we got some action, sir," he told the lieutenant colonel. "Two vehicles approaching."

The lieutenant colonel glanced at his watch. "They're early."

Before he could say more, Kamigami's voice came over the radio. "The package has arrived, the delivery team is right behind, in sight."

"Start pulling in," the lieutenant colonel ordered. He could not believe their good luck.

Two minutes later, Nikki Anderson was on board and the four men who had rescued her were piling out of their car. The helicopter rocked as the landing zone team ran on board. "All accounted for!" the gunner responsible for the first head count shouted over the intercom.

But nothing happened as Kamigami and another sergeant ran their independent head counts. When they both agreed that everyone was aboard, Gillespie gently applied left pedal as he pulled the collective up, increasing pitch in all six rotor blades to get the lift needed for takeoff. As the helicopter broke away from the ground, he squeezed the cyclic forward and to the left for a smooth climbing turn away from the LZ.

Gillespie's copilot radioed Hammer, telling the colonels that Nikki Anderson was on board and Rascal One was launching from the LZ. Mallard acknowledged and continued to work the most pressing problem—extracting the five remaining men of Pogo Two.

"Rascal Three is airborne and will be on station in sixty-eight minutes," Mallard told Trimler. "Can you get Pogo Two into position for a pickup?" The maintenance crew from the 1st SOW had worked a minor miracle in fixing the backup Pave Low helicopter and getting it launched. The other helicopter, Rascal Two, had never made it back to base and had made an emergency landing at Uttaradit. Mallard decided to let General Mado worry about explaining the presence of that helicopter with its twelve heavily armed passengers to the local authorities.

Trimler talked to Pogo Two's leader over the FM radio and motioned for Mallard's attention. "Our maps show an open area here," he said, pointing at the chart. "They'll be there." His voice became very hard. "We've got a KIA and it's slowing them down." The impersonal acronym KIA, killed in action, helped them put aside the reality of the man's death so they could concentrate on terminating the mission without further casualties. They would deal with Joey's death later in their own personal terms.

Gillespie's voice came over the Have Quick radio. "I don't think we've got sixty-eight minutes to get Pogo out. I can land, drop off Anderson with half the men and go in after Pogo." Gillespie did not elaborate—there wasn't time for lengthy discussions. But for the young helicopter pilot, all doubt had been erased; they were up against a well-organized and competently led force of men. "I can be over Pogo Two in twelve minutes."

The Beezer came on frequency. "Spectre can return to station."

Mallard considered it. Hal Beasely was superaggressive and his fangs grew with each challenge. But flying an AC-130 gunship in combat on three engines and with a controllability problem was a high-risk venture. It was a risk Mallard did not want to take but at the same time he wanted to keep the firepower of the gunship in reserve in case it was needed. "Negative Spectre, remain in holding," he commanded.

E-Squared sat in the left-hand pilot's seat of the MC-130 wishing they had the latest Fulton surface-to-air recovery system that could snatch up to six men off the ground with one pass. He cursed his luck that they were only equipped with the older system that allowed them to snag the lift line that a balloon held aloft with a single person attached to the other end. He had enough recovery kits to get three men out, but it would take some time doing it one at a time.

Now it was up to Mallard and Trimler to put it all together. But when it came to the final decision, it was Mado's to make.

Mallard keyed his mike and outlined the options to Mado. He finished with a strong recommendation to go with Gillespie's suggestion.

Mado was certain the mission was turning into a disaster. But he could see definite possibilities to save his career, if he played it right. "Colonel Trimler, what do you recommend?" Mado finally asked.

The Army colonel did not answer for a moment. "Pogo Two will reach the open area in thirty minutes. I'd like to extract them immediately."

Mado made the decision. "I don't see Pogo Two as being under direct pressure at this time. Further, we can't be certain how soon they will reach the clearing. Rascal Three is now inbound and there will not be any appreciable delay in extracting them. Our objective was to rescue Anderson. Let's not lose what we've got." He double-checked to be sure the recorder was still on. There would be many Monday-morning quarterbacks in the Pentagon and Congress to replay this one.

With the decision made, Mallard keyed the Have Quick radio. "Rascal One, return to base. Repeat, RTB." Gillespie acknowledged the order.

Trimler was on the FM radio, telling Pogo Two to press ahead to the landing zone and rendezvous with Rascal Three for extraction in sixty-one minutes.

The man carrying Joey's body paused to catch his breath. The sounds of a helicopter passing to the north caught his attention. "He's a persistent bastard," he grumbled to his leader as he started to move again.

"Hammer, Pogo Two," the team's leader radioed. "A helicopter is in the area, doesn't sound like ours."

"That helicopter is hostile," Trimler answered. "How far are you out from your objective?"

"Almost there."

"Continue," Trimler told him. "ETA for Rascal Three is now forty minutes." The team had made better time than predicted and was going to have a long wait for the pickup.

"Roger," the team leader answered. Then a new sound assaulted him. "Hammer," he transmitted, "that helicopter is landing in the clearing."

"Copy all," Trimler answered. "Stand by."

"Stand-fucking-by," the team leader grumbled to himself.

Trimler's voice came back on the radio. "Hold your position.
Spectre is inbound to clear the area."

Pogo Two's leader directed his men to take cover and the man
carrying Joey gently laid his burden next to a tree before he
disappeared into the underbrush. They could hear the drone of
Spectre's three engines as the gunship approached. But it was not
loud enough to drown out new sounds coming from behind
them—men moving through the jungle. "Spectre," the leader
radioed, "you're passing overhead our position now. Gomers
moving in behind us, estimate their position less than a hundred
meters to the west."

"Roger," Beasely answered. "Gotcha. Stay put. There's a
chopper on the ground where you want to go. Will clear the LZ
first and then do an attitude adjustment on your other guests."

The spirits of the five Americans soared when they saw the
dark shadow of the gunship in the night sky set up a thirty-degree
left-hand turn—the classic firing orbit for a gunship. A tongue of
flame belched from aft of the left main gear wheel well as the
105-millimeter Howitzer fired. Ten seconds later it fired again.
Then the explosion from the first round echoed over them and
they heard a secondary explosion. The first round had missed the
helicopter but a shower of frag had cut through the helicopter
and hit a fuel cell.

"The chopper's dead meat," Beasely told them, "but we're
monitoring movement in the vicinity." Spectre's sensor operator
was feeding the Beezer a constant flow of information. The gunship's highly sensitive infrared had picked up three men running
away from the destroyed helicopter. "Hold on a minute while we
have a come-to-Jesus-meeting and clear the LZ." The Beezer
descended and tightened his orbit, bringing his two 20-millimeter
cannons to bear, pressing his three good engines past their normal
operation limits, driving the turbine inlet temperatures well into
the overheat range. Fortunately, he was turning into two good
engines and the feathered engine was on the outside of the turn.
The gatling guns gave out a loud buzz as the Beezer peppered
the area around the helicopter, saturating it with high explosive
rounds. "Looks quiet now," he told Pogo Two.

Faint sounds of movement kept Pogo Two from answering.
Then a uniformed figure emerged from the underbrush, saw the
American, and yelled a warning. The American reacted auto-

matically and blasted the man with his MP5. Another soldier popped out from behind a tree with an AK-47 and squeezed off a short burst, only to die as a hand grabbed his hair, jerked his head back and a knife flashed across his neck.

The fight was short, intense and impossible for one man to follow. The sharp staccato bark of AK-47s mixed with the faster and smoother, more rolling sound of MP5s. A frag grenade exploded.

"Fuck! I'm hit!"

"Stan! Where are you!"

A loud scream—not an American. More shouting and gunfire. Then someone tossed a smoke grenade, adding to the confusion. Pogo's leader cleared an empty magazine from his MP5 and jammed a fresh clip into the weapon. A burst from an AK-47 cut across his stomach, throwing him into the brush. He rolled over and shoved his left hand into the gaping wound, trying to stop the bleeding. A hard silence came down.

Four soldiers stepped into the killing ground and looked around. One was heavily bandaged and half-carried by a comrade. Pogo Two's leader tried to focus through the fog of shock and approaching unconsciousness. He had a sense that the wounded man was in command. One of the soldiers pointed to Joey's body and jabbered in a language the American did not recognize.

The wounded man was helped over to Joey's body. "Americans," he growled. One of the other soldiers poked at the body with the toe of his boot before he drew his machete and gave it a hard cutting blow in the neck, almost decapitating it.

Anger flashed through Pogo Two's leader and a killing urge swept over him. Caution and survival were not part of the game and a primordial thirst for blood and revenge ruled. He readied a target flare and mashed his transmit button for one last radio call. "Spectre! Hit my flare!" He fired the flare at the soldiers, barely five meters away, as they raked the underbrush with long bursts from their AK-47s. He never heard the cascading sound of the twenty-millimeter high-explosive rounds that walked over the killing ground.

"Hammer," Beasely transmitted over the Have Quick radio net, "we've lost contact with Pogo Two. No movement in the area." The metallic sound of his voice carried its own message of defeat.

"Copy all," Mallard answered. "RTB."

The National Military Command Center, the Pentagon

The mission controller in the NMCC flicked the transmit toggle on the console. "Udorn, this is Blue Chip. We understand the mission is terminated."

"That is correct," Mado replied. "All elements are returning to base at this time." The satellite relayed communications between the NMCC, the National Military Command Center, in the Pentagon, and Mado had a slight tinny sound owing to computer-driven encryption, but were otherwise crystal-clear. Mado could have been in the next room.

The mission controller swiveled her chair to look at the four-star general sitting in the rank behind her before she spoke into her boom mike. "Sir, the reconnaissance platform is on station and ready to launch a drone to sweep the area."

The general stared at the big mission boards and video screens on the wall in front of him. "Launch the drone," he ordered. The mission controller turned back to her console and keyed another circuit. Halfway around the world, an Air Force sergeant aboard a matte-black RC-130 orbiting near Chiang Mai, Thailand, went through the routine to drop a multisensor drone off the RC-130's wing and send it over the last-known position of Pogo Two. A lieutenant colonel sitting at the console beside him gave the order and the sergeant punched the launch button.

In the NMCC, a light on the general's communications panel flashed. Someone in the Command and Authority Room wanted to speak to him—probably National Security Adviser Cagliari. The general reluctantly picked up the receiver and listened. The serious Monday-morning quarterbacking had begun.

Mackay sat quietly in the chair he had drawn up alongside Mazie Kamigami's position in the far corner of the NMCC. He had monitored the mission with her and was still digesting what he had learned. It had been a revelation. Mackay had toured the NMCC and the other command facilities of the Pentagon in the past, but he had never been on the floor during an exercise or actual mission. It was not what he had expected. The atmosphere had been businesslike and calm when things started going wrong, with none of the frantic shouting and gesturing conjured up in the public's mind by the entertainment media. Mackay's overwhelming impression had been one of professional competence and, for the first time, he sensed the extent of the resources commanded from this room. It was a sobering experience.

His relentless mind probed into the mission—what had they learned? General Chiang Tse-kuan had created a well-trained, well-led, well-equipped, and well-motivated force. Too many "wells" on the wrong side, he calculated. What did all that mean for him? Cagliari had been very specific in telling the CAT that this was not the end of it even though they had lost the element of surprise. Chiang would be an idiot not to be expecting a follow-on mission to rescue the remaining hostages now. Mackay drew deeper into himself. An image of a football game played out. The other side is always expecting a pass, he thought. So what do you do? Pass anyway. But it helps to fake it first. What had Cagliari said about losing the element of surprise? Mackay recalled the national security adviser's exact words: "Now how do we get around that problem?" Mackay explored the possibilities in front of him and started making connections with what Mazie had extracted from the NSC's System 4. How fortunate, he thought, that she knows how to read between the lines of a computer data base. I've got to get out of this place, Mackay warned himself. Too much politics and not enough reality. This isn't for me. But, he finally decided, there were things he could make happen before he left.

Mazie Kamigami shoved the pile of papers and hastily scribbled notes she had been working on into a folder stamped "Secret" that would be hand-carried to her office along with a stack of other classified information from the mission. She was acutely aware of Mackay's brooding silence next to her.

"Mazie," he said, "I think there's a way to get the others out."

"Please don't smile," she told him.

Fort Bragg, North Carolina

Three men wearing Navy issue UDT shorts were running down Chicken Road when Trimler drove up to Delta's compound. The colonel recognized them immediately as part of the team who had been on the helicopter that had made an emergency landing at Uttaradit and had returned the night before. He hadn't heard the details on how they had shrugged off the local Thai authorities and only knew that they had not used any of their gold Krugerrands for bribes. Sergeant Dolores Villaneuva, Delta's unofficial chief of administration and controller, would have given them fits making them account for the gold. A jagged smile played at

Trimler's mouth. People normally don't give receipts for taking a bribe. It was the first bit of humor he had experienced since the termination of Operation Dragon Noire.

Trimler glanced at his watch—6:15 A.M. Since he was early and dressed in sweats, he decided to do a quick stint in the weight room. For reasons that escaped him, pumping iron focused his thinking. Kamigami was already there, his T-shirt drenched in sweat, with seven other men. Trimler stepped up to the Nautilus machine next to his CSM, adjusted the weights, and grunted a "Good morning" at the men. He was greeted with vague responses and within minutes, he and Kamigami were alone in the room.

"Notice the tension?" Trimler ventured.

"They're grim," Kamigami answered.

"I expected that."

Kamigami didn't answer and pumped his arms, increasing the tempo of his bench presses. The veteran sergeant could read men who chose combat as their profession easier than most people can read a book. He didn't like the message he was getting. The men should be reacting to the loss of six of their compatriots, but he sensed more to it than that. Hell! he raged to himself, six was a large number for a small unit like Delta. He had heard all the standard words and phrases that marked how men come to terms with combat losses: "For damn sure Joey didn't go a virgin"; "I prefer to go out with a bang myself"; "You hear how they nailed a Gomer with a flare and turned him into a crispy critter?"

He knew what was wrong. Combat losses extract a hurt that is the price to be paid for being what they were. But at the same time, there should be a renewed commitment to their job. He wasn't sure if the grimness that pervaded the compound was a mark of that renewal. Well, Colonel, he thought, we need to work this problem. He sat up at looked at Trimler. "We need to lay it all out for them," he said in his soft voice.

"I was thinking about that myself," Trimler said.

An hour later, the two men were closeted with Delta's staff. They sorted through the mass of photos and reports that would eventually end up in an after-action report. At first, they had concentrated on the infrared photos taken by the reconnaissance drone. These were the safe pictures because they chronicled a scene of widespread death and it was impossible to separate the casualties. The bodies were all the same. Kamigami calculated an exchange rate of thirteen to one, thanks to the gunship. Finally, the Intelligence officer produced the report of a Thai ground team that had entered the area two days later. The Thais had found the killing ground, taken photos and brought out what was left of Pogo Two.

"These are grim," Kamigami said, passing the photos around.

"That seems to be the operative word these days," Trimler allowed. Silence. The photos and report told a story of viciousness that was beyond the experience of the men. The bodies of the Americans had been hacked to pieces and then scattered in the underbrush. The Thais had taken photos and collected what they could before leaving the area. They had not wanted to linger any longer than necessary. Trimler was not a religious man, but he prayed the men had all been dead before they had been dismembered.

"What motivated the bastards to do this?" he asked, not expecting an answer. "Do we show the men this?" Now he did expect an answer.

"Do we have a choice?" Kamigami asked. The silence came back down.

Trimler knew the answer. "We tell them," he said. "Never hide the truth from a bunch of pit bulls like Delta. Let 'em know what they are up against. Give 'em more meat."

"Will it affect their performance?" This from the lieutenant colonel who led A Squadron.

It was a question the men could not answer.

Late that afternoon, Trimler sat in his office, piecing together the day's events. The men of Delta had reacted to the photos that detailed the fate of Pogo Two much as he had expected. If anything, their humor had taken on a more grim cast. Sergeant Villaneuva knocked on his open door and came in, cleaning up before knocking off for the day. "Are you finished with your classified, sir?" Trimler nodded an answer and she scooped up his folder marked "Secret" and locked it in the office's safe. She waited, knowing he wanted to talk.

Trimler studied the sergeant for a moment, considering his words. "What is that sensitive antenna of yours telling you, Sergeant?" he asked.

"Mostly what you know," she answered. "The prevailing attitude is grim but it's business as normal. They'll be okay"—she decided he was ready for the news—"in time." Trimler's eyebrows shot up but he didn't say anything. She took a deep breath. "Which we're in short supply of."

"Time?" he asked. She nodded an answer. "What makes you say that?"

"We're going back in, Colonel. I just don't see any way out of it."

"Where did such a beautiful woman ever get so many brains," he replied, not wanting to believe her.

"Flattery isn't going to make it go away, Colonel. I figure you got two weeks at the outside." She turned and walked out of the office.

She's right, Trimler thought, and reality's a bitch. He forced his own emotions aside, making himself become a commander, a man capable of making the hard decisions, taking losses, and then, if need be, ordering his men back into harm's way again. But he had the responsibility to protect those men and not waste their lives needlessly. Could he do all that? Rather than work that problem, he turned to the letters he had to write. Six letters to next of kin. Villaneuva had produced a file of condolence letters she had rat-holed to help him. But the phrases seemed too trite and polished and he had pushed them aside. He tried to finish the one he had been working on. " . . . I knew Joey and had come to depend on him. His unfailing sense of humor will be missed." No! he thought, that won't work. Too many images assaulted his memory—crisp color photographs courtesy of the Thai government.

Out of frustration, he selected one of the letters out of Villaneuva's file and copied it, changing it to fit the circumstances. He quickly worked through the other letters. A knock at the open door caught his attention. It was Villaneuva. "Finished?" she asked. He nodded and she picked up the letters. "I'll get them in the mail tonight."

"That's not necessary," he told her. "Tomorrow will be fine. It's late. Go on home." She ignored him and set to work.

Okay, Trimler thought to himself, I can't avoid the question any longer. What did I do wrong? He sat in his chair and ran through every decision he had made and tried to reconstruct what had conditioned his thinking at the time. He knew what the mistake was. They should have used Spectre with its highly sensitive detection systems to monitor the road for the trucks. If the trucks had arrived early, then the mission should have been aborted. Why hadn't he brought it up at the time? A shuffle caught his attention and he looked up. Villaneuva was standing there, the letters complete, her eyes full of tears.

"Were they hard to type?" he asked.

She nodded. She knew that he, along with some other ranking officers, had screwed up. She waited while he signed the letters. She spun and left the office, only to return almost immediately. "Colonel, it isn't all your fault. Remember that." Then she was gone.

Trimler returned to his private hell and he turned his searing intelligence inward. You didn't want to use Spectre, he berated himself, because you wanted it to be an all-Delta show. You wanted to hog all the glory for yourself. You sacrificed six men to your ego! Now what are you going to do about it?

For a moment he considered resigning. But was that the answer? If Villaneuva was right, Delta had to be ready again. Soon. Could he do the job? He bowed his head, wishing some general would make the decisions for him.

The White House, Washington, D.C.

Charles, the President's valet, hovered outside the small office on the second floor of the White House that Pontowski liked to use at night. The old man glanced at his watch, not really concerned about the late hour, and wondered how much longer his charge would be working. He touched the transmit button on the small radio on his waist and checked in. "Still awake, A-Okay." He took pride in the service he gave to the President and was fully trained and prepared to be a human shield if he had to. Besides being a gentle and considerate valet, Charles was a dedicated Secret Service agent.

He knocked at the door of the small office and entered when he heard "Yes?"

"Is there anything you need, sir? Perhaps tea?" He took in the condition of the room at a glance and studied the President's face. Other than being a little tired, Pontowski was fine.

"Thank you, Charles. Tea would be fine." The words were enough to reassure the valet that nothing was amiss. If he sensed anything unusual he would immediately relay it to his control and the watch over the President would shift gears and become more attentive. Charles noted that the President was watching TV and that two news commentators were analyzing the recent rescue of Nikki Anderson. They were questioning if the action had been rash since six men had been killed in the rescue.

"What do you think?" Pontowski asked.

Charles was taken aback that the President should ask him such a question. "It's not really for me to say, is it, sir?" he hedged. The gentle look on Pontowski's face told him that was the wrong answer. The President knew who he was and what he did. Charles gave it to him straight. "The men knew the risks, it was what they volunteered to do, and the objective was accomplished."

"Were their lives worth the rescue of one young girl?" Pontowski asked.

"Who knows what that particular young lady is worth," Charles said.

Pontowski smiled. "Yes, who knows her value." Charles excused himself and went for the tea. Pontowski gazed at the TV, not thinking about Nikki Anderson, but of the past and the value of another young lady.

1943

Bletchley Park, Buckinghamshire, England

The mist came at night, settling over the grounds and casting a gossamer haze over the ugly red-brick Victorian mansion and the village of prefabricated huts and buildings that surrounded it. There was no wind to drive it away and no moonlight to infiltrate its spidery clutches. Slowly the mist thickened and the buildings faded into a gentle obscurity. An occasional voice could be heard as the dense ground fog cast an unearthly silence over the big house in Buckinghamshire, forty-five miles northwest of London. The fog was a perfect and most suitable cover for what went on inside. Outside, armed guards dressed in camouflage uniforms continued their patrols, moving silently through the trees and along the paths that surrounded the estate known as Bletchley Park.

Lights were on throughout the estate as work continued around the clock. In one of the most closely guarded rooms, Colossus, the world's first electronic computer, whirred under the watchful eyes of British and American scientists as it wreaked havoc on the enemy. The destruction caused by Colossus was much greater than that caused by any conventional bomb for it had broken the German code known as Enigma. The intelligence gleaned from Colossus was labeled Ultra and was passed on to a small group of Allied leaders who used it to slowly turn the tide of war.

Outside, a man-made forest of antennas plucked radio signals out of the air for Colossus. Highly skilled radio operators, many of them with years of experience in the merchant marine, could chase a faint signal across the wave bands, determine if it was "hostile" and feed it to the cryptanalysts who tended Colossus. But one group of huts was occupied by radio operators and controllers who were only concerned with listening for "friendly" transmissions from agents deep inside German-occupied territory. Those transmissions were not fed to Colossus but passed to Special Operations Executive, the branch of the British government that carried out sabotage, subversion, underground activities, and assassinations in occupied Europe. This strange collection of military professionals, historians, linguists, scientists, mathematicians, musicians, and the occasional oddball were called the Baker Street Irregulars by those in the know.

"You had best get her," one of the SOE radio operators said as she copied down a message. "Rebecca is calling."

The young woman who was Rebecca's controller did not hesitate and reached for the phone, quickly relaying the message. "It's fortunate that she's here tonight," the controller said after completing the call. "I had given up on Rebecca." The radio operator gave a noncommittal click of her tongue and fine-tuned the receiver. The door swung open and Wilhelmina Crafton hurried in. She was wearing a khaki uniform of the First Aid Nursing Yeomanry, or FANY, and her hair was pulled severely back from her face and fastened in an untidy bun that still glistened with moisture from the fog. The speed of her arrival and the rumpled look of her uniform indicated she had been sleeping fully clothed. But she was fully awake now as she adjusted the short jacket and straightened her tie and trousers.

"How long has she been transmitting?" Willi asked.

"She's off the air now," the radio operator said, handing the transmission to the controller for decoding.

"Was it her?" Willi asked.

"It was her 'fist,' " the radio operator confirmed. She was Rebecca's "godmother" and had recognized the distinct but subtle way the agent had worked her key. It was her personal signature that identified her to the telegraphist.

Willi bit the inside of her cheek as she waited for the controller to decode the message. Rebecca's last transmission had been nineteen days ago and had omitted the code set LS8B that should have been inserted after the third group. The omission meant

that something had gone wrong. The controller finished the decode and handed the message to Willi. Tears were in her eyes.
"It's in the wrong place," she said.

A numbness froze Willi's face as she read the message. It was
a request for another pianist, or radio operator, to be parachuted
in with additional explosives. All was correct except that LS8B
was inserted after the fifth and ninth group. It was an obvious
mistake and the message was clear—Rebecca had been "burned"
and was now under the control of the Gestapo. But she was still
trying. "We will have to send an answer," Willi said. It was the
only way they could keep Rebecca alive and it offered a means
of feeding misinformation to the Germans. "When would she
normally expect a reply?"

"On the first BBC transmission of 'London Calling' seventy-
two hours after this message."

"I'll arrange it," Willi told them. Her right fist balled into a
tight knot. "I must return to London." She walked out of the
hut, her face set in a grim mask.

"No wonder they call her the Ice Queen," the radio operator
said.

"This is the third 'Mistral' pianist she's lost," the controller
agreed. "You would think she'd feel something."

The khaki-colored BSA motorcycle and sidecar emerged out
of the thick London fog and rattled to a stop next to the St. James
underground station in Westminster. "That was sporting, miss,"
the Army private said as Willi unlimbered her long legs from the
cramped confines of the sidecar. She was numb from the cold.

"Thank you," she told him. "But it is important." She gave
him a smile that made up for the difficult journey from Bletchley
Park. He nodded, wondering what a volunteer nurse could be
doing that was important enough for his sergeant to dispatch him
so early in the morning. Probably some general's popsie, he
thought as he gunned the engine and disappeared into the dense
fog. She watched him go and then hurried across the street to the
Broadway Buildings. She walked briskly up the steps past the
bright brass nameplate that announced the headquarters of
the Minimax Fire Extinguisher Company.

She made her way to the sixth floor and walked down the
narrow corridor crowded with a menagerie of people. While all
of them were concerned with putting out fires, none were in the
fire extinguisher business. It was the headquarters of the British

Secret Intelligence Service—the organization the world mistakenly called MI-6. A secretary glanced up from her work when Willi entered the crowded office that she shared with four other Baker Street Irregulars from the Special Operations Executive who coordinated activities with the Secret Intelligence Service. "Miss," the secretary called, "the general wants to see you immediately."

"Do I have time to freshen up a bit?"

"I don't really think so," the woman answered. Willi hung up her heavy overcoat, tucked her shirt in, glanced in a mirror, frowned, and hurried out of the office.

The dapper and slender man who looked up from his work when Willi entered his office looked more like an academician than a general. He motioned her to a seat while he finished signing the documents a secretary had handed him. For at least the third time, Willi wondered if he was really the illegitimate son of Edward VII. Well, he has the connections, she thought, recalling the succession of high-born wives he had married. This was "C," the legendary chief of the Secret Intelligence Service—Major General Sir Stewart Menzies.

Finally, he turned his attention to her. "More bad news, I hear."

"Yes, sir. We've lost our third pianist in the Pas de Calais area in less than two months."

"That's Mistral, as I recall. Was she good?"

"Very." He didn't like that answer, Willi thought, watching his face.

"Can SOE set up a new circuit?" Menzies asked. "Obviously, Mistral has been penetrated and we need to effect a bypass."

"That will take resources we don't really have," Willi told him.

"Can you make them available? It is important, you know."

Willi knew the area must have taken on added importance for Menzies to make such a request. She tried to think of what was going on around the Pas de Calais to make the creation of another underground network so critical. "The invasion?" she asked.

"Obviously," he said.

"I'll see what we can do."

"There's another matter that needs tending. Can you and Combined Operations do something about those confounded E-boats operating out of Dunkirk?"

"I'll talk to Commander Bertram and see what we can arrange."

"Barmy mentioned that Roger was back in hospital."

Willi frowned. Menzies and his cronies seemed to have unlimited sources of information and gossiped about everything. "He should be out today. He had a nasty fall."

"From a horse in a polo match, I hear. Who was the American?"

Where did he learn that? she wondered. "I don't recall his name. He's in the RAF."

"Ah, I see," Menzies said. "Let me know about the new circuit and those E-boats." She stood up and left, fully aware that Menzies was mentally undressing her as she walked out.

When Willi entered the Combined Operations Headquarters Building in Richmond Terrace, she was wearing the dark blue uniform of an officer in the Wrens, the Women's Royal Naval Service. The well-tailored uniform caused more than one male to turn and watch her walk purposefully down the hall to the operations section, where she sought out the chief of current operations, Commander Roger Bertram.

Roger looked up from his crowded desk and eyed her approvingly. "Smashing," he said. "You should wear that one more often."

"It does seem to be the perfect cover for over here," she allowed. "It fits right in." In addition to the FANY and Wren uniforms, Willi would occasionally wear a WAAF, Women's Auxiliary Air Force, uniform. The proper uniform simplified matters as she went about her duties.

"Please." Roger smiled at her. "No interservice rivalries are allowed in Combined Operations. Mountbatten would have my liver if I was the least bit partisan towards the Senior Service. But you do give us an advantage."

"Roger, I'm not here to discuss internal politics."

Bertram adopted a serious face and waited. Like most of his colleagues, Bertram considered the Baker Street Irregulars and the SOE not quite "top form" and condescendingly discounted their work. But considering the personal relationship he wanted to keep on track, he did have to humor the beautiful and headstrong girl. "C called me in this morning," she told him. "He wants to do something about the E-boats out of Dunkirk."

"Now why should they concern him?" Roger wondered. He pushed his chair back and stood up. Willi could tell that he was still moving carefully and favoring his right side. She followed him into the next room where navy yeomen constantly updated the latest changes in the disposition of German forces on large maps that covered every wall. "Peterson," he called to one of the yeomen, "what's been brewing in the Pas de Calais sector?"

The short and pudgy former schoolteacher scurried over to them. "Interesting force dispositions," he told them. "Whenever we turn up our level of attention, a slight increase in bombing raids, or more aggressive air patrols, the Boche respond with increased defenses. They take anything we do there very seriously. The night intruder missions by Mosquitoes appear to be most effective in eliciting a response. The Germans have their own name for Mosquito ops now—*Moskitopanik*."

"That will be all, Peterson," Bertram said, dismissing him. Like most of his social class, Bertram instantly cast the lower ranks into a special limbo where they were expected to wait until needed. It was a totally natural order to Willi and she thought nothing of it. Peterson waddled away, but stayed within earshot in case they called.

"I think it's very clear," Bertram said. "This is the area where the invasion can be expected. We need to soften their defenses."

"Obviously," Willi parroted, imitating C's reaction. "But we don't have the resources to do anything about those E-boats. Can you do it?"

"Difficult," he said. "After the raid on Dieppe, we avoid well-defended areas like Dunkirk. No," he decided, coming to a conclusion, "it's just not on for us. Perhaps those Mosquitoes"—his voice had a condescending tone—"can do something."

"I'll let C know and speak to the RAF," Willi said.

Roger gave her his most charming look now that business was taken care of. "Tonight?"

"Oh, I'd love that." She gave him a smile that reached out and captured the nearby Peterson. "Are you up to it so soon?" she asked.

"Perhaps we can make medical history."

Peterson watched them walk out of his room. "They bloody well deserve each other," he muttered to himself, hating them for what they were, living examples of the British upper class. George Peterson was a loyal British subject and a dedicated communist.

The sixth floor of the Broadway Buildings had settled down into its usual midafternoon routine and Willi had the office to herself. She used the privacy to change into her WAAF uniform for a visit to her RAF contact in Whitehall. If Special Operations couldn't handle the E-boat problem at Dunkirk, the RAF would. A slipped word about Combined Operations declining the mission would whet their appetite. She calculated that Menzies would owe SOE a favor if they solved whatever problem he was having with the E-boats. She chalked it all up to the conflict of interest SIS was having with SOE. Menzies had never been happy when the covert action arm of intelligence had been split off from his SIS and given to the Baker Street Irregulars. But it made sense to her; the Special Operations Executive tended to make loud noises when they went to work and many of their agents were captured. Those were two conditions that the gatherers of intelligence like the SIS should avoid.

"Willi," one of her office mates called when she entered, "good news. There might be an agent available. You need to get right on to Anna, otherwise you may be too late. Establish your claim now." Willi thanked the woman for helping with Menzies's request for a new network and then asked her if she would approach the RAF about striking at the E-boats. "That means Reggie, doesn't it?" Willi nodded. Reggie was the RAF officer who handled special requests from the SOE. "He'll ask me to sleep with him, you know."

"Well," Willi replied, "there might be a bottle of champers in it."

"Lovely," the girl said, rushing out of the office. She did like champagne. Willi watched her go and decided not to waste time changing uniforms. If Willi wanted to break free an agent and the resources to set up a new network, Anna would be a hard nut to crack. But Menzies was right, Mistral was being rolled up and if the Pas de Calais was the site of the invasion, they would need a healthy circuit in place.

Anna Fredericks was the power that guided the SOE's operations in France. Her title indicated that she was a mere administrative assistant but, in reality, her recommendations drove any decision. Only twice had the higher echelons disregarded her advice, and twice the results had been an instantaneous disaster. Never one to bite her tongue, Fredericks had promptly told her superiors, "I believe I had raised that possibility." But there had been no joy or self-satisfaction in the telling. Agents had died with each failure. When Willi walked into her office, Fredericks came right to the point. "C is interfering in our operations again."

"He interferes in everyone's," Willi replied.

"Why the insistence on throwing resources away in the Pas de Calais?" Fredericks wondered. "Surely the Germans are not so stupid as to believe it's the invasion site."

"Perhaps," Willi speculated, "by our showing a continued interest in the Pas de Calais, the Germans cannot discount it."

Fredericks said, "I see your point. We continue to sacrifice agents and the Germans must ask why. The only logical answer being that it is the site of the expected invasion. At the very least, it causes them to split their forces." Fredericks stared at her hands. "But what a damnable price to pay."

"Yes, it is," Willi said. "You know Mistral has lost its third pianist in two months."

"Yes. I heard," Fredericks said. "I hope she still has her L pill." The L pill was the suicide capsule all agents were issued. "Well then, perhaps you had better see what's available." She pushed a thin folder across her desk to Willi. "I would be willing to set up another circuit in the area operating independently of Mistral. But I want you in charge, controlling the operation." Willi lifted an eyebrow at this. "Bletchley Park is saturated and you would have to set up a new station," Fredericks continued. "Why don't you take a look at Manston. It does offer some possibilities."

"Humm," Willi said, as she read through the document. "Her cover could prove a bit dicey."

"It's not a cover. She is a doctor."

"Yes, she would do nicely," Willi allowed. "Any problems?"

"A few. She's been dark for a time and only recently resurfaced. Her circuit was rolled up three months ago and she was reportedly picked up—we don't know by whom. Since we have no photos, we're not sure if she's the same person. She could be a plant. Also, she might have been turned while in captivity. Lastly, she is reported to be absolutely stunning."

Willi stiffened at Fredericks's last comment. It was the reason she had been rejected as an agent. She had wanted to go inside occupied France and had even gone through the first phase of training. Although her French was perfect and she had lived in France for a number of years, her instructors had disqualified her because she was too pretty. German officers would have been instantly attracted to her, destroying the anonymity an agent needed to move freely about. Instead, the SOE had sidetracked her into coordination duties and kept her available in case they needed someone with her special qualifications. Willi shifted her attention to the file again and finished reading it. A name near the end caught her attention. "Why don't we bring her in for training and vet her?"

"It would be worthwhile if we had someone who could verify she is the legitimate article," Fredericks said.

"We might have. There's a reference in her file to a Pontowski."

"I saw that. It would be the very devil to find an American with that name." Fredericks paused, thinking. "I suppose we could, given time."

"My grandfather," Willi said, "knows a Flight Officer Pontowski. He's an American flying with the RAF. It's possible that he might be the same Pontowski."

Later that evening, Willi had changed back into her Wrens uniform and met Roger Bertram at his office in Richmond Terrace. As they left for dinner at a nearby Navy officers mess, they passed George Peterson, the intelligence yeoman who worked in Combined Operations. They didn't even see him. Peterson accepted his invisibility. "Bloody aristocrats," he muttered.

Peterson left work early that night just after nine P.M., the time he calculated Bertram would be undressing Willi. He was wrong because that event would not occur for another two hours. He made his way to a small apartment in Soho. A tall and slender man let him in and offered him a cup of tea. While the tea brewed, Peterson related all that had transpired in his office over the last few days. The man listened quietly and noted two items of importance; the reference to the Pas de Calais as the invasion site and the interest in the Dunkirk E-boats. "Then you think the RAF will go after the E-boats?"

Peterson nodded. "With Mosquitoes." When he had finished his tea, Peterson left.

The man carefully composed a detailed message for his control. He would deposit it that night in a dead drop for dispatch, not to Germany but to Moscow. Both he and Peterson were dedicated to their cause and would have gladly sacrificed themselves in the fight against German fascism. Because of that fanatical hatred, the message was safe from the Germans and it reached Moscow late the next evening. There it was decoded by a short rotund woman who worked for the NKVD. But she had another employer, the German Abwehr that had recruited her years before. Thirty-six hours later, the contents of the message had reached

Berlin. There, two things happened; the Luftwaffe and the military commander of Dunkirk were alerted to expect an attack by Mosquitoes on the E-boats and the German high command received one more item that pointed to the Pas de Calais as the landing site for the invasion.

The intelligence officer was waiting for Zack and Ruffy when they entered the room of the big manor house at Church Fenton that 25 Squadron had turned into its operations briefing room. The other pilot and navigator who would fly on their wing for the mission were right behind them. "Ah, yes," the Intelligence officer said when he saw Zack and Ruffy, "I'm told you're slated for Intruders." Intruder missions were single-ship night missions for which a Mosquito crew was assigned a specific area to patrol at night with the express purpose of disrupting German flying operations. "Very good progress for such a young crew," he said. "Normally, crews are much more experienced before being assigned to night ops."

"Well," Ruffy told him, "we were on night ops in Beaus. I think we have an idea of what's out there."

"Ah, yes, I see," he said. They could hear skepticism in his voice. "Well, to matters at hand. Your target is the airdrome at Soesterberg in the Netherlands. Quite heavily defended and their JU-Eighty-eight night fighters have been a concern to our bombers on their way to Germany. Please see what you can do about them." The Intel officer spent some time going over the local defenses and what they could expect on their way in and out of the target area. He ended with "Operation Starkey is in full swing and the Eighth Air Force is throwing as many B-Seventeens as it can against German fortifications and supply lines in the Pas de Calais region. They shouldn't be a factor, but if you see any stray B-Seventeen in need of help, please lend a hand. While the weather is proving most cooperative, even for August, it is also making it most easy for the Germans to find the bombers. The 'boys from Abbeville' are extracting their pound of flesh."

The men dutifully filed that information away and made no comment. Unknown to them, Operation Starkey was an attempt by the Allies to convince the Germans that an invasion in the Pas de Calais area was imminent and take the pressure off the hard-pressed Russians on the eastern front. But the "boys from Abbeville," the nickname given to one of Generalmajor Adolf Galland's Luftwaffe wings that was based at Abbeville, France, were creating havoc among the B-17s. Flying Focke-Wulf 190s, the "boys" had turned the skies over the Pas de Calais region into one of the toughest zones in Europe.

The navigation officer took over and laid out their route. "Please remember," he said, "the primary rules for daytime—in fast and out fast—don't go around for a reattack—those who fight and run away, live to fight another day. This will be your area for Intruder so mark the defenses well. You'll find it's easier to avoid them at night when the buggers can't see you."

Then they emptied their pockets, collected their parachutes, Mae Wests, dinghies, and the rest of their flying kit before going out to dispersal to the waiting aircraft. At the last moment, they were told that their aircraft was u/s, unserviceable, and that they would be flying number 529. "Luck of the draw," Zack said. Number 529, better known as *Romanita* in the squadron, was the best aircraft assigned to 25 Squadron.

As usual, the two-man ground crew who tended the machine, a fitter for the engines and a rigger for the airframe, were there. The two young men took extraordinary pride in their aircraft. "Please bring 'er back, Mr. Pontowski," the rigger said as he helped Zack snake his six-foot frame through the small hatch on the right side of the aircraft located just forward of the navigator's position. Zack had to crawl across Ruffy's seat to settle into the pilot's seat. The sergeant's grinning face beamed at him from the hatch. "*Romanita*'s like a virgin, sir, hard to get into but lovely once you're there." Once he had nestled into the seat, Zack found the small cockpit comfortable enough, except that the rudder pedals were slightly displaced to the right. He heard an "Ouch!" from outside followed by a muttered "Bloody airscrews." Ruffy had bumped into one of the propeller blades that were close to the hatch before he climbed the boarding ladder.

Ruffy's head emerged through the hatch as he wiggled his way on board and into his seat which was to Zack's immediate right and set slightly back. Then the rigger passed his navigation board and chest-pack parachute in after him for storage at the navigator's feet. Zack sat on his parachute and seriously doubted that he would ever be able to bail out of the cramped cockpit since there was no autopilot and the controls needed constant tending. Then the hatch was closed.

"Whackin' great engines," Ruffy muttered, rubbing his head.

Zack's hands moved over the switches and controls, setting them for engine start. He yelled out the open side window that he was starting, switched on the ignition, and pressed the starter and booster-coil buttons. The left propeller moved suddenly as the starter-motor sent out a thin, discordant wail. Since the ground crew had warmed up the engines earlier, the twelve cylinders of the Merlin 21 roared to life and the three blades of the propeller disappeared in a whirl. They repeated the procedure for the right engine and Zack checked the hydraulic pumps, made sure the right generator was on line and charging, and checked the operation of the constant-speed propeller. He motioned the chocks away and the last physical human contact with the ground was broken. Now only the radio would keep that contact alive.

They taxied out of dispersal, lined up on the runway and ran through the takeoff routine: elevator trim slightly nose-heavy, slight pressure on the right rudder, ailerons neutral, flaps up, prop controls full forward, fuel cocks to outer tanks, superchargers to MOD, radiator switch to open. . . . Straighten the damn tail wheel, he reminded himself. Now a green light from the tower. "Let's go," he told Ruffy as he inched the throttles forward, making sure the left one was slightly forward to counter the Mossie's tendency to swing on takeoff. When the rpm were hovering on 3,000, he released the hand brake lever on the control column and they thundered down the runway. At 120 mph, the aircraft wanted to fly but Zack held it on the ground. At 130, he lifted the Mossie smoothly into the air with its two-thousand-pound bomb load.

Ruffy gave him a heading for the coast as the other Mosquito joined on their right. Then they coasted out over their checkpoint two hundred feet above the deck and headed out across the North Sea for Holland at 300 mph.

This was the Mosquito, a flying anachronism of wood that relied on pure speed for defense. It was the most versatile and fastest fighter-bomber of its time. And while the Mosquito was a light-weight, weighing in at less than twenty thousand pounds fully loaded, it was able to carry as much death and destruction to the enemy with greater accuracy and fewer losses than its big brothers flying massed raids into the heartland of the enemy.

Zack and his wingman coasted in over the Dutch coast south of Haarlem and headed straight for Hilversum. They wanted to make it look as if they were going after the antennas and communications facilities clustered around that city. Both Zack and Ruffy kept a constant lookout for enemy fighters, confident that they could only be intercepted by a fighter diving down on them from above. At low level, they could outrun anything the Germans had flying. At one point, Ruffy slapped Zack on the back and pointed to four Messerschmitts on patrol to the north. "Me-One-oh-nines," Zack told him. "I don't think they've seen us."

Zack pushed the throttles up and increased their speed to 320 on "the clock" as they arced around the southern edge of Hilversum. Ruffy picked out a landmark and gave Zack a new heading, pointing them directly toward the Luftwaffe base at Soesterberg. Squashed flies and dust had smudged the windscreen and Zack was hard-pressed to see the field.

"The city on your left is Amersfoort," Ruffy told him. "The aerodrome should be on the nose in that wooded area." Like Zack, Ruffy could not pick out the camouflaged German air base and was navigating from checkpoint to checkpoint. "Climb now," he said as the last checkpoint flashed by underneath their right wing. Zack honked back on the stick and climbed to fifteen hundred feet for a low-angle bomb run. His wingman would go in straight and low at fifty feet above the ground and drop bombs fused with an eleven-second delay. He would toss them straight ahead much like a rifle bullet—and with the same accuracy. Zack would be coming down the chute and release his bombs from a shallow dive angle. But his timing had to be perfect and he had to be off target before the bombs from the first Mosquito exploded. The maneuver called for extreme precision but the results were devastating.

When Zack rolled in, he saw the runway and the other Mossie at the same time. His partner was going to put his bombs right into the entrance of an underground command bunker. Then he saw the noses of three JU-88s hidden in the trees. It was pure luck, the right combination of sun angle, shadow, and the fact that he was looking more out the side window than straight ahead—thanks to the smashed bugs. His feet twitched on the rudder pedals and he sighted on the trees where he had seen the snouts of the JU-88s. Ruffy counted off the altimeter as it unwound. He mentally calculated the lag in the instrument and when he figured they were at the release altitude of eight hundred feet, he shouted, "Pull out!" over the intercom. Zack's thumb flicked on the bomb button and they were off, running to the south at treetop level. Ruffy twisted in his seat in time to see a huge secondary explosion mushroom into the sky behind them.

"Tallyho!" Zack shouted as he threw the Mossie into a hard left turn and then skidded it across the treetops. He jammed the throttles full forward and set the rpm at 3,000. Crossing directly in front of him was a Junkers 88 with its gear down. The exploding bombs had discouraged the pilot from making a landing and he was circling the field. The German pilot saw Zack and accelerated as Zack zoomed up behind him, ninety degrees off the Junkers's heading. The Junkers's gear was coming up when Zack pulled down behind him. They closed and Zack concentrated on the GM-2 gunsight the Mossie shared with the Spitfire, lining up on the wildly gyrating Junkers. His thumb mashed the cannon trigger and the four 20-millimeter Hispano cannons under the floorboards erupted, shaking the Mosquito. Pieces flew off the Junkers and it careened to the right, crashing into the center of the city of Amersfoort.

"Oh my God," Zack groaned.

"Set course two-three-five degrees," Ruffy snapped, all business. Zack did as he said and tried not to think about what he had just done. How many innocent Dutch did I kill? he thought.

"Not your fault," Ruffy said, knowing what his pilot was thinking. "We're only doing our job."

They only encountered one patch of light flak on their way out of Holland.

The two men could feel the tension from the mission slack as they raced across the North Sea, alone now as they had lost contact with their number two man coming off the target. "No time for get-home-itis," Zack mumbled as he scanned the skies, looking for trouble.

"Beg pardon?" Ruffy replied.

"Get-home-itis," Zack told him, "is the head-for-the-barn complex when you forget about business. Horses get it." Then he saw the trail of smoke far to his left and slightly above them. "Someone's in trouble." He studied the smoke trail. "It's going in our direction. Must be one of ours. Let's check it out." The old tingling feeling scratched at him, sending its vague warnings. He had learned not to disregard it and climbed into the sun, gaining altitude.

"It's a Flying Fortress," Ruffy said, making out the heavily damaged B-17. "Bandits! Two Focke-Wulfs! They're on the Fort."

"Got 'em," Zack said. He pushed the nose over into a steep dive and slashed down on the two Focke-Wulf 190s, still hiding in the sun. The airspeed climbed to 460 mph. "Too fast," he grunted and pulled the throttles back. Now he was stabilized at

450 as the trailing Focke-Wulf filled his gunsight ring. His right thumb pressed the gun camera button and then moved over to the button that fired the machine gun. He hesitated before mashing it. The four Browning .303 machine guns mounted in the nose cut loose and he walked the stream of bullets across the 190's cockpit. The German fighter pitched over in a steep dive and crashed into the sea. He pulled off straight ahead and zoomed, trading off his airspeed for altitude, clawing for every bit of height he could gain before turning back into the engagement.

"Jerry's running for it," Ruffy told him. The other Focke-Wulf had seen his wingman crash and, not being able to find the cause, had turned tail and run. It was exactly what Zack would have done. They pulled alongside the stricken Flying Fortress and looked it over. The pilot gave them a wave and pointed to his mouth and ears before making a slashing motion. "They must have lost their radios," Ruffy said.

"I think they're going to ditch," Zack said. The B-17 was slowly descending toward the sea. "Call Manston and tell them what's going on," Zack said. Ruffy checked his list for Manston's call sign and made the radio call.

Manston, the emergency recovery base located on the eastern coast of Kent near Ramsgate, acknowledged the call. They would notify Air-Sea Ops for a pickup. "Coastal Command," Manston warned them, "reports an E-boat operating in the area."

"We'll fly cover as long as we can," Zack told Manston. They watched as the B-17 settled into the water and, for one sickening moment, Zack was certain that its nose was going to dig in and it would pitch-pole onto its back. A huge cascade of spray hid the B-17 and then collapsed over it like a falling curtain. In the mist, they could see the B-17 at rest in the water, still right side up. "Lucky bastards," Zack muttered, remembering when he and Ruffy had ditched in the North Sea. Three dinghies popped out and they counted four men as they scrambled out of the aircraft. Then two wounded were passed out, followed by four more men. "They all got out," he said.

They loitered over the dinghies until Ruffy said, "Fuel." They had to go. Zack flew one last turn over the men and wagged his wings. Then he saw it. A low gray silhouette in the water was moving toward the men in the dinghies. "Oh, Jesus," he moaned as they flew closer. "It's an E-boat."

"Fuel" was all Ruffy said.

"One pass," he promised. "We've got to discourage that bastard." He headed for the E-boat, turned the gun camera on, and walked a string of twenty-millimeter cannon shells across the boat. He pulled up and headed for England.

Zack and Ruffy were walking into the anteroom of the mess the next afternoon when they were told to report to their squadron commander at station headquarters. "He's probably read our combat report by now," Zack said. Ruffy gave him a worried look.

The squadron leader who commanded 25 Squadron was a no-nonsense, thirty-two-year-old from Yorkshire and he came right to the point. "The bomber chaps reported that not much was going on over Holland last night, probably due to the dents you made at Soesterberg." It was the closest thing to a compliment they had ever heard him utter. "Impressive," he continued. "Two kills. I hope the film from your gun camera bears that out." Now they were hearing absolute praise. Zack was certain the film would catch up with him in a few days and support his claim. After attacking the E-boat, they had run dangerously low on fuel and had made an emergency diversion into Manston. They had de-briefed Intelligence while the ground crews refueled their aircraft and developed the film. But they had been ordered back to Church Fenton before the film was processed.

"But"—the squadron leader glared at them, not about to let them off the hook—"if you ever land on one engine again because you've run out of petrol and then have to be pushed off the runway because there is absolutely nothing left in the tanks, I'll have your guts for garters."

Both men relaxed. This was more like it. "Manston didn't seem to mind refueling us," Zack said. "And it was only a short delay."

"Fortunate for you there was no damage to Five-twenty-nine," he grudgingly admitted. Zack buried his smile. His squadron com-mander had been as worried about *Romanita* as he had for the crew. "There's an Intelligence type up from London . . . flew in twenty minutes ago . . . who wants to talk to you about your mis-sion. They must have discovered something important in your report or on the film." He tried to fix them with his sternest look, but his pride in what they had done wouldn't allow it. "Dis-missed," he muttered. Then he added, "And well done, lads."

Ruffy led the way out of the door and stopped dead in his tracks. "Smashing," he mumbled, "absolutely smashing." Wil-helmina Crafton was waiting for them wearing her WAAF uniform, holding a slim black leather portfolio.

"Mr. Pontowski," she said, "so good to see you again."

Zack stumbled over his words, searching for the right thing to say. After a few "ahs" and "ums," he said, "This is my nav—"

"Yes," she said, cutting him off short. "We do need to talk in private."

The arrogant, in-charge attitude he had experienced before was back in her voice. He didn't like it. "Yeah, sure," he muttered.

"I'll see if I can find something," Ruffy said.

"Alone, please, Mr. Ruffum." It came as a surprise that she knew Ruffy's name. Ruffy shrugged his shoulders and went in search for a vacant office.

Zack liked her patronizing way of speaking even less than before. "What is this all about?"

"I'll explain in private."

"What the hell," he said, gesturing at the busy office, "these people are on our side and they read every combat report. They know what goes on."

"Really?" she said, condescension dripping from the word.

Ruffy returned and motioned them down the hall. "Where did you meet her?" he asked. Zack could hear a Norfolk inflection in Ruffy's question. Where had that come from? Why was this the first time he had heard it? "In here, miss," Ruffy said, holding the door open. They entered and he started to leave.

"You too, Ruffy," Zack said, waving him to join them.

"We do need to speak privately," Willi said, bestowing a gracious smile on Ruffy, dismissing him.

Zack walked out the door. "Nice seeing you again, Miss Crafton. Have a nice trip back to London."

"Must I have your squadron commander order you . . ."

"To do what?" Zack was tired of her lordly manner and the way she automatically expected everyone to jump to her slightest wish or whim. "To talk to you 'in private'? I don't think you have the slightest idea what we do. For your information, we kill people, some who deserve it and others who are quite innocent."

"Mr. Pontowski . . ." she protested, not hearing the pain in his voice, not aware of the emotional turmoil that bound him with images of the JU-88 crashing into the middle of Amersfoort.

He cut her off with an angry gesture. "And we do it as a team. So if you want to talk to us, you'll talk to us as a team."

"I take it that you know each other," Ruffy said.

Willi ignored Ruffy. "You will talk to me or I'll see you up on a charge."

"Really?" Zack said, his tone matching her use of the word. They exchanged cold stares.

Ruffy took charge. "I hope this is not a silly lovers spat." Willi flinched at the thought and turned away. She would not dignify that remark with an answer. "Why don't you ask us whatever concerns ops," he offered, "after which, I'll leave. Then you can discuss whatever else is on your mind."

"Yes, why don't we?" Willi replied.

"That's agreeable," Zack muttered, sinking into a chair. How in the hell did we reach this state? he wondered. The sparks had flown from the first word and he felt like a hopeless teenager.

She turned to them and pulled a set of photos out of her portfolio, now all business. "These are for your Intelligence officer, but here, you can see them now." She handed them a set of glossy, black-and-white photos. "These were enlarged from your gun camera film developed at Manston," she told them. "Here"—she pointed to the photos from the bomb run—"are at least six, possibly eight, German night fighters hidden in the trees. Some of our people are wondering how you found them."

"Squashed bugs," Zack said.

Willi assumed he was wisecracking like so many of the Americans she had met. "Yes, of course. I can see that."

"I doubt that you do," Zack shot at her. "Since it's summer, dust and bugs are a problem when flying fast at low level. I could hardly see out of the windscreen by the time we arrived over Soesterberg. I was constantly looking out the side window. By pure luck I saw these," he pointed to the three aircraft snouts barely visible underneath the trees. "I was in a position to switch targets and did so."

She nodded and showed them the next photo. It was the JU-88 he had shot out of the sky when he came off target. The photograph captured the doomed aircraft as the right wing folded up, broken apart by twenty-millimeter cannon fire. "It crashed in the center of Amersfoort," Ruffy told her.

"Oh, I didn't know." Silence. "These are from the engagement over the North Sea," she continued, not so sure of herself now. "The markings on the Focke-Wulf you destroyed indicate it was from the Jagdgeschwader at Abbeville."

"One of the 'Abbeville boys,' " Ruffy said.

"And the photos of the Schnellboote you strafed are most interesting," she said, showing them the last photo. "We believe this figure"—she circled the blurred image of a man standing in the open cockpit—"is Ernst Hofmann. At least, it is his boat."

"Young Ernst," Ruffy said, studying the photos.

"Yes," she continued, "he is a problem. He has made the English Channel his private hunting preserve and comes and goes at will. He's playing the devil with our operations and has torpedoed at least eight freighters."

"He probably machine-gunned those poor bastards in the dinghies," Zack said.

"No, he did not," Willi said. "He doesn't work that way. We have reports that he has been in trouble with his superiors for not doing exactly that. The B-seventeen crew reported that he threw them an inflatable when he couldn't stop to pick them up. Some of our chaps in Beaufighters showed up after you strafed him and chased him back to Dunkirk."

"Not your normal Hun," Ruffy allowed.

Zack sensed the woman was more than she appeared and was deeply involved in Intelligence. "I find it hard to believe that these photos are the reason they, whoever *they* are, sent you here. It would have been almost as fast by regular courier."

Willi stared at him for a moment. "Mr. Ruffum, would you be kind enough to leave us a few moments?" Ruffy nodded and made a quick departure. "You are quite right, of course. There is another reason." She collected the photos and arranged them in a neat stack. "I must give these to your Intelligence section. I brought them since I happened to be coming this way." She seemed relieved as she turned to the real purpose of her visit. "Do you know a Frenchwoman named Chantal Dubois?"

A hard silence came down. The part of his being that Chantal had claimed, and that he had written off as another casualty of war, came surging out of its hiding place. He had never expected to see her again and had consoled himself with vague promises that he would go looking for her after the war. For the second time that day, he couldn't find the right words. "Chantal. . . . Where?" Coherent thought was slow to return.

"Then you do know her," Willi said, not satisfied that she had been successful in finding the only person who could identify the woman. The look on Zack's face made her strangely uncomfortable. Then it came to her—this was a man deeply in love. She had received more than her share of attention but most of the looks directed at her were either lust, envy, or jealousy. Not this.

"Where is she?"

"I'm sorry, I can't say any more at the moment. But we would like for you to come to London."

"When?"

"Now," she replied. "I'll arrange it with your commander."

"He may be reluctant to let me go. We're shorthanded."

Willi allowed a tight smile to cross her lips. "I assure you, he won't cause any problems. Why don't you gather your kit while I arrange it." She sounded extremely sure of herself.

Zack ambled back to the room he shared with Ruffy and started to pack. Ruffy meandered in and leaned against the door jamb. "Hope she's not in the family way," he deadpanned.

"Not hardly," Zack snapped.

"She is a bit offputting."

"A real bitch," Zack added. "I wonder why she's like that."

"Who knows. She doesn't need a reason." Ruffy shook his head at Zack's lack of understanding. "She's some lord and lady's daughter. One of our so-called betters." Zack could hear sarcasm in his voice. "Class distinction," Ruffy explained, "is the true vice of the English. One of the many things we need to change when we're finished with Herr Hitler."

"How will you do that?" Zack asked.

"Politics. We need to change the government."

Zack was astounded. One of the forbidden subjects in an RAF mess was politics. He had no idea that his best friend was so fiercely opinionated. "Does that mean you'll vote against Churchill after the war?"

"Right. He's one of them, one of our so-called betters."

It was all very confusing to him and, like most Americans, he thought the English were one hundred percent behind their prime minister. "But you and everyone else seems to be for him now."

"Because there simply isn't any-bloody-one else who can do the job."

He zipped his bag closed and stood up. "Ruffy," he said, changing the subject, "I could have sworn I heard a Norfolk accent when you were talking to her."

His navigator blushed brightly. "It comes out when I get around them. It's part of my upbringing. My family is what *they* call one of the lower orders." Zack could hear a deep anger behind Ruffy's words. Or was it hurt? Andrew Ruffum had never told him that he had been a "scholarship boy" at one of the English public schools that were anything but public. They were reserved almost exclusively for the British upper class. By hard work and brilliant academic achievement, he had broken out of the class mold his parents had been caught in and one of the first things he had discarded was his Norfolk accent. The war had ended his college studies, and like many of his contemporaries, he had joined the RAF.

"I've got to go," Zack told him. "I should be back in a few days."

Ruffy walked with him back to station headquarters and waited while he picked up his pass. Back outside, he said, "Have a good time. I'd stay clear of our Miss Crafton if I were you." Ruffy doubted that his friend would understand the warning. Wilhelmina Crafton was a product of her social class and would not tolerate any man who tried to rise above his position. She was clearly miffed because she didn't know what Zack's place was. For that matter, neither did Zack.

Ruffy smiled to himself at the thought.

SEVEN

The Golden Triangle, Burma

Chiang's majordomo hovered on the other side of Heather's desk, ready to be of instant service. Normally, the portly and white-haired old Chinese gentleman was the perfect English butler, but he was anything but reserved and calm now. "James," she said, "please sit down. You're flapping." He looked at her reproachfully, as if she should understand the gravity of what they were doing. He forced himself to sit down. Heather immediately stood up and paced the priceless Persian carpet that Chiang had given her for her office that adjoined his. "James," she ventured, "is that your real name?" Heather wanted to make him part of her growing entourage. She liked giving orders.

"No ma'am, it is not," he answered in his impeccable British accent. Then he did something totally out of character—he became less stiff. "It is the name General Chiang wishes to call me."

She bestowed a smile on him, sensing the break in his rigid austerity. "Well, it does match your accent—which is perfect. Where did you learn to speak English?"

"I was born and educated in Hong Kong," he told her, as if that fact alone accounted for his fluency. "I later became an air traffic controller for the British."

"How did you become a butler then?" she asked. Hong Kong and air traffic control was a long way from Burma and being Chiang's majordomo.

"General Chiang heard me speak over the radio when he was flying his private jet into Hong Kong and sought me out." A knock at the ornately carved doors that connected the two offices slashed across his words, cutting them off. He sprang to his feet and opened the doors, bowing as he pulled them back.

"Ah, yes," Chiang said as he entered, ignoring the man. "I was wondering how the arrangements for the conference were progressing."

Heather stepped over to the antique writing table she used for a desk and picked up a leather-bound folder. "I think we've thought of everything," she told him. "James has been most helpful and I've learned so much." She tried to be all business, but excitement caught at her voice as she outlined the details of the meeting between Chiang and the leaders of two other drug cartels. From the moment Chiang had told her about his idea for a merger that would unite them into a "consortium" that would control a large percentage of the world's drug traffic, she had wanted to be part of it. She had coaxed him into letting her help and had seen yet another side to Chiang; he could have been the chief executive officer of any large and successful international corporation as he modernized his production base, secured his distribution net, and exploited his markets.

She held a gold-filigree-covered fountain pen and ticked off the details. "There are some minor points to be worked out," she concluded. "The number of bodyguards they travel with is a problem. We don't have enough rooms for them all in the guest houses and I would like to split them up. But we must keep their numbers balanced so one group doesn't outnumber the other." Chiang nodded his approval. "And I am arranging companions and entertainment to keep them occupied."

"James has a portfolio of escorts," Chiang told her. "I would suggest two for one and about ten percent should be young men and boys. We have some new cottages in the village. Why don't you see if they can be made suitable while James and I discuss other matters."

"I'll get on it right away," she said, beaming with pride and success as she hurried from her office. This was her first opportunity to leave the compound on her own, proof that she was becoming more than just his mistress.

Chiang walked back into his office and James followed, closing the door behind them. Both men sat down. James was much more than a majordomo in charge of the domestic affairs of the compound. He was Chiang's chief of security and second-in-command. "She is proving very helpful," James said in Chinese. "It is a sad thing to lose her."

"It was your idea," Chiang replied. "Besides, it will provide a certain entertainment for our guests. And the other two?"

"They are in the cells," James said.

"I was listening in on your conversation," Chiang said. James's expression did not change. He had supervised the installation of the hidden microphones in the villa and was mindful of how Chiang eavesdropped at will. "I would rather you did not discuss your past with Miss Courtland." All color drained from James's face. In all the years he had been in Chiang's service, this was the first time he had been criticized. It was a warning. "Please make the other arrangements." Chiang gave him a pleasant smile.

James stood and left, his knees very weak. He had been granted a reprieve.

The Executive Office Building, Washington, D.C.

Mazie's stubby fingers flew over the keyboard of the computer as she switched scales on the map. The video screen flashed and the map changed, showing a larger area around Chiang's compound. "I don't think it will work," she told Mackay, who was peering at the screen over her left shoulder. She used a pencil as a pointer. "The distances are too close together where they should be farther apart and too far where they should be close together."

"Trust me," Mackay said. "It can be done."

"First you tell the President that we need a cast of thousands to crack this place open and now you're telling me you can do it with a small unit."

"With the right group, you bet."

Mazie drummed on the video screen with the pencil's eraser. "Let's run it past the boss and see what he says. Personally," she groused, "I think you're simply looking for a way out of here." He only grinned at her. "Please stop smiling," she told him.

National Security Adviser Cagliari's first reaction to Mackay's proposal had been a simple "That's dumber than dirt." Mazie got up to leave, satisfied that it was a dead issue. But the lieutenant colonel would not give up easily.

"Sir," Mackay persisted, "the reason we keep doing pushups on our sword in small-scale rescue operations is because our government is too damn big and we keep having problems with duplication of effort and jurisdictional disputes."

Cagliari relented and motioned for Mazie to sit back down. "For example?" he asked.

"We cannot do a damn thing in Burma without the ambassador's approval. Then the CIA gets involved and makes sure that all intelligence is funneled through their Far Eastern Division. CIA division chiefs run the show like feudal barons and nothing gets by without their approval. By this time, the whole operation starts to resemble a bureaucratic nightmare as everyone starts to get a piece of the action."

"I see you've learned how this place works in a very short time," Cagliari said. "So how do you intend to get around all this?"

"Simple," Mackay replied. "We don't tell anyone what we're doing and keep the operation small and under close wraps until we're ready to execute. Then we chop to the normal chain of command."

"Chop?" Mazie asked.

Mackay explained, "Chop means change of operational command to another authority."

"And who exercises that tight control until we chop?" Cagliari asked.

"You."

"You're asking me to take one hell of a chance," Cagliari growled. "This place has infected you with delusions of grandeur and you seem to have forgotten what happened the last time the NSC got involved in covert operations."

"But I can make it work," Mackay interrupted. "And we only get the operation ready. We never assume the authority for execution."

"Details, I need details," Cagliari said. He was intrigued and saw possibilities where none had existed twenty minutes before.

"I don't have the details all worked out . . . yet," Mackay told him. "Let me put together a small unit disguised as routine training. All I need is to get the right people talking to each other and we'll fill in the details."

"And who are these right people."

"Well, we'll need one squadron from Delta, the same contingent from the First SOW that rescued Anderson would be preferable, and some help from the ISA. . . . " He hesitated when he saw Cagliari stiffen. The Intelligence Support Activity was so secret that even most of the intelligence community did not know it existed. Mackay plowed ahead. "Specifically, I want the ISA's shooters."

"That tears it," Cagliari said, slapping his desk with both hands and coming to his feet. "How in God's creation did you learn about them?"

Mackay grinned. "Mazie has access to System Four and worked it out. There is only one possible explanation for what happened in Beirut—the ISA has shooters—very good ones."

Cagliari sat back down. "You snookered me. You weren't even sure they existed until I confirmed it. How do you propose to fund this operation?" he asked.

"By using the funds that were sequestered during the Yellow Fruit investigation and court-martials."

Cagliari only shook his head and did not bother to ask how Mackay had learned about Yellow Fruit. Yellow Fruit was an Army special operations unit that had gone astray in the mid-1980s and its officers had been court-martialed for misappropriation of government funds. When the bureaucrats started scrapping over the carcass of Yellow Fruit with its huge multinational secret bank accounts, the attorney general had ordered all moneys impounded and held in a special account until the investigation was complete. The account had grown and in the last secret budget for clandestine operations, it had been transferred to Cagliari as part of the NSC's contingency fund. "Is there anything else?"

"I want one other person," Mackay concluded.

"Why not?" Cagliari conceded. "You seem to have this all worked out. Now you only need my approval."

"Have I got it?" Mackay asked.

"You have my limited approval to put a team together, plan, and train for the operation. That's all."

"Thank you, sir." Mackay smiled as he bolted from the office, anxious to get out of Washington.

"I wish he wouldn't smile," the national security adviser told Mazie before she followed him.

The Capitol, Washington, D.C.

Senator William Douglas Courtland sat in his office hurrying his way through the stack of documents and reports on his desk.

The task never took much time since his staff had reviewed and prepared a three- or four-paragraph summary cover sheet for each one. Then the summary had been further distilled to a three- or four-sentence minimemo that was stapled to the top. Like all good staffers on the Hill, Courtland's people knew what would upset the senator and had carefully massaged each summary and memo, presenting unpalatable topics in a way that would not scratch his prickly personality too deeply.

"Goddamn it," he growled, becoming more frustrated as he worked his way into one report that detailed the recent successes of the Drug Enforcement Administration in rolling up a major Canadian-based drug ring. His face flushed when the report covered the evidence that tied the drug ring to Chiang Tse-kuan. *How does that dumb Polack do it?* he raged to himself. The senator had focused on the DEA as a prime political issue for his upcoming drive for the presidency and had planned to beat Pontowski about the head and shoulders with it, claiming only he could turn the DEA around. But the President had honed the DEA into an effective law enforcement agency and ripped the issue out of Courtland's hands. Courtland's mental political calculator tallied it up, giving Pontowski another credit. *Not good,* he cautioned himself, coming so hard on the heels of Nikki Anderson's rescue. A warning light was flashing on the calculator, telling him that he had to do something very soon as Pontowski's side of the balance sheet was much longer than his.

His intercom buzzed, demanding his attention. It was Tina Stanley wanting to see him. The senator scribbled a "no action" note across the memo and tossed the report into his out basket, glad for the chance to shift his attention. A secretary announced Tina and held the door open. A tall, immaculately groomed and handsome Air Force three-star general preceded her into the office.

"Senator Courtland"—Tina smiled—"I'd like you to meet Lieutenant General Simon Mado."

Courtland stood up and extended his hand. "I am glad to meet you, General. I've heard some good things about you." They shook hands and exchanged the customary courtesies, each sizing up the other. Courtland was struck by the man's presence, for the general was in excellent physical condition that complemented his reputation as a first-class intellect. He started to add up the political possibilities.

"General Mado," Tina said, "the senator is very worried about his daughter and we would appreciate your personal assessment of the situation."

"Needless to say," Courtland interrupted, "I applaud your rescue of Miss Anderson and wish to offer my congratulations."

"Thank you, sir," Mado replied. "Your support is greatly appreciated. As you know, we did experience high casualties and are being severely criticized by the media and a few of your fellow senators. Of course, I am not in a position to set the record straight in public, nor will I since I am a subordinate officer."

It was the response Courtland wanted to hear. "I am appreciative of your position," Courtland reassured him. The two men nodded at each other, both considering an alliance. No deals would be cut and no promises exchanged; however, both men were aware of how they could help each other. Open collusion was out of the question; active support of each other's goals was not. But they had to reach an understanding. The senator adopted the look of a concerned parent. "General, I would like to know the truth about that rescue and my daughter's situation."

Mado carefully considered his reply. "Sir, given my position, I'm not sure what I should say at this time."

Courtland nodded understandingly. "My committee will be conducting hearings into the matter. As chairman of the Armed Services Committee, I must oversee the effectiveness of our defense establishment." The senator watched Mado's face as he offered the bait. "Without the right leaders in command of our military services, we become a paper tiger."

"If I am called on to testify," Mado said, "and I am asked the right questions, the truth will come out."

"And what is the truth?" Courtland asked.

Mado ran through his own decision making process and decided to commit. "It was my intention to free all the hostages simultaneously. I was overruled and Operation Dragon Noire was executed prematurely. If my recommendations had been followed, we would have freed all the hostages and I am confident that six members of Delta Force would still be alive." He fell silent, letting them digest his "revelation." "Your daughter's release will have to be negotiated now because another rescue operation is out of the question. By going after Nikki Anderson when we did, we lost the element of surprise and Chiang will be expecting another attempt. He's ready and waiting for us."

"I think," Tina said, "that thanks to the recent activities of the DEA, Chiang is in no mood to negotiate." She had read the same report that had caught Courtland's attention earlier.

"So, my daughter's continued captivity is the price we paid for rescuing Miss Anderson." The senator was not upset by this latest calculation and saw some new equations forming, creating definite political opportunities. "But surely," he continued, "we are capable of mounting another rescue. What with the forces available to us . . ."

"Senator," Mado said, "I cannot encourage you on that point. We were lucky in getting Miss Anderson out with only six casualties."

Courtland fixed his gaze on Mado. "General, I would like for my committee to hear what you've told me." He held up his hand. "Before you make that decision, I want you to know that I appreciate your position and understand that your testimony could hurt your career. But I protect those loyal Americans who put duty and honor above career."

"Thank you for your concern, Senator," Mado said. "I will answer any questions from your committee with candor and honesty. I won't pull any punches."

"That's all I can ask," Courtland replied, his face serious and full of concern. The alliance was signed, sealed, and delivered.

Tina escorted Mado out of the senator's office. "General," she said, "perhaps you can tell me the exact questions the senator should be asking during the hearings."

The White House, Washington, D.C.

"You see what the newspapers are calling us these days?" Bobby Burke, the director of central intelligence, asked Michael Cagliari as they entered the Oval Office.

"It could be worse," Cagliari replied. "They could have called us the Three Stooges." They exchanged brief smiles, both accepting the recent spate of publicity that the President's top three advisers had been getting in the press. One reporter had labeled Burke, Cagliari, and Leo Cox, the President's chief of staff, as the three most powerful men in the United States. Burke and Cagliari were smiling because the reporter obviously didn't appreciate just how strong-willed and independent their chief was. The reporter had misread the President's courtly and gracious manner as a sign of indecision. In reality, no one controlled the President of the United States or set his priorities.

Cox was already there, going over the day's schedule with Pontowski. "We're here to do our 'daily number' on you," he told the President, quoting the same reporter.

"Do your damnedest." Pontowski smiled, waving Burke and Cagliari to seats. "What nefarious schemes are you three trying to perpetuate on this poor old unsuspecting soul today?" He had read the same story in the press. The three men briefly expounded on their favorite schemes before turning to business. For the next forty minutes they covered the most pressing concerns the White House was addressing that spring day. Finally, they turned to the matter of the three hostages and the rescue of Nikki Anderson.

"The Senate Armed Services Committee hearings are turning into a bloodbath," Cagliari said. "Courtland is treating our people from Defense like hostile witnesses and ripping them apart. He really grilled General Mado."

"I thought Mado held his own and came out looking pretty good," Burke said.

"He personally looked good," Cox interrupted. "He passed the buck up the chain of command. Wait until Courtland starts grilling the NMCC. And you're next, Mike."

Cagliari accepted the prediction calmly. "I expected to be called to testify," he said.

"The trouble," Cox continued, "is that Courtland is asking all the right questions. It's as if he has an inside line to our decision cycle."

"Some one is feeding him," Burke grumbled. "He's making the rescue of Miss Anderson look like a complete fiasco. It would help if Anderson presented a better public image. She looks and talks like a freak."

"That," Cox interrupted, "is exactly how heavy-metal weirdos want to look. But what happens when Courtland starts probing for the reasons we ordered Delta in when we did? That has me worried. We need a way to muzzle him."

"There is a way," Pontowski said. The men fell silent and waited. From long experience they knew that the President had reached a decision and they were about to get their marching orders. "First, send word to the committee that Bobby is available as a witness only for today. They will jump at the chance to get the head of the CIA on the stand. Once you're there, Bobby, force the committee into closed-door session so you can discuss classified information. That will muzzle Courtland. Tell the committee everything except our sources. We don't need Willow-branch compromised. There are some good men on the committee and they can accept the truth.

"Second, have Special Operations Command start working on a rescue mission. I want this to be a major effort and all concerned agencies involved. The State Department will veto any large-scale military action and claim it would totally destabilize the new Burmese government, which it would, and which we do not want. But we will override State's objections and press ahead with the planning. Another leak will magically appear and the word will be passed to the press, forcing us to cancel the operation."

"Isn't it wonderful how decisions are made in our government?" Cagliari complained.

A disgusted look played across Cox's face. "We're wasting a lot of time and effort on this when we've got more pressing problems."

"That's politics, Leo," Pontowski said. "Rationality and logic have nothing to do with what's important. While all this is going on, I want to explore every contact we have to negotiate for the hostages' release. Get the DEA and the FBI involved. They've got contacts inside the drug cartels. Finally, I want to get a second rescue operation on the boards and keep it totally dark." He pointed at his national security adviser. "Mike, see what you can do."

"I do have something in mind," Cagliari said. "But if we opt to use it, it will have to be transferred to the normal chain of command. We can't afford another Iran-contra affair."

"That's what I had in mind," Pontowski said. "But we do that at the last possible moment." He brought the meeting to an end. "Do I have time for a walkabout?"

Cox stood up. "Yes, sir. You're free for the next thirty minutes. Who's the lucky target for today?"

Pontowski smiled and led them out the door. "Guess." He headed for the Office of the Budget.

Navarre Sound, near Hurlburt Field, Florida

Gillespie sat at the Pagoda's bar taking in the sunset. He took a long pull at his beer and drained it, appreciating how peaceful it was; the quiet waters of Navarre Sound, a lone sailboat silhouetted by the setting sun. *Will I be doing this again?* he thought, pondering the orders that had come down that were sending them to train with Delta Force. The Beezer's curt remark that "we might be doing some Chiang chopping" had sobered the captain and E-Squared hadn't helped with his observation that "he'll be expecting us this time." An F-15C cut across the sky, bringing him back to the moment as the old longing came back. "That's what I should be doing," he muttered to himself.

"Doing what?" Mike the bartender said, automatically drawing another beer for him.

"Flying those." Gillespie nodded toward the F-15. "I'm not cut out to be a rotorhead."

Another voice interrupted their conversation. "I didn't know you flew helicopters?" It was Allison, the beautifully stacked volleyball team captain who headed Allison's Amazons. Both men turned and smiled at her, pleased by her unexpected appearance. As usual, Gillespie's stomach did a quick two-step and he could feel the makings of an erection. She gave her hair a well-practiced toss and moved against the bar, deliberately brushing a breast against Gillespie's arm. "I was married to a fighter pilot once," she said.

Allison's closeness left Gillespie gasping for words. "I didn't know you'd been married," Mike the bartender said, breaking the silence. What's the matter with you Gill? he thought. You should be jumping on her like a bear on honey. She's sending signals. Your tongue got stiff all of a sudden?

"Actually, twice," Allison told them. "My second husband was also in the Air Force but he flew B-Fifty-twos. They both were first-class dorks." She gave Gillespie a thoughtful look. "They both claimed that only pree-verts flew helicopters."

Gillespie managed a smile. "Oh, I hope so," he finally managed.

Allison gave her heavy mane of hair another toss and bestowed a smile on him. "You seem different lately," she said.

Mike the bartender found an excuse to leave. "Hey, would you mind watching the bar until I get back?" He headed for the office. I'll be damned, he thought, the bimbo noticed. A few of the more astute volleyball leaguers had mentioned the subtle change that had come over Gillespie since his return from Thailand and Mike had heard some rumors about the little captain having balls that he needed a wheelbarrow to carry around.

"How come so serious today?" Allison asked.

"The Air Force. . . . You know . . . the usual thing," he answered, trying to make light of it. He sensed that a serious conversation was not the best way to keep Allison engaged. It was out of the question, he reasoned, to tell her about the orders that detailed him to train with Delta and how he was worried. She wouldn't understand, he decided. He was wrong.

"Yes, I do know," she said, suddenly wanting to cuddle and stroke him. "Dinner?" she offered. "My place?" He nodded, and as soon as Mike returned, they left.

Donna Bertino was driving off the bridge that spanned Navarre Sound when she saw Allison's flashy Mustang convertible pull away from the Pagoda with Gillespie in the passenger seat. Her pretty mouth pulled into a thoughtful pout. She decided she wasn't in any hurry to get home and pulled into the parking lot. Maybe Mike the bartender could tell her what was going on.

"Sock time," Allison murmured as she rolled over Gillespie and sat on the edge of the bed.

"Sock time?" he asked and stroked her bare back. Allison turned and glanced over her shoulder as she fumbled for her high-heeled slippers. Then she leaned into his touch, pressing the smooth warmth of her body into the palm of his hand. She pulled back and walked away as his eyes followed her across the room, taking in every detail of her naked body. The high heels made her legs look even longer, more delicious, and he could feel the start of a fresh erection.

She paused and looked at him. A slight smile played across her mouth when she saw the renewed interest in the lower regions of his body. "Keep that thought coming," she said. She rummaged through a drawer, finding what she wanted.

Gillespie half-faked a groan. "Have mercy. I don't think I'm up to four times in one night." He was a little sore.

She held up a pair of the long white tube socks she wore with her running shoes and studied his crotch. "You're up to it." She ambled back to the bed, casually swinging a sock in each hand. She stepped out of her shoes with a fluid motion and rolled over him into the bed, rubbing her breasts against his chest and drawing a leg over his crotch. "I think," she nipped at his right ear with her teeth, "that you're part goat. Are you rotorheads really pree-verts?"

Allison dropped the socks across his chest and lay on her back, bent the knee closest to him, and drew her left leg up, her foot brushing against his thigh. She reached down with her left hand and drew her fingernails over his stomach before she stroked his erection. Then she grabbed her foot. "Tie me up," she whispered, her voice suddenly low and very husky. He fumbled with a sock and tied a loose knot, binding her ankle and wrist together. He was excited by her rapid breathing and trembling breasts. "Tighter," she urged. "Now the other." He lay across her and tied her right ankle to her wrist. Allison gave a little twist and wiggled under him, clamping him with her inner thighs, holding him tight. "Now!" she urged, thrusting her hips against his, making him enter her. "Yes!" she shouted, threshing about under him, not letting him go. She pressed her mouth against his neck and her thighs beat at him. "HELP ME!" She sank her teeth into his neck, drawing blood.

"What is the matter with you," Donna Bertino mumbled. Normally, she had no trouble falling asleep but an inner need was tormenting her, not letting her escape images of Allison and Gillespie making love. Out of frustration, she threw herself out of bed and walked out onto the balcony of her condominium. The cool night breeze moving in off the Gulf of Mexico washed over her. "Quit being a silly cow," she scolded herself. "He's just another man out chasing poontang." But Donna was too honest with herself to let it go. She was more than passingly interested in one Captain S. Gerald Gillespie and she did not like Allison infringing on her territory. But what could she do? Allison had the stuff *Playboy* centerfolds were made of and the disposition of a porn star. "And men are so damn stupid," she announced to herself. She gazed up into the clear night and plotted her strategy, hoping that they were at least practicing safe sex. With her mind made up, she went to bed and immediately went to sleep.

Fort Bragg, North Carolina

The doubting ate at Mackay, consuming his self-confidence, making him question even the reason he was sitting in Delta Force's conference room. He willed himself to stop obsessing and concentrate on what Colonel Robert Trimler was saying. The words were right, but Trimler's southern accent had stirred deep-seated feelings and old fears. Listen to the man! he reprimanded himself. Everything the colonel was saying indicated that he had bought into the operation. So why the doubts? Why couldn't he accept the man for what he was? A competent and professional officer in command of Delta Force. Come on, Mackay told himself, old prejudices die hard, so spike this one in the heart.

But it was hard.

"Your timing couldn't be better," Trimler told him. "B Squadron's CO is being reassigned so it will be a simple matter for you to take his place and we can fit ISA into your squadron. No problems." He turned to his CSM, Victor Kamigami. "You've been working with them, Sergeant Major. How are they stacking up?"

"They are an extremely professional group of shooters," Kamigami said. "They are showing us action and maneuver in the Shooting House that make us look like amateurs. And they do things with C Four that I've never seen. They can blow the front end of a car over a building without the two teenagers copulating in the backseat missing a stroke." His face was expressionless and brown eyes passive. "But they can't hump Alice the Wart worth shit."

"The sergeant major does have a way with words," Trimler told Mackay. "But I have learned to listen to him." Mackay found the soft humor in his voice reassuring and he started to relax. "I take it they didn't keep up on one of your fun runs," Trimler observed. The daily five-mile march that Kamigami led with full gear and the heavy rucksacks called Alice the Wart had become the common denominator for determining if a Delta commando was in shape. The troops referred to it as "K's fun run in the sun" and the ISA shooters had failed miserably, not even finishing.

A new doubt started to gnaw at Mackay. Success depended on the team being able to make long marches through jungle. "I'll have to sort that one out when we reach Entebbe," he told the men. Entebbe was the name they had given their training site.

"The First SOW is airlifting us there tomorrow to start training," Trimler said. "Sergeant Villaneuva jumped at the chance to volunteer and I'm quite sure the CSM would be more than willing to help you whip our friends from ISA into shape."

"That would be appreciated, sir," Mackay replied, "and there's more help on the way."

Bethesda Naval Hospital, Maryland

The medical officer of the day bolted out of the elevator as soon as the doors had cracked open wide enough to let him escape. He scurried down the corridor, looking for Edith Washington, the big black woman who served as the head nurse on the floor.

He reached the nurses station, puffing heavily, all too aware that he needed to get into better shape. "First time you've had the duty when the President has been on the floor?" Washington asked. She knew the answer. The young doctor nodded, still working to catch his breath. He had never been on duty when President Pontowski had been to Bethesda Naval Hospital and, even if he had, the senior members of the staff who looked after the President and his family would have shuffled him off into a corner. "Relax," Washington told him. "Just be available if he wants to talk before Captain Smithson gets here. He's been called and is on his way but I doubt if he'll get here before the President." The nurse gave a tight smile as she thought about Smithson, the pompous Navy doctor who served as the President's personal physician. Smithson hated it when Pontowski dropped in on short notice to visit his wife. Personally, Washington would have preferred the young MOD as her own doctor.

"Is Mrs. Pontowski awake?" the doctor asked.

"She was asleep when I last checked with Margaret." Edith Washington glanced at the wall clock—it was 10:34 P.M. She ran her floor with military precision. "That was four minutes ago. Here"—she handed him Tosh Pontowski's file—"review this while I see if there's been any change." She hurried off to talk to the duty nurse sitting in Tosh's room.

The doctor appreciated the trust. Like everyone on the staff, he knew that the President's wife was being treated for lupus and was in serious condition, but only the few doctors and nurses who were directly concerned with her care ever saw her files. When the nurse came back, the doctor handed her the thick folder. "Does the President know how bad she is?" he asked.

"I don't know what Captain Smithson has told him," she answered, "but I suspect he knows." She took a deep breath and looked at the doctor. They both knew that Tosh was near death. "He comes every chance he can get and sits with her, even if she's asleep."

Three Secret Service agents stepped out of the elevator and scanned the hall. One spoke into his radio while the others opened doors and checked the rooms. One of the agents assigned to the floor appeared and the four talked quietly. The first agent spoke into his radio again and a few moments later, the elevator door opened and Pontowski walked out. He headed directly for the nurses station. "Hello, Edith," he said to the nurse. "How's Tosh tonight?"

"Resting comfortably, Mr. President," Washington said, heaving her bulk out of her chair. She was almost as tall as Pontowski.

Pontowski nodded and walked into his wife's room. "Hello, Margaret," he said to the on-duty nurse. "Mind if I sit in your chair?" The nurse rose and left, understanding the President wanted to be alone with his wife. She closed the door behind her. Pontowski sat down and buried his head in his hands. After a few moments, he lifted his head and relaxed back into the chair.

He ran the day's events through his mind, sifting the wheat from the chaff, focusing on the major problems, forcing them into perspective. Then he relaxed, able to renew his strength for what the next day held. Tosh, he thought, I don't know if I can do it without you. They won't tell me how long we have. Oh, I know that young doctor out there would if I asked him a direct question; so would Edith, but that wouldn't be fair to them.

The President sat there, hoping he would have another chance to tell his wife how much he loved her. He knew it wasn't necessary, but he wanted that chance. He had only known one other woman in his entire life and he had loved her as much as he loved his wife. Tosh also knew that. It amused him to think of the opportunities that had come his way to sleep with other, equally beautiful and worldly women. . . . They seemed to come with the territory. . . . But only two . . . the most important two . . . and he had no regrets.

A movement caught his attention. "Zack," Tosh said, reaching out to hold his hand, "go home and let these poor people get some rest."

"I love you," he whispered.

"I know."

1943

RAF Fairlop, Essex, England

"Warts on a bullfrog's ass," Zack mumbled to himself, dropping the newspaper he had been reading onto the table in front of him. He glanced around the reading room of the officers mess on RAF Fairlop, the base ten miles northeast of London where the Lysander had dropped him and Willi two days ago. He wondered when she would reappear.

"Sir?" the mess steward asked, not able to decipher the American's words.

"Oh, sorry," Zack answered. "Just feeling useless, hanging around like this."

The steward sympathized with him. The young flying officer had been cooling his heels for two days, waiting for a summons that had not come. Speculation around the mess had it that he was in some sort of trouble, up on a charge or awaiting a court-martial. Personally, the steward suspected that he was at RAF Fairlop for another reason, for while the American was anxious, he was not worried. The steward had long recognized the different mental states fighter pilots were subject to. Over the past two years he had seen a succession of squadrons rotate through Fairlop and had become very adept at gauging their moods. This particular officer, he judged, was quietly competent and not the type to get into trouble. "Lovely day outside," the steward told him, calculating that a walk and some fresh air would do the man good.

Zack took the hint and walked out of the two story red-brick building that served as the officers mess. He ambled by the sports field and headed for the main hangars. There, he walked through a hangar and studied the sleek fighter aircraft undergoing repairs or inspections. The 239 Squadron was flying the new Mustang, recently delivered from the States. "A real beauty, sir," a voice said behind him. The flight sergeant in charge of the hangar was standing there.

"I'd love to try one out," Zack said.

"You'll be Mr. Pontowski, yes?" the sergeant asked. It amazed Zack how everyone on base seemed to know who he was. He nodded a reply. "I don't think the CO would be too keen on that," the sergeant said, "but why don't you see how it fits." He motioned toward an open cockpit. Zack climbed over the left wing and settled into the cockpit. The flight sergeant was right behind him. "Do you fly fighters?"

"Mosquitoes." Zack studied the controls and instruments, liking the cockpit layout.

"Ah. Same engine, you know."

"I've heard she's fast," Zack said.

"Faster than a Spitty and she has a decent range. The chaps are giving the Luftwaffe some nasty surprises." For a few moments, Zack sat there, feeling pride in what his countrymen had built. The cockpit was nicely finished and functional. He tested the canopy and it slid smoothly back and forth onto the fuselage. The early Mustang did not have the clear bubble canopy that became one of its trademarks, but had a raised spine, much like the Spitfire. "The hood doesn't jam like on the Spitty," the sergeant explained. "An excellent machine."

"I've heard some of the pilots talk," Zack told him. "They seem to really like it." He heaved himself out of the cockpit. "Thanks for the tour, Flight. I hope you won't take offense, but I think I'll stick with the Mossie."

The sergeant escorted Zack out of the hangar and studied the pilot's back as he headed for the perimeter road that surrounded the huge triangular patch of grass that served as the runway. "Is that the Yank?" a fitter asked the flight sergeant.

The sergeant nodded an answer. "A decent type," he allowed. "All right," he bellowed, "get the finger out! We've got work to do."

Zack walked briskly around the perimeter, enjoying the light exercise. He paused for a few moments when he reached the southwestern end of the new concrete strip that stretched for four thousand feet parallel to the hangars. He watched as three of the new North American Mustangs taxied out and ran up, not using the concrete runway but taking off across the grass instead. Old habits die hard, he thought as the three made a formation takeoff, but that's the English. He watched with a professional interest as the three aircraft lifted smoothly into the air and then moved closer together, collapsing their formation into a tight vic. I guess they want to impress the locals, he laughed to himself. At least they no longer engage in that formation like they did in the Battle of Britain. He wondered why the British had been so slow to change tactics when it must have been painfully obvious that what they were doing wasn't working.

He walked more slowly now, past the dispersal pens and the squadron's crew huts on the far side of the field. From the activity going on inside the huts, it looked like the squadron was packing up for a move. That was not unusual as the RAF constantly moved its squadrons about, flying the aircraft and pilots out. Some of the maintenance personnel would follow but the rest of the base would stay behind, ready to accept the next squadron that would arrive shortly. Zack wondered when his squadron, 25, would be moved. They had been at Church Fenton since May of 1942. A long stay by RAF standards. That makes sense, he reasoned; move the aircraft to where they can work most effectively.

It took him an hour to make the circuit of the field. Finally, he was headed back for the officers mess, feeling more relaxed. A staff car he hadn't seen before was outside and the old tingling sensation brushed his senses. Willi was back and his brief vacation was over.

"You were told to wait here," Willi said when she saw him.

"What a pleasant surprise." He smiled, ignoring her reprimand. "You'd like it here—many nice people."

"Get your bag," she ordered. "We're leaving."

The mess steward suddenly appeared, carrying Zack's bag. "Here, sir," he said. "I took the liberty of packing when the young lady asked for you." He gave Zack a bland look that said, "Off to a dirty weekend, I take it."

Zack played the game to Willi's obvious discomfort. "Thank you. We really don't want to waste any time."

"Yes, I can imagine," the steward replied. Willi stomped out of the mess while Zack settled his bill and thanked the steward.

The driver loaded Zack's bag and they headed out the gate, turning toward London. "The house at Wimbledon," Willi told the driver.

A polite "Yes, miss" answered.

Zack arched an eyebrow. "Tennis this time?"

"Don't be stupid," she snapped.

A cold silence hung over them as the driver headed into London. This was the third time Zack had been to London and, as before, he found the city depressing. War had made the huge metropolis even more drab and dirty. He wondered if this was the fate of all big cities. Maybe Ruffy's right, he thought; we are going to have to change things after the war. He looked skyward, searching for relief in the clean and simple sky. Then he saw them and smiled. "I see you've taken precautions against sinking."

"Whatever are you talking about?" Willi asked.

He grinned at her and waved out the window. The sky over London was stacked with tethered barrage balloons. "You have so many balloons tied to the ground that your lovely little island is bound to stay afloat under the weight of all us Yanks."

The driver laughed. "I think he's right, miss." Willi looked out her side of the car. It did indeed look like London was suspended from under a canopy of bloated silver sausages, each anchored to the earth by a slender cable that stretched earthward from the underbelly like an umbilical cord.

"They serve a very real purpose," Willi told him, disapproval in her voice. Then she saw the humor of the sight. "You do have an odd way of looking at things," she said, her voice softer now.

"It makes things much more interesting," he told her.

"Miss," the driver said, "there's a diversion ahead." A traffic warden was standing in front of a barricade. "I'll ask for directions." He pulled up beside the woman who gave them precise directions around the area that had been bombed the night before. "It would be best to take the Waterloo Bridge," he explained and pulled back into traffic.

"Yes, do that," Willi said, giving Zack an odd look. She settled back into her seat and studied the American's face, waiting for a reaction. As they neared the River Thames, more and more American GIs packed the streets, moving aimlessly about.

"How long has it been since you were in London?" Willi asked.

"Eighteen months ago," he answered.

"It's changed since then."

"All the Yanks?" he asked.

"And the tarts."

Zack studied a number of women on the sidewalk mingling with the GIs. "My God! They can't all be . . ."

"Most of them are," she told him. "It's so bad that a decent woman can't walk the streets without having one of your countrymen wave two pounds in her face. It is not pleasant to see so many of our women turned into prostitutes."

"Where did they all come from?" Zack asked.

"They've always been here, sir," the driver said. "Before the war, the newspapers claimed there were over seventy-five thousand of them in London alone. We call 'em Piccadilly Commandos. Their ranks have swollen a bit and they are more open about it now. Probably does 'em good, open-air work and the like." Zack saw what he was talking about—standing back in an alley was a GI. A woman was kneeling in front of his open fly, her fist guiding him into her mouth. Zack's head jerked away from the sight and he stared into the car.

You're blushing! Willi thought. Then it came to her—he was also ashamed.

The driver pulled into the drive of a big house set well back from the road. He hurried around to open the door for them but Zack was already out of the car. "That was quite a maze you drove through," he said. "Thanks."

"Piece of cake," the driver said, beaming at the praise. He ignored Willi and handed Zack his bag.

Willi led the way into the house. A dumpy, nondescript woman came rushing up. Zack recognized her as the woman he had mistaken for Willi at the duke's country estate. "They got her out last night," she said. "She's here." Zack stood frozen in his tracks.

"Good," Willi told her. "But first we need to explain the drill to Mr. Pontowski." She motioned Zack into the lounge and sat him by the bay window overlooking a large, unkempt garden.

They were joined by a middle-aged, balding, round little man who had a pipe permanently stuck in his mouth. "We brought you here for two reasons," he said, not bothering to sit down. "First"—a big puff of acrid tobacco smoke swirled about his head like a fog—"we want you to identify Mrs. Bouchard—"

"I thought . . ." he stammered, interrupting him.

"Yes, her maiden name was Chantal Dubois," the man explained. He paused at the stricken look on Zack's face. "Can we continue? Good. We could have done this with a photograph. It is really the second task that is much more important. We want you to help us determine if she has been turned by the Germans . . . that is . . . we need to know if she might be a double agent."

"How do I do that?"

"By spending some time here, of course," he answered, puffing lustily at the pipe.

"Alone?"

"Impossible, old chap. Out of the question." More smoke.

"What happens if she has been turned?"

"Then we try to convince her to be turned again."

"And if you fail?" Zack asked.

"Don't think about that, old chap. Ready? Good." He waddled to the door leading into the next room and held it open. Zack stood up, seriously doubting if he could take the next step. He didn't have to. Chantal Dubois, now Mrs. Bouchard, walked in.

"*Mon Dieu,*" she whispered.

They were walking in the overgrown garden late the next day. Zack scuffled his feet, deep in thought as he and Chantal walked the path that led around the high walls. He glanced at the big house and saw Willi standing in an upstairs window watching them. He wanted to take Chantal's hand but thought better of it. So much had changed since he had last seen her.

"There is much you want to ask," Chantal said in German, still their best language for communicating.

"I wish I spoke French better," he told her. "I don't think it would sound so hostile, considering where we are."

"And I, English," she replied. "Your Miss Wilhelmina would not look at us with so much disapproval." She laughed at the thought of Willi's stern looks whenever they spoke together. Her laughter was clear and bell-like, echoing through his emotions. "It is strange that the English would give one of their children a German name. After all, she must have been born after the Great War. She looks so young, like you."

"I was born in November of 1918," Zack told her. "On the eleventh, to be exact."

"On Armistice Day," she said, a twinkle caught in her voice. She was doing some mental arithmetic. "I am two years older than you." She watched his face and then laughed at his discomfort. "Please, don't be so embarrassed. It is acceptable to be seen with an older woman."

"I seem to be in love with one." He felt much better for having said it.

"Oh." So much in that simple word—but no other reply. They walked in silence while Zack cataloged the way his world had changed. Chantal had matured during the seven months they had been apart. The months might as well have been years. Her age had exploded like a bombshell, and yet it changed nothing. Chantal had only become more beautiful—and confident. And she was married.

"We must talk," Chantal finally said, breaking the silence. She took him by the hand and guided him to a garden bench. "What is bothering you?" she asked, sitting him down.

"Your name," he managed to blurt out.

"Ah, that." Her voice had that flat, practical tone only the French can master. "It is really quite easy to explain." She smiled at him and he felt his legs go weak. "But matters like this are very difficult for Americans to understand. You remember Leonard?" Zack's chin came off his chest at the mention of the English agent who had helped them escape out of France. "His name," she said, ignoring his reaction, "or at least the name he was using, was Leonard Bouchard." She put her fingers to his lips, not letting him speak. "Leonard came back for me . . . " She spoke slowly, carefully choosing her words, and told how Leonard had returned to Zaragoza and waited until General Alphonse de Larida y Goya was done with her. She didn't bother to explain how the old man was nearly impotent and had taught her how to help him achieve an erection. Under the best of circumstances it never lasted long. "Goya became bored with me very quickly and threw me out— after taking my papers. Leonard decided that marriage was the quickest and safest way to create a new identity and get me out of Spain. So we were married."

"Was that necessary?" Zack asked.

"You Americans are so naive. You have no idea what it is like to be without papers in Europe." She told him how Leonard had bought a forged French passport for her that wouldn't stand up to rigorous scrutiny but was sufficient to get them through an official Spanish marriage ceremony. They had then taken the false passport and very real marriage certificate to the French embassy in Madrid where she applied for a legitimate French passport under her married name. A substantial bribe had been passed to facilitate matters and the consular official had issued her a real passport and French identity card with her new name. It had been amazingly easy.

"Did you . . . " He blushed brightly. "Ah . . . sleep with . . . "

Chantal held his hand in both of hers. "We were married and shared the same bed." Tears filled her eyes. "He was kind and gentle . . . a very good man. We returned to France and I helped him as a courier until he was picked up by the Gestapo. He had an L pill . . . " She explained how he had crushed the capsule between his teeth and died within seconds before the Germans could interrogate him. "I was picked up as a matter of routine by the French authorities and held for three days. They released me when my papers held up and did not turn me over to the Gestapo. I went into hiding to avoid the Germans until I could establish contact with the Resistance."

"Were you interrogated?"

"It was worse when we were captured by the Gestapo in Germany. The French only wanted to check my identity." She smiled. "I was most believable as a hysterical young bride."

Inside the house, Willi waited until the short fat man removed the headset he was wearing. The bench that Chantal and Zack were sitting on had been bugged. "What do you think?" she asked.

"It checks," he answered. "We can use her. Get rid of Pontowski." He puffed a blue haze into the room. They didn't see the couple gently kiss and embrace.

Late that same afternoon, the driver who had chauffeured Zack and Willi from Fairlop appeared at the door. Willi told Zack to pack. The driver would take him back to the RAF base. "You don't waste any time discarding people when you're done with them," Zack said. "Am I allowed to say good-bye?"

"Of course," Willi replied. She could understand why he was disturbed, perhaps angry. Still, she had her job to do and listened discreetly at a distance while Zack and Chantal spoke. It disturbed her that they were speaking German and she wished her pipe-smoking superior hadn't left for the day. He spoke fluent German.

"They're sending me back tonight," Zack said. Chantal said nothing and stared at the floor. "I was hoping we'd have some more time . . . " He didn't trust himself to say more. He touched her cheek and she raised her chin, looking directly at him. Her eyes were filled with tears. "I don't want to go," he finally managed.

"There is never enough time," she murmured. "Perhaps . . . after the war . . . "

"Yes, perhaps." They knew the dangers they faced. Neither had a good chance for survival.

"I love you," she said in French. The soft words seared his soul. "I wish we had one night." This last was in German.

"Maybe," he said, his mind racing, "there's a way we can arrange that. If we can get you out of the house and you had something else to wear . . . "

Chantal's eyes widened at the thought. She and Willi shared the same bedroom. "There is a spare uniform hanging in Wilhelmina's closet."

"Borrow it," Zack said. "Go down the back stairs, sneak out the rear, and wait at the gate by the road for the car to leave. I'll keep Wilhelmina occupied. Hopefully, she won't notice you're gone. Make this look like a real good-bye." Chantal gave a slight, almost imperceptible nod. Her lips brushed against his, sending him a promise of warmth and love. Then she pulled back, gave him a long look, and ran from the room.

Zack shot Willi a sad look and walked past her, heading for his room. "I'll pack now." Halfway up the stairs he paused, turned, and looked back down at her. "Is a little more time together out of the question?"

"There is a war on, Mr. Pontowski."

"I suppose that's the right answer. But I sometimes wonder what you English use for hearts. Carburetors?"

"Please hurry." Her face was impassive but something caught in her throat. Their good-bye had touched her and she understood his anger. It upset her to know that Chantal would probably suffer the same fate as most of their agents sent into France—capture, interrogation, and torture. The Gestapo would end her ordeal by marking her *"Nacht und Nebel—Rueckkehr Unerwuenscht,"* "Night and Fog—Return Not Required," and transporting her for execution.

"Time for an oil change, Miss Crafton. You're starting to sound gritty. That might make it difficult for you to slip around and use people. Don't worry, I'll be quick."

Do you think I enjoy this? she raged to herself. But she refused to be baited. Her mouth hardened into a tight line. She decided to wait where she was and not lower herself to his level or argue. But why did his words cut so deep? Before she realized it, he was back, bag in hand. "Ready," he said. "I don't want to delay the war."

"This is not called for," she said, following him out to the waiting car.

"Again, the right answer from one of my betters. I am put in my place." There was a power in his voice she had not experienced before and his words cut deep.

"Please take Mr. Pontowski away," she told the driver. "We are quite finished with him here." She stared at the departing car and walked back into the house, determined to keep her dignity intact, not thinking about Chantal.

"Bit of a row back there," the driver said as they drove away. "Never seen her so upset. Normally, she's a cool one." The American must have put her in her place, he decided.

"Can you stop here?" Zack asked. The driver braked, coming to a halt at the gate. Chantal stepped out of the bushes.

"Sorry, sir," the driver said. "Service personnel only. They'd have me on the peg."

Zack opened the rear door from the inside and saw that Chantal was carrying a uniform in her arms. "Not even for a Piccadilly Commando?" he asked. "She's got a uniform."

"Bloody hell," the driver said. "Are they callin' 'em up now? I've got to see this." Chantal climbed into the car and they headed for London. She quickly changed into the uniform she had taken from Willi's closet. The driver kept looking over his shoulder. "A FANY!" he roared with laughter. "I should have known that."

Chantal finished tying her shoes and looked up at him, a beautiful smile lighting her face. She told him how much she appreciated the lift—in French.

"And a bleedin' Frog to boot!" He shook with laughter and almost ran off the road. "Well, in for a penny, in for a pound." He thought for a few moments. "We'll never get 'er past a sentry. Where would you like to go?"

"I thought you had to take us to Fairlop?"

"I was detailed to make a run to Fairlop and I'll do that," the driver explained. "But my last orders were simply to take you 'away.' I was never told 'where' to take you. So, where would you like to go? Within reason, mind you."

"Someplace in London, I guess." He stuffed Chantal's clothes into his bag. "I need to do something with this."

"I can drop it off, sir," the driver offered.

"Can you leave it at the officers mess at Fairlop?" Zack asked. "That way, they'll know we're coming back."

The driver nodded and said he would do that. Then: "I know just the place. Grosvenor Square. Lots of foreign types around there. You'll mix right in." When he reached the square, he pulled to the curb. "If you need a room, try the Swan, a pub on Bayswater Road. My uncle's the publican. Say you know me and he might have something. Be there by closing."

"What is your name, monsieur?" Chantal asked in halting English.

"Peter Abbott," the driver said.

She gave him a kiss on the cheek as they piled out of the car. "*Merci,* Mr. Abbott."

The driver beamed and looked at Zack. "She's no Piccadilly Commando, sir." He sat at the curb until they had walked away. "Cor, that's a piece of nice," he muttered. Then: "I hope he makes it." The driver was thinking about when the war ended.

They wandered in the direction of Hyde Park, talking in low voices when no one could overhear them. The quiet conversation bound them more closely, making the moments more intimate. The weather had turned unseasonably cold and damp and they huddled together for warmth. Willi's well-tailored uniform fit Chantal perfectly except for the long pant legs. The cuffs kept coming unrolled. Finally, Chantal found a bench and rummaged through Willi's musette bag that she had also borrowed, looking for a sewing kit. She smiled and brought out a thin packet of condoms. She dangled it daintily from her thumb and forefinger. "I see our Miss Wilhelmina travels prepared," she smiled. Zack blushed furiously and she dropped it back into the bag. Then she found a sewing kit and quickly tacked up her pant cuffs. "Come, let's find something to eat. I'm famished." They started to walk again, searching for a restaurant and warmth.

Much to Zack's surprise, there were many restaurants, but all were jammed with people seeking a table. He was about to give up and go directly to the pub the driver, Abbott, had told them about when a familiar aroma caught his attention. "Chorizo," he said, following the smell into a narrow lane. "Mexican sausage," he explained. "I haven't had any in years."

"I don't doubt it," she said, wrinkling her nose up at the foreign smell. Soon they heard the sound of Spanish voices. "That's a strange accent," she said.

"It's Mexican, not Castilian," Zack said. He knocked at the narrow door where the smell was the strongest. A robust and heavily built woman in a black dress answered. Her hair was pulled back into a severe bun and she was wearing an apron. *"Señora, por favor,"* he stammered.

"I speak English," she said.

"Gracias," Zack said. "I smelled your sausage cooking and . . . "

"A gringo," she said, "wearing an English uniform who smells chorizo and who comes knocking." He could hear humor in her voice.

Chantal interrupted with a flood of Spanish. The woman smiled and motioned them into the kitchen. She and Chantal carried on an animated conversation for a few moments before the woman disappeared. "What did you say?" Zack asked, bewildered by it all.

"This is the back kitchen for the Mexican embassy," Chantal explained. "She's the cook. I told her we were married yesterday and you're on a three-day pass before leaving on a new assignment." Chantal waved her hand, flashing the wedding ring she still wore. "I told her the smell of her cooking made you very homesick."

"I didn't know you spoke Spanish."

"There are many things about me you need to learn." She came to him, sat on his lap and gave him a soft kiss. When she felt him respond, her mouth grew more hungry. Then she drew away and looked at him. "Many things," she whispered. "But I learned something from Leonard." Her voice low and sad. "We may only have this one moment to share. I don't want to lose it."

The cook came back. "Come," she ordered. "You'll eat with us." She led them into the servants dining room, where they joined four others at a large table. Within minutes, they were diving into a steaming platter of enchiladas, tamales, and beans spiced with hunks of chorizo. The cook kept smiling at them and commenting on Chantal's appetite. "That's good, that's good," she kept saying. Occasionally, she would ask Zack a question and learned he was from Oakland, California, and had developed a taste for Mexican food when he worked on a ranch during his summer vacations. That was also where he had picked up a smattering of Spanish.

Chantal watched as Zack slowly drew the five strangers to him; even the sour chauffeur joined the conversation and lingered over coffee. Since she spoke little English, she concentrated on their gestures and facial expressions. What is it about you that draws people so? she thought. Is it that crooked grin? The way it seems to wander all over your face? Perhaps it is those blue eyes. Yes, she decided, those eyes. Perhaps it's the way you listen to what people have to say. You listen much more than you talk and you are genuinely interested in what they do say.

Suddenly, she wanted him all to herself. "Zack," she said, claiming his attention, "we must go if we're to find a room." She almost laughed at the startled look on his face. Then it came to her—this American had never been with a woman before. That worried her. Was he some kind of prude? Americans were notorious for being quirky.

"Señora Pontowski," the cook said, "Perhaps I can arrange something." She barraged the chauffeur with a torrent of Spanish that was too fast for Chantal to fully understand.

The chauffeur nodded and stood up. "Please come with me. We must go now before the fog gets too thick." The cook told them to go and after a shower of good-byes and thanks, they were in an embassy car and headed for an unknown destination. They were surprised that a heavy mist had developed so early in the evening, casting a mantle of silence over the city. The drab ugliness of wartime London had changed into whispering, ghost-like shadows. Images would move and materialize into people or another car, slowly making their way to some unknown destination. "I like London like this," the chauffeur told them. "Besides, Jerry will stay home tonight."

The chauffeur drew up outside a small hotel and gave them a key. "Room three on the second floor," he said. "Leave the key on the table." For the first time he smiled. "We keep it for visiting guests who need privacy." Then he eased the car into the fog and disappeared. A curious rule of life had attached itself to Zack: Things are often given to people who can easily afford or do for themselves while other, much less fortunate people, are rarely given such presents. And this was one gift that was embarrassing him.

"There's a pub across the street," he said. "Care for a drink?"

Chantal took him by the hand and led him across the deserted street as the fog grew even more thick. They passed a couple locked in a passionate embrace in a dark doorway, barely visible as they walked by. Chantal gave his hand a squeeze and pulled him against the wall, pressing her body against his. She pulled his face down to hers. "I want to be like them," she whispered. "Nameless people lost in a fog, without a tomorrow and only now." She kissed him, her mouth open, her tongue hungry for his. She caressed his neck, her lips brushing against his ear. "I love you, Zack, always." It was a whisper, warming his soul, driving the fog of tomorrow away from them. "I knew from the first."

"The first?"

"When we were in the train at Düsseldorf and the bombs were falling all around us, your bombs." He could feel her body shake and drew her to him. "You would not move away from the window and I watched your face," she said. "You were afraid, but I remember thinking that you had to witness the death and destruction around you. You were horrified but I also saw compassion in your face for our enemy." She clasped his hand to her cheek and led him back across the street, into the fog, toward the hotel.

Her movement roused him from a deep slumber, the best sleep he had experienced since leaving the duke's country house. He watched her walk across the floor and throw the curtains back, letting the morning sun stream into the room and wash over her. She shimmered in the light, her nude body glowing. "Come back to bed," he said. She twisted in the light and looked at him, not smiling, just looking. Then she took the few steps back to the bed, her hips swaying and provocative, and slipped back under the blankets. She reached for him and stroked until he was hard.

"That didn't take long," she said and rolled on top of him. She drew her fingers up his side and rubbed the nipples on his chest. Then she kissed each one and nuzzled his neck. Then she worked her way down his body, her tongue tickling his navel. "It was sweet being the first one," she said, casting her eyes lower, eyeing her next objective.

"Was it that obvious? Ouch! Don't bite."

"You are so embarrassed about some things. I was afraid you might be one of those American prudes." Now she was working her way back up his body. "I'm glad you're not. But why?"

"Why what?" he asked, confused.

"Why was I the first?"

He pulled her up and rolled over, resting on his elbows, pinning her to the bed. "I don't really know why." His face was inches from hers as he looked inside himself for an answer. "Maybe it just didn't seem right before."

Her hands stroked his hips and she pressed her stomach against his. "It is unheard of that a man should save himself for the marriage bed. But I'm glad." Her hand wedged between their stomachs as she reached down and guided him as her legs lifted to draw him into her.

"I love you," he said, never so sure of his feelings and how right it was.

The bus dropped them at the gate to Fairlop and the sentry on duty would not let them enter until after he had made a phone call. Then he waved them through. "Sir," he said, pointing at a low building. "You're wanted at Station Headquarters."

Zack gave Chantal what he hoped was an encouraging grin as they neared the entrance. The driver, Peter Abbott, was standing by his staff car. "I think they're expecting us," he told her. "Good morning, Peter," Zack called. "I hope we haven't caused you too much trouble."

"Not too much." Abbott grinned. "Other than taking a strip out of my backside." He pointed inside. "In there, sir. Never seen 'er ladyship so worked up. He's taking it calmly enough, though. I'll take you in."

The civilian from the house at Wimbledon was sitting on a couch in the room when Abbott opened the door. He glanced up from the newspaper he was reading, took a big puff on his pipe, and turned the haze in the room a darker shade of blue. He laid his paper down but didn't move. Willi came to her feet with a forced, icy composure. "Just what do you think you were doing?" She stared at him, expecting an answer. Zack only returned her look and said nothing. It made her even more angry. "This," she spat at him, "raises the question of her reliability."

"She has a name," Zack said. "Chantal, in case you've forgotten, and she is in the same room with us."

"We may not be able to use her now," Willi said, determined to make her point. "Of all the utter irresponsible . . ."

"She's been used enough," Zack said. "Hopefully, you'll be decent about it and not send her back." He couldn't keep from smiling at the stunned look on Willi's face. "I owe you an apology for last night," he added. "I had to distract you so Chantal could slip out."

"You succeeded," she admitted, ice still in every word. She didn't like how easy it had been for him to manipulate her . . . them. Damn, she fumed to herself, it's his voice. He uses it like a weapon. "Still, that doesn't change the trouble you've caused . . . I just don't see of what use she can be now." Then it came to her. The American had planned it from the start. He had no intention of letting SOE use Chantal as an agent and had deliberately planted a seed of doubt as to her reliability. Not enough to get her in trouble, but enough to cast suspicion in their minds.

"Not to worry, Wilhelmina," the man on the couch said, heaving his bulk into a standing position. "It all depends on what we need her for, does it not? Come, my dear." He held the door open for Chantal, gave her an encouraging smile, and walked out into the hall.

Chantal turned to Zack and touched his lips with a finger, silencing him. "*Adieu,* my love." Her lips brushed his and she followed the man out the door.

"Is she that valuable?" Zack asked. There was no answer.

EIGHT

The Golden Triangle, Burma

Heather was working in her office when Chiang and James, his majordomo, knocked and entered. She was wearing a businesslike straight gray skirt, white silk blouse, and for all appearances was the successful corporate executive. "James tells me," Chiang said, "that the arrangements are completed."

"I think," Heather replied, her voice full of confidence, "that we have done everything we can to care for our guests." She spread a map across her desk for Chiang and pointed out the various houses and bungalows in the nearby village that she had appropriated for their "guests." "I've grouped them into separate areas and arranged all the necessary transportation."

"It is a most clever solution," James added. As Chiang's chief of security, he had been worried about allowing such a large group of armed men inside their defenses. One group, sensing a temporary advantage, might decide to dispose of their competition in short order. But Heather had housed the leaders with a small number of their personal bodyguards in the compound under Chiang's immediate protection and then separated the others in the village.

"The entertainment," Heather continued, "has been arranged

264

and the chefs will arrive the day before." She had saved the best for last. "The, ah, escorts are here and in isolation. They have all been given a thorough medical examination and we are waiting for the test results to be sure none have AIDS."

"You have done well," Chiang said, "considering how critical this meeting is to the Consortium." He had made it abundantly clear that the Japanese and Colombian-German ringleaders who were coming to the meeting were vital to the new enterprise he was putting together. He estimated that if he could get them to agree to join with him, they would control between 60 and 70 percent of the world's drug traffic.

But there were dangers. If the men sensed any weakness on his part, they would brutally eliminate Chiang's organization and take over his operation. Yet, the combination of money and control flowing from the Consortium held the promise of real power on a global scale, and that outweighed the dangers.

"Now," he said, "please undress."

Heather was confused and embarrassed. They had been discussing business and James was still in the room. What had changed? She slowly shed her clothes until she was standing in front of the two men only wearing her shoes. "Turn around and bend over," Chiang ordered. She did as he commanded, her eyes fixed straight ahead while he walked up to her. She felt his hands spread her buttocks.

"Most interesting," James said, inspecting the tattoo of the coiled snake. "At least one of our guests will be fascinated by this." She started to cry.

"Please excuse us," Chiang said. James gave a bland nod of his head and retreated out of the office. Chiang led her to a couch, dropped his pants and sat down, pulling her onto his lap. "There, there," he said, kissing and wiping her tears away as he entered her. "Daddy will take care of you."

Samkit found Heather curled up in the corner of the couch, shaking and sobbing incoherently. She ran into the bathroom, moistened a face cloth, and snatched up a bath towel before sitting down and taking her into her arms. She covered the girl and bathed her face, speaking softly and trying to calm her.

"It was horrible," Heather gasped between sobs. "He was like my father when I was eleven. I don't understand. I thought I was special to him." Slowly, she recounted all that she had done to help Chiang with his Consortium.

"He's using you," Samkit said, all traces of her pidgin English gone, "like he has used the others."

Heather clung to the woman, numb, drained of emotion. Her life had come full circle.

The lighted windows in her hooch hurried Samkit up the steps to the small bungalow she called home. Weariness from the long day slipped away as she entered the single room and saw her son. She made a graceful *wai* as a serene feeling captured her. "My humble home is yours," she said, not looking directly at him, not caring that their connection might be exposed. Her son was with her.

The Buddhist monk motioned her to a seat, not touching his mother. "It was necessary that I come," he said. "We have an ally." The heavyset German anthropologist stepped out of a shadowy corner. "You can trust him."

"How will I explain his presence?" she asked.

"You are still a beautiful woman, Mother, and he is older than you. He can be your lover."

"That is acceptable," Samkit said. "I have much to tell you." She recounted all that Heather had told her. Then the monk rose and disappeared into the night. She glanced at the stranger and started to cook them dinner.

Pope Air Force Base, North Carolina

The Pave Low MH-53 helicopter approached Pope Air Force Base from the south. Gillespie called the tower for an approach and landing and was cleared in perpendicular to the main runway. He hovered over the grass, not crossing the Active until the tower cleared him to taxi to the ramp. He eased the cyclic forward and, firmly touching the ground, taxied in. Ground control cleared him to Base Ops and he guided the twenty-ton goat down the taxipath until he parked in front of the canopy that marked the entrance to Base Ops. The crew shut down the two turbo shaft engines and the six-bladed main rotor spun down, its incessant beating fading away.

"Cheated death again." Gillespie grinned at his copilot.

"There's our passenger," the copilot said, pointing at the English Army officer standing under the canopy.

Gillespie grunted and turned toward the cargo compartment. "Colonel Mackay, I think your exchange officer is waiting for you."

E-Squared released his lap belt and made his way forward. "Smooth landing, kid." He grinned. "Why don't we hit the greasy spoon for something to eat while they refuel? A touch of civilization would be nice." After exercising with Delta for three days in the field, the idea appealed to Gillespie.

"Why did you get tapped for this one?" Gillespie asked.

E-Squared shrugged. "I guess they wanted the Air Force represented. Mackay seems to think this guy is a high roller." They jumped off the ramp at the end of the cargo compartment and headed for Mackay and their passenger.

"He's only a captain," Gillespie said.

"How can you tell?"

"The three pips on his epaulet," Gillespie told him. "That's the insignia for a captain in the English Army—I think." They walked up to Mackay, who introduced them to the Englishman. Neither of the two Air Force officers were impressed with the man. He was nondescript, of average height and on the stocky side. The only feature that distinguished him were his cold blue-gray eyes. He wore a beige beret with an unusual device—it looked like a dagger with wings—and his khaki service dress uniform had been tailored to give him a well-turned-out appearance.

"Major Eberhard," Mackay said, "I'd like you to meet Captain Peter Woodward." Woodward snapped an open-handed salute. E-Squared returned it with his normal awkward wave that he tried to pass off as a salute. "Captain Woodward," Mackay continued, "this is Captain Gillespie, our pilot." Again, salutes were exchanged and Gillespie wondered why Mackay was being so correct in his introductions. This guy is only a captain, Gillespie reminded himself.

"We'll be about forty-five minutes," Gillespie explained, "while we refuel and refile. Then it's a two-hour flight to Entebbe."

The Englishman looked puzzled. "Entebbe," Mackay explained, "is the name we've given to our training site."

Gillespie and E-Squared excused themselves to take care of the paperwork and get something to eat. "You ever see that badge on his beret before?" Gillespie asked.

E-Squared shook his head. "He doesn't look like much to me."

"Yeah," Gillespie agreed.

They discovered how wrong they were the next night.

* * *

The Pave Low MH-53 approached the clearing from the south, but this time no radio clearance was needed to land. The noise split the night air, and like a giant wasp, the helicopter settled into the small landing zone, its whirling, thirty-six-foot-long blades barely clearing the surrounding trees. The ramp at the rear of the aircraft was down and, before the wheels touched, twelve men piled out and disappeared into the dark, securing the perimeter. Then Mackay stepped off the back and waited. Quickly, the men reported in—the landing zone was secure. Gillespie cut the engines and silence came down. Gillespie, his copilot, and flight engineer ran a checklist, cocking the aircraft for a quick engine start and takeoff. Then they waited, ready to crank engines and launch on a moment's notice.

E-Squared stuck his head onto the flight deck. "I mean to tell you, boy, flying this thing at night is an unnatural act. What do you tell your mother you do for a living?"

"Something respectable," Gillespie answered, "like playing piano in a whorehouse."

"I've been meaning to ask you about that," the Combat Talon pilot said. "Is that where you got the hicky?"

Gillespie touched the square bandage on the side of his neck. "It's not a hicky."

"You consorting with vampires then?"

"In a manner of speaking."

"The boy's becoming a pree-vert," E-Squared chortled as he disappeared out the back of the plane. He felt a definite urge to put his feet on solid earth. He didn't like being an observer and would have preferred piloting his own plane, something respectable like an MC-130. But Colonel Mallard had insisted that he be familiar with every detail of the training going on with Delta and to keep him informed. He joined Mackay and checked his watch. "They're late," he said.

"They've got a twenty-minute window to rendezvous for the extraction," Mackay explained. "We're only two minutes into it." The colonel tried to hide the worry in his voice. The exercise he had laid on was not that difficult. A team was to bring two individuals, one friendly and one a hostage, through a heavily wooded area at night to rendezvous for a helicopter extraction. Woodward had volunteered to be the hostage and Sergeant Dolores Villaneuva, the friendly. Mackay was now worried because he had told the British captain to "throw them a curve" and Woodward had allowed that he "would love to oblige." Mackay found some comfort in the fact that Kamigami was part of the team.

"Hell," Mackay said, more to himself than E-Squared, "Kamigami can carry him if he has to." But there was no trace of the team and the radios were silent.

Seven minutes later, Mackay monitored a single radio transmission; something about closing in on the hostage. Then silence. Mackay's worry increased—captors don't normally "close in" on their hostage. A slight movement in the low brush near the helicopter caught Mackay's attention. He motioned E-Squared to cover and moved away from the helicopter. Woodward stepped out of the brush and walked directly over to Mackay. "What in the hell happened?" Mackay asked.

"Incredibly loose security on the march," Woodward explained, "so I escaped. But Sergeant Villaneuva was spot on. She slowed us down as expected."

Mackay gritted his teeth. Well, he had told Woodward to throw them a curve. "How did you penetrate our perimeter?"

"One of your chaps was making a bloody great noise so I convinced him that he was dead."

"Is he okay?"

"Of course. I trussed him up. He should work himself free in a few minutes."

The radios came alive as the landing zone security guard cleared the missing team through the perimeter. Kamigami's huge bulk was the first to materialize out of the darkness as he slowly made his way to the helicopter. When he joined the group, they could smell dampness. More of the men came straggling in. Many flopped to the ground, exhausted and bruised from the chase through the woods. The last of the team came in, carrying Villaneuva. "Thanks for the lift, fellas," she told the men brightly. It was the first time she had been in the field with Delta and was enjoying herself.

"Believe me," came the reply, "it wasn't our pleasure."

"What happened, Sergeant Major?" Mackay asked.

Kamigami didn't answer at first as he considered his answer. "Captain Woodward managed to escape," he explained.

"Like fuckin' Houdini," a voice from the ground said.

"And we couldn't recapture him," Kamigami continued, ignoring the comment. "At one point, I thought I had him trapped against a river, but without backup from my team"—he paused for effect—"I was forced to take an unscheduled swim." A stunned silence settled over the men. They could not believe what they were hearing.

"Swim?" Mackay asked.

"To be exact, sir," the big sergeant said, "Captain Woodward threw me in the river."

Mackay stifled a smile, remembering another patrol in Malaysia. "He does have a penchant for that." Mackay made a mental note to ask Kamigami in private how the captain had managed such a feat. It was a question the rest of Delta Force would be asking before too long.

"He was threshing around a bit," Woodward said.

Kamigami said, "He told me I was making too much bloody noise and wouldn't let me out until I promised I'd give him a head start."

"Couldn't let the chap drown," Woodward allowed.

"He was holding on to me, sir," Kamigami admitted. "Otherwise, the current would've carried me away."

"And you negotiated with him?" Mackay said, now totally incredulous. Kamigami's legendary reputation was taking a severe hit.

"Yes, sir," Kamigami replied. "It seemed like a good idea at the time since no one on the team had kept up during the chase." That answered Mackay's unspoken question as to what had happened to the rest of the men.

E-Squared couldn't help himself. "Sounds like you got in over your head, Sergeant Major." No one laughed.

"I think," Mackay said, "that we had better find the hamhock Captain Woodward tied up. I don't think he'll work himself free." He detailed two men to follow Woodward and they set off while the security guard pulled in and the men climbed aboard the helicopter. Mackay pulled Kamigami aside. "What the hell happened out there, Sergeant Major? Why did you let him get away with it?"

"Sir, no one let him get away with anything. He made it happen." There was respect in his voice.

"And what does all this prove?" Mackay snapped, frustrated with the turn of events. "And just what message do you think the men are getting?"

"It proves that there's someone out there who's a lot better than us. The message is that we"—Kamigami stressed the "we"—"have to get better. Fast." The last word did not need emphasis.

* * *

How many times have we been over this, Mackay thought. He was sitting in the command tent at Entebbe reviewing the plan named Operation Loose Red with Mallard and Trimler. He was impressed with the two colonels and how they worked together and had mastered every detail of the planned operation on Chiang's compound. Mackay glanced around the tent, trying to gauge the reactions of the other men who had gathered for a last review of the plan before they took it to Cagliari. The three Air Force pilots seemed more bored than concerned and Mackay could understand their feelings. Their part was uncomplicated and straightforward, which, in his opinion, was good.

The plan called for helicopters to insert two assault teams at separate landing zones. The LZs were set well back from Chiang's compound so the helicopters could escape detection by Chiang's air defense net. The teams would then move independently into position for the attack. The first assault team, Fastback, would be responsible for freeing the hostages while the other team, Bigboot, blasted holes in the wall and kept Chiang's security forces occupied. Although Colonel Trimler seemed satisfied, a nagging worry keep itching at Mackay, demanding a scratching. Rather than fight it, he decided to ask Kamigami a direct question. "Sergeant Major, do you have any reservations?"

"As long as we can deliver maximum surprise with maximum violence, it will work," Kamigami replied. "But to get the violence, we got to surprise them. The closest any chopper can get to the compound without being detected by radar is about twenty miles and that means Fastback and Bigboot have to make long overland infiltrations to get under Chiang's air defenses. Plus we have to do it in the rain to sneak past his observation and listening posts on the ground. That's going to take time. The longer we're on the ground, the greater the chance for discovery. Then once we attack, I figure it's got to be by the clock—in and out fast."

Mackay glanced at Peter Woodward, trying to gauge his reaction to what Kamigami had said. It was the first time the British officer had seen the entire plan and Mackay wanted his opinion. While he had never come to terms with the vicious streak he had seen in Woodward during the interrogation of the three pirates in Malaysia, Mackay needed a coldblooded bastard like Woodward to help him. Woodward arched an eyebrow at him. "Captain Woodward," Mackay said, "we would appreciate any comments you might have to offer."

"Beat the clock and it should work," Woodward said.

The Executive Office Building, Washington, D.C.

Heads turned and stared as Mazie Kamigami led the three officers through the halls of the Executive Office Building to the secure conference room where they would meet with the national security adviser. There was a brief pause when she held the door open and the men waited for her to enter first. She sighed and waddled in ahead of them. Once inside, Mackay could see the northeast corner of the White House through the windows. "Well, Colonel," Mazie said, "welcome back."

"Not for long I hope," Mackay said. "By the way, your father sends his best and says he hopes to be in town this weekend."

Mazie gave another mental sigh—that was her father, a man of few words and more than willing to let others pass messages on to her. Family togetherness by rumor, she thought. Nothing had changed. She settled into a chair. "You ready to sell it to the boss?"

"Loose Red is ready to go," Mackay assured her.

"Where do you get these names?" she asked.

"The Pentagon has a computer that spits out random names for exercises or operations so the name won't serve as a tip-off to the objective."

"Oh, like Desert Storm or Just Cause."

"Well," Mackay admitted, "sometimes politics does get involved."

National Security Adviser Cagliari walked in. "Good morning," he said, sitting down. "What do you have?"

"Good morning, sir," Mazie replied. She introduced Mallard and Trimler to her boss. "The situation with Chiang is still very fluid," she told him. "The DEA has evidence that the Colombian and Japanese drug cartels are forming an alliance with Chiang called the Consortium. The DEA estimates that between the three, they will control over half of the world's heroin production along with all the major distribution nets and approximately seventy percent of the cocaine traffic."

"Anything from Willowbranch?" he asked.

"Willowbranch confirms it and reports that the leaders of the two cartels are scheduled to meet with Chiang in his compound in the near future. No firm date as of yet." She went over the details of the latest report.

"What an opportunity," Trimler said, unable to contain himself. "We initiate the attack when they are there."

"Chiang has some formidable resources available to him," Mallard reminded Trimler.

"True," Trimler shot back, all eagerness. "But look at his guests. If I were Chiang, I'd have my forces more aligned for internal security so they would feel secure from each other. We go in and there will be so much confusion as to who's doing what to who that we will be well inside their reaction cycle. By the time they get it sorted out, we're out of there. Hell"—Trimler grinned—"we might even be able to service a few of the bastards."

"What does that mean?" Mazie asked.

"The good colonel means," Mackay explained, "that it is an opportunity to put a well-placed bullet into a few brains."

"Anything else new?" Cagliari asked.

"Yes, sir," Mazie said. "We received confirmation that the earring found on the body thrown over the embassy's wall in Bangkok was Heather Courtland's. This is getting very weird. Does Chiang want us to know that he has Heather?"

"Chiang is one the most devious and clever bastards that I have run across," Cagliari said. "My best guess is that he's inputting noise into the system. Treat it that way."

" 'Noise'?" Mallard asked.

Now it was Mazie's turn to explain. " 'Noise' is information that masks the important facts."

"I see, the fake stuff," Mallard said.

"Nothing fake about it at all," Mazie told him. "Because noise is valid, we have to analyze it to determine if it's relevant. That's what makes this job so frustrating—too much noise. In this case, we're going to ignore it."

"Let's cut to the chase," Cagliari told them. "I want to see what you've come up with to rescue Heather Courtland."

Twenty minutes later, Cagliari made his decision. "I think we need to take this to the President."

The men and Mazie were standing behind their chairs in the White House's Situation Room when Pontowski entered. Leo Cox, his chief of staff, introduced Mallard and Trimler before Mackay presented the plan called Loose Red. When he was finished, Pontowski said nothing and stared at the large-scale map Mackay had used for his presentation.

"He's got to be expecting us," Pontowski finally said. "Without surprise this could backfire and turn into a disaster." He paused, recalling the lessons of Eagle Claw, the abortive attempt to rescue the fifty-two Americans held hostage in the United States embassy in Teheran. Eagle Claw had spelled the end of the Carter administration. Then he remembered another raid years before: a raid that no one in this room had ever heard of. Was he about to repeat history? So be it, he thought. But it saddened him that the crisp, clear call to duty that he had felt before was missing.

"How is Special Operations Command progressing with their plan to rescue the hostages?" the President asked.

"It's ready," Cagliari answered. "As expected, it's a massive attack with Stealth fighters leading the way to take out the radars and surface-to-air missiles followed by a vertical envelopment."

"If we go in like that, the hostages will be dead by the time we get to them," Cox predicted.

Pontowski made his decision. "We'll do this one by the book. Place Loose Red under the operational control of USSOCOM." He rose to leave. Then another thought came to him. "I would like to change the name Loose Red to Operation Jericho." He disappeared out the door.

"And the walls came tumbling down," Mallard quipped.

"That's probably what he was thinking of," Cagliari replied.

Mazie sat frozen to her chair, trying to calm the rolling emotions that beat at her, threatening to break like a tidal wave over the breakwaters that kept her safe. Oh, Pop, she thought to herself, matching a face to the cutting edge that was now called Jericho.

1943

RAF Church Fenton, Yorkshire, England

I've lost her, Zack thought as he poked at the unrecognizable mess on his plate. He ignored Ruffy, whose appetite never failed him, not even when the cook had committed an unspeakable crime on their food, shoved his plate away, excused himself, and left the mess. He walked outside and shivered in the cold night air as he ambled toward the operations building. The dark sense of loss that plagued his spare moments was back. "Hold on," Ruffy called, catching up with him. "Still thinking about her?" he asked.

"I can't seem to think about anything else," Zack admitted. Unbidden, the image of Chantal standing in front of the window as the morning sunlight washed over her bare body came back, driving a sharp ache into his chest.

"This will all come to an end and you'll find her again." Ruffy was an incurable optimist. "At least it hasn't affected your flying." He gave Zack a light slap on the shoulder, trying to encourage him. They walked into the briefing room and the gloom that had been hanging over him vanished. The routine of operations, the building tension of a mission, and the immediacy of combat had all asserted their priority as they went about the business of preparing for another Intruder mission.

Their squadron commander was waiting for them. "Well, this is it," he told them. "You two have been posted to Four-eighty-seven Squadron at Sculthorpe."

"Isn't that a New Zealand squadron?" Zack asked.

"Correct. The Kiwis need some experience to bring them up to snuff in the kite. You're it. You'll take your Mossie with you to bring them up to full strength. Four-eighty-seven Squadron has been made part of Two Group, which falls under the command of the new Allied Second Tactical Air Force. You lucky buggers are going to have a serious go at Jerry." He started to leave but halted at the door. "Jones is on leave and has offered you *Romanita* for tonight—since this is your last with us."

"That's decent of him," Ruffy said, truly impressed with the favor.

"Don't prang. The fitters would mutiny. Don't need that."

The briefing was routine and the weather over their area and the latest disposition of enemy defenses occupied most of their attention. This was their seventeenth Intruder, the name given to the night missions where a lone Mosquito was assigned to patrol an area over occupied Europe with the single purpose of attacking enemy night fighters on or over their own airfields. By repeatedly going back to Soesterberg in the Netherlands, they had become intimately familiar with the area and were experts at disrupting German night operations against RAF bombers. They had spread so much *Moskitopanik* around that the Germans were forced to take off by flying a few feet above the ground until they were far away from their airfield. Only then could they climb to search for the bombers flying overhead on their way to targets deep in Germany. The German pilots said that by flying so low during a night takeoff they automatically earned a Knights Cross.

The two ground crew were waiting for them when they reached *Romanita* and, as usual, the aircraft was in immaculate condition and ready to go. Engine start and takeoff were routine and they were soon well out over the North Sea, skimming under the bottom of a cloud deck at five hundred feet. For reasons that totally escaped him, Zack was always relaxed during this part of a mission. The waiting tension had shredded with the satisfying feel of the wheels breaking free of the runway, and a comfortable warmth engulfed him. Perhaps it was the smooth-running machine that surrounded him like a cocoon that did it. Unlike the Beau-fighter, the Mosquito was a warm aircraft, its heater worked fine, and he did not have to bundle up against the cold. Or maybe it was the ease of handling the aircraft, its controls responsive and alive to his touch. Without a doubt, the Merlins, those magnificent V-12 engines with their unforgettable, heart-throbbing roar, made him feel secure. The throttle quadrant did not require the huge jabs that the Beaufighter demanded. A slight movement, and the engines responded with a crispness that made him think of a superb polo pony charging after a ball.

But the aircraft did have its vices, like all high-strung and beautiful ladies, and a stall was an invitation to disaster. The aircraft simply fell out of the sky. It was not very stable and he had to tend the stick constantly. But he liked that, for instability was the handmaiden of maneuverability, which was one of the Mossie's virtues. He chewed on that seeming contradiction. Maybe, he thought, there's a price to be paid for every virtue. No wonder men named their aircraft after women. What a dumb tradition! he laughed to himself; the Mossie was only a flying collection of wood, glue, screws, metal, and ideas. Still, he loved the aircraft for what it was.

This is a strange way to live, he thought. Here we are at a few hundred feet above the sea, flying below a cloud deck, ready to go about the deliberate business of killing other men. Yet he had never felt more free of responsibility. Other men had assumed the burden of ordering him and Ruffy into the killing arena and taken the weight from his shoulders. He was an agent of their will and his only duty was to deliver death and destruction on the enemy. His only concern was his and Ruffy's survival. He did not even have the responsibility for the fate of his targets, for if he didn't fly the mission, someone else would. It was a dangerous, but very simple, uncomplicated life.

So far, he had lived a charmed existence and he fully expected to live through the war. What then? What would he do when the world returned to normal? Or could it ever resume its old, ordered ways? What would happen after the victory parades and shouting died down? Would he ever find Chantal again? He forced that thought away, back into its own hidden niche.

"There," Ruffy said, pointing to a faint fluorescent line of surf in the dark below them, the coast of Holland, bringing Zack back to the job at hand. They threaded a narrow corridor between The Hague and Rotterdam that the Dutch Underground had reported to be relatively free of German defenses, skirted to the south of Gouda, and headed for the town of Doorn, looking for the big house where Kaiser Wilhelm II, the emperor of Germany during World War I, had lived in exile until he died in 1941. The Germans had made it into a shrine after they occupied the Netherlands in 1940, but the Dutch Underground used it to send messages to the RAF. Zack racked the Mosquito up into a sixty-degree pylon turn as they overflew the town. The distinctive sound of the Merlins announced they were British. A light blinked twice at them from an attic window of House Doorn, the Kaiser's shrine. The Dutch caretaker who lived in the attic was a member of the underground and was the end destination of a telephone relay. "Set course zero-one-zero," Ruffy said. "Jerry's taking off to the east tonight."

Zack turned to the new heading and rooted the airspeed indicator on three hundred miles per hour. By going at exactly five miles per minute, one mile every twelve seconds, it was easier for Ruffy to navigate. They were less than one minute away from Soesterberg. They had no black boxes that could replace the Mark I eyeball or the intimate knowledge the two men had of the area and how the Germans operated. A flicker of light caught Zack's attention—an aircraft's exhaust. It was little more than a short stub of blue flame knifing the darkness. "Tallyho," Zack called over the intercom. His hands flew over the controls, automatically configuring the Mosquito for combat: supercharger switch to Auto, increase rpm to 3,000, set the throttles to climbing gate, pull the boost control cut-out. Ruffy hit the gun master switch, making sure it was down. "Guns are hot," he told Zack who was concentrating on their target. They were less than fifty feet above the ground, the airspeed indicator touching 330.

A shadow materialized in front of them and instantly grew into a JU-88 night fighter. "Oh, shit!" Zack shouted as he yanked back on the stick. They ballooned over the Junkers in an overshoot.

"He's turning into us!" Ruffy shouted.

"Got the bastard," Zack grunted. He barrel rolled, arcing over the German's turn, and disappearing into the low cloud deck above them. He continued the roll and sliced down out of the overcast, anticipating the German's position. He guessed correctly and slid in behind the Junkers. His thumb brushed the twenty-millimeter trigger and the four barrels mounted under the nose flashed. The heavy shells ripped into the aft fuselage and walked forward across the greenhouse canopy. The crew were dead before they hit the ground.

"We took a hit," Ruffy said. "We may have picked up some frag when he came apart."

Zack headed to the south and checked the instruments. "Port engine temperature gauge is climbing."

"Radiator must have packed up," Ruffy said. Rather than risk blowing the engine from an overheat, Zack shut it down. He could always restart it in an emergency. They headed for home on one engine, maintaining 200 mph until well out to sea. They had been over the Netherlands less than thirty minutes, destroyed an enemy aircraft, killed two men, and caused the Germans to stop all operations out of Soesterberg for the next two hours. Now all they had to do was to convince the two young men who tended *Romanita* on the ground that they hadn't damaged her unnecessarily.

"Sandringham should be to starboard," Ruffy said. Zack did a quick check of his blind-flying instruments, looked out the windscreen, and tried to find the royal family's country home in the thick haze. No luck. "Remember what the Old Man said," Ruffy reminded him. The station commander at Church Fenton had sent them on the way to their new assignment with a simple warning, "They'll have your guts if you fly over the place." Both men tried to find a recognizable landmark on the ground but the flat Norfolk countryside lacked sharp definition. The weather was not cooperating. "On the nose!" Ruffy warned him. A large multistory stone house was directly in front of them. Zack rolled the Mosquito onto its left wing and flew around the palace.

"I expected walls and a moat," Zack said. "Well, at least we know where we are." They headed due east and entered the circuit around RAF Sculthorpe, waiting for clearance to land.

"They'll be watching us," Ruffy said. "Make this a good one." The Mossie had one very unpleasant vice: It swung badly to the left on landing and new pilots were watched closely to see how they tamed that particular tendency.

Zack gave a noncommittal grunt and turned final. "Lots of runway," he said. He eased the throttles back and touched down at 120 on the main gear and then dropped the tail wheel for a smooth and perfectly controlled landing.

"That wasn't what I had in mind," Ruffy grumbled. Neither did their new squadron commander and he dispatched a car to pick them up at the dispersal where they parked their Mosquito. They barely had time to retrieve their bags from the bomb bay before they were hustled into the car.

"Bad day to show up," the driver told them. "Squadron Leader Bonder is right brassed with some wallahs up from London. He can't do anything about them but say, 'Yes sir, yes sir.' Now you, on the other hand, he can do something about."

"We probably flew too close to Sandringham," Zack told him.

"We never get a complaint from Sandringham," the driver replied. "Occasionally, they'll ring up with a 'Good show.' It'll be the landing, I expect." Ruffy gave Zack an I-told-you-so look.

Squadron Leader Bonder came right to the point when they reported in. "RAF flying techniques are very specific and not subject to debate, at least not while you are under my command." His voice was strained and high-pitched. "Three-point landings are required and you will follow standard procedures."

"Sir," Zack protested, "I always make a three-point landing on short runways, but you've got lots of runway here and—"

"Mr. Pontowski," Bonder interrupted, "I'm fully aware that a rumble landing with touch-down on the main gear is one way to handle the Mossie's wretched tendency to swing. But I thought I made myself quite clear that the rules are not open to question."

"Sir, are those rules man-made or God-made?" Zack asked.

"In your case," Bonder replied, "they are quite celestial." He was about to say more when the telephone rang, its insistent ring cutting him short. He snatched it out of the cradle. "Bonder here," he said. It was not the call he had been expecting and for the next few moments he listened. "Why, yes, thank you very much," he said before hanging up. He relaxed into his chair and gave them a long look. "That was Colonel Denham, one of the king's equerries, a decent chap. The king saw you maneuver to avoid Sandringham and said it was a "good show." He paused, deep in thought. "Now what am I going to do with you? Look"—

his tone had changed and was much more relaxed—"I'm having trouble with some types up from London. We're flying an op for them that must be done their way . . . not the way I'd have gone about it."

Zack understood immediately; their squadron commander was sweating out the return of his men and aircraft from a mission he did not want to fly. "Right then," Bonder said. "From now on its a three-pointer during the day and save landing on the mains for at night—when nobody can see you." After a slight pause he added, "That's the way most of the lads do it."

The telephone rang again and he grabbed it. This time it was the call he was expecting. He slammed the phone down and rushed out the door. They followed him to the tower where a large group of men were waiting for the returning Mosquitoes. Zack wanted to climb the steps to the tower but saw that the outside catwalk was already jammed. He counted five aircraft enter the circuit and circle to land. "We launched nine," an armorer told him.

"My God," Ruffy whispered. The mission had been a bloodbath for 487 Squadron.

What went wrong? Zack thought. He looked up at the catwalk, trying to find Bonder. How would I handle the responsibility he's burdened with? he wondered. Then he saw Bonder working his way through the crowd to the stairs. Following him was an RAF wing commander and a tall Navy lieutenant commander—Roger Bertram. He sucked in his breath when he saw Wilhelmina Crafton. "I think I know what went wrong," he muttered. He edged toward the steps.

"We need to discuss this," Bertram was saying.

"There's bloody nothing to talk about," Bonder snapped as he walked away from them, his back a rigid spike. Willi saw Zack and jerked her head away.

"What the hell were they going after?" Ruffy asked from behind him.

"Rumor had it some E-boat pens," a voice told him.

"At Dunkirk?" Zack asked.

"That was the word going about," the same voice confirmed.

The officers mess that night at Sculthorpe was unusually quiet and after dinner Zack had gone to his room to unpack. When he was finished, he lay on his narrow bed and read. Ruffy came in and started to undress for bed. "She's in the bar getting absolutely smashed," he said.

"Crafton?"

"Of course. Someone needs to look after her."

"She's got her own friends here."

"They seem to have disappeared along with Squadron Leader Bonder."

Zack sat up and pulled his shoes on. "Why me?" he muttered under his breath.

He found Willi sitting at a table in the bar. At first, she looked normal, but the moment she lifted her glass, he could tell from her rigid movements that she was stoned. "Another, please," she said to the barman.

The barman looked at Zack who shook his head. He sat down across from her. "You've had enough. It doesn't solve anything."

"What would you know about it?" she demanded. Her words were carefully enunciated and drawn out. "Yes," she decided, "what could you possibly know about it?"

"There's no way I can," he admitted. "But I've lost friends before."

"Your friends? This isn't your squadron."

"It is, as of today," he told her.

"Then how can they be *your* friends?"

Zack had tried to reason with drunks before and knew it was a hopeless cause. "You need to get to bed and sleep this off."

"Your bed, Mr. Pontowski? I imagine you are quite good in bed."

"I wouldn't know."

"Ah, but Mrs. Brouchard would know, wouldn't she?" Her mouth bent into a smile when she saw Zack flinch.

He ignored her and went looking for the barman. "Does Miss Crafton have a room here?"

The barman shook his head, said that he would arrange something, and disappeared. A few moments later he was back. "We have four empty rooms tonight," he said. "As long as she doesn't mind sleeping in a room with a dead man's belongings."

"I think she's too blotto to notice." Zack returned to the table and scooped her up. She protested weakly. "Lead the way, MacDuff," he said.

"The name's Higgins," the barman said, showing him the way to the empty room.

"Thank you, Higgins," he said when they had deposited her in bed. He removed her shoes and spread a blanket over her.

"Yes," she said, tears streaming down her face, "what could you possibly know about it?" Her words were almost inaudible. "We had to do it that way. Intelligence, you know . . . that's what I do . . ."

He sat down beside her and touched her lips with a single finger. "Don't say anymore. I know what you do. And like those men who died today, you have to do your job the best you can. That's all anyone can ask of you." He withdrew his hand—she had passed out. He stood up and quietly closed the door. "Well, Higgins, she'll have one hell of a headache tomorrow."

"We'll take care of her, sir." He watched Zack walk down the hall. "You're the lucky one," he said to the closed door. "A few of the blokes here would have had it off with you, drunk, passed out and all."

The message was waiting for him in squadron operations the next morning after he had landed from a short flight with Squadron Leader Bonder. The commander had been impressed when he reviewed Zack's record and was even more satisfied with the way he handled the Mosquito. The American was a welcome addition to his squadron.

Zack read the note on the short walk to his room in the officers mess. "May we talk after you land?" was all it said. It was signed with a distinctive "W." He gave a mental shrug and asked Higgins if she was in the mess. He pointed to the reading lounge and said that she had asked after him.

"She thanked me quite nicely," he told Zack. "Normally, they don't bother."

When Willi saw him, she folded her newspaper and stood up. "Would you mind walking?" she asked. She looked tired and drawn from the monumental hangover that was still marching around in her head. Outside, the weather had started to clear and patches of blue were breaking through the heavy clouds. "I think it's going to turn into a nice day," she said, making small talk. She glanced at him. "I want to thank you for last night, I don't normally drink—at least not that way."

"It was obvious," Zack said. "But sometimes it's the only way to hang on to your sanity."

"Sanity," she said, wanting to talk, "I think we've all lost it. It was those damn E-boats and Hofmann. Two weeks ago, he attacked an amphibious training exercise on the coast of Devon. Sailed in bold as brass, torpedoed two ships, machine-gunned six landing craft, killed I don't know how many people, all Americans."

They walked in silence. There was more that she wanted to say but could not. SOE had become deeply involved in the operation because the Gestapo had moved numerous French prisoners to serve as human shields into the buildings built on top of the pens where the E-boats docked. Unknown to the Gestapo, some of the prisoners were part of the Mistral network that had been inadvertently picked up. "We had information," she continued, "that dictated the attack be extremely precise." Part of the attack called for the Mosquitoes to hit the building where the Mistral agents were being held to kill them before the Germans discovered what they had. But by the same token, they had wanted to spare as many Frenchmen as possible.

And they wanted Hofmann. His boat had also been identified inserting German agents along the British coastline and SIS was positive that he had picked up a group of Luftwaffe officers who had escaped from a POW camp. "Hofmann's the very devil," she said. She gave him a plaintive look. "We had to select the targets."

"Is that why you're here?" he asked. She nodded. "And Bonder thought it was too risky?" Again she nodded. "Do you remember last night?" She shook her head no. "We all do the best we can," he repeated. "It's as simple as that." Then he added, "I would have volunteered for the mission."

Willi stopped dead in her tracks, a great weight lifted from her shoulders. "Why?"

"Because it's something we have to do—you, me, Chantal— all of us. Your grandfather says it's the 'call to duty.' Perhaps it's our fate, I don't know." He paused for a moment. "But I do know that we can't run from it."

She felt a quiet resolve pull her back from the chasm of doubt where she had been tottering. "Thank you," she said. "I was very near the edge."

"Self-doubt and a sense of responsibility can do that to you." Then he looked at her. "Shall we get on with it?"

"Yes, let's do that."

They walked back to the officers mess, a fragile peace established between them.

NINE

Morgan Adams, Washington, D.C.

The song's rock and roll lyrics rang out through the apartment and Mazie did a clumsy little spin as she half-danced and half-tripped across the room to turn up the volume on the stereo. Then she pranced back into the kitchen, stomping her feet as she worked at cleaning it up. *"La danse de la petite elephante,"* she laughed, wondering if she had said it right. French was her weakest language but she liked to play with it as a distraction. She surveyed her handiwork and decided that it would do. Her father always wanted to do the cooking when he came to visit, claiming that she delighted in poisoning him with her cooking. So, she always cleaned the kitchen first. It will be stir-fry tonight, Mazie calculated. She surveyed the clutter in her large three-room apartment on the third floor of an old house off Columbia Road. Like her office, it was a study in disorganization and drove her father wild. But she knew where everything was. "What difference will ten minutes make?" she muttered, checking her watch. A knock on the door ended any further agony over her sloppy housekeeping.

Kamigami's huge frame filled the doorway and she was in his

arms, making him drop the two bags he was carrying. "Hi, Pop," she said, content just to hug him. A slow smile spread across Victor Kamigami's face as he held his only child. He was home.

Later, after they had finished the dinner he had cooked and after she had put the kitchen back in order, mostly to satisfy his sense of discipline, she joined him on the comfortable old couch she had rescued from the Salvation Army. "I was looking at this the other night," he said, pulling an old family photo album out of a bag, "and thought you might like to have it." They leafed through the pages together and he again called up the personalities and places that went with each photo. She hadn't seen the album in years. When they got to the last page, a heavy silence came down. There was only one photo. A young and beaming Kamigami was holding a cherubic baby in his left arm and his right arm encircled a rotund young woman. She could have been Mazie's twin sister.

"You really loved her, didn't you?" Mazie could not remember her mother and only knew her through his memories.

"Still do," he said. The pain of his wife's death soon before Mazie's first birthday had long died and there was only an occasional sadness when he thought of what might have been.

"Why didn't you ever remarry?"

Kamigami didn't have the answer. "The Army, I suppose. It seemed to fill a gap, and with your grandmother to help raise you, I couldn't see changing. . . . " His voice trailed off.

"What are you going to do when you retire? Move back to Hawaii?"

Kamigami tried to look at his future and be honest with himself. "I don't know what I'll do and since your grandmother died, there's no one left on Maui. The family seems to have scattered." It made him sad to think about it, but the Kamigami family had broken apart, fractured by the pressure of modern society.

"Why don't you move in with me?" Mazie asked. She quickly added, "At least until you get settled and decide what you're going to do." Mazie had seen how her father's stubborn pride drove his decisions. "You're too young to retire and vegetate."

"I'll think about it," he replied.

"I'll put out some feelers. . . . "

"Mazie, don't go worrying about me. I'll work it out. There's something out there I can do." It amused him when he thought how a prospective employer would react to his qualifications as a professional warrior. "Sometimes I wish that I hadn't stayed so focused and branched out more," he allowed.

"It's not too late to change," she said. "You can take classes. . . . "

"I wonder." He stared at the album, still open in front of him. "The Army is all I've ever been. It's what I am."

Bethesda Naval Hospital, Maryland

Captain Smithson had received the alerting phone call that Pontowski was on his way to the hospital. He reached the third floor in time to make sure everything was in order before the President arrived to visit his wife. "We're looking good, Edith," he told the head nurse. She peered over her reading glasses at the President's doctor, wondering if the man would ever learn that her ward was always in good order. Smithson hurried off for one last check and to chase away anyone the President might stop and talk to. It was another opportunity to be in the limelight that he didn't want to share.

Edith suppressed a smile and made no move to page Smithson when she saw the Secret Service agents come out of the elevator and do one last sweep before Pontowski arrived. Two minutes later, she looked up and saw the tall figure of the President coming toward her. They went through the greetings that had become a ritual when he came to the hospital late at night. Then he said, "Edith, you're always on duty. Don't you ever take a night off?"

"Of course, Mr. President." She smiled, touched by his concern. The nurse would never tell him that as long as his wife was on her floor, she would cover every night shift.

"I brought this for her room," he said, holding up a framed photograph for her inspection. A middle-aged Pontowski was holding a baby and standing next to a young version of himself. "Tosh took this," he explained. "That's my son, Zack Junior, and my grandson, Matt." A gentle smile spread across his face as he looked at the picture.

"There's a strong family resemblance," the nurse said. She and Tosh had talked about their families and Edith knew that Zack Junior had died in a fiery crash in Vietnam when his F-4C Phantom had crashed into a hill. Now the President's grandson, Matt, was in the Air Force and, like his father, flew fighters.

"There's going to be a new addition to the family," Pontowski explained. "Matt called tonight. His wife, Shoshana, is expecting and they'll be here Friday. I want to tell Tosh."

"She's asleep, Mr. President," Edith said.

"I'll wait until she wakes up," he said. "Hope it's a boy." He turned and walked down the hall.

"So do I," Edith whispered.

Smithson scurried up to the desk in time to see Pontowski disappear into Tosh's room. He hurried after him, dismissing the nurse with a contemptuous glance. "And that, Dr. Smithson," she murmured, "is the difference between you and a great man." In her mind, she ranked Pontowski with Winston Churchill and FDR, the two great wartime leaders of the twentieth century.

1943

Stowmarket, Suffolk, England

The old coachman stomped up and down the train platform to keep warm. He kept glancing at the clock over the waiting room entrance and urged the minute hand to touch twenty-two minutes past the hour. It did. "Late, as usual," he groused to the middle-aged woman who was serving as a porter until the war ended.

"Wait inside, dear," she said. "They're always late now." The clanging of a nearby crossing guard bell announced the imminent arrival of the train. "Only four minutes late," the woman porter said. The train pulled into the station amid smoke, steam, wheezes, and grinds. "Good as on time, these days," she announced. A compartment door swung open and Zack stepped onto the platform. Ruffy followed by a few steps.

"Over here," the coachman called.

Zack smiled and walked briskly over. They shook hands and he introduced Ruffy. "How's everyone?" he asked.

"Most about the same. The duke's been under the weather and the doctor won't let him out. Just as well—the bloody old fool wanted to drive over to meet you himself. He always did fancy himself a coachman. I brought the trap today." He guided them to the light one-horse carriage waiting outside the station. They bundled in and the old man set the horse at a brisk pace toward Sherston Hall.

Zack asked about the duke's old mare. "How's Nancy doing?"

"The duke had to put 'er down . . . twisted bowel. Damn painful. It about killed the duke, but he did it himself. He's been going downhill ever since." They rode in silence the rest of the way.

The duke was waiting in the library for them. As usual, he was impatient and not content to sit comfortably in front of the fire. Instead, he hobbled around on a walking stick, ignoring the pain in his legs and hip. "About time," he said when Zack and Ruffy entered the room. Zack introduced Ruffy and the duke waved them to nearby chairs while he settled into the large overstuffed wingback chair he always claimed. Zack could see that he was in pain and much weaker. "Glad you could join us," he told Ruffy. "Sorry to hear about your family." There was genuine concern in his voice.

Zack had written how a stray German bomber had crashed near Norwich and destroyed Ruffy's home. His parents had been asleep and never knew what killed them. The duke had sent a letter in his almost illegible handwriting inviting them both to visit on their next leave. At first, Ruffy had been hesitant to accept the offer but Zack had convinced him. "Look," he had argued, "Sherston Hall is close to Norwich so if it gets too much for you, claim family business and go visit your aunt or sister."

Within a few minutes, Ruffy found that he was enjoying the old duke's company and they found themselves in a rousing argument about how to treat the Germans after the war. Much to Ruffy's surprise, the duke argued for a much more lenient peace than after World War I. "Reparations, punishment, all that nonsense last time didn't work. Got to try something different.... Maybe we should listen to your chap." He waved his walking stick toward Zack. "Amnesty, forgiveness...that sort of thing ...when we can."

"That was Abraham Lincoln," Zack told him, "and we didn't listen to him then."

The duke grunted an answer. "Damn colonials. Don't know when they've got it right."

"Grandfather!"—the familiar voice captured their attention—"Will you please be nice to our guests?" It was Willi. The old man humphed and settled back into his chair. Ruffy caught the wicked gleam in his eye.

"What a coincidence," Ruffy said.

"Hardly," the duke conceded.

"Some leave," Ruffy groaned as he and Zack entered the dining room after a long day cleaning out the stables. "You damn Yanks have this thing about hard work being good for the soul."

"We got the idea from you," Zack reminded him. They waited

for the duke and Willi to enter. She walked beside him, arm in arm, trying not to be obvious as she steadied him. The duchess was right behind them. The duke sat at his customary place at the head of the table and urged them to enjoy the meal.

"My, but you're being gracious lately," Willi said.

The duke grunted an answer and shot a glance at Ruffy, who was closely watching him. The old man waited for the right moment to make his next move. "The quack," he grumbled, "says Chartwell is out of the question—at least for me." He lifted a bushy eyebrow and waited for his wife's reaction. They had received an invitation from Clementine Churchill, the wife of the prime minister and the duchess's cousin, to spend a long weekend at the Churchills' country home in Kent. As usual, the duchess knew her husband had some devious plot in mind. She said nothing. "Of course," he growled, "you and Wilhelmina should go without me."

You old fool, the duchess thought, you are so transparent. She decided to play along with him. "Really," she said, "it is out of the question. We'd have to go by train and I don't fancy London these days. Why, just the thought of managing our bags from Liverpool to Waterloo Station to change trains is frightening."

"One of these chaps can do bearer duties," the duke said, glancing at Zack.

So that's it, his wife thought, you're throwing Zack to Willi. Well, she decided, that is a fate he doesn't deserve. She gave her husband a sweet smile. "Well, if it wouldn't be an imposition and if *they*"—she stressed this last word—"wouldn't mind helping us through London, we could manage on our own." The duke shot his wife a withering look and it was decided that Zack and Ruffy would escort the two women through London. When Zack discovered that Chartwell was only twenty-five miles south of London, he volunteered to travel with them all the way. Ruffy said he'd be glad to tag along and help carry their bags.

Later that night, the duke cornered Ruffy and asked if he would mind only going as far as London. When Ruffy looked confused by the request, the old man had said, "Confound it, I've got to patch things up between those two." Ruffy stifled a laugh and said that wasn't in the nature of things but that he would only go as far as Waterloo Station. The gleam was back in the duke's eyes.

The train trip to Liverpool Street Station was uneventful but the train was packed and they were hard-pressed to find a seat for the duchess. Willi and Ruffy sat on the women's two suitcases in the narrow corridor and Zack stood so he could better see the passing countryside. He grew depressed as they pulled into the outskirts of London and passed street after street of bombed-out buildings.

They unloaded from the train and had to take the Underground to Waterloo Station to catch the train to Sevenoaks, the nearest train station to Chartwell. It had turned into an adventure for the duchess and Zack was shocked to learn that it was the first time she had ever taken the "tube." At Waterloo Station, Zack fought the ticket line to get a ticket for the duchess. Since Ruffy, Willi, and he were wearing uniforms, they traveled free. When he came back, Ruffy was gone. Willi explained that he had seen some old friends, made his apologies, and left. "He said that he'd get a room at the Imperial Hotel in Russell Square and for you to meet him there," she told him.

"And with some encouragement from you, no doubt," Zack said. She gave him a puzzled look. "We can't have you and the duchess showing up at Chartwell in the company of one of the working class, now can we?" he asked.

"You don't understand anything about us," Willi snapped. The fragile peace between them was shattered and they made the rest of the trip in strained silence, finally arriving at Chartwell late that evening. The duchess and Clementine Churchill were obviously very close but took time to properly thank Zack and see that he had a "proper meal" and a place to sleep. He thanked them and headed for the small two-bedroom cottage at the back, where he could spend the night. He had a hard time falling asleep and kept thinking about Willi. She had disappeared with the suitcases immediately after their arrival and Zack wondered if he had misread Ruffy's disappearance and had been too quick in his judgment.

The dull, distant echoes of bombs woke Zack from a fitful sleep. The luminous face of his wristwatch told him it was 1:50 in the morning and he tried to ignore the bombing. But the much fainter sounds of antiaircraft artillery blended with the sporadic explosions to trap his attention. He rolled over to go back to sleep. But sleep eluded him and, frustrated, he got out of bed and walked across the cold floor to open the blackout curtains. He could see a dull red glow outline Chartwell's roofline. Now, wide awake, he quickly dressed and stepped outside into the cold night air. He picked his way along the path and followed it to a better vantage point. The northern horizon was glowing. The Germans had bombed London again.

He whistled a long, low "Oh-oh."

"Goddammit!" a voice rasped behind him. "Stop that confounded noise."

Zack twisted around to see a dark shadow standing behind him. The famous outline was topped by a bowler hat and only needed the cigar to complete the image. It was Winston Churchill. "Sorry, sir," he said. "I thought I was alone."

Churchill's bodyguard emerged out of the shadows and a flashlight blinked over him. "It's Flight Officer Pontowski, sir. He's one of the house guests."

Churchill said nothing, pulled out a cigar, and went about the process of lighting it with a long match. This is something to write home about, Zack thought. He cataloged his impressions, not wanting to lose the details. The man was short, perhaps five foot seven inches tall, must have weighed two hundred pounds, and had massive shoulders. The match flared and Churchill puffed, bringing the Romeo y Julieta to life. For an instant, the prime minister's face glowed in the surrounding darkness and Zack thought how much he looked like the cartoon character John Bull, the English equivalent of Uncle Sam. He is the ultimate English bulldog, Zack decided—squat, solid, and tenacious.

"There is nothing," Churchill said, drawing on the cigar, "that can redeem one who whistles."

Without thinking, Zack turned back to the red glow and gestured at the horizon. "I kill the people who drop those bombs," he said. There was no reply and the three men stood in silence gazing at the horizon. Then the young American remembered the question that had puzzled him. "Sir," Zack ventured, "how did you know Hitler was the enemy when most of your countrymen sought appeasement?"

"Is this of importance?"

"Perhaps only to me," Zack replied. "I was thinking of the future."

"There is always evil in this world and it is only a matter of recognizing it." Churchill stared at London's glowing skyline. "Evil"—he warmed to the subject—"is one of the absolutes of our existence, yet the twentieth century has convinced itself that it does not exist. What fools. Hitler smacked of putrid corruption from the very first and I became certain of it when I read *Mein*

Kampf. It is a pity that you Americans have not read it."

"I have," Zack told him. "I found it bloated and heavy going, especially in the original German. He did give us fair warning that he is a bloodthirsty killer."

There was no answer and he heard a shuffling sound. When he turned, he saw Churchill's back as he walked toward the big house. The detective who served as his bodyguard spoke in a low voice. "Whistling drives him round the twist but you're fortunate—he likes Americans." He followed his charge down the path.

Zack didn't move, thinking about the chance encounter. The prime minister had not been at his home when they had arrived or, for that matter, when he had gone to bed. Churchill must have driven in from London during the night. A young woman came scurrying down the path, her arms crossed in front of her against the cold. "The prime minister asked if you would please join him," she said. It was not a request and Zack followed her into the big house. "He likes to speak to the men who actually carry out his orders," the woman explained.

Churchill was standing at a high podiumlike desk when Zack was ushered into his study, the cigar clenched in his teeth. "You were impertinent," he said, not looking up from his work.

"Please accept my apologies—I didn't mean to be."

Churchill grumped, seemingly satisfied. "You're the American who plays polo. Not well, I might add, but aggressively. Where did you learn?"

"I worked on a ranch near Santa Clara, California, during my summer vacations. I was an exercise boy and played occasionally when they needed a fourth for an impromptu match."

"Why haven't you transferred to your forces with most of your countrymen?" Churchill asked.

"I decided to see out what I had started." He thought for a moment. "Besides, I like my squadron."

"Which is?"

"Four-eighty-seven, sir. New Zealanders. We fly Mosquitoes."

Churchill's massive head came up and he shot Zack a hard look. "Were you on the raid against the E-boats at Dunkirk?"

He was surprised that Churchill followed operations so closely. "No, sir. I arrived just in time to see them recover."

"A damnable waste," the prime minister muttered. "The Germans were expecting an attack." Zack wanted to ask how he knew that but thought better of it. "There must be a way," Churchill said.

"There is," Zack told him. "We just have to be more devious about it next time." They talked for a few moments before Churchill dismissed him.

Willi was waiting for Zack when he came out of his bedroom later that morning. He was carrying his musette bag and ready to leave. "What happened last night?" she demanded.

"Nothing that I know of."

"With the prime minister, you fool," she retorted.

"Oh, that. We talked."

"Well, he left word for you to be available when he wakes." She glared at him. "Apparently, he wants to 'talk' some more." Zack shrugged and followed her into the main house for breakfast, amused at her discomfort.

The summons came for him two hours later. Churchill's valet, David Inches, held the door to the master's bedroom open and closed it behind him. Churchill was propped up in bed like an oriental potentate, newspapers on the floor. A battered red dispatch box was open on the bed beside him. Churchill came right to the point. "Last night," he growled, "you asked a question because, as you said, you were thinking about the future. Pray tell, why are you concerned about impending tomorrows that you may never see?"

"If I do live that long," Zack said, "I don't want to make the same mistakes that got us into this mess."

"Then you plan to enter politics?"

The idea surprised Zack; he hadn't thought it through that far. It shocked him that the answer was formed and immediate. It must have been hovering in his subconscious, waiting for the right moment to explode into his life. "Yes, sir. I suppose that I will try. It's going to be a difficult course to navigate."

Churchill's face came alive at this and he rummaged through the papers that littered his bed. He found what he wanted—a batch of papers held together by a string threaded through holes punched in the upper left-hand corner of each page. He read, "The oceans we travel on are storm-tossed on the surface and dangerous with shoals and barrier reefs. Yet with cunning navigation we will reach safe harbor. But the ever-changing oceans move with a force beyond our feeble imaginations and we must

contend with this force as it is—not as we would want it to be."
He looked over his reading glasses at Zack, expecting to find an
admiring audience. Instead he saw a grin on the young man's
face. The prime minister's lower lip jutted out in petulance.

"A speech about the future?" Zack smiled.

"Of course."

"Your audience will love it," Zack told him.

"Mr. Pontowski," Churchill said, settling back to work, "I hope
you survive this war. I can see a future in you." When Zack left,
one of Churchill's aides entered. Churchill did not look up from
his reading. "A most unusual young man," he said. "He has a
sense of presence and surety unusual in one so young. You can
hear it in his voice. Very captivating." He paused and read a
report about the disruption the German E-Boats were causing
with channel shipping and training exercises. Under the leader-
ship of Ernst Hofmann, they alone were able to still disrupt Allied
operations in the English Channel. "Christ! Those E-boats are a
menace totally out of proportion with their numbers. I want them
eliminated well before D-Day."

He thought for a moment. "Perhaps Four-eighty-seven Squadron would like another go at them."

TEN

Training Site Entebbe, North Carolina

Woodward and Kamigami maintained a discrete distance from the three Intelligence Support Agency operators working their way up the hill on a night training exercise. Like the three men, Woodward and Kamigami were wearing night vision goggles and were easily able to follow them as they moved through the heavy foliage of the North Carolina countryside in nearly total darkness. The three ISA agents were moving with a new confidence and Kamigami was pleased with their progress. The agents were in much better physical shape and had cross-trained so they could take over for any member of the team who might go down. On this exercise, they were functioning as a mortar team.

"Baulck just got a stick in the face," Kamigami said, his soft voice almost inaudible. The ISA team was experiencing the usual problems wearing NVGs—lack of depth perception and losing details in heavy shadows.

"I think they missed their objective," Woodward said. On cue, the three-man team stopped and retraced their steps, finding the exact spot that had been identified as their objective. They quickly set up the M224 sixty-millimeter mortar tube and readied the twenty rounds they had been carrying. Two men stayed with the tube while the third man, Andy Baulck, disappeared, moving into cover to provide security for the other two. Kamigami surveyed the terrain and calculated he would find Baulck twenty meters down the hill with his back to the mortar team.

"Baulck and Wade were Rangers," Kamigami said. "I wondered what had happened to them. Time to find out if Baulck has learned anything." He removed his bulky NVGs and waited for his eyesight to adjust to the darkness. "Never could patrol with these," he explained. Then he disappeared into the brush.

Woodward moved to a new position where he could see the ruins of a large building on the firing range in the valley below them. He estimated the distance at five hundred meters, well within mortar range. He waited while the seconds ticked down. He checked his watch and focused his attention. At the exact time to open fire, the loader dropped a round down the tube and a dull "whomp" reached out. The round was on target. The loader quickly fed round after round into the mortar while Wade walked the point of impact across the building. Woodward was impressed. He had seen what these men could do with C4 explosive and every weapon they got their hands on. He was going to arrange for them to train some of his men in the SAS.

"Where's Baulck?" the loader said when the last round was expended. "It's time to boogie." As the security man, Baulck should have counted the rounds in order to know when to rejoin. But the missing Baulck did not appear. "Damn," Wade, the team leader, groaned. "We'll have to go get him." They quickly booby-trapped the mortar tube by placing a small charge of C4 explosive with a pressure release switch under the base plate.

Baulck appeared out of the underbrush pushing Kamigami ahead of him. "Look what I found," he said, "sneaking around in the dark. What do you think we ought to do with him."

"Well," the loader said, "we could strip him bare and paint him pink."

"I only brought green paint this time," Wade said. "But I don't think I've got enough. A half-green Jolly Green Giant is not a pretty sight."

"Consider yourself dead," Woodward said from the shadows.

The three men turned toward the voice. "Ah, what the fuck, Captain," Wade complained.

"Never let up for a moment when you're on patrol," Woodward said, his point made.

"Secure the tube and let's move out," Kamigami said. The ISA team deactivated the booby-trapped mortar tube, packed up, and moved confidently into the night. Woodward and Kamigami followed them, again at a distance.

"Excellent work with the mortar," Woodward told him. "All they left of the target was a smoking hole. By the way, did you let Baulck get the drop on you?"

"Sort of," Kamigami replied. "I didn't push too hard."

A shadow separated from a tree behind them. "If you talk, you die," Baulck said.

"They're ready," Kamigami allowed.

The White House, Washington, D.C.

The shortness of the walk from Michael Cagliari's desk to the Oval Office was ample indication of his importance in the Pontowski administration. Only the chief of staff, Leo Cox, stood between him and the President. Few men have such access to power and the national security adviser was careful not to abuse it. So when the shaggy, bearded academic shambled down the hall into Cox's office and said he had something of importance, Cox immediately escorted him into the President. "Courtland's at it again," Cagliari said. "He's on the floor of the Senate right now. I think you should hear what he's saying." Pontowski nodded and Cox switched on the TV set and punched up the closed circuit channel to the Senate.

"Is Bobby watching this?" Pontowski asked.

Cagliari nodded. "I called him." The President's three main advisers were a close-knit team, and with Bobby Burke in his office at the CIA's headquarters in Langley dialed in, all would be on the same wavelength. They listened as Courtland demanded that the United States government act to counter the increasing flow of drugs out of the Golden Triangle, protect American citizens, and hold Chiang Tse-kuan accountable for his barbaric actions. He claimed that the government's antidrug policy was a total failure and that Congress would have to force the administration to act.

"So far this is classic Courtland," Cagliari observed. "Now here comes the bit about his own personal suffering."

But the senator surprised them by doing the unthinkable. He revealed in open session what he had learned from behind his committee's closed-door hearings concerning the rescue of Nikki Anderson.

"That son of a bitch," Cagliari growled. "I can't believe he's doing this."

Courtland's face filled the TV screen, full of concern and indignation. "I am asking for legislation that will permit my committee to appoint the armed services foremost expert on special operations, Lieutenant General Simon Mado, as an overseer of any future rescue operations. We must act to prevent such ill-planned, hastily executed, and uncontrolled covert missions in the future." Courtland was now looking directly into the camera, his voice was more sad than indignant. "This is a perfect example of how inept and lax this administration has been in responding to such situations and I assure you that no one would like to see a rescue operation mounted more than me . . . my own daughter is held by Chiang . . ." He choked off his words with a visible show of emotion and returned to his main point. "But I cannot allow more American lives to be needlessly wasted."

"That's enough," Pontowski said.

Cox flicked off the TV as the intercom buzzed. He picked up the phone and listened. "It's Bobby Burke," he said. "He's on the way over. I've never heard him so angry."

When Burke arrived, he was furious. "That son of a bitch," he said. "He knows what we're doing. My God! What the hell is the man thinking of?"

"It's simple enough," Pontowski explained. "He keeps short circuiting our plans and we end up looking like fools."

"That's so obvious," Burke snorted, "that he can't get away with it."

"It doesn't play that way to the press," Pontowski said. "What with his own daughter a hostage. Courtland makes sure that someone feeds the reporters the story on what's happening to his daughter as deep background. Then when he criticizes what we're doing, it looks like he's putting the general good above his own personal concerns. We're talking the stuff of tragedy here. Makes good copy for the seven o'clock news."

National Security Adviser Cagliari stood and paced the floor. The men had all seen it before; when Cagliari paced and talked, he was most dangerous. "Perhaps this could be turned to our advantage. But we need to act now." He laid out his reasoning and, twenty minutes later, the secretary of defense was ordered to deploy Mackay's contingent to its forward operating location and await an execute order.

The Golden Triangle, Burma

Samkit was the first to sense the new presence in the heart of Chiang's fortress compound and within minutes the servants were pleading illness, begging to be sent home. The news then rippled out, spreading outside the walls and into the villages that surrounded the compound. Demons were about.

She forced an outward serenity over her features when James, Chiang's majordomo, ordered her to fill the gaps as more and more servants retreated to safety outside the walls. Samkit calmed those who remained and took charge of the young girls serving Chiang and his foreign guests. It was a rare chance to watch Chiang firsthand even though her oriental sense of balance was offended by the presence of both the Colombian-Germans and the Japanese at the same meeting. It was that imbalance, she cautioned herself, that had allowed the spirits and demons to enter.

She quickly inspected the three girls as they gathered outside the massive doors that led into the drawing room, making sure their trays were correct and the portable bar was properly stocked. Satisfied that all was ready, she pulled one of the kitchen staff aside. "Tell Miss Courtland that we are serving early. She should come now." The older woman responded to the anxiety in Samkit's voice and hurried to deliver the message. Samkit knocked discreetly and opened the doors. Her senses jangled as a strong force engulfed her—danger, disruption, and death were present in the room—but she didn't know for whom. She would have to visit the temple outside the compound that night and make an offering to the *nats*, the ancient spirits who had never yielded sway to Buddha.

The servants entered and went about their duties while Samkit hovered at the door, making herself invisible, memorizing the features of the four Japanese who led the four major families of the Yakuza and the three Colombian-Germans who controlled the Medellin cartel. Heather walked through the open door wearing a simple black off-the-shoulder cocktail dress with a full skirt. The room fell silent as she moved across it. Samkit continued to take the measure of the strangers. All were expensively dressed in dark silk suits and hand-sewn Italian shoes. Their hard and dispassionate faces did not match their clothes. A cold shiver of fear shot through Samkit as Heather selected a glass of wine from a tray and joined Chiang.

He stared at Heather impassively, not returning her greeting. An inner voice told her to be attentive and submissive and she sank to the floor beside his chair, curling her legs underneath, leaning against his leg. It was a graceful gesture that was not lost on the men. One of the Colombian-Germans smiled at her and asked her name.

"May I introduce Miss Heather Courtland?" Chiang said in English, his manner as charming and sophisticated as ever. "The daughter of Senator William Douglas Courtland." The men stared at her in silence. They all knew of her captivity. One of the Japanese said something in his own language. Heather focused her attention on the man and noticed a solid ring of tattoos showing just above his collar and at his wrists as Chiang answered him in Japanese. Then, in English, "Mr. Morihama says you are a most beautiful insurance policy." He reached over and stroked her hair. "Gentlemen," he said, "it is because of Miss Courtland that I can guarantee there will be no interruption in the 'traffic' at my end. She is, indeed, an insurance policy." His fingers tightened in her hair, pulling hard. "Please stand up, Heather," he said, slowly untangling his fingers.

She did as he ordered and stood beside his chair. His hand ran up the inside of her leg, stroking her inner thigh. He continued to speak in carefully modulated tones, his actions at odds with his words. "I am confident that as long as Heather is my guest," he jerked at her panties, aware that the men were more interested in her humiliation than his words, "the DEA will not interfere in my operations here." She gasped as he dug a finger into her. "Of course, I cannot extend such a guarantee beyond my area of control. But then you, without doubt, know how best to neutralize the Americans who intrude in your own provinces. Acting in concert is our strength." Then he dropped his hand. "You may go," he told her.

Heather walked with as much dignity as possible past the seated men. Morihama stopped her. "Yes," he said in heavily accented English, "you are a most beautiful insurance policy." Then he ran his hand up her leg.

"I am given to understand," Chiang said, "that you have an interest in tattoos." Morihama jerked his head in a sharp nod, his face rigid. "If you wish," Chiang continued, "she's yours tonight. You will discover that Miss Courtland has a most interesting tattoo. But you must search for it. Be kind enough to return her undamaged. Shall we consider it part of our 'arrangement'?"

The men were laughing and talking as Heather retreated from the room, shaking with fright and humiliation. Samkit wanted to follow her, but her instincts warned that much more was to be learned by remaining. The men resumed their discussion as if she weren't there. Finally, Chiang brought the meeting to an end. "Why don't you discuss the details with your counselors and we can gather tomorrow. Perhaps we can come to a final agreement at that time."

Samkit motioned the servants to leave. She was closing the door when Chiang said, "Entertainment has been arranged for tonight, should you care to partake. Perhaps you would also be interested in what has been arranged for the day you leave." Samkit could not see the men but sensed their interest. "Have you ever seen a Kran execution?" Chiang asked. "It is a very ritualized beheading with a sword in which the executioner must first demonstrate his expertise by cutting off the head of a bullock with one stroke—one bullock for each of the condemned. The executioner and two bullocks arrive tomorrow. I think you will find it most entertaining."

Samkit slipped the doors closed and ran from the compound, seeking out the anthropologist, her contact. The demons were thriving on the evil imbalance that had descended over them.

Bethesda Naval Hospital, Maryland

The reading lamp was turned down low as Pontowski gazed at his sleeping wife. As at all hospitals, a stillness had descended over the corridors in the late evening and only an occasional hushed footstep could be heard passing in the hall. Pontowski calculated that Dr. Smithson was hovering outside, hoping to talk to him and bask in the glory of advising the President of the United States. How silly, he thought. Matthew Zachary Pontowski did not have a vain bone in his body. Age had done that to him. But at times he delighted in being contrary and pricking the bubble of self-importance that some people inflated around their egos. Smithson was one of those people and only his undeniable competence kept him in Tosh's service. Pontowski preferred the company of people like Edith Washington, the head nurse on the floor, Mazie Kamigami, or Leo Cox.

He wasn't drowsy in the least and wondered if the need for

less sleep was one of the compensations nature gave the old in their last years when time was most precious. He savored the quiet hours when he had time to think and it was comforting that he could remember recent events and new facts with the same clarity as a thirty-year-old man. He knew he was lucky in that regard but worried that the years would dim his judgment.

Oh, Tosh, he thought, how much longer do we have? Where's the justice in it all? I never understood what love meant when I was young. Can I do this alone? I do need to talk to you for I'm not sure if I'm doing this one right. Bobby Burke may have assassinated two people, one his own employee. It was too convenient and solved too many problems. I can't allow that and will nail his hide to the wall if it is true. Or should I ignore it for now? Is that the wise thing to do? And with the next election just around the corner, I've got to derail Courtland— this country doesn't need a packaged demagogue for President— and I'm too old to run even if the Constitution allowed a third term. This could be a rare opportunity to get him. Nothing kills a controversy like success. But what a game to play with those kids caught in the middle. I do want to get them out, but not at the expense of more lives.

But long and hard experience would not be denied and Pontowski knew there was a price to be paid regardless of what course of action he chose. Well, get on with it, he chastised himself. You know what has to be done. If Mike Cagliari's right, we can pull it off. That would nail Courtland's hide to the wall. But Chiang has got to be expecting another rescue attempt now.

Then he remembered another time when the enemy had been expecting him and his mood brightened. There was nothing wrong with his memory or judgment. He finally dozed off, thinking about lighthouses in the night. The door cracked open and nurse Edith Washington looked in. She slipped into the room and checked on Tosh. Then she spread a blanket over the sleeping President of the United States and quietly left, leaving the light on low.

"I don't care what your orders were about not being disturbed," she mumbled to herself. "That was for that fool Smithson." Edith Washington had long ago claimed Matthew Zachary Pontowski as one of her patients.

1943

RAF Hunsdon, Hertfordshire, England

Zack led the four-ship contingent of Mosquitoes on the short flight from Sculthorpe to RAF Hunsdon. The weather was cold and clear and they flew at a leisurely 250 mph, taking twenty-five minutes to make the hop. They entered the circuit and Zack decided to land last, after the other three ships were safely down. He was on downwind when the first ship touched down. From his vantage point, it looked like a perfect three-point landing and the tail wheel came down with the mains. Suddenly, the Mosquito ground-looped to the left. The Mossie had just stung one of its more experienced pilots. "What the hell," Zack muttered. "Not a good first impression." The 487 Squadron was scheduled to move from Sculthorpe to Hunsdon in a few days to join with 21 and 464 squadrons. The three squadrons made up 140 Wing, which was part of the RAF's 2 Group, which, in turn, was part of the newly formed allied Second Tactical Air Force.

"I hope he didn't bend the oleos," Ruffy said, thinking about how the oleo struts on the main gear could collapse on a ground loop.

Zack radioed the Mossie on the ground. "Sammy, are you still in one piece? What went wrong?"

"It was worse than it looked," came the answer. "There's a blasted dip in the runway short of the halfway mark. Watch for it."

"Tango aircraft," Zack radioed to his other Mosquitoes, "land on the mains." By changing to the nonstandard landing technique, he was certain that they would all land without further incident.

The Mosquitoes landed smoothly and all four taxied into the same dispersal area. A small van was waiting and bused them the five miles to Uxbridge, the headquarters for Second Tactical Air Force. Their station commander from RAF Sculthorpe, a tall, blond-haired group captain, was waiting for them in the briefing room. Sammy, the pilot who was still smarting from the good-natured kidding he had been subjected to for his spectacular landing, was the first to enter the room. "My God," he said in a loud stage whisper as they shuffled into chairs, "it's the movie star." The group captain was the legendary Percy Charles Pickard, the star of the documentary movie *Target for Tonight*. Pickard had four years of continual operational experience and was one of the best pilots that ever climbed into a Mosquito. With the exception of Zack and Ruffy, the men were all well-acquainted with Pickard.

Pickard came right to the point. "It appears that Four-eighty-seven Squadron"—he checked them over with a stern look—"has been given a singular honor, not withstanding its, ah, unusual landing techniques."

Zack stood up. "Sir," he said, "that was my decision."

"A bit much," Pickard deadpanned, "for a new flight lieutenant, don't you think?" Zack had sewn on his new rank two days before the flight. He blushed brightly. Pickard let him off the hook. "In my wing, the goal is to get safely down. Do that and I'm happy. Shall we get on with why you're here?" He called the room to attention and the commander of 2 Group, Air Vice Marshal Basil Embry, entered the room. Two men followed him carrying a cloth-covered board. The men immediately recognized it as a target model and sucked in their breath. Scale models were only built for extremely important and hard-to-hit targets.

Embry was even more direct than Pickard. "The powers that be at Two TAF have decided to give you a chance to even the score with Jerry at Dunkirk. Word has it that the PM himself has taken an interest in the operation and specifically requested that Four-eighty-seven Squadron do the honors. Why he should be so personally involved escapes me, but, needless to say, it does show considerable high-level interest in the target. That's why Group Commander Pickard and you are here. We've got to do it right this time."

Zack gave an inward groan and stood up again. "Excuse me, sir. But I may be responsible for that."

"Now that is a bit much for a new flight lieutenant, don't you think?" Pickard quipped and the men roared with laughter. Zack related the part of the conversation he had had with Churchill about the E-boats and sat down.

Embry thought for a moment and then whipped the cloth cover off the target model. It was the harbor at Dunkirk. "Perhaps, Mr. Pontowski," Embry said, "you have some ideas on how to successfully strike this target?" He motioned for the men to gather around the model. It was a scale replica of the harbor that simulated what the crews would see from an altitude of one thousand feet four miles away. The E-boat docks were in man-made caverns buried under what looked like a peninsula crowded with low buildings. The peninsula stretched eastward into the water from the western side of the harbor and ended in a forty-foot concrete cliff that dropped straight into the water. Embry pointed to two tunnels that were set in the water at the base of the cliff. "These are the entrances to the pens," he said. "The pens extend approximately two thousand feet back. Your task is to toss your bombs into the entrances." A half-smile cracked his face. "They do expect miracles now. But you only have yourselves to blame for it. You chaps have become too good at low-level bombing, especially when the target has vertical development against which your bombs can be thrown." He pointed to the low buildings on top. "The Gestapo has discouraged bombing by crowding French workers and prisoners into these quarters, which makes pinpoint accuracy mandatory."

"How many aircraft will attack the target?" Zack asked.

"You four," Embry answered.

"Can I pick the time?" Zack asked.

"Certainly."

"Then we can take them out."

Zack had reasoned that since the Germans had been expecting the first attack on the pens, they would be expecting a second. In order to unlock the door to the E-boats, it would be necessary to get the Germans looking elsewhere. He had sold Embry and Pickard on the idea that the four Mosquitoes should enter the area single-ship at night and act as Intruders. "We need to spread a great deal of *Moskitopanik* around," he had told them. "Once the Jerries are convinced we are Intruders operating single-ship, we rendezvous and go against Dunkirk at first light. We come at them from the south, a direction they are not expecting." The crews were enthusiastic and all were confident they could navigate with the precision necessary to make the rendezvous in the early-morning dark.

Zack and Ruffy were flying *K for King*, their own Mosquito, and for once, it performed like *Romanita*. "That new fitter," Ruffy said over the intercom, "did wonders on the Merlins." The two 1,460-horsepower Merlin Mark 21s were singing in perfect harmony, performing as never before.

"His name is Brian," Zack said. "It's hard to believe that an eighteen-year-old kid can be a first-class mechanic. He says he wants to work on race cars after the war."

"He's got the talent," Ruffy allowed. He made a mental note

to pay more attention to the way Zack drew the best out of those
around him. Ruffy had seen how most everyone was attracted to
the young American; everyone except Wilhelmina Crafton. He
bent over the new bomb sight that had been recently installed on
K for King and checked their drift as they coasted in over Holland.
He then ran a check on the indices. "Spot on," he said. "Much
better than the old Mark Nine." He sat upright and concentrated
on finding identifiable landmarks in the night: a unique set of
locks on a canal, a bend in a river, or a certain bridge. Within
minutes they were approaching Doorn and looking for House
Doorn, the Kaiser's old residence. Zack wracked the Mossie into
a tight turn, skirting the edge of the town. "Break!" Ruffy
shouted. A stream of tracers reached up toward them from the
grounds of House Doorn. "Jerry has moved in a damn ack-ack
battery," Ruffy groused.

"I can't believe it," Zack said. "We got three flashes from the
roof. The Germans are taking off to the west out of Soesterberg.
Someone is taking a hell of a chance to send that signal."

"Or it's a setup," Ruffy warned.

"I wonder?" Zack said. His inner warning bells were quiet and
he decided to trust the signal. He headed to the west.

An old man sat in the attic at House Doorn and listened to
the sound of heavy footsteps run up the stairs. He made a hurried
phone call and uttered the code word that meant the Germans
were onto him and he was in imminent danger of being captured.
Then he ripped the special wiring out of the telephone and draped
an orange banner, the forbidden color of the Dutch royal family,
over his shoulders and waited. He smiled at the soldier who
clubbed him into unconsciousness.

"Tallyho!" Zack called, catching a glimpse of a dark shadow
at his ten o'clock. His hands automatically flew over the controls,
setting *K for King* up for combat. The aircraft leaped forward
and the airspeed indicator touched 340 mph. "Hot dog!" Zack
shouted. "We're hauling bombs and she's going like a striped-ass
ape!"

"Don't get too enthusiastic," Ruffy warned him. But he was
also impressed.

Zack rolled in behind the shadow and closed for the kill. But
now his inner warning bell came alive and he hesitated. Ruffy's
hand flashed out and hit the gun master switch, disabling the

machine guns and cannons as he yelled, "It's a Mossie! One of ours."

"Roger," Zack replied as he pulled off. "That was a close one."

Ruffy hit the gun master switch again. "Guns are armed." He checked his watch. "We've still got ten minutes to use up. We can't use House Doorn as a departure point now." The plan called for them to use DR, or dead reckoning, to navigate to the rendezvous point with the other three Mosquitoes. But for DR to work, they had to start at a known point. In this case, Ruffy had picked House Doorn as the departure point. They discussed alternatives, but the points that could be easily found at night, such as bridges, were also heavily defended and it would be very difficult for Ruffy to rework the route in the cramped confines of the cockpit at night.

The decision was simple. "Better the enemy we know," Zack said. "We'll start at Doorn and fly right over them as low as possible. They might think we're one of theirs."

"Don't bet on it," Ruffy said. They made one more circuit of Soesterberg looking for activity. "Well, they should definitely know we're here by now," Ruffy said. Again, he checked his watch. "Time to head for Doorn."

Zack turned to the south for their departure point, trusting his instincts. He was prepared to change course at the slightest tingle of that strange inner warning. Nothing. He set the rpm at 3,000 and dropped to fifty feet, skimming the treetops. Again, the Merlins willingly responded and the airspeed indicator climbed to 360. The machine seemed to be working better and better as the mission went on. "Brian has performed magic on these Merlins," he quipped.

"Set course one-nine-zero," Ruffy said as they approached House Doorn. They flashed over a few feet above the rooftop and Ruffy started his stopwatch. The crew tending the antiaircraft battery was totally surprised and there was no reaction. Zack honked back on the throttles and rooted their airspeed on 300. "New course one-six-five in five seconds," Ruffy told him. He counted the seconds down and when the hand on the stopwatch touched twenty-four seconds into the leg, Zack turned to the new heading. "Crossing the Rhine in thirty-six seconds," Ruffy said. They saw the silver band snaking across the flat Dutch country side and crossed it two seconds ahead of schedule. For the next thirty minutes they worked their way southwest to the rendezvous point over the flat fields of Flanders in Belgium. Sweat streaked Ruffy's face as he used time and heading to navigate. He would strain to find some feature on the ground that would confirm they were on time and on course. He trusted Zack to keep the airspeed riveted on 300 and the course indicator welded to each new heading that he gave him. The faith the two men had in each other was absolute and unshakable.

Finally, Ruffy said, "We're there." Zack turned to the left and entered a racetrack pattern. They strained to see, hoping the first streaks of morning light in the east would help them find the other three Mosquitoes. The radio came alive. "I've got you in sight." It was Sammy. Elation replaced worry when the other two Mosquitoes checked in. Now they could see better in the growing light.

"I hope Jerry hasn't tumbled to this yet," Ruffy said.

"We'll know in about four minutes," Zack told him. He could see a small town emerging out of the morning mist coming under the nose. "I hope that's Leper," Zack said. The small town of Leper had been chosen as the checkpoint to start their ingress into the target area. Ruffy told him that it was.

"This is Tango leader," Zack radioed. "Dance time starts in twenty seconds." He firewalled the throttles and flew over the town with Sammy on his right wing. The second element of two Mosquitoes fell in behind them.

When the Mosquitoes were three minutes out, the German air defense warning system received a warning that four unidentified aircraft were operating in the area well inland from Dunkirk. Since the German radars had not picked up any inbound hostile traffic coming from across the Channel into the sector since midnight, the plot officer hesitated. It had been the first quiet period they had experienced in over three weeks and everyone was exhausted, including him. The German major suspected the reported aircraft were Focke-Wulf 190s out of Abbeville on a dawn patrol. Rather than send a full alert out over the net, he brought the system to standby and had his telephone operator call the Jagdgeschwader at Abbeville for confirmation.

When the Mosquitoes were two minutes out, the telephone operator told the major that the Focke-Wulfs were still on the ground and taxiing out for takeoff. Then a second report came in that four Mosquitoes were spotted nine miles southeast of Dunkirk and headed directly toward the port. "Four Mosquitoes in that quadrant?" he shouted. "That is not possible!" Despite his doubts, he put the system on full alert and sent the ack-ack crews scrambling for the gun pits. The Mosquitoes were seventy seconds out of Dunkirk.

Zack had planned to start the attack with a run-in from the southeast just as the sun broke the eastern horizon. They dropped down over the town and cleared the rooftops by a few feet. At one point, Zack and Sammy bracketed the spire of a cathedral by flying around it on opposite sides. When they reached the water's edge, they turned left forty-five degrees to a westerly heading, paralleled the docks and dropped even lower, barely ten feet above the smooth water of the inner harbor. For the first time, they could see the cavelike arched entrances to the pens set in the base of the concrete cliff. The low sun angle at their back spotlighted the tunnels and gave them a perfect aim point. Zack was going for the left entrance, Sammy for the right, and they would drop their bombs at point-blank range—seventy yards. The bombs would fly straight ahead like a rifle shot into the darkened tunnels while they pulled up to clear the forty-foot wall in front of them.

"Bomb bay doors open!" Ruffy yelled. He glanced at the concrete dock they were paralleling and saw dark figures running for the sandbagged gun emplacements. They were too late. Ruffy glued his right eye onto the bombsight. The cross-hairs were fixed on the tunnel opening—Zack had killed the drift and lined up perfectly. "Spot on!" he yelled as the indices started to align. When they came together, their two 500-pound bombs would automatically release.

Tracers erupted from a gun emplacement that was on top of the wall and directly in front of them. "Nail those bastards!" Zack yelled as he lifted *K for King* up to fifty feet. He had shifted targets. They had to get the four barrel Vierlings-Geschutzen cannon or the two Mosquitoes running in behind them would be setting ducks for the gunners.

"Come right, come right," Ruffy told him. "Steady, steady." The indices came together and the Mosquito shuddered as the bombs fell free. Zack mashed the trigger on the twenty-millimeter cannon and flew directly at the rapidly firing cannon. Then they were off, skimming over the low sheds on the roof of the pens that housed the French workers and prisoners. They didn't see their bombs explode. Zack wracked the Mosquito into a hard left turn over the town to check on his flight and saw the second two Mosquitoes that were still inbound on their bomb run.

"Where's Sammy?" Zack asked. A deep sense of worry for his

wingman drove out any concern for his own safety. He had planned this raid, led it, and felt a deep responsibility for all his wingmen.

"I lost him," Ruffy said. "But we got the bastards." He could clearly see a smoking hole where the antiaircraft battery had been.

The two Mosquitoes lifted over the high concrete face of the pens and raced for open water and safety. Smoke belched out of the tunnel entrances as Zack turned to follow them, three miles in trail.

"Bandits ten o'clock high," Ruffy called. Swooping down onto the two Mosquitoes in front of them were four Focke-Wulf 190 Butcherbirds. The boys from Abbeville had arrived.

"Bandits at your eight o'clock high!" Zack called out on the radio. He altered course to the left, splitting the distance between the Focke-Wulfs and the two Mossies and firewalled the throttles. As expected, the two Mosquitoes accelerated straight ahead and moved farther apart, relying on their superior speed at low level to outrun the Germans. But the 190s had the height advantage and were screaming down in high-speed dives with enough speed to catch the Mosquitoes. But they would only have one pass and then the Mosquitoes would have the speed advantage and be able to scamper home free. Zack watched in horror as the engagement developed and, with a sickening finality, realized the 190s would gun the two Mossies out of the sky. I won't lose any more! he swore to himself.

"Turn into 'em!" he yelled over the radio. He pushed *K for King* for all it was worth and hit the button to the nitrous oxide bottle, overboosting the two engines. The two Merlins responded, howling in a high-pitched wail.

"Understand, Tango Leader," came the cool reply as the two Mosquitoes turned into the threat. Both started to jink back and forth as the planes rushed at each other. Now all six planes were firing as they merged in a head-on cannon attack. One Focke-Wulf disintegrated in pieces as twenty-millimeter shells slammed into its engine. The Mossie flew straight through the debris.

"Oh, my God," Ruffy said, just loud enough for Zack to hear. Then: "He made it!" The Mossie was still flying and disengaging, apparently undamaged. The second Mosquito was also clear but was trailing a white contrail of glycol from the port engine. "They got his radiator," Ruffy said. They could see the Mosquito slow when it lost the engine. Two of the Focke-Wulfs turned on him, once again able to close.

"Hang on!" Zack yelled as he closed the distance. They were only a few feet above the waves and the rough ride was slamming them into their seats and throwing them against their lap and shoulder harnesses. "Where's the other fucker?"

"No joy," Ruffy said as he tried to get a visual on the one unaccounted-for 190.

"He's in the sun," Zack said. He sensed, rather than knew, that was where the third 190 would be.

"Tallyho!" Ruffy shouted. "Coming out of the sun! At four o'clock, on us."

Zack turned right fifteen degrees to get a visual on the 190 coming at them and immediately turned back onto the other two Germans. The one look had been enough for him to sort out the geometry of the developing engagement. He would close on the two 190s that were converging onto the damaged Mossie before the lone 190 could reach a guns-firing position on him. "Watch him," Zack grunted as he concentrated on the two 190s that were closing on the damaged Mosquito. He was certain that the two 190s hadn't seen him. Why doesn't the bastard coming at us warn them? he thought. He would never know that the German pilot was a nineteen-year-old boy fresh out of pilot training and on his first combat mission. In the heat of the battle, the teenager had target fixation on *K for King* and had lost track of the fight.

What happened next had none of the chivalry or gallantry the public imagination credited to pilots. Unseen, Zack closed to the seven o'clock of the nearest Focke-Wulf 190 and gunned him out of the sky with his machine guns. The German pilot never saw what killed him. It was the work of an assassin and Zack felt no sense of elation. The other Focke-Wulf did see *K for King* and turned into the new threat. They passed head-on, guns firing, both missing. Zack skidded *K for King* across the wave tops, certain that the 190 on his tail was now in range. He wracked the throttles back and pulled back on the stick, causing the Mosquito to suddenly slow and balloon. The novice 190 pilot had not been expecting that maneuver and was spit out in front, passing underneath. The American kicked the pedals, ruddered over and squeezed off a gunshot. The .303 Brownings did their work and tore into the Focke-Wulf. The agile German fighter disappeared in a blazing explosion. But *K for King* was too close and flew through the fiery cloud, momentarily blinding Zack.

Instinctively, Zack pulled back on the stick, gaining height. He felt Ruffy's hand over his on the stick. "It's all right," the navigator said as he leveled them off. A red glow burned into Zack's returning eyesight. His vision cleared and he gasped. A red haze was licking over the front of the windscreen and the tops of the wings. They were on fire—the one thing he feared most in the wooden aircraft. But the controls and instruments were perfectly normal.

"I've got it," Zack said and Ruffy's touch disappeared. Again, he scanned the instruments and the wings. Instinctively, he jammed the throttles forward. The Merlins responded and they accelerated crisply to 270 knots as he dropped them back onto the deck. He was hoping speed or spray from the ocean's surface would snuff out whatever was burning. It worked. Then he noticed that the rudder was not responding to commands from the pedals. He wanted to weave to check his six o'clock position and see if the one remaining Focke-Wulf had found them. But without the rudder, it was not to be. He inched the throttles forward as he checked the Mossie's controls. Other than the dead rudder, they were fine. Now speed had to save them. He lifted *K for King* up to two hundred feet and ran for home as an acrid smell invaded the cockpit. Were they still burning? "What's the closest airfield?" he asked. "We need to get on the ground."

"Manston," Ruffy answered. "Set course two-nine-zero. Five minutes to landfall. Use the lighthouse as an initial approach fix. Piece of cake." He hit the IFF switch so they would be identified as a friendly aircraft to British radar.

"Stalwart fellow," Zack mumbled. He punched at the buttons on the TR.1133 radio control unit and changed to the recovery frequency.

The sharp smell was still with them when they saw the low headlands of the English coast and overflew the lighthouse. Magically, the wide expanse of concrete that was the runway appeared in front of them. Because Manston was the primary emergency recovery base for battle-damaged aircraft returning from raids over the continent, the British engineers had made the runway as wide as it was long. It was a simple matter of flying over the lighthouse, dropping the gear, and descending. There would be a runway wherever they touched down.

Zack dropped the undercarriage and they made a smooth landing on the mains. The numerous crash wagons and ambulances spotted around the field were reassuring. He braked to a halt and shut the engines down. Ruffy popped the hatch and clambered out in a headlong rush. He was careful to avoid the right propeller that was still spinning down. Zack was right behind him. They ran away from the Mossie, afraid that it would explode. Nothing happened and they stared at the aircraft. It was totally blackened like a scorched potato. "We were damn lucky," Ruffy said. "I could have sworn we were on fire."

"We were," Zack said as they cautiously approached their Mosquito. Zack ran his hand over the plywood fuselage and examined the linen fabric that covered the plane like a thin outer layer of skin. "I'll be damned," he muttered. "The madapalon burned, nothing else." He checked the rudder. The fabric covering the framework of the tail fin was totally burned away. "There's the control problem with the rudder," he said. "That shouldn't take long to fix."

They retrieved their flying kits out of the cockpit and started the long walk into the operations section. A maintenance officer gave them a lift and discussed the condition of their aircraft. He told them that the plane would be flyable in two or three days as soon as the tail surfaces were recovered. "It happens all the time," he told them. "The Intelligence wallahs will want your combat report. Then call your squadron and report in. They'll probably have you sit on your finger here until we get it fixed. All very routine."

A scholarly-looking flying officer in his early forties met them for the debrief with Intelligence. Cups of tea appeared when he sat them down and he methodically recorded their answers to his questions. "When did you last observe your number two?" he asked. Zack hesitated as he sought the answer. When had he last seen Sammy? Then it hit him. His wingman had simply disappeared. What had happened to him?

Ruffy answered. "On the run to target. We were abeam the concrete loading piers and he was to our starboard, on the seaward side, slightly behind us."

"Then you were definitely ahead of your number two."

Still Zack could not answer. "That's correct," Ruffy said. He then described how they had dropped their bombs on the cannon that was shooting at them from the roof of the E-boat pens. "We had to get those bastards," Ruffy explained, "or they would have gotten our number three and four."

"So you released two bombs on the gun emplacement?"

"That's correct."

"And for what time delay were they fused?"

"Four seconds to allow time for us to escape the frag pattern if we missed the entrances and they exploded in the open."

"I see."

And so did Zack. "Sammy was behind us and could have flown right into the frag from our bombs." His voice was little more than a whisper.

"If he were lagging too far behind, yes, that is a possibility."

"Oh my God," Zack moaned. "*K for King* was going like a . . ." Words failed him and he stood up, knocking his chair over.

"It is only a possibility," the older man said. "Luck of the game."

Zack bolted to his feet and hurried from the room. Outside, he fought for breath. With a will he did not know he possessed he forced himself to move, to think of other things. He found a telephone in a nearby Nissen hut and called his squadron. As the maintenance officer had predicted, they were told to wait until *K for King* was fixed and then fly to their new base at Hunsdon. He went in search of Ruffy, thankful for the activity, the need to do anything however trivial. He found Ruffy outside the officers mess talking to Wilhelmina Crafton. Damn, he thought, what the hell is she doing here? She keeps coming back like the plague. He turned to walk away, not wanting to speak to her.

"Zack," Ruffy called, "please. Over here." His voice was strained.

He walked over to them. "Well," he said, putting a front over his feelings, "what brings you here?"

"I'm posted here now," she said, "and I happened to see Mr. Ruffum . . ." Security barred her from revealing that she had set up a station at Manston to monitor the Pas de Calais operation. The SOE had discovered that because of a fluke in the frequency wave propagation of the radios their agents in France were using, the best reception was in the vicinity of Manston or Belfast, Ireland. The SOE had never considered the latter location.

"There's bad news," Ruffy said. He shook his head and walked away to give them some privacy.

"My grandfather . . ." she began, "passed away." She turned her head so he wouldn't see her pain. "I know that you were fond of him. . . ." She couldn't say more.

"What happened?" he said, his voice a hoarse whisper.

She steeled herself to tell him. "A Doodlebug . . . one of those damn pilotless rockets. . . . He saw it when the motor cut out and it fell on our village. He turned into a madman and was everywhere . . . organizing the firefighters, digging people out, making sure all the children were safe. He . . . he wouldn't stop until everything that could be done had been done. He finally went home to bed. He died in his sleep."

"Why did he do all that?" Zack asked. "He was a sick old man."

Then it came to her. The American didn't really understand. She had to explain it to him. Now her own hurt and frustration came out and focused on him. "They were his people and he cared for them. He knew their names, their problems, their children. All you saw were people divided by class . . . a duke surrounded by privilege and comfort while the common people around him struggled to get through each day. He wasn't wealthy. In fact, he was nearly bankrupt and deep in debt. He did what he could for them and tried to provide them with a livelihood. But the modern world was beyond him and he hated the twentieth century. All he could do was give them a sense of belonging and place." She paused to let that sink in. "Two values you Americans . . ." She bit her words off when she saw the stricken look on his face.

"Go ahead, say it," Zack said. "Two values we wouldn't understand." He looked at her and raised his hand, wanting to touch her, not sure how to say he was sorry. "You're right, I didn't understand." He looked away and stared across the field. "I am sorry." When he turned, Willi had disappeared into the building. He suddenly felt drained of emotion and purpose. Sammy, now the duke, how many more? he thought. Chantal? A sense of loss engulfed him and he froze, unable to move.

Men react to combat in different ways. Some slowly disintegrate under the pressure and horrors, develop a telltale twitch or weird behavior, and with luck are rescued before they totally break down or are killed. Others, like Zack, go steadily along at a normal pace, seemingly unaffected by it all. They can survive if they can get out before their inner emotional reservoirs are swamped with the shocks and horrors of war. But Zack was not to be that fortunate. He had reached his limits and was engulfed in a tidal wave of emotional despair. He had seen too much death and destruction and could no longer contain it all. For one desperate moment he doubted his own humanity.

Ruffy's voice touched him. "It's time to get on with it," he urged.

Automatically, Zack placed one foot in front of the other and followed his friend. The movement helped. "I don't know why this should hit me so hard," he said. "For a moment, I thought

I'd lost it. I wasn't sure if I could make my body or mind work again."

"You need a good booze-up," Ruffy told him. "Or a roll in the hay with some popsie. Preferably both."

The air in the radio hut at Manston was filled with blue smoke as Willi's superior puffed on his pipe. He heaved his rotund body into a standing position and walked to the door. "There's not going to be any more transmissions," he told the three women clustered around the radio. "The Gestapo has us in a bog in northern France. Our networks are being wiped out in areas we can least afford to lose. We need to unstick things. I don't think I have to tell you that we're in danger of a complete collapse and what that means to our invasion plans." He disappeared out the door into the early-morning dark.

Anna Fredericks looked to the radio operator who served as Chantal's "godmother" and arched an eyebrow. The radio operator only shook her head. The pattern spoke for itself and the conclusion was inescapable—they had lost another "pianist" to the Gestapo. "I think we need to talk," Fredericks said to Willi. The two women walked outside. "We cannot be positive what's happened to her at this time," Fredericks said. She did not see Willi's right hand slowly clench and relax, only to ball into a fist again. "But we must continue. I have another team ready for insertion. I want you to handle them from here."

"More sheep for the slaughter?" Willi asked.

Fredericks gave her a hard look. "Yes, if need be." She turned and walked away, leaving Willi alone.

Anger and misery tore at Willi as she walked toward the Nissen hut where she was quartered with the rest of the SOE team at Manston. She almost bumped into a shadowy figure crossing her path. It was Andrew Ruffum. "Sorry," she said.

"You're up early," Ruffy ventured. "Or is it late?"

"And you," Willi said. She needed human company, someone to talk to.

"I needed a breath of fresh air," Ruffy said. "We had a difficult mission yesterday and Zack took the news of the duke very badly. I've been seeing to him. This is one of those times when the bottle helps."

"I wish it were always that easy," Willi said.

Ruffy heard the hurt in her voice and sensed she needed company. "Shall we get some breakfast?" He led her into the officers mess.

The empty bottle of Scotch that Ruffy had produced from some mysterious source lay on the floor beside Zack's bunk. He stumbled over it in his hurry to reach the latrine and fell on his face, retching and heaving until his stomach was empty. Then he passed out. The young batwoman who looked after the officers in that room heard the noise and found him facedown in his own mess. She had seen it before and dragged him back into the bed. Then she went about the business of cleaning up him and the room. When he awoke, a glass of water and four aspirins were on the stand waiting for him. An hour later, he managed to get out of bed and stagger downstairs, looking for food to quell his churning stomach.

Ruffy and Willi were alone in the lounge, sitting and talking quietly in a corner. Ruffy's voice had a warm and comforting tone. "Nothing is certain," he was saying. "We can only keep muddling on, hoping this nightmare will end." Willi looked up and saw Zack standing in the doorway. Her eyes were bloodshot and tears streaked her face. She stood and, for an instant, was on the verge of saying something. Instead, she clasped her arms in front of her and walked briskly from the room.

"What was that all about?" Zack asked.

"She couldn't tell me . . . but her operations have gone terribly wrong. . . . She's devastated. The game can be brutal."

"It's no game, Ruffy," Zack muttered.

After lunch, Zack walked briskly around the base, enjoying the bright, cool day and a chance for some exercise. The one good thing about waking up with a hangover, he thought, is that you know you'll feel better before the day is over. Since he was on the base, he didn't pay attention to the sentry standing guard near a set of Nissen huts with a canopy of aerials. He turned down a side path that led into a thick clump of trees behind the huts. Another guard emerged out of the bushes and halted him, demanding to see his pass. "Sorry, I don't have one." Zack explained how he had made an emergency landing the day before and was waiting for his plane to be repaired. The SOE had trained the guard to be suspicious of anything unusual and he thought it very strange that an individual with an American accent was wearing an RAF uniform. He placed Zack under arrest and called his superior. A few minutes later, Willi emerged on a bicycle from behind the huts and pedaled toward them.

She came to a halt beside the guard and explained that she would take custody of the miscreant. The guard gave Zack a hard look and disappeared back into the bushes. She motioned him to come with her and pushed the bike back down the path, away from the huts. "You were fortunate," she explained, "that I was just coming off duty. What were you doing in this sector, anyway?"

"Walking. I needed some exercise. That's all." He eyed her bike. "If I could get my hands on one of those and a pass, I wouldn't even be on the base."

"Then you'd like to see the countryside?"

"Sure. What I've seen from the air, it looks gorgeous."

"I'll see what I can do," she said.

"Please don't put yourself out."

Willi stopped and looked at him. "Ruffy told me about your last mission. An outing will do you wonders."

"And he told me about you. Can you find another bike? A break would do us both some good."

She gave him a thoughtful look. "Yes it would. I'll see what I can arrange." Twenty minutes later, they pedaled through the main gate and into the quiet countryside. "Well," she said, "what would you like to see?"

"The coastline," he answered. "I saw a lighthouse when we landed."

"You like lighthouses?"

"Don't know. I've never met one before."

She smiled at the thought of meeting a lighthouse. "I can introduce you. You'll like the keeper, Tory Chester." She treated him to a delightful laugh. "I've done some exploring on my own. Come on, then. It's farther than it looks." They set off down a narrow lane, the fragile peace that eluded them back in place.

The scenery delighted Zack and he would stop frequently, pointing out whatever caught his attention. At one point she laughingly called him the "mad geographer" and discovered, much to her amazement, that the gloom and stress that bound her life had eased its shackles. They had stopped on top of a small hump-back bridge that crossed a rail line and watched a train barrel past, the steam and smoke engulfing them for a moment. She pushed off, heading down the bridge but lost her balance and landed with a hard thump on her rear end. The pout on her face told Zack that she wasn't hurt.

"Right on the old tosh," he laughed.

"It's 'tush,' you fool," she said, getting back on the bike.

"I like 'tosh' better."

Willi laughed. "So do I."

Twenty minutes later, they reached the lighthouse that stood on a small point of land that jutted out into the Strait of Dover. Zack stood silent, transfixed by the view while Willi knocked on the door. The old man who answered could have been straight from the pages of a Somerset Maugham novel: craggy face, bright blue eyes, a wispy gray beard, slightly hunch-shouldered. He wore a thick Aran sweater that had seen better days and smelled of stale cigarette smoke. "Hello, lass," he said, obviously pleased to see her. She introduced Zack to Tory Chester and produced two packs of Players cigarettes. He held them for a moment, one in each shaking hand, weighing them. "You shouldn't waste these on an old geezer like me. Filthy habit, but thank you." He ripped open a pack, offered his guests one, which they declined, and lit one for himself, inhaling deeply. He was an addicted chain smoker and had suffered greatly due to rationing.

Zack was intrigued by the relationship between Tory and Willi; he had always thought of her as too snobbish to establish a friendship with someone like a lighthouse keeper. But they were clearly good friends. Tory took Zack on a tour of the lighthouse. The living quarters consisted of two rooms: a combination kitchen-living room and one small bedroom. A door off the kitchen opened onto the tower stairs, which they climbed to the top. Tory paused on the landing below the beacon. It was neatly stocked with an old morris chair and a set of shelves loaded with rags, tools, and a radio. Tory let Zack go up the ladder first onto the platform that surrounded the big lens. He waited for a reaction. Silence. Finally, Zack whispered a single word, "Magnificent." Zack found the word inadequate to describe the seascape stretched out below him. Satisfied that he had not misjudged the young American, Tory climbed through the hatch and joined him.

"It's a first-order Fresnel lens," he explained, pointing out the 666 hand-ground glass lenses that focused the light into a powerful beam. The glass parts and brass framework sparkled like crystal in the sunlight, spotlessly clean and free of dust. "It's about six feet in diameter, weighs over two tons," he explained, "and with those two electric lamps"—he pointed to the pair of huge one-thousand-watt electric lamps in the center—"it can be seen for twenty miles."

"When do you turn it on?" Zack asked.

"When this bloody war is over," Tory growled. There was a deep hurt or bitterness in his voice; Zack couldn't tell which. "I still clean it every day so it will be ready." He stared out to sea. "We've reached an unspoken agreement with Jerry—we don't turn our beacons on and he doesn't turn his on."

"What happens if you do?"

"Then we can expect a visit from the bloody Germans... Sometimes a bomber but most likely an E-boat would shell us." Zack almost interrupted to tell him that that was much less likely now, but he said nothing. "We do the same to them," Tory continued. "At least, the lighthouses will all be in a piece when this is over, ready to go again." He stared out to sea, seeing something that wasn't there for Zack. "I've tended a beacon most of me life. It's all I know. Now I sit up at night and listen on the wireless as you blokes come home. I hear it... the SOS calls, the Mayday calls, some pilot hopelessly lost... and I can't do a bloody thing except listen. That's not what a Fresnel is for. It should be turned on and sweeping the sky when souls are in distress. All I want is for this damn war to end so I can light the beacon and do what I've always done." The old man climbed down the ladder to the landing and led the way down the stairs. "The fishing was good today and I've got plenty if you'd like to keep an old 'un company for dinner."

"I think we have to get back to base before it gets dark," Zack told him.

"Rain's on the way. You'll be soaked through before you do that. It'll clear out before morning."

They found Willi in the small kitchen cleaning the fish and Zack repeated Tory's offer and his weather forecast. "Tory's an infallible weather prophet," she allowed. "If he says it's going to rain, it will be a monsoon." Tory settled the matter by telling them that they could spend the night and Willi could sleep in his bed. "You"—he pointed to a big chair by the small fireplace—"can doss there."

"Where will you sleep?" Zack asked.

"I don't sleep at night," Tory told him. "Too old to change me habits. I'll be up on the landing."

"He listens to the radio there," Willi said.

It was all agreed on and Tory proved that he could cook fish. Before they had finished eating, the rain was pelting down, driving against the small windows. They could hear the gusting wind pound at the door. "I don't think there'll be much flying tonight," Zack observed.

"You never know," Tory said and made his way up the tower steps.

Zack and Willi talked for a while and could hear the radio echo down the tower as Tory changed from one frequency to another. Zack closed the door to the stairs but Willi said to leave it open so they could hear. Finally, they heard music. "You were right," Willi said, "not much flying. But he'll keep a listening watch and scan the emergency frequencies from time to time." She thought for a moment. "If you don't mind, I'm going to bed. I could use a good night's sleep." She found him some blankets and a pillow and disappeared into the tiny bedroom, closing the door behind her. Zack poked the coals in the hearth to life, tested the big overstuffed chair, and stretched out under a blanket.

He wasn't sure what woke him and he listened. The rain had stopped and he could see moonlight streaming through the windows. A faint melody echoed down from the tower. Then he saw her standing next to the kitchen window, looking into the night. She was wearing an old duffel coat and was barefoot. "Are you okay?" he asked. He could see her head nod.

"They'll fly now, won't they?" Her voice was little more than a whisper.

He joined her at the window. "Yeah." There was a finality in his voice. It was a bomber's moon. "They're out there right now." Tears filled her eyes and Zack knew that a deep hurt was hovering just below the surface, ready to make its presence known.

An old English music hall melody drifted down from above. " 'After the Ball Is Over,' " she said, naming the song. A bitter irony in her voice. "Just like this war."

"This will be over," he told her. "These are the wasted years."

Willi stared at him, her mouth slightly open. "The wasted years," she repeated, her voice barely audible. He did understand. "We've been at this for over four years now. Four wasted years. Our youth gone. How many more years? We won't be young anymore. These years should have been filled with parties, pretty dresses, picnics, boys lined up in a row and dances. . . . I was so looking forward to the dances when I was seventeen. Because of this war, this damnable, bloody war, we've lost all that . . . the years . . . the dances . . . our youth. We won't get them back. And there's no end in sight."

"It will end," he said and folded her into his arms. She held on to him and wept. Now the gentle and haunting voice of Vera Lynn singing "I'll Be Seeing You" echoed down from the tower. "Miss Crafton," he said, "may I have the honor of this dance?" She held on to him and he could feel her shake. Then her mouth was on his, her lips full and trembling. Her hands were on his neck, holding his head, not letting him go as her tongue searched for his.

"Oh, damn you," she moaned and pulled away. He wanted to protest that he hadn't done anything. "You don't know what you are," she said. "Damn you." Then she was back in his arms.

"Who would have believed?" Zack said as he felt Willi's arms reach over him and her warm body cuddle against his back. Then her tongue brushed his neck and sent tingles down to the lower regions of his body. But he wanted to talk. "I can hardly credit this," he said and rolled over so he could see her face. The blankets pulled away and cold air washed over his bare skin. He tugged the blankets back into place. She wrapped a leg around his and pulled herself to him. Her arms snaked around his neck and she buried her face against his neck.

"Talk later," she commanded and rubbed her breasts against his chest. Her hand worked between their stomachs and inched lower. She stroked him until he was hard. "Yes, we'll talk later," she whispered.

"You were always so angry," Zack said. He was propped up on an elbow, still in bed. "And so hostile. It was almost as if you were mad at me for breathing English air."

Willi stroked his cheek. "It wasn't you—personally. Well, maybe it was. You are so much like your countrymen: an un-bounded free spirit. I sometimes wonder how you Americans ever agree on anything. You assault life, determined to win. You never accept anything the way it is. If you don't like something, then you change it, as if the changing will make it better. And you"— she was now talking about him personally—"never seem to bloody your head. That is what happens to normal people, you know." She gave his chest a little thump with her fist. "You Yanks play at this war. Look at what you bring with you. I'm surprised your musette bag isn't stuffed with chocolates, cigarettes, and nylons."

"I am in the RAF," Zack reminded her.

"Yes, you are," she conceded.

Zack said, "I suppose this war extracts a different price from each of us."

She rolled out of bed and searched for her clothes. He watched her as she dressed, captivated by her graceful movements. He hadn't noticed that before. "I suppose it's time to get back to the real world and continue paying the price," she said. Then she sat on the edge of the bed, not touching him. "I'm not sure when it happened, but I love you, Zack Pontowski." She stood and walked out of the room, shutting the door behind her. He lay there, still propped on one elbow, trying to understand what he was feeling.

Then it came to him. He was in love with two women.

ELEVEN

The Executive Office Building, Washington, D.C.

The situation went critical when Mazie's contact with Bill Carroll at the Air Force's Special Activities Center hand-delivered the latest report to her. "Tell General Carroll," she told the handsome black woman, "that I appreciate him keeping me in the loop." Mazie had been told that Carroll's operatives were now working with the CIA, and reporting through Willowbranch. But it took the CIA at least twenty-four hours to process any message and pass it on.

She switched on her computer and read the latest intelligence summary issued by the DEA. It confirmed that the meeting with Chiang and the other two cartels was still in progress. Mazie chewed her lower lip and waddled down to the basement for a private chat with the DEA's liaison officer. "How reliable is your source?" she asked the man.

"Pretty good," he replied. "The PUSIO has an informant inside the Yakuza." Mazie's lips compressed into a thin line as he filled in the details. She was one of the few Americans who knew about the shadowy Japanese intelligence organization that carried the bulky name Public Security Investigation Office, or PUSIO for short, and hid in the Japanese Ministry of Justice. It was the Japanese equivalent of the CIA and produced excellent intelligence. The PUSIO had recently penetrated the Yakuza, the largest criminal organization in Japan, and had discovered that the Yakuza was considering joining Chiang's consortium. At that point, the PUSIO started cooperating with the DEA in an effort to stem the growing drug trade in Japan. That liaison had just paid a dividend.

Mazie picked up the phone and called Cagliari's office for an immediate appointment the moment he returned from a meeting with the President. She hurried through the tunnel to the White House and was still puffing from the run when he walked into his office. Cagliari recognized the signs and told her to follow him into his private office. Mazie did not sit down and cut to the heart of the matter. "Chiang is going to execute at least two of the hostages. It could happen any time after tomorrow."

Cagliari's face turned to ice. "When did this come in?"

"Less than fifteen minutes ago."

Cagliari asked the critical question. "Sources?" He stared at his hands and fought down an urge to scratch them as Mazie answered. "I'd feel much better about this if we had a second confirming source," he said. Mazie only shook her head. Cagliari took a deep breath. "How do you rate the report?"

"It fits the picture," she said. Then she added, "Sir, the PUSIO gave the DEA another item. The Yakuza are going international. They have plans to flood the market with below-cost, good-quality drugs to undercut their competition. Then once they've got the market cornered, to set the prices they want. But the DEA says the cartels won't roll over and play dead for that. This could get very bloody."

Cagliari frowned. "I'll take it upstairs." He meant down the hall and into the Oval Office.

The Capitol, Washington, D.C.

General Simon Mado was whistling a tuneless melody when he reached Courtland's offices. The secretary told him he was expected and he pushed through the door into Courtland's office. "Things are heating up," he told the senator. "It looks like we're going in after your daughter." Courtland pulled a slight grimace but said nothing. "I can't figure out exactly what's going down," Mado explained, "but there are two groups in on this. One is a large unified force in training at Eglin Air Force Base in Florida and the second is a small composite group deployed to Udorn in Thailand. That one looks like a repeat of Dragon Noire."

Courtland thought for a moment. He supposed he wanted his daughter rescued and paid lip service to the idea. But at the rock bottom of his calculations lay one singular fact—he didn't really like his daughter and only saw problems with her in the future, especially if he was successful in his quest for the presidency. And more than anything else, he wanted to be President of the United States. The idea planted months ago that a failed rescue attempt would rebound to his advantage had grown and was now bearing fruit. He fixed Mado with a hard look. "What chance of success do you give a rescue attempt now?"

Mado did not respond immediately. Courtland was his ticket to a fourth star and, if he read the signs right, to becoming the Chairman of the Joint Chiefs of Staff. What a coup that would be. Promoted over at least seventy more senior generals to become the youngest Chairman of the Joint Chiefs. His ambition burned as hot as Courtland's but every instinct he possessed shouted that the senator would dump him in a moment if his advice proved worthless in military matters. "I'd give the small group deployed in Thailand less than a twenty-five percent chance of pulling off a rescue. As for the large group at Eglin, even less. It has the mass and firepower to wipe Chiang off the face of the earth, but it cannot get into the compound fast enough to rescue the hostages before the guards shoot them."

The senator could live with that. "Perhaps our best course of action is to see how this plays out," he said. Then another thought occurred to him. He hit a button on his intercom panel and summoned an aide. In a few moments, Tina Stanley walked into the room. "Tina," Courtland said, "I'd like you to get in contact with one of your, ah, more reliable journalist friends. Have General Mado provide some deep background on what's going down, very deep background." He meant the leak had to be buried deep and not traceable to him.

Udorn, Thailand

The rain sheeted down, drenching the two men, seeping inside every opening in their ponchos, soaking them to the skin. "I wonder why we even wear these damn things," Mackay muttered.

It was his first experience with the full-blown fury of an Asian monsoon and he could hardly credit the force of the rain as it dumped on the airfield at Udorn, Thailand.

Kamigami didn't answer and hunched against the downpour, maintaining an even pace as they headed for the building where Mallard and Trimler had set up a temporary command post. He had experienced the monsoon years before when he was a seventeen-year-old private, newly enlisted in the Army and on his first tour in South Vietnam. He didn't recall it being as bad. Since the visibility was the same then as now, he chalked it up to old age. They stomped their way into the building and shed their ponchos.

A very wet E-Squared burst through the door followed by a half-drowned Gillespie. "My God," E-Squared laughed, "talk about a two-cunted cow pissing on a flat rock!"

"Can you take a C-One-thirty off in this?" Mackay asked.

E-Squared looked out a window and studied the rain. "I can launch between the breaks. Don't know about shooting an approach and landing in this shit though. It's pretty heavy." Gillespie said nothing and followed the three older men into the command post.

Inside, Trimler handed Mackay the yellow copy of a message stamped "Secret" at the top and bottom. It was an execute order by the authority and direction of the secretary of defense. It was the first one that Mackay had seen. "I know we need the weather on our side," Trimler said, "but this is too much. Colonel Mallard is on the SatCom right now explaining the situation to the NMCC."

They were joined a few moments later by a worried-looking Mallard. "It's pretty simple," he explained. "Recent intelligence indicates that Chiang is going to execute the hostages. They think he's lost his marbles. They agree that the weather is bad but it will give us the cover we need to move into position." He looked at them. "Since I'm the mission commander, the ball is in my court. If I think we can hack the weather, we go. Your thoughts, please."

It was a council of war. Only this time the men who were the cutting edge were making the decision, not some old men safe in their comfortable chairs in a warm and snug office. Trimler's lips compressed into a hard line and he said nothing.

"We can launch the C-One-thirties," E-Squared said.

"Can the helicopters hack it?" Mallard asked. He was looking directly at Gillespie. It was an awesome responsibility to lay on a young captain.

Gillespie hesitated. Then: "Yes, sir. We can insert the teams."

"Colonel Mackay, can the teams move into position in this rain once they are on the ground?" Mallard asked.

The tall black man moved to the window and stared at the driving rain. The reasoning behind the order made sense—it was the cover they needed to gain the element of surprise. But the deluge belting down from the heavy clouds was much worse than he had expected. He didn't like what that did to their chances of success. During the buildup they had never practiced in the rain for one simple reason—it hadn't rained. Now the rain was the critical element. He wanted to shout "How should I know!" But that option was denied him. Now the lives of his men depended on his judgment. His voice betrayed none of his doubts when he said, "I think we can do it." A slight smile flickered across Kamigami's lips.

Mallard looked at Trimler, his ground commander. Now he had to commit. "I agree with Colonel Mackay, we should be able to do it. If our intelligence is correct, we don't have a choice."

The burden of command now came squarely onto Mallard's shoulders. The final decision was his to make. "We go" was all he said. He left to relay the decision over the SatCom to the NMCC.

Kamigami joined Mackay by the window as they waited. "It's a good decision," the CSM told him.

"We've got to tell the teams to get ready," Mackay allowed. He fell silent, thinking. "Aren't you worried?" he finally asked.

Kamigami's answer was a simple "I'm worried." The sergeant was an inarticulate man and could not tell Mackay about the deadly virus known as doubt and how it affects combat readiness. He had done all he could and now they had to enter the crucible of combat for the final test. "I'll tell the captains to get their teams ready," he said.

"It's getting worse," Gillespie said to the Beezer and E-Squared. They were standing inside a hangar less than two hundred feet from the helicopter he would fly. The driving rain had obscured the taxipath leading to the runway and his aircraft was fading in and out of the rain.

"Visibility is too damn low," E-Squared grunted. "Way below

minimums." He judged the forward visibility to be less than three hundred feet and he was having second thoughts.

"What's this?" the Beezer said, a mock-concern in his voice. "A belated worry over weather minimums? Getting too old to hack it?"

"Air off," E-Squared shot back. He didn't feel like taking any flak from his old friend.

"I remember when weather minimums were just an excuse for not flying when you were hung over," the Beezer said. Then he grinned at Gillespie. "The boy must be getting old."

"For Christ's sake," E-Squared groused, "knock it off."

But the Beezer was relentless. "Do you suppose it's because he just got engaged? He wants to make an honest woman out of the poor woman...."

"Hey," Gillespie interrupted, "that's great. Congratulations. Who's the lucky—"

"Lieutenant Colonel Leanne Vokel," the Beezer told him.

"Our Intel officer?" Gillespie couldn't believe it. He had always thought they were good-natured rivals.

"Yep," the Beezer replied. "He did the deed last night. I can just see it now, the oldest pregnant lieutenant colonel in the Air Force. Sure you're up to fatherhood?"

Gillespie half-listened to the two men banter as he watched Delta Force start to load his helicopter. The rain momentarily slackened and he saw the SAS captain, Peter Woodward, climb on board the second helicopter farther down the ramp. It must be some screw-up, Gillespie thought; Woodward isn't a player on this. Then he remembered how the SAS captain had always traveled on a backup helicopter during training. It would be an easy matter to sort out.

Before he could say anything, E-Squared said, "It's almost block time. Got to kick the tires and light the fires." Then he turned and whispered to Gillespie, "You didn't see what you thought you saw" before he walked rapidly into the rain, heading for his MC-130.

The Beezer watched him go. "He is one crock of shit," the gunship pilot grumbled good-naturedly. Gillespie pulled on his poncho to make the dash to his helicopter. The Beezer grabbed him by the arm. "Tell Kamigami what you didn't see. He's the only one who needs to know."

The White House, Washington, D.C.

WAIT:

OPERATION JERICHO

flashed on the big video display screen at the far end of the
Situation Room in the basement of the White House. A message
was coming in. Pontowski tried to relax into his comfortable chair
but his restless mind would not allow him that luxury and too
many old memories kept demanding his attention. Fifty years
before he had been in a similar position and he knew what he
was ordering this new generation of young men to do. Jericho!
The name he had given the operation kept pounding at him, not
letting him rest.

He remembered the time when he had sat in the cramped
cockpit of a Mosquito with Ruffy, waiting for a break in the
weather to launch. A fleeting image of his friend flashed across
his memory, still sharp and clear. Again he felt the same building
tension, the worry that clamped his chest with a viselike grip when
he had time to confront his own mortality. It was all back, even
the slightly coppery taste in his mouth and the urge for action.
Normally, he was a very patient man—another gift of age—but
now he itched for movement to break the tension, the same as
then.

But he did nothing and, like then, he waited.

Words flashed on the screen.

OPERATION JERICHO

LAUNCH AT 1430 ZULU

LANDING ZONE TIME: 1720 ZULU

With no conscious effort, Pontowski translated the first time,
1430 Zulu, which was Greenwich mean time, into local time in
Thailand and Washington, D.C. It was 2130, or nine-thirty in the
evening in Thailand, and 0930, nine-thirty in the morning in Washington—exactly twelve hours' difference. "What's the weather
like?" he asked.

The Army colonel who ran the Situation Room when military
operations were under way spoke into the boom mike on his
headset and the screen flashed, this time displaying a weather
map. The monitor on the left side of the big screen scrolled up
and a detailed readout of the weather appeared. "Ceilings less

than one hundred feet, forward visibility one sixteenth of a mile," Leo Cox, his chief of staff, read out. "My God," he added, awe in his voice, "that's little more than a football field."

It all had meaning for Pontowski. He knew what it was like to fly at low level in weather like that. He could remember the constant jolting and twisting as the aircraft banged about, the dryness in your mouth, the sweat, and the chafing of your beard's stubble under the oxygen mask. Jericho!

"Well, Leo," he said, pushing himself to his feet, "there's nothing we can do but wait now."

"The hardest part," Cox conceded.

"I'd like to monitor Jericho when it goes down," Pontowski said.

"The Battle Staff at the NMCC will be fully manned until the helicopters have landed and gone into hiding," Cox explained. "After that, the Battle Staff will be reduced and a general will monitor the situation until the attack starts. You can bet they'll all be back then. Where would you prefer to be?"

"I'll be here," Pontowski said. "I want Mike Cagliari in the NMCC when it goes down. Have him talking directly to the generals and experts. Have Bobby Burke there, too." He thought for a moment. "In the meantime, I'd like Mazie Kamigami to monitor things from this end." Cox raised an eyebrow at this. "She's got her head screwed on straight and probably knows more of the big picture than anyone else," Pontowski explained.

"Mr. President, why did you change the name of the operation to Jericho?" Cox asked. He was keeping a daily journal of his tour as the President's chief of staff and planned to publish his own account. He already had a title, "A Time of Honor."

"Since we're blowing some walls down, it seemed appropriate." And, he mentally added, like I did in World War Two on my own Jericho. Silence came down in the room.

The Army colonel spoke into his boom mike again, paused, and then said, "Sir, you have a message from Dr. Smithson at Bethesda. He says your wife is awake and requests your presence, if possible."

Pontowski rose to his feet, suddenly feeling tired and very old. Smithson might be an ass but he would only have sent that message if Tosh had taken a turn for the worse. A bitter panic touched his heart when he thought that this might be the last time he would ever speak to his wife. "I'm going to the hospital," he said. Cox followed him out of the room. "History won't let us go," the President told him, "and keeps repeating itself, reminding us that the human condition hasn't changed. I just wish it would let up on me." But he knew it wasn't to be; his past was his fate and now he would have to experience it all again, reliving that day in February of 1944.

1944

RAF Hunsdon, Hertfordshire, England

What will the censor do to this? Zack mused, thinking of the pompous officer who read all the mail leaving RAF Hunsdon. Zack was sitting in the reading room of the officers mess writing a letter to Willi. They had not seen each other since he had flown out of Manston after *K for King* had been repaired. But not before they had spent one more night together. The room she had found for them over a pub had been much more comfortable than the lighthouse and the negligee she had produced from her bag had been a work of art. He had no idea that clothes could be so provocative. The next day she had seen him and Ruffy off to their new base at Hunsdon with a cheery good-bye. Two days later her first letter had arrived and they started an almost daily correspondence. Not even the war had diminished the efficiency of the Royal Mail. Her last four-page letter had sent scorching shivers through the lower regions of his body and he wanted to get an answer in the mail immediately—before she changed her mind. Her last word had been "hurry," and he wanted to do exactly that.

He wrote:

> After reading your last letter, I am surprised that the envelope was not singed. You English have a much maligned reputation when it comes to l'amour and give nothing away to the French. I'm going to keep your letters and see that they are published a hundred years from now. They will give new meaning to the term "the good old days." But we must protect the innocent—namely me—for now.
>
> And yes, I'll try to get leave and meet you on Saturday, the 19th of February, in London for what you so intriguingly refer to as a "dirty weekend." I am due some leave so there shouldn't be a problem, unless some op gets in the way. But the lousy weather this time of year has been the deciding factor.

The censor will no doubt razor that out, he thought. Time to get even with the pompous bastard. He scribbled:

I need to change the subject. I'm writing this in the mess and keep getting strange looks. I'm either moaning too much when I reread your letter or I'm panting with my tongue hanging out.

Now that will get you wondering what was in Willi's letter, Zack mused.

I just returned from a course on munitions.
    Actually, it was more like a research project than a formal class. I've become some type of "Bomb Wallah" and supposedly know all there is to know about the subject. I suppose it helps to do the job more efficiently. But I don't think a future employer will be impressed. Did you know there is a special tribe of Gremlins that inhabits all bomb dumps? Those little buggers do nothing but sit around all day and think up things that can go wrong. Then they go and test their latest theory on some poor hapless guy or airplane. Damn bombs can be as dangerous to us as to the Germans.
    One of those Gremlins was hard at work yesterday. The armorers were winching a big bruiser into a bomb bay when the machinery went totally wrong. The bomb dropped to the ground and went rolling out from under the aircraft and merrily along the ground. They had a devil of a time getting it stopped. "As usual, P. was there and when they asked him what to do, all he said was 'Put it back on.' Problem solved. He's a cool one.

Zack knew the censor would have fits if he mentioned that it was a four-thousand-pound bomb that looked like a huge garbage can and he and Ruffy were testing it for the first time in combat. The brass had thought it was too heavy for the Mosquito, but 140 Wing had proven them wrong.
    He would tell her more in person about what he had learned from watching Group Captain Percy Charles Pickard. In Zack's estimation, Pickard was the best leader he had ever met and was directly responsible for the outstanding success of the wing.
    Oh, the bomb worked very well, he recalled, his pen still. What death and destruction had he and Ruffy caused when they dropped that bomb? It was all so clean and antiseptic for the crews. All they saw of the target was smoke and maybe some flames. Later, Intelligence might show them reconnaissance photos of bomb damage. But those photos were impersonal and could have been taken over London. It was the same with his squadron mates. Impersonal. A person was there in the morning and then

he was gone, never to return. No mess, just pack up his things while the commander wrote a letter to his wife or parents. For a time, the others might remember him; what he looked like, his personality, his voice. But because of some unwritten rule, the men would not talk about him, probably because it would remind them of their own mortality. Then the memory would fade, saving them from confronting the reality of his death; the charred remains, a dismembered body so totally smashed and pounded into the aircraft's wreckage that the two were inseparable.

Sammy, the wingman he had lost over Dunkirk, materialized in Zack's mind. Every detail was there, his face, the wispy mustache, the way he left the top button of his tunic undone, and his bright blue eyes. Zack could hear his voice as clear and true as if Sammy were with him. He closed his eyes, leaned back into his chair, and let the memory carry him. I hope it wasn't my bombs that killed you, he thought. I'm glad I haven't forgotten, he said to himself. And I won't, he promised.

A whiff of a half-remembered tobacco smoke assaulted his nose. He glanced up and saw the rotund figure of a man standing in the foyer—the man from the house at Wimbledon. Images of Chantal came rushing back and a longing hurt mixed with guilt feelings beat at him. It wasn't right that he should be involved with Willi while she was in danger. He forced himself to concentrate on the man and masked his guilt feelings. What the hell is he doing here? he thought. Why am I caught in a vicious circle and keep running into people I'd like to avoid? What the hell is going on?

Slowly, he reasoned it out. It was not a vicious circle or some perverse fate, but one of the ironies of life that the phrase "it's a small world" becomes especially true in wartime. In spite of the scale of the war and the millions of people involved, certain operations overlapped geographically and Zack figured that because he was occupying the same space and time, they were likely to run into each other. A change in assignment could alter all that. But that would mean he would not see Willi until the war ended. Did that mean he was betraying Chantal? Damn, he thought, I haven't practiced guilt in a long time.

He finished the letter, stuffed it in an envelope, and dropped it unsealed in the box for the censor. Ruffy found him an hour later. "Pick wants you over in operations. Seems there's an ops on. Must be a bit of a flapper because Embry's here from Two Group."

"It's a small world," Zack said, mystifying Ruffy.

The acrid aroma of the pipe smoke and the light blue haze tinting the air hit Zack the moment he walked into the room. An uneasy feeling of foreboding captured him and he half-expected the portly little man from the house in Wimbledon to be there. But only the squadron leaders who commanded the three squadrons that made up 140 Wing were in the room with Pickard and Embry. Then he saw it, a cloth-draped target model sitting on a table, waiting to be revealed. But why had he been called in? He sat down in the rear of the room and waited. The tingling sensation that had always warned him when something was wrong stirred.

Embry stood up. "Right then, we're all here. The French Resistance has made an unusual request." He pointed to a map of northern France that was tacked up on the wall and circled the town of Amiens. "The Gestapo is holding over seven hundred Resistance workers in the jail at Amiens and are being their normal bloody selves and have sentenced a hundred of them to death. Needless to say, the Resistance would like to do something to prevent that but find themselves powerless. Jerry has been most adept at penetrating their operations in this sector. That's why so many Resistance workers are in the bloody place to begin with.

"The Resistance has asked the RAF to bomb the jail, blow the walls down, kill a few guards, and effect a jailbreak to allow the poor bastards a chance to escape." Embry was looking directly at Zack and watched the young pilot stiffen. "This is where you come in, Mr. Pontowski. You do seem to have some skill for this type of thing. The French have assured us that the prisoners would much prefer to take their chances with our bombs than die at the end of a German rope or in front of a firing squad. This is a chance to do something very worthwhile and send the Gestapo a message they won't forget." He walked over to the scale model and whipped the cover off. "Gentlemen, your target." It was an exact replica of the prison at Amiens.

The three squadron leaders crowded around the model, looking at it from different angles, picturing a bomb run. "Which squadron leads the attack?" one of them asked. Pickard smiled, his faith in his men reaffirmed. The 140 Wing was made up of three squadrons: 21 being British, 464 made up of Australians, and 487 from New Zealand. They all wanted to go and he would not show favoritism.

"I'll flip a coin later," Pickard said. "Right now, each of you pick your six best crews while we work out the navigation and details. It should be on within the next forty-eight hours. I don't need to remind you that mum's the word."

"You'd never do that," one of the men laughed. They filed out of the room to see what crews they had available and check on the status of their aircraft. Zack's commander, a cool New Zealander, stopped and said, "If you want, you're on."

"I want," Zack replied, ignoring his inner alarm bell.

The squadron leader nodded, pleased that his best pilot was volunteering. He pointed at the model. "You best get on with it. Please see that they don't have us doing anything stupid."

Embry turned the mission planning over to Zack and two navigation officers and retreated into a nearby office. The man from Wimbledon was waiting for him, puffing on his pipe. "I hope it went well," he said. Embry nodded. "Make sure you attack at lunchtime. Most of the prisoners should be out of their cells and in the dining hall, which should make it much easier for them to escape. Also, could you pay special attention to the guards quarters? The Germans will be sitting down to dinner and it would be nice to dispatch a few of them." He gave Embry an encouraging smile. He had no intention of telling Embry that many female prisoners, the young and pretty ones, were kept in the guards' quarters to serve as prostitutes. "We do have another reason," the pipe smoker added. "The French collaborator who has sold many of our agents to the Gestapo has been invited to lunch. We don't know which day, but then we mustn't overlook any opportunity."

"I'm sure we can spare a SAP or two," Embry said. "A SAP," he explained, "is a semi-armor-piercing, hard-nosed bomb. It should do the job."

"This raid is more important than you know," the man told Embry. "The collaborator has managed to feed most of our new network, code name Sosies, to the Gestapo. Sosies has a priority one." He puffed on his pipe and let that sink in. Priority one meant that the Sosies network was critical to the Allied invasion preparations. "The Germans don't know it, but they have captured Sosies's leaders. Quite a gold mine of information there. We must get them out." Or kill them with our bombs, he mentally calculated.

"I'll have Mr. Pontowski make sure we target the guards' quarters," Embry promised. "He is very good at that type of thing."

TWELVE

The Burma ADIZ

It was a three-way battle—Gillespie versus the goat versus the weather. The captain's strategy was simple, make the goat his ally, his friend. He wasn't fighting the heavily loaded MH-53, the twenty-two tons of metal, fuel, mechanical gadgetry, electronic wizardry, and human flesh called Rascal One. Instead, he was seducing the beast to his will, making it want to do what he wanted. The designers of the helicopter thought in aerodynamic terms: the control of pitch, roll, and yaw; thrust vectors, stress analysis, center of lift versus the center of gravity, translational lift; and thousands of other technical concerns, all capable of being reduced to mathematical abstractions and force-fed into a computer. Now the young captain was living with those results and he made no attempt to recall the formulas or forces at work on his machine. He had mastered them all in pilot training and they were part of his nature. Now, Gillespie concentrated on what the goat was telling him, instinctively understanding the signals and coaxing the beast to do the right thing, which in this case was to stay airborne and on course.

And Gillespie was winning. But the weather was not going to give the two MH-53s an easy victory as they beat their way into

337

Burma's airspace, penetrating Burma's ADIZ, the Air Defense Identification Zone.

A steady stream of water was leaking out of the overhead panel onto the center console. An electrical short was the last thing he needed. "Can you cover it up?" Gillespie asked the flight engineer. The sergeant grabbed a poncho and spread it over the console. "I thought these puppies were watertight," Gillespie mumbled. "We're leaking like a sieve." A hard bump punctuated the light turbulence they were flying through, twisting and shaking the aircraft. Gillespie automatically stroked the flight controls, coaxing the goat to do the right thing. He was flying totally on instruments, relying on the magic that went on behind the instrument panel and in the black boxes that gave the MH-53 the ability to penetrate a monsoon rainstorm flying three hundred feet above the terrain.

The copilot concentrated on navigating, constantly cross-checking the Doppler/inertial navigation system with the ground mapping radar and the Global Positioning System monitor, GPS, to keep them on course. He kept hoping for a break in the rain so he could rely on old-fashioned map reading to fix their location. But it was not to be, so he kept up the cross-check, trying to keep everything in agreement. He kept the whole system honest by relying on DR—dead reckoning—as the final arbiter. The old, time-tested technique of flying a compass heading for a specified time was still basic to navigation. Another hard bump lifted them out of their seats and drove them against their lap and shoulder harnesses.

The stream of water stopped. "Something must have snapped back into place," the flight engineer allowed. He removed the poncho.

The intercom crackled. "We're drowning in water and puke," one of the gunners complained. "I'm talking Niagara Falls back here."

A shudder twisted the helicopter to the right. Again, Gillespie compensated. Sweat, not water, was oozing out from under his helmet. His eyes darted from the horizontal situation indicator to the terrain-following radar to the altimeter and then across the engine instruments. All was well. "A few of the troops sick?" he asked.

"About half," came the answer. "The big colonel is chucking his guts all over the floor." Mackay was suffering from a violent case of motion sickness and adding to the mess in the cargo compartment. "The sergeant major is sleeping like a baby," the gunner added.

"How we doing on fuel?" Gillespie asked. The copilot and flight engineer conferred, checking the fuel remaining against what the flight plan called for. Again, all was well. They had enough fuel to make their landing zone and then extract Delta Force, but they would have to refuel on the way out. "No way we can hook up in this crap," Gillespie said. If fuel did become a problem on the way home, he would find an isolated clearing in the jungle and land to wait for a break in the weather. Then they could take off and join up on E-Squared's MC-130 for a drink of JP-4.

"IP in one minute," the copilot said.

The gunner in the rear passed the word when he heard the copilot announce they were one minute out of the initial point. The flying time from the IP to their landing zone was two minutes and fifty-seven seconds. Relief spread over the sick men as they realized their ordeal was almost over.

The rain came down harder when they overflew the IP, a sharp bend in a river with a prominent rock. No one saw it. "It's okay," Gillespie said. He sensed it was all coming together. He turned to a new heading as the copilot started the elapsed time hand on the clock. Gillespie peered into the weather, trying to get a visual on their landing zone. Nothing. But he wasn't worried. At exactly two minutes and fifty-seven seconds, Gillespie pulled on the collective and reduced airspeed with the cyclic. Instinctively, he compensated and kept them from sinking like a rock. They hovered. "We're here," he announced.

"Yeah, but I don't see a goddamned thing," the copilot growled. They were hovering over a solid canopy of trees and blow-drying the green foliage beneath them. There was no sign of the clearing that had been chosen as their LZ. A quick check of the GPS monitor indicated the LZ was at their three o'clock position.

"We'll circle in an expanding search pattern," Gillespie said as he pivoted the helicopter to the right. They had barely entered the first circuit when the clearing appeared. Gillespie calculated they had missed it by less than two hundred meters after flying blind in a driving monsoon rain, at low level, for three hours. He'd settle for that any day of the week.

He settled the MH-53 into the clearing and the security team ran out the back to secure the landing zone. Rascal One had landed and within two minutes, he had a thumbs-up from the team. A sergeant directed him to taxi the goat closer to the trees, where they could better camouflage and hide it. Just before he cut the engines, the copilot broadcast the code word telling the orbiting MC-130 carrying the two colonels that they had safely landed. Then they heard Rascal Two, the second helicopter, report in, also safely down.

"Check that out," the copilot said. The rain had slackened off to a slight drizzle and the low clouds were clearly visible, four hundred feet above their heads. "Someone up there likes us."

Orbiting at thirty-four thousand feet and a hundred miles south of their position, a USAF reconnaissance RC-135 monitored the two transmissions from the helicopters, which were immediately followed by a short message from the command MC-130 to the NMCC in the Pentagon reporting that the teams were safely inserted. Since the RC-135 had not monitored any "hostile" transmissions that indicated the helicopters had been detected, it maintained radio silence. The aircraft commander moved the RC-135 farther south and reestablished a new orbit as the MC-130 returned to Udorn. The recce bird would continue to monitor Chiang's communications while the two assault teams moved into place. If it detected any sign that the Americans had been discovered, it would immediately down-link with the NMCC. The first phase of Operation Jericho had been successfully completed. The assault teams had been inserted without being detected by Chiang's defense net. Now phase two began. The two teams, Fastback and Bigboot, had to move through the jungle to reach their initial positions for the attack.

Landing Zone Alpha, Burma

"You're looking better, Colonel," Kamigami said.

Mackay was glad to admit that he was feeling much better after getting off the helicopter. His queasy stomach settled down almost immediately once his feet were on solid ground and was demanding to be fed. He gingerly nipped at one of the granola bars he liked to carry in the field and waited to see if his stomach would accept it. No problems. He took a bigger bite and checked his watch. They had been on the ground six minutes and should be moving out.

The captain leading Fastback reported in. "We'll be ready to move out shortly," he said. "One of our shooters is still puking his guts up. Severe motion sickness. I had to replace him with Marston from the LZ team."

"Good choice," Mackay said. Kamigami nodded his approval. The intense training program he had put Delta through had anticipated using the LZ security team as a backup to Fastback and every member had cross-trained to be part of the assault team. Mackay checked the clearing one last time. Camouflage netting had been spread over the helicopter; foliage had been carefully cut and placed, further concealing the aircraft; the LZ team was out of sight, already established in covering positions where they could intercept anyone approaching the clearing. Fastback formed up and moved silently into the jungle. Mackay, his RTO, and ammo bearer were sandwiched in the middle. Kamigami attached himself to Mackay's small command and control unit for the first part of the trek. They maintained radio silence, confident that Bigboot, the second half of the assault force that had been inserted by the other helicopter, was also moving.

The first two hours went smoothly and Mackay calculated they had covered about a mile. They were making unbelievably good time. They worked hard to move silently, for only stealth could preserve the critical element of surprise. The men were little more than shadows as they penetrated the darkness, moving parallel to a stream. Their night vision goggles helped them to some extent and the rain was cooperating. Then the terrain grew rough and they started to slip and fall in the darkness. "Better call a halt," Kamigami said. Mackay agreed but the captain leading the team chose to press on for another hour before establishing a bivouac until morning. The captain keyed his GPS to check their position. They were in a valley seven miles from Chiang's compound. Kamigami checked his watch—they had twenty-five hours to cover those seven miles.

"If we move out at first light," Mackay said, "and reach here"— he pointed to a spot five miles away where the valley they were in opened onto a flood plain less than two miles away from Chiang's compound—"we can hunker down for the rest of the day before moving into position under the cover of darkness. That'll cut down our chances of being discovered and still give us plenty of time to make contact."

"If this rain keeps up, that's going to be a pretty hard five miles tomorrow," the captain said. He gave a little snort. "We can always put the sergeant major at the head and let him lead."

Not a bad idea, Mackay thought.

The fourteen men that made up Fastback were ready to go at first light but the rain was driving down again. The men moved out. It was not the jungle underbrush that hindered their movement but the mud. Their boots were sticking and sliding and every step was an effort. It became a slogging contest and the men were rapidly tiring. The spot they were trying to reach was on the slope of the limestone ridge, called a karst, that formed the northern wall of the valley they were in. Kamigami studied his map as they moved and calculated their progress. We ain't going to make it, he thought. Then he slipped and fell, splattering the man behind him with a barrage of muck. He heaved himself to his feet and wiped his plastic-covered map clean. It was time to change. Then he saw it. On the map, two contour lines about one third of the way up the slope of the karst widened, telling him that the slope was not as steep. There's a shelf up there paralleling our direction of travel, he decided, remembering his last tour in Vietnam. Probably much more rocky up there with better drainage and less foliage. Time to do some mountain climbing.

At the next halt, he showed Mackay and the captain his map. "If you're right," the captain said, "there won't be much canopy to hide under."

"Who's going to be up there with us?" Kamigami asked. "And no one is going to be flying around in this weather." Five minutes later, Fastback was moving up the ridge, Kamigami in the lead. The mud quickly gave way to more solid footing as the vegetation thinned out. He set a blistering pace, making the men follow him. Soon they were angling along the ridge making good time.

Six hours later they were nearing the end of the karst formation and almost at the spot where they wanted to hide when Kamigami caught the smell of cooking. His left hand shot up above his head, his arm fully extended and palm forward. The men halted and silently took cover. They watched as Kamigami crouched then disappeared into the underbrush. Within minutes he was back and raised his MP5 submachine gun above his head with one arm, the barrel parallel to the ground and pointing in front of him. He had the enemy in sight.

Kamigami lowered the MP5 and raised his right fist to his waist and rotated his forearm several times in a horizontal clockwise circle. It was the signal to prepare for action. He drew out the black anodized Bowie knife he preferred to carry in combat and held the blade upright with the forefinger extended. He was ordering an immediate action drill they had practiced many times.

Silently, two men shed their rucksacks and moved out, one above the trail and one below. Kamigami moved forward in a crouch, becoming a shadow. His eyes drew into a narrow squint when he could see the lean-to where the cooking aroma was coming from. One of the men appeared on his right, gave a slight nod, pointed to the lean-to, and held up two fingers. He could see two people inside. Kamigami passed the signal to the man on his left, who could not see the lean-to but was contracted to keep Kamigami in sight. Kamigami moved closer to the rear of the lean-to. Now he could see that it was an observation post that in good weather had a commanding view of the valley and flood plain. That meant there was a radio inside.

A happy babble of laughter erupted from the lean-to and a young boy, no more than fifteen or sixteen emerged. He tugged his poncho into place and took a few steps down the slope, toward the number two man. Kamigami didn't know or care why the boy had come out, probably to answer a call of nature, but it was a mission he would never complete. A dark shadow moved from behind a large bush and fell in behind the boy. Kamigami saw an arm come up and jerk the boy's head back as a knife flashed across his throat. Then the shadow dropped the body. It was a mistake. The man should have supported the body and lowered it silently to the ground, holding the chin back so the neck would be stretched tight. With the tension released, Kamigami could hear a loud gurgling sound much like a perking coffeepot.

Shit! he raged to himself. He credited it to "buck fever," the first-time eagerness when a hunter botches the kill. But their luck held and the second person in the lean-to, puzzled by the unfamiliar noise, scrambled out and ran directly into Kamigami. She was a pretty young girl, no older than the boy, only wearing a T-shirt that barely covered her bare bottom. Kamigami didn't hesitate and before she could scream, his huge fist smashed into her chest, crunching bones and knocking all her breath out. He held her up by the hair as he drove his knife into her body, slightly below her heart, the tip angled up. He lowered the body carefully, his face an expressionless mask.

The third man was into the lean-to. He came out holding a radio still buttoned in its case. "She never thought of using it," he said.

The second man came up. "You'd make a good rattlesnake, Sergeant Major," he said. There was respect in his voice. "What were they doing up here?"

"An observation post," Kamigami said. "He probably brought his girlfriend along to help pass the time. Just two kids looking for a chance to screw." They scouted the area to make sure they were alone.

Mackay came up with the rest of the team and checked their position on the GPS. They were less than a hundred meters from their objective. "They must have chosen this place for the same reason we did," he said. "We can stay here until it's dark." The captain ordered two men to reconnoiter the trail that led down to the valley and to set up an outpost to make sure they would not receive any unannounced visitors. Most of the men were silent, their faces stone hard, as they stared at the two dead teenagers.

The tension eased when Kamigami picked up the two bodies, one under each arm, and carried them down the slope. He found a fold in the terrain and gently laid them out before covering them with the boy's poncho. He spread some brush over the shallow grave and sat down. For a few minutes he stared into the mist that obscured the flood plain and Chiang's headquarters below him. The rain started to come down again, this time a deluge. Then: "I'm sorry." He rose and rejoined the men.

Over Thailand, South of the Burma ADIZ

The second RC-135 monitoring Chiang's communications had been established in the same orbit for over six hours and the first ship had returned to Kadena, its base in Okinawa. It was a boring mission and so far no unusual transmissions had been detected and all was normal. The tedium was broken and the technicians in the rear perked up when they monitored encrypted SatCom transmissions from the two teams updating their progress with situation reports. Fastback was safely concealed two miles from Chiang's headquarters, and Bigboot was in trouble.

The White House, Washington, D.C.

Leo Cox was a tired man and he envied the President's ability to go to bed and fall instantly asleep. During all his years in the Air Force, he had never been able to sleep when an operation was under way and some deep inner need drove him on. Nothing had changed. He had gone home the previous evening but rest had eluded him and he had finally returned to the Situation Room in the White House at midnight, sent Mazie home to get some rest, and he monitored Jericho's progress. Some progress, he told himself, as he waited in the hall outside the President's bedroom with the morning's news. The door opened and Charles, Pontowski's valet, motioned him in, directing him to the small office off the bedroom that the President liked to use in the morning. Cox found him looking fresh and rested but far from relaxed. "It's going to be a long day, Mr. President." Pontowski nodded in agreement. "Tosh had a comfortable night," Cox continued, "and is still asleep."

"Was that from Edith Washington or Dr. Smithson?" Pontowski asked. He had discovered that Washington's observations were as reliable as Smithson's and much more concise.

"Smithson," Cox replied. "He's staying at the hospital now around the clock." Cox eagerly accepted the cup of coffee Charles handed him. He needed the caffeine jolt to stay alert. "The rest of the family arrived last night."

Pontowski drew in a deep breath. "Not much longer," he said, his voice low and dark.

Cox turned to the next subject. "Jericho is in trouble. One of the teams has not reached its initial position."

Pontowski glanced at the carriage clock on the mantel and quickly made the conversion to local time in Burma—six-forty-five in the evening—which meant they had nine hours and fifteen minutes to get into position if the attack was to go off on time. Should he abort the raid before then? Not yet, he decided, only if they are discovered and lose the element of surprise. "What's the problem?"

"Rain, sir," Cox answered. "It gave us the cover we needed to insert the assault teams but it has slowed them down moving into position."

"The rain slowed only one team, Leo, only one. Who's experiencing difficulty?"

"Bigboot, sir. They're the team that initiates the assault, blows one of the walls and seals the compound off."

"Are the hostages still alive?"

"At last report," Cox answered.

"We'll let it run for now. Stay on top of it." He didn't tell Cox that he had made the decision to abort the raid at the first sign of serious trouble. Bigboot's delay in moving into position was about all he would tolerate. The two men went over the day's schedule before they walked down to the Oval Office.

Six hours later, Dr. Smithson called Cox. He was worried about Tosh's condition and asked for the President to come to the hospital.

The distance from the White House to the Naval Medical Center at Bethesda, Maryland, is seven miles, perhaps twenty-five minutes by motorcade or a few minutes by helicopter. Pontowski's staff opted for helicopter because the flying weather was good and security was easier to provide. Only a few minutes in a northwest direction. Pontowski appreciated the dedication and expertise that went into the planning and execution of that short flight. It was a lesson he had learned many years before.

1944

RAF Hunsdon, Hertfordshire, England
The telephone call for Zack came at nine-thirty in the morning. "Zack, darling," Willi said, her voice captivating and thrilling him with its hidden promises. "I'm on an errand today and will be free tonight. It would be a shame to waste it, don't you think?" He stammered out a reply, certain that he sounded like an inane idiot. He knew he was blushing. "Good," she continued, satisfied with his reply—whatever it was. "Can you meet me at the Swan and Partridge in Rickmans Worth? It's a pub in the center of town. You can't miss it. Say seven o'clock? I'll arrange dinner, if you're hungry."

He told her that he would be hungry and she hung up, leaving him filled with anticipation and guilt. He couldn't put aside the vague feeling that he was betraying Chantal. Does love always get so mixed up? he thought. Or is this just sex and lust? He was a very confused young man and thankful that he had work to keep his mind occupied. Pickard had detailed him to work on the Amiens raid and he had to make the short trip to 2 Group headquarters at Uxbridge to finish planning the attack.

The man in charge of the planning was a tall squadron leader with a classic RAF handlebar mustache. Heavy burn scars on the right side of John Maitland's face had destroyed his good looks but not his buoyant personality. Zack wasn't sure if the constant tick that played at Maitland's right eye was due to neurological damage suffered when his Mosquito crashed and burned on landing or the result of combat fatigue. Still, he enjoyed working with Maitland and had learned much about the details that went into a successful mission. When the planning was complete, the two men sat in the room cluttered with detailed charts and reconnaissance photos. At the center of the room was the target model of the prison. "What have we overlooked?" Maitland asked. He ticked off the attack:

"Weather—wretched but out of our hands.

"Timing—dinner starts at noon and the attack is scheduled to come off at twelve-oh-three. Right at the conclusion of the blessing no doubt.

"The bomb run—three squadrons, six Mossies from each squadron, attack in sections of three. Three minutes between squadrons. First squadron breaches the outer walls, second squadron goes after the main building at a right angle to the first's attack, and the third squadron held in reserve to clean up what is missed.

"Enemy defenses—expect Focke-Wulfs out of Abbeville. The ack-ack at the Luftwaffe base at Amiens-Glisy will present a problem to your second squadron when they make a left-hand circuit to get the spacing they need. That will bring them fairly close to Amiens-Glisy but heads up, please, and you should be fine.

"Fighter escort—twelve Typhoons from One-ninety-eight Squadron stationed at Manston, rendezvous over Littlehampton. The Tiffies should discourage any Luftwaffe interest while you're over the target and most vulnerable. Also, they can escort any stragglers back to Manston for an emergency landing.

"Deception—we need to keep Jerry guessing as to the target. He will know we're out and about but if we've done the navigation right, he won't tumble to Amiens until the last possible minute. And then he will probably decide that we're going after the railroad marshaling yards.

"Coordination with the Maquis—a chap will be here who can relay the word to the Resistance when you launch. The French have to be ready to move into the area five minutes after the bombing to assist the lucky bastards that make it through the walls."

"It should all work," Zack allowed. "Was all this your idea?"

"Not quite," Maitland replied. "Pick had a hand in it. The

guiding hand, you might say. All very brilliant." Maitland turned his attention to the scale model. Amiens prison was a sixty-foot-high building shaped like a cross that stood in a rectangle of walls twenty feet high and three feet thick. "I'm quite beyond it when it comes to the 'cookies,' " he admitted.

Zack was an expert on bombs, or "cookies" as the RAF called them, and blast effects. "Each Mossie will be armed with four, five-hundred-pound semi-armor-piercing bombs fused with eleven-second-delay detonators," he explained. "I read an inspiring report on some of the colorful things that can happen when a SAP is tossed at speeds greater than two hundred and forty miles per—fractured bomb casings or it bounces back up at you. Still, a very nice present for the Germans. We'll have to tell the pilots to keep their release airspeed under two-forty. The walls should not present a problem." He pointed to the spots on the northern and eastern walls where they planned to punch holes for the prisoners to escape. "Bombing the guards' barracks," he said, pointing to the one story building tacked onto the head of the cross-shaped main building, "will be more of a problem. The aircraft will have to lift over the walls and then immediately skid their bombs into the barracks.

"But it's the collateral damage we can expect when we bomb the main building that has me most worried. The most critical place is here." He pointed to the corner where the long and short arms of the prison building formed a cross. "We've got to hit it here to free the Resistance workers and at the same time give them an exit close to the breaches in the walls. Our bombs are going to kill many of the very people we are trying to save."

Maitland stared at the model. "Is there an alternative?"

"No, not really," Zack admitted. They dropped the subject.

"Anything else?" Maitland asked.

"I'm worried about the 'boys from Abbeville.' I was wondering if we could have a Mossie or two do a daytime Intruder mission on their base and spread a little *Moskitopanik* around. It would keep them preoccupied."

"Not a bad idea," Maitland said.

"By the way," Zack asked, "will you be going on the raid?"

"I would if the quacks would let me," Maitland replied. His right eyelid twitched furiously and Zack could see his hands shake. "They say my nerves are shot. Probably right."

Am I going to end up like Maitland? Zack thought, shaking,

scarred for life, willing to carry on but sidelined. How much longer do I have?

Maitland's face cracked into a grotesque smile. He knew what Zack was thinking. "Not to worry, this won't happen to you. You're a survivor, old boy. Obviously, meant for better things than this. Come on, let's run your latest brain wave about a daytime Intruder mission by Pick."

Group Captain Percy Charles Pickard listened quietly as the two men recapped the planning and Zack presented his idea about using Mosquitoes on a daytime Intruder mission to distract the German wing at Abbeville. He stood and walked to the window, thinking and taking the gauge of the weather. "No, it's not on," he finally said. "The Intruder mission, that is. A day Intruder is too dangerous and the Tiffies can do the job. I was hoping we could do it tomorrow but the weather is beastly and the weather prophets don't see any improvement in the next forty-eight hours." They discussed a few more details and Maitland said he would have the Navigation Section finalize the route into and out of the target area. On the way out of Pickard's office, Zack asked if Maitland would drop him off at Rickmans Worth.

"The Swan and Partridge, no doubt," Maitland said. "Lovely place to meet a popsie. Use it myself from time to time." He laughed at the bright red that spread across Zack's face.

Maitland pulled in behind a bright red roadster parked in front of the Swan and Partridge. "Nice machine, Morgan," he said. "I make it a 1937 Four-Four. Wouldn't mind having one myself. Wonder where they came by the petrol?" Zack had never heard of the car but did like its classic lines. Maitland waved him good-bye and pulled away, heading back to Uxbridge.

Willi was waiting for him in the lounge. She was dressed in her Wrens uniform and smiled in relief when he sat down. "You would be late," she said. "An American colonel"—she glanced at a man standing at the bar—"was most annoying."

"My fellow countrymen," Zack grumbled and headed for the bar to get them drinks.

The colonel summed Zack up with a quick look and decided to pull rank. "You're not wanted here," he said.

"Then we'll leave," Zack replied.

Zack's American accent surprised the colonel. "What the hell! A Yank in the RAF. If that don't beat all. Ashamed of your own country, mac?"

"No," Zack replied. "Not at all."

"Look," the colonel said, "why don't you go back to whatever rock you crawled out from under and I won't turn you in as a deserter. Leave the bird here."

"As you wish," Zack said and returned to the table. "I think we had better leave," he told Willi. "He's been drinking and is in an ugly mood."

"Yes, let's," she said and stood up. "I do have plans for us—elsewhere."

Zack helped her on with her coat and they headed out the door. The colonel was right behind and caught up with them outside. "Hey, mac!" he yelled. "I thought I told you to leave the bird here. You stupid or deaf?"

"Are you talking about me?" Willi asked, her voice arched and frosty.

"Yeah," the colonel grunted.

"Really," she said, "if you are in rut and do wish to stand at stud, may I suggest a barn down the road. I'm quite sure you will find the beasts there most appealing. But on the other hand, they don't really deserve someone like you, do they? So please feel free to take matters into your own hands."

It took a moment for the words to sink through the man's drunken stupor. His face flushed. "British bitch . . . " He swung his arm to slap Willi.

Zack's left hand flashed out. He grabbed the colonel's arm and twisted, almost dumping him to the ground. "You had better go back inside," he said.

"Who do you think you are?" he growled and jerked free. He started to walk away and then turned and swung a haymaker at Zack's head. It was a clumsy move and Zack stepped back, easily avoiding the punch. The man tried again but this time Zack blocked it with a hard sideways chopping motion to his forearm. The man grunted, surprised by the pain, but he was persistent and swung again. Zack dodged the punch and snapped two rapid jabs to the colonel's right biceps. It was beyond the colonel's experience that two such quick and easy-looking punches could hurt so much. He tried to raise his right arm but it wouldn't respond.

"Let it go, Colonel, while you can still walk and talk at the same time." The hardness in Zack's voice drilled through the alcoholic haze in the man's brain. For the first time the colonel really saw his adversary. Zack was standing perfectly still, at ease, his face impassive. A well-founded fear gripped him with the sure knowledge that he was overmatched and that the young American would maul him unmercifully. He retreated into the pub.

"Get in the car," Willi said. She ran around to the driver's side of the red Morgan.

"Your car?" Zack asked.

"I borrowed it from Roger."

"Bertram?"

She nodded. "But he doesn't know it." She gunned the engine and spun a tight U-turn.

"Where are we going?" Zack asked.

"Roger's family home."

Then they chorused in unison, "But he doesn't know it."

Willi drove fast and competently, sure of the road. But she far exceeded the reach of the shaded half-beam headlights. "Zack, would you have hurt that drunken sod?"

"The choice was his, not mine."

She wheeled the car into a narrow lane and pulled up in front of a gate house guarding the entry into a big country estate. "The Bertrams gave me a key," she explained. "The main house is closed for the duration. It's a drafty old place, but this is very cozy." She unlocked the door and let them in. Inside a coal fire was going in the fireplace and a note was on the table. "I called ahead and told the housekeeper I was coming. The old dear started the fire and left dinner in the cooker." She smiled at him. "Hungry?" He nodded. "I'll be right back."

Zack settled into a comfortable couch in front of the fire. As she had advertised, the room was warm and snug. "This is the first time I've been warm this winter," he called.

"Make yourself comfortable," Willi sang from the kitchen. "I hope you like shepherd's pie. And there's a bottle of wine." He shed his coat, loosened his tie, kicked off his shoes and stretched out. Willi brought a tray through and they ate in front of the fire. After they had finished the wine, she curled up on the floor beside him, cuddled his legs and stared into the fire. "This is so peaceful," she murmured. A feeling of contentment and warmth swept over him and he dozed.

He was vaguely aware of movement. "How long have I been asleep?" he asked.

"About an hour." She was still curled up on the floor at his feet but was wrapped in a blanket. She had stoked the fire and the room was still cozy and warm. "I let you sleep. You needed the rest."

"You've let your hair down," he said. He reached and stroked her hair. She held his hand to her cheek and then gently kissed his palm. She looked at him, her face serious, her lips slightly parted. Zack pulled her up to him and the blanket fell away. She was naked and her skin glowed in the soft firelight. She sat on his lap and he tenderly kissed her. "Is it that warm?" he wondered.

"It will be," she said and nipped at his ear. She wiggled around to face him and her long legs straddled his hips. Her arms encircled his neck and she hungrily kissed him, her mouth open. "Oh, it will be." Her hands pulled at his tie and she slipped it over his head. Then her long fingers undid the buttons on his shirt and reached inside, stroking his chest, before she dropped the shirt to the floor. She slipped to the floor and undid his belt and loosened his pants. Her fingers danced over his crotch and she pulled his pants free. She tickled at his feet as she tugged his socks off. "I love your body," she whispered. Her tongue explored his thighs as she pushed between his legs and worked higher.

Zack groaned and stood up, pulling her with him. He scooped her up to carry her into the bedroom. "No," she whispered. "By the fire." They sank to the rug and he laid her on her back. Her legs lifted as he entered her and then wrapped around his, claiming him. "I do love you," she murmured.

The fire was dying. Willi unfolded from the couch and tossed the blanket over Zack. She dumped the last of the coal out of the bucket onto the fire. "There should be more in the shed," she said.

"You can't run around outside naked as a jaybird in this weather," Zack said from under the blanket. "It's raining cats and dogs." She arched an eyebrow and darted out the door, bucket in hand. She was back in a moment, her skin moist from the rain. She fed the fire and jumped back under the blanket. "My God!" he yelped. "You're freezing!"

"Stimulating, yes?" Her mouth was on his neck and her hands roving over his body.

"You're insatiable," he told her.

"Only around you. Now pay attention." He gladly complied.

* * *

Zack shifted his arm into a more comfortable position. It had gone to sleep and tingled. Willi moved and readjusted to the change. He stroked her back and stared into the fire. "You're worried about something," she said. "I can tell."

"I was just thinking."

She sat up, curled into the corner of the couch and studied his face. Willi was a clever strategist and consummate tactician when it came to bending others to her will and she had given hours of thought to the problem of Zack Pontowski. She knew that she loved and wanted him more than anything else in her life. Yet she realized the peace between them was very fragile and could be shattered again. She had used lust and sex to draw him to her and loosen the bonds that Chantal had woven around him. But had she been too aggressive in their lovemaking? She had to show him another side to prove that she was the right woman for him. I will marry you, Zack Pontowski, she promised herself.

"I hope you're not feeling guilty," she ventured. No answer. She was certain she had hit the truth and warned herself to avoid mentioning Chantal. "Zack." She reached out and touched his cheek, turning his face to look at her. "I do love you." Damn you, she thought, say the words too—make yourself commit to me. She pressed ahead. "And I'm willing to settle for this moment, or the next one, or however many we can have."

"What happens if you should, ah, become, ah . . . " he searched for the right words.

"Pregnant?" She supplied the missing word. He nodded. She bit her cheek to suppress her laughter. He was so typically American, so prudish, so determined to do the right thing. "Then I will name him Zack."

"And if it's a girl?"

"You are sure of yourself," she chided him. "There are no strings here." She sensed immediately that she had said the wrong thing. He did want commitment and strings. She opted for the truth. "I do want you—forever and ever. But our future is on hold and until we are free again to make our own decisions and get on with our lives, I want these moments with you."

He accepted the truth of what she was saying and fell silent. She waited, knowing that his restless mind was still questing down some unknown path, chasing an illusive thought, cornering a problem.

"Willi, what was the errand that brought you here?"

Her carefully guarded world crashed down about her. He was thinking of Chantal and probably suspected that her duties with SOE had brought her to 2 Group headquarters at Uxbridge.

"I'm on leave," she lied. "I had to take care of some family business."

THIRTEEN

Sixteenth Street, Washington, D.C.

General Simon Mado whistled a tuneless melody as he walked down Sixteenth Street near the National Geographic Society building. A dark gray town car pulled to the curb beside him. The front-seat passenger window rolled down and a voice called him by name, telling him to get in. Very fancy for a reporter, he thought. The rear door swung open and he got in. A small-caliber handgun was jammed into his ribs as the car moved into the midday traffic. "You bastards made a bad mistake," he growled.

A needle jammed into his arm was his only answer.

Consciousness came slowly and Mado fought the fog that swirled through his brain. His first clear impression was of a very bitter taste in his mouth. Slowly another sensation came to him: He was lying naked under a blanket in a narrow berth. I'm on a boat, he thought. The soft light streaming through a porthole and a gentle rocking motion told him it was afternoon and that they were in smooth waters. Now where are my fuckin' clothes, he thought. Since he still had his watch on, he checked the time. "Been out about three hours," he mumbled and stood up to look out the porthole. They were anchored in a small cove that made him think of Chesapeake Bay. Apparently he hadn't been taken too far. He wrapped the blanket around him toga-style and checked the cabin door. It was unlocked. He pushed it open and stepped into the main salon of the boat. The sole occupant was Tina Stanley, Senator Courtland's aide. Like him, she was wrapped in a blanket. He ignored her and tested the door leading to the deck.

"It's locked and they're outside," Tina told him. He could hear panic in her voice.

"Who are they?" he asked.

"I don't know." Her panic was building.

"What the hell happened?" Mado growled. "I thought you had set up a meeting with a reporter." She gave a little nod, looked away, and jammed a fist against her teeth. She started to shake. Mado turned it all over in his mind. What the hell was going on? What wires had been crossed? He was supposed to be providing a friendly reporter with "deep background" on the rescue mission that was about to be launched or was already in progress. That was all. If the mission failed, the reporter would have a ready-made exposé with which to embarrass the Pontowski administration. But this was not a situation that a general officer wanted to be caught in. "I've got to talk to them," he said, pounding on the door.

"I don't think they want to listen," she said, tears flowing down her cheeks, ruining what was left of her makeup.

The door flew open and three men walked in. One dropped two small clear plastic capsules on the table next to Tina. "What are those?" Mado asked.

"Bullets," Tina whispered. "Coke."

One of the men ripped their blankets away and pushed them together. The other man started taking photos.

New Downtown, Washington, D.C.

Bobby Burke, the director of central intelligence, was not surprised that Charlie Bonazelli was waiting for him in the office the CIA used as one of its fronts in the New Downtown section of Washington, D.C.

"How they hanging?" Bonazelli asked in his friendly way. He handed Burke an envelope with four very clear and unambiguous photos.

"As usual," Burke replied. He didn't know how to reply to

the crude greeting. He examined the photos. "Have these been given to the right people?"

"Of course. They're front-page stuff."

"Then all is well?"

"Of course."

"Then why are you here?"

Bonazelli made a thoughtful face. "The families owe you big-time and all parties are aware of our debt to you," he began. "But we don't know how you want to end this."

"Let them go tomorrow morning."

Bonazelli's bushy right eyebrow shot up. "A very simple thing. And if it becomes complicated? Very complicated."

"Then they should be discovered together."

"Yes, I see. If we have to do that, the debt would then be—"

"Settled," Burke said in his pompous, most bureaucratic, voice.

The White House, Washington, D.C.

"Almost noon," Mazie said to herself. She had been on duty in the Situation Room since six A.M. and was hungry. "Well, why not?" She jabbed at a button on the intercom panel and called the kitchen for lunch. Twenty minutes later, a steward brought her a tray and a newspaper.

"I thought you'd like to see this," he said with a tight grin. It was one of the sleazy tabloids she had seen at the checkout counter of her local market. The front page was packed with headlines and a delicately censored photograph of two nude people locked in an embrace. The headlines proclaimed that a general had been discovered in a drug and sex tryst with a senator's aide aboard a yacht on Chesapeake Bay. Story on page two. Mazie opened the tabloid to page two and smiled as she read how one General Simon Mado, United States Air Force, had been discovered with his paramour, Tina Stanley, an aide to Senator William Douglas Courtland, on board their love boat. The boat was aptly named *Bustin' Loose.* So much for the career and credibility of Mado, Mazie decided as she dropped the paper and devoured the sandwich. Men! she laughed to herself, always thinking with their peckers.

Then another thought came to her. I wonder if Mado was set up? It could not have happened at a better time. This is exactly what the media loves, sex and scandal, and it turns public attention away from us and onto Courtland. Who would do that?

She turned her attention to the green numbers on the master clock on the wall. They were marching with a relentless pace toward 2100 hours Greenwich mean time. Two smaller clocks read out the local time for Washington, D.C., and Burma. "Noon here and midnight in Burma," Mazie Kamigami said to herself in a vain effort to break the building tension. Then: "Only four hours to go." The attack was scheduled to begin at 2100 hours Greenwich mean time or four in the morning in Burma. A video screen flashed WAIT, telling her a message was coming in. She toggled the key that routed SatCom transmissions to the small speaker set in the telecom console in front of her.

"Hammer, this is Fastback." It was Mackay and even the encryption/decryption cycles of the SatCom could not completely distort his voice. They were using the SatCom because Hammer, the MC-130 carrying Mallard and Trimler, was still on the ramp at Udorn waiting to launch two hours prior to the attack. Mazie listened to Mackay's situation report, updating his commanders on the progress of the mission. Fastback had moved out of its hide, reached its initial position but had not yet made contact. But Bigboot was mired down six miles short of their objective.

Relief engulfed Mazie. Bigboot did not have enough time to move into position and the attack would have to be aborted. Delta would be extracted. Then a sickening feeling swept over her. Innocent lives were at stake and she was willing to sacrifice them because her father was in danger. She felt like a traitor. She punched at a button on the telecom console in front of her and buzzed the national security adviser's office on the secure line. Her voice was under tight control when she said, "Mr. Cagliari, we have a situation that requires your attention. Bigboot is still not in position."

Three minutes later, Cagliari barged into the Situation Room. He listened impassively while Mazie detailed the situation for him. Before he could respond, Mackay's voice came over the SatCom. "Hammer, this is Fastback. I've ordered Bigboot to move out of the jungle and run the road. They've been told to commandeer a vehicle if possible."

Cagliari stroked his beard. "It might work," he finally allowed.

"Are you going to tell the President?" she asked.

She didn't like the answer. "No . . . you are. . . . As soon as he returns from the hospital. I'm going to the Pentagon and I'll link up with you when I'm in the NMCC." He was out the door.

The sick feeling in Mazie's stomach was back.

The Golden Triangle, Burma

The compound was quiet when Heather returned to her room. She sat down in front of a mirror and stared at her reflection. Slowly she rubbed her cheek. Then she saw Samkit sitting in a corner. "You didn't have to wait for me," Heather said tonelessly. Samkit rose and padded across the room, picked up a brush and started to stroke her hair. The heavy odor of sex was still on her. "Morihama likes me" was all Heather said.

"You should sleep in another room tonight," Samkit said. Heather stood up and followed Samkit to the servants' wing. She moved automatically, without emotion, not questioning, only obeying. Samkit pushed her into a deserted room and helped her into bed without undressing. Samkit waited until the girl's breathing smoothed and drifted into the comforting currents of sleep. She left, locked the door behind her, and hurried into the kitchen to see if there was more news. A cook told her that a stranger had arrived and was demanding a huge meal and a girl for his bed. Another servant reported that he was sharpening a long sword and asking about the two Americans he was to "test."

"He's the executioner," the cook announced, sure of himself. He repeated all the rumors coursing through the compound.

Samkit yawned and left, telling them that she was tired and going home. Outside, she hurried across the compound to the barracks where a gardener had told her the two condemned Americans were being held. A soldier stopped her at the entrance and shoved her into the guard shack. He was bored and studied Samkit. "What are you doing here so late?" he demanded.

"They say the Americans are going to be separated from their heads tomorrow and I wanted to see them." She studied the guard, gauging his reaction. "Maybe I can get a lock of their hair," she whispered.

The guard nodded, understanding. He had heard of different potions that could be made with such ingredients. "The general has given orders not to let anyone see them. He'd have my head with theirs if he heard. . . . " He stroked her shoulder.

Samkit moved to him and rubbed her body against him, knowing what the price was. He pulled her blouse open and stroked her breasts. Samkit closed her eyes and waited until he was finished. She tried to make the right sounds and movements at the proper time. It was over in less than two minutes. "Now get out of here, old woman," he growled as he buttoned his pants.

Her fury blazed as she tugged her clothes in place. She started to leave, only to whirl on him. "A curse brews strong when I have part of you in me," she snarled. He backed away as a white-hot wrath built in the small woman. She started the chant that would call down a *nat,* one of the ancient spirits that inhabited their world. Fear and superstition held a primitive power over all the soldiers, and the image she evoked was real for the simple and illiterate man.

"Please," he begged, offering her all his money and possessions. But there was no mercy in Samkit as she conjured the *nat.* The soldier collapsed to his knees, wailing his own death lament.

"If you do what I ask," Samkit said when she had finished, "I will release the *nat* and lift the curse." He begged her to tell him what she wanted. "Show me where the Americans are being kept and let me talk to them." He jerked his head in agreement and led her to the cells. He opened the door and let her in. "Go," Samkit ordered. The guard hurried back to his post. "Listen carefully," Samkit whispered to DC. "After I leave, lie on the floor and pull the sleeping pallet over you for protection. If you hear anything, be very quiet, close your eyes and open your mouth. Yawn deeply and cover your ears with your hands." DC told her that she understood. "I need a lock of your hair," Samkit said, pulling out a small pair of scissors from the black bag she carried. Then she moved over to Ricky's cell, repeated her instructions, and clipped a lock of his hair.

On the way out, Samkit showed the guard the hair she had taken and told him that she would release the *nat* when the Americans were dead. Once out of sight, she slipped off her sandals and ran for the service gate on the other side of the compound. When she reached the outside, the rain came down, soaking her to the skin as she ran down the road. She was barefoot and her saronglike tubular skirt snapped against her legs. In frustration, she pulled the skirt up to free her legs and ran faster. Through mist in front of her she caught a glimpse of three trucks parked beside the road. She recognized them as the supply trucks that arrived early every morning at the compound. A hand reached out of the shadows and grabbed her. "Samkit," a heavy male voice growled. It was the German anthropologist.

"The general is going to kill the Americans tomorrow," she gasped.

The German did not question her information. He had learned from long experience that Samkit, as were many servants in this part of the world, was an unimpeachable source of information. He unsnapped a small radio from his belt and spoke rapidly into the microphone.

The monkey of command was firmly on Mackay's back as he talked to the two colonels still orbiting in Thai airspace in E-Squared's MC-130. "Hammer copied all," Mallard said, confirming that he had all the details.

Mackay looked at Kamigami and the captain who was to lead Fastback into the compound and storm Chiang's villa. "Decision time," he told the two men. They all appreciated that the two colonels were waiting for Mackay's recommendation as the on-scene commander. "No word from Bigboot and we have to make contact with the trucks now. I'm going to recommend an abort." It pained him to say it and fatigue drew his face into tired lines. The captain's lips were compressed into a tight line and he said nothing.

"Sir," Kamigami said, "Captain Woodward is with Bigboot." Mackay shot the sergeant major a hard look. But he said nothing, waiting for Kamigami to make his point. "If anyone can get Bigboot into position, he can." The sergeant shut up. He had said enough.

Mackay's eyes drew into narrow slits. He would find out later how the British captain had managed to come along but for now, he evaluated how his presence changed the situation. Woodward had repeatedly proved himself to be the most resourceful special forces operative Mackay had ever met. It was a new factor in the equation. "We could slip the attack thirty minutes," he said, "so Woodward can get Bigboot into place. While he's doing that, we make contact with the trucks and move into position. If Bigboot doesn't do their thing, we know that they didn't make it. Then we abort, cut and run. Hammer can coordinate it, have the helicopters moving toward us for a rapid extraction if things go to shit, and have Specter ready to give us cover. Your thoughts."

Fastback's captain allowed a terse, "Hell, plans are man-made, not God-made. Run it past Hammer."

Kamigami gave a sharp nod and Mackay's radio operator

handed him the mike. In their own way, the men of Delta had voted. They weren't about to let it go after coming so far.

The White House, Washington, D.C.

"Put me in contact with the national security adviser," Pontowski told the staff officer managing the Situation Room.

"Mr. Cagliari is in the NMCC," the lieutenant colonel said, "on line one."

Pontowski picked up his phone and motioned for Mazie Kamigami and Leo Cox to do the same. "We've seen the message recommending the attack be delayed thirty minutes while Bigboot moves into place," he said to Cagliari. "What do you and Admiral Scovill think?" Scovill was the Chairman of the Joint Chiefs.

"I recommend we abort now, Mr. President," Cagliari answered. "Admiral Scovill says to give them the thirty minutes and if it doesn't go down then, to get the hell out of Dodge."

The President held the phone lightly on his shoulder, suddenly feeling his age. The ultimate decision was his to make. He had set the operation in motion, had given the orders that put Delta Force in harm's way, and now he had only minutes to decide if it should continue. No matter what he decided, someone was going to die. How perverse life is, he thought, just like the run on Amiens jail in 1944. Would his history never let him go? He remembered the time he sat in a Mosquito fighter-bomber on Hunsdon Airfield in a driving snowstorm that threatened to turn to rain. And he remembered wanting to go regardless of the risk.

Cox caught his eye. "Sir, Dr. Smithson is on line two. He says it's urgent."

The bulldog image of Winston Churchill standing alone in his library came to him. "You always saw their faces, didn't you?" he muttered aloud. He scratched a brief one-line message on the note pad in front of him—his decision—and handed it to Cox. The chief of staff read the message and looked at him. "I'm going to the hospital," Pontowski said. "Will you please stay on top of things here." He rose and walked out of the room, now an old man, but still upright and walking alone.

1944

"Mr. Pontowski," the voice urged, dragging him out of a deep sleep. He was vaguely aware that it was still very early and, as usual, the central heat in the room was off. He could see an image standing in the partially opened door to the room he and Ruffy shared in the officers quarters. His vision cleared. It was his batwoman.

"What is it, Barnes?"

"You're wanted in the Operations Block, Mr. Pontowski." She hesitated to be sure he would not fall back asleep. "Just you, sir. Mr. Ruffum isn't needed." When he sat upright and placed his feet firmly on the floor, she closed the door. "Coo," she mumbled to herself, "wouldn't mind him getting a leg over." She had a vision of herself as the other participant in that activity. A few minutes later, he was fully dressed and headed out the door. Barnes was waiting with his overcoat. "Nasty outside," she told him as he put it on. He nodded and disappeared into the early-morning dark. "Please come back, sir," she whispered.

Squadron Leader John Maitland was waiting for him. Fatigue and strain had turned his fire-scarred face into a hard mask. "Pick's inside with Embry," he said. "Well, old boy, it's today or not at all." It was Friday, the eighteenth of February, 1944.

"Christ," Zack swore, "have you seen the weather? It's miserable. Driving snow and rain."

"I do look out the window" came the answer.

Inside the office, Pickard paced slowly back and forth, puffing on his pipe. Air Vice Marshal Embry, the commander of 2 Group, sat quietly at the desk, staring at the message in his hands. He came right to the point when the two men entered. "The Gestapo has set the executions for tomorrow. We don't know the times and the French Underground has sent a desperate appeal. It must be today."

"The weather is absolutely rotten," Maitland said.

"I am aware of that," Embry said. "Met says it should be clear over the Continent. So it's really a matter of launching, isn't it?"

Pickard puffed on his pipe. "And joining up in formation, and navigating at low level to avoid Jerry's radar, and making rendezvous with the Tiffies, and finding the bloody place." The men could tell he was straining at the leash, wanting to have a go at the prison.

"What does Bill say?" Embry asked. Flight Lieutenant J. A. "Bill" Broadley was Pickard's friend and navigator.

"You know Bill," Pickard answered. "If I can get the Mossie into the air, he can get us there."

"What about your man?" Embry asked Zack.

"Much the same story," Zack replied. He almost added that the ability of the crews was not the deciding factor—it was the lousy weather. He had seen it before and fell silent. The two commanders were caught up in the agony of decision, a decision that spelled the death of some of their men. It was a personal equation that each had to work through, weighing factors that could not be quantified, visualizing how each man selected for the mission would perform, wondering if one or two was nearing the "twitch," that nervous tic that warned of combat fatigue, calculating if the cost was worth the result.

"There really isn't a choice," Pickard finally said. "If this bloody weather cracks and we can get off the ground, we go." Embry nodded in agreement. "I'd like to lead the mission," Pickard said. Embry's face froze but he said nothing. "I'll go in with the second squadron," Pickard continued, "and see if we need to call in the third squadron to complete the job. If the walls have enough holes in them and I see prisoners escaping, we'll all scamper for home."

Embry drummed his fingers on the table. "Charles," he said, before biting his words off. Embry had originally intended to lead the wing himself but was sidelined by his superiors. Now he was worried because Pickard had recently come off night ops and had only flown six daytime missions. Was he fully tuned into daytime operations like Zack was? Again, Embry ran through his personal agony. Pickard was a natural leader, that rare combination of skill, personality, and physical presence that men trusted and would follow through hell. He sensed that Pickard's presence on the mission increased the chances of success. And that was the bottom line. "Well, then," he finally said, his decision made. "Which squadron shall do the honors and lead the attack?"

"We'll toss a coin at the briefing," Pickard said. Zack felt better knowing that Pickard would be leading the mission.

"When shall we rouse the crews?" Embry asked.

"I had planned for a six o'clock call with the briefing at eight," Maitland replied.

"I'll be at the briefing," Embry told them. "Please keep an eye on the weather."

The word went out and the crews were awakened at exactly six o'clock. Most of them glanced out of the window in disbelief. Blinding gusts of snow obscured most of the base. The meteorological staff was on the short end of many obscene comments as the men made their way to the dining room. They fell silent when healthy servings of eggs were ladled out. Eggs and the number of crews called out meant a big op was in the making. At ten minutes before eight o'clock, the Tannoy squawked and sent the crews to the briefing room in the Operations Block.

The men were numb from the cold and were slapping hands and stomping their feet when Pickard entered. They came to attention when Embry followed him into the room. He took the low stage and began with the traditional first words. "Gentlemen, your target for today is Amiens." The surprise came next. "We are going to attack not the railroad marshaling yards, which you have all come to know intimately, but the prison." Pickard removed the sheet over the papier-mâché model. Embry said, "The Gestapo is being its usual bloody self and is going to execute more than a hundred French Resistance workers tomorrow. Both men and women. We are going to breach the walls, break Amiens wide open, and give them a reasonable hope of escape. I asked the weather prophet if God was helping with the weather and he reports moderate visibility in the target area. I do hope that is the case. The French tell me that the prisoners would rather be killed by our bombs than German bullets.

"We're calling it Operation Jericho, very appropriate under the circumstances. Group Captain Pickard will be leading the wing"—the quiet looks and nodding of heads among the eighteen crews indicated it was the right choice—"and Squadron Leader Maitland will cover the details. Right, then. John, it's all yours."

Maitland stood up and covered the attack and the route that had been selected to ingress the target area. "We want to keep Jerry guessing until the last minute as to the actual target. Even when he identifies Amiens as the target, he should be looking at the marshaling yards, not the prison. But the "boys from Abbeville" should be up and about. So remember the daytime rules: in fast, out fast. Don't go around for reattack. Those who fight and run away, live to fight another day. We've seen some recent improvements in the Focke-Wulf. The kite is definitely faster than a Mossie above twenty thousand feet, so don't go there. You still have the speed advantage down low. Use it. By the way, there will be a Mossie from the Film Unit going along to see what job you make of it. Look pretty, please."

There was no doubt in Zack's mind that every man in the room wanted part of the action. "No doubt," Pickard said as he stood up, "you've been wondering who will go in first. He looked at the three squadron leaders who commanded 21, 464, and 487 squadrons. "Coins please, gentlemen. First toss for who flies in reserve. Odd man out." They flipped the coins and 21 Squadron, the British component of the wing, came up odd. Rude remarks from the British pilots. "It's between the Aussies and Kiwis," Pickard said. "I'll call it in the air." The two men flipped their coins. "Heads leads the attack," Pickard said. The New Zealanders won the toss and a grim feeling of determination washed over Zack. His squadron, 487, would lead the attack and go after the walls while 464 Squadron, the Australians, would bomb the main building.

"Makes one proud to be an honorary Kiwi." Ruffy grinned. "Good thing the Aussies got part of the action," he added.

"Why's that?" Zack wondered.

"This is all red meat. Look at them. They would have skinned and tanned their commander if he had come up reserve." Ruffy was right. The Australians were definitely out for blood on this one. The British pilots did not look happy.

Call signs were given out next. "Four-eight-seven Squadron is Dypeg," Maitland said. "Four-six-four Squadron is Cannon and Twenty-one Squadron is Buckshot. Your Typhoon escort is Garlic. Navigators, you have the list of all other call signs you might need so please use them properly. The brass is concerned your R/T procedures have been getting sloppy." Rude comments from the crews echoed around the room and for the next two hours they pored over charts, photos, and the papier-mâché model, memorizing every facet of the mission while the armorers loaded the Mosquitoes. Then the Tannoy ordered them to their aircraft. By ten-thirty, the aircrews were at their aircraft, ready to start engines. Only Pickard had not manned his aircraft.

"Miserable weather," Zack complained. "But I think we can take off."

"Landing might be a bit of a problem," Ruffy replied. "This is no weather to go flying in."

"We've got to do this," Zack said.

"More red meat, no doubt," Ruffy said.

Zack thought about it for a moment before replying. Was there a killing lust on him? "Not this time," Zack replied. "It's not a killing heat spurring me, not now. All I want to do now is to survive and get on with my life."

"What will you do after this is all over?"

"I'm thinking of law school and maybe running for office."

"Politics?" Ruffy was astounded. "You must be mad."

"Perhaps." Zack grinned at him. "But then war does that to a person, doesn't it? Do you still plan on going back to Cambridge?"

"Should do," Ruffy answered. "An inheritance from my parents will see me through. I am thinking more and more of taking a degree in psychology."

"The disturbed science? And you accuse me of being crazy!"

"All the better to study the aberrations of our elected leaders," Ruffy told him.

"Ah, I can see your thesis now," Zack kidded him. " 'Aberrant Behavior and Low Intellect Among Politicus Animus.' "

"It does have potential," Ruffy laughed. "But intellect has little to do with being a politician. It's more a matter of temperament."

"Then I'm dead in the water," Zack replied.

"Oh, I don't think so." Ruffy's voice was serious.

The two men fell silent and waited. From their position, Zack could see the main operations building and Pickard's car parked in front. Then a bright red roadster drove up and parked beside Pickard's car. He could make out the figure of a tall woman getting out of the car. Willi! he thought. Then it came to him—Chantal was one of the prisoners. Zack felt as if all the air had been sucked out of his lungs. "I think it's slacking off a bit," Ruffy said. Then they saw Pickard come out of the building and hop in his car. The car sped across the ramp toward them and Pickard jumped out. Zack watched as he climbed through the hatch of his aircraft, *F for Freddie.*

The mission was on.

FOURTEEN

The Golden Triangle, Burma

The German anthropologist rechecked the three trucks parked alongside the narrow road to make sure the Burmese drivers with their ever-present family members had left. Satisfied that all was secure, he walked fifty meters back down the road and lit a cigar. He puffed the cigar down and lit another, worried about the long delay. He was about to leave when he heard a whispered "Daisy cutter" from the shadows. It was the code word he had been expecting and replied with "War rose," the only acceptable response. He braced himself. If the exchange of bona fides was screwed up, he was a dead man. A huge figure materialized out of the deep shadows—Kamigami.

"You're late," the German said. "The trucks"—he gestured at the waiting vehicles—"are the same ones that come every morning. The service gate won't be opened for about another hour, but the guard won't be surprised if one or two arrive early. The Burmese are pretty casual about it all. The keys are in the ignition." He made a come-here motion at the shadows. "There's someone here you should talk to." Kamigami shot his right arm straight up above his head and made a circular motion, the signal to assemble. Then he pointed up the road to the trucks, the assembly point. Dark figures moved out of the shadows and trotted to the trucks while Mackay, his radio operator, and Fastback's captain joined Kamigami and the German. Samkit emerged from the shadows. "She's my contact inside the compound," he told the men. To Samkit, he said, "Tell them what you told me."

The frightened woman looked at the wet and hulking figures in their jungle fatigues and boonie hats. For a moment she couldn't speak. Then it all came in a rush. "An executioner arrived late yesterday. He uses a sword. I heard the general say he will cut off the head of the man and the woman called DC to entertain his guests." She used a diagram of the compound to show them where she had moved Heather and where the cells were located.

"This helps," Fastback's captain said. "The cells are in a building that is part of the outer wall. We can go through the wall to get them out. That only leaves Courtland and the third objective. This is exactly what we needed," the captain said, "if it's true."

Kamigami drew his Bowie knife and purposely examined its edge. Samkit almost fainted. "It is the truth," she moaned.

It was the sergeant's way of confirming what they were hearing. The intelligence Samkit had provided was critical and they had to be sure she was telling the truth—their lives and the success of the mission depended on it. It is a rare thing when the cutting edge, the operators, the men who must do the job talk face-to-face with a primary intelligence source. Normally, the intelligence they receive is funneled to them through a variety of agencies and bureaucratic levels where it is evaluated, analyzed, correlated, confirmed, and massaged. Too often, basic information takes on the "spin" the bureaucrats want, making it conform to their view of the world. Kamigami cut through all that and reduced it to basics. "She's been dead on, so far," the German reassured them. Kamigami jerked his head and sheathed the knife.

Mackay rallied his team leaders around him and they quickly modified the attack to exploit Samkit's information. While the team leaders briefed their men, Kamigami checked on the demolition team rigging the lead truck. "How soon?" he asked.

"Almost done," the demo man answered from under the hood. He was double-checking the platter charge he had rigged on the back side of the radiator next to the fan. The steel plate that was backed with a heavy charge of C4 explosive was securely clamped in place and he jammed an M-122 remote detonator into the heavy charge of C4. He lowered the hood. "God, I just love demo," he told Kamigami.

"Your job is to blow the gate down, not make a parking lot," the sergeant told him.

"No problem," came the reassuring answer.

The two colonels sat in the small command module that had been loaded on board E-Squared's MC-130, which had seemingly become a permanent fixture of the aircraft. E-Squared was tired of serving as an airborne taxi driver for the command element called Hammer and longed for some action. "I wish we could eavesdrop on the SatCom," the copilot told him, showing the same boredom.

"It would only scare the shit out of you," E-Squared replied. The copilot shot him an inquisitive look. "Because," the pilot continued, "you'd see how fast the heavies can screw things up and get our sweet asses in a crack."

In the command module, Mallard and Trimler were trying to avoid that particular predicament as they conferred with the NMCC over the SatCom radio. "I'm not going to push for an abort until I hear it from Mackay on the ground," Trimler told Mallard as they waited for the decision on the mission from the NMCC.

Then the NMCC relayed the President's decision. "Well," Mallard said to Trimler, "they got it right this time." Trimler only nodded and hit the transmit button to give Mackay his marching orders.

Mackay was tethered to his radio operator by an eight-foot cord that ended with the handset grasped firmly in his hand. His face glistened black, wet with sweat and rain but impassive, giving no indication of what he felt. "Roger, Hammer," he said. "Copy all. Stand by." He cradled the handset against his shoulder and motioned for the captain and Kamigami to join him. "Hammer says the 'go/no go' decision is ours. Your recommendations." He felt an explanation was in order. "Apparently, that decision came from the White House."

"No change," Kamigami counseled. "Go if Bigboot can make it. No more extensions."

The captain stared at his boots, trying to weigh all the things that could go wrong since they had already slipped the attack thirty minutes. "We can handle the thirty-minute delay," he said.

But he was still worried. "Colonel, I know we got to be flexible and worship Gumby. But this time it's got to be by the clock. No more fuckin' around."

Mackay nodded and spoke into the handset.

The men were little more than flickering shadows moving down the side of the road. Most were bent forward under the weight of their eighty-pound rucksacks and only the soft pad of their footfalls and heavy breathing broke the dark stillness of the early-morning dark. Every head was mounted on a swivel as each man scanned the darkness looking for some signs of life—anything that would indicate they had been seen. Peter Woodward kept checking his watch as he maintained the pace, driving Bigboot on, determined to reach the compound in time. He couldn't believe their luck since they were violating every known rule of special operations by running the road so near their objective. He tried to find some consolation in the fact that they hadn't been discovered—yet.

"Fuckin' A, Captain. This sucks," the man following Woodward grumbled. Then he fell silent, conserving his breath, determined to keep up the relentless pace the British SAS officer was setting. Woodward picked up the faint outline of a shack set back from the road and he slowed, being careful to sneak the men by. He used the break to check his position and again glanced at his watch. We're not going to make it, he raged to himself. Got bogged down too long in the bleedin' jungle.

Headlights flickered on the road behind them and the men disappeared into the foliage beside the road. A few moments later a mini pickup truck that had been converted to taxi duties passed them. The rear guard keyed his Motorola 360 radio and told Woodward that it was transporting people, probably the first of the workers who arrived at the compound every morning from the nearby villages. Then he reported a second set of headlights coming down the road. Woodward made his decision. "If it's a truck, stop it." One of the men spotted a water buffalo tethered near the shack and led the animal onto the road while four men moved into position.

On cue, another pickup truck appeared and slammed to a stop amid a babble of voices from the rear. The driver jumped out to shoo the water buffalo off the road. He never saw the man who grabbed him from behind and ripped a knife across his throat. The six passengers were frozen into silence when four men materialized out of the shadows and motioned them to get down. "What do we do with this group?" one of the men radioed.

Woodward glanced at his watch. Did they have time now that the situation was back in control? He didn't want to kill people needlessly. His reply was a terse "Jab 'em." The six Burmese were quickly bound with plastic flex-cuffs and an adhesive bandage was slapped over their mouths to gag them. Then they were led into the foliage beside the road and a needle was jabbed into each's arm. The knockout injections worked quickly and they would be out for at least four hours. The four Americans ran for the road and were the last to pile into the overloaded pickup. The delay had cost Bigboot ninety seconds. "Go!" Woodward barked at the driver. "We've got seven minutes and three miles to go."

The second and third trucks in line were loaded and waiting to go. Only Mackay, his RTO, a sniper, and Sergeant Jim Isahata, the small and wiry Japanese-American who had volunteered to drive the empty truck in front had not mounted. Isahata finished stripping off his equipment, cammy makeup and shirt and pulled on a dark, loose-fitting shirt the German had given him. Mackay stood back and checked him over. "You'll pass for a Burmese in the dark. Just do it like the man said—drive the truck right up to the gate, kill the engine, switch the lights off and get out like you're going to take a leak. If the guard yells at you, wave at him and keep moving. If he doesn't buy it, we'll take him out. Get back to the trucks because we're moving in exactly six minutes, into the compound if Bigboot does their thing, or beating feet for an extraction."

Isahata gave Mackay a hard look. "Got it all, Colonel." Then he grinned. "Trust me."

"And I'll respect you in the morning," Mackay grunted. He gave Isahata a sharp slap on his backside when he swung into the cab. Isahata started the engine and moved out while Mackay waited for the two other trucks to drive up. He spoke to the drivers, gave them their final instructions, and hopped in the back of the last truck. Then the two trucks followed Isahata with their headlights off, giving him a two-hundred-meter head start. The two trucks stopped just short of the last bend before the straightaway that led up to the service gate at the rear of the compound and waited.

Within moments, Isahata appeared. "Piece of cake," he told

Mackay. "It went as advertised. I drove it right up to the gate, got out, and walked away. It's parked right up against the gate." He was scrambling back into his gear, anxious to be ready in time.

Mackay rechecked his watch and got out of the truck. He would remain outside the compound with his RTO and his ammo bearer, who was also a very proficient sniper, when Fastback went in.

The pickup carrying Bigboot coasted to a stop, its lights out. Silently, the men jumped out and moved into the wet foliage. Woodward followed two shooters, one a sniper who was carrying a carefully wrapped and camouflaged rifle, and his security man. The three men moved through the bush and made for a small hill that was less than three hundred meters from the south side of the compound. They reached their position within minutes and the shooter stripped the camouflage wrap away from his rifle while Woodward checked his watch. The sniper braced the rifle's bipod on a fallen log and sighted through his night scope while the other shooter covered. "Get ready, mate," Woodward said in a low voice.

The sight picture was exactly what the sniper had expected. He could clearly see the main gate and the high guard tower that rose above it. He switched to a higher magnification and laid his cross hairs on the lone guard pacing slowly around the small platform. Woodward again glanced at his watch, waiting. He steadied his own night scope on the watchtower, seeing the same greenish-yellow image the sniper saw. The bright spots glowed in the scope, making him think of a photographic negative, and he could see the guard lean over the edge of the railing, obviously bored. Then he checked his watch one last time—ten seconds to go. He did a mental countdown as he refocused on the guard. "Now," he said, his voice dead calm. The sniper squeezed off a shot.

The key to the compound was surprise and it was inserted by that single shot. The same shot also started the attack clock. Woodward watched as a greenish haze erupted from the guard's head. The sensitive scope had captured the guard's head coming apart as the bullet penetrated the right cheek bone and blew out the left side of the head. The force of the impact knocked the guard back onto the platform, out of sight. A second shot was not necessary. "Spot on," Woodward allowed.

"What the fuck did you expect?" the sniper growled. Two teams of sappers keyed on the rifle shot and ran out of the shadows as Bigboot unleashed a mortar barrage on the compound. The sapper team from Fastback made for the east wall while the team from Bigboot crossed the open area in front of the south wall. The first two mortar rounds struck the guards' barracks inside the compound as the sappers placed the charges and retreated to safety. The charge placed by Bigfoot's team blew a hole in the south wall large enough to drive a truck through. The hole made by Andy Baulck, the ISA operator, for Fastback was more surgical. A four-man team darted through the small breach in the wall and directly into the building that contained the cell block. They knew exactly where they were going as Bigfoot's next two mortar rounds impacted inside the compound.

Now the two trucks carrying the rest of Fastback moved around the bend in the road and headed for the supply gate. "Make it look like we're trying to make the compound for safety," Kamigami told the driver.

"I know the goddamned drill," the driver replied as he honked his horn and flashed his lights, trying to get the attention of the guards inside the compound. Kamigami counted down from five. When he said "One," the driver slammed on the brakes and ducked as Kamigami fell on top of him. The truck Isahata had parked against the service gate moments earlier erupted in a fireball as the platter charge was detonated. A fireball charged with metal fragments from the steel plate and the truck mushroomed out, blowing the gate down and vaporizing the guard who was trying to open the gate and let the trucks reach safety inside. The windshield of Kamigami's truck shattered over him and showered his back with harmless shards of glass. The concussion of the blast had killed the engine and the driver ground the starter.

The surveillance camera that monitored the service gate shot up out of its hidden niche. The camera pivoted from right to left as its telescopic arm reached full extension. Then a single shot rang out from the shadows and the camera exploded, leaving only the headless stalk of its support arm standing. "Good shooting," Mackay said, relieved that his sniper had gotten it with the first shot. The last image the man monitoring the camera inside the compound's command bunker had was of two trucks trying to reach safety when the parked truck exploded as if it had been hit by a mortar round. Mackay, the sniper, and his radio operator pulled back into the shadows, well back from the compound where they could monitor all radio communications and coordinate the teams storming the compound. They would also be the observation post that kept the back door open.

The engine of the stalled truck roared to life and the two trucks raced across the last two hundred meters to reach the gate. Both trucks slammed to a halt and the men piled out, streaming into the compound.

While Fastback penetrated into the northern half of the compound, twelve men from Bigboot ran through the breach they had just blown in the south wall. They went through in groups of four and headed off in different directions, each element to its assigned objective. Two more mortar rounds slammed into the guards' barracks as two teams reached their positions. They were in time to catch most of the guards running from the barracks. Staccato bursts of submachine-gun fire raked the open quadrangle as they cut into men fleeing the burning structure. "We didn't get 'em all," a corporal told his team leader. The leader keyed his radio with a heads-up call.

Bigboot stopped its mortar barrage as its three teams moved into position inside the southern half of the compound, sealing it off from any uninvited visitors and looking for Chiang's guests. Woodward followed the team called Bigfoot One into a guest house and ran into a hail of small arms fire. The first two men in were hit and he flattened himself against the floor, raking the big room and hall with submachine-gun fire. A squat, heavily tattooed figure came out of a bedroom, his hands in the air. "Morihama?" Woodward asked. The man nodded. Woodward stood, snapped his MP5 up, and blew Morihama's head apart. He jammed in a fresh clip as the team searched the guest house. Two more shots rang out. Then he keyed his radio and told Mackay that the Japanese delegation was accounted for. When Mackay acknowledged the transmission, he told his team to tend the wounded and withdraw. He checked his watch and slipped into the shadows.

The White House, Washington, D.C.

The Air Force lieutenant colonel coordinating the flow of information into the Situation Room drew Mazie's attention to the latest message from Hammer flashing on the video screen.

OPERATION JERICHO:
ATTACK ON COMPOUND INITIATED AT 2130 ZULU.

The words hammered at her as she fought to control her breathing. She looked at the clocks on the wall: 2130 Zulu, Greenwich mean time, was 4:30 P.M. in Washington, D.C., and 4:30 A.M. in Burma. Two minutes ago, she thought. Damn that satellite radio! I didn't need to know this. When her breathing had slowed to a more normal rate, she picked up the secure phone that linked her to Leo Cox. "General Cox," she said, her voice calm and measured, "the attack on Chiang's compound started three minutes ago. I thought the President . . . Yes, sir . . . I understand. We can expect him here within twenty minutes."

"Oh, Pop," Mazie whispered, "what's happening to you?" She resolutely fought the tears back.

The Golden Triangle, Burma

The captain leading Fastback was with the first team to reach the villa's heavy doors. As expected, they were sealed and he pointed at the team's demo man. The sergeant slapped a C4 ribbon charge around the door, jammed in an M1 detonator with a fifteen-second delay and tugged on the pull ring to fire. The team stepped back and the captain checked the second hand on his watch, satisfied they were still on schedule. He looked up in time to see two of the escaping guards from the mortared barracks charge around the corner of the building. A hail of gunfire from the team cut them down before they realized the team were intruders. A third guard was far enough behind to avoid the fate of his comrades and skidded into the shadows. He swung his AK-47 around, ejected the old clip, jammed in a fresh clip loaded with dum-dum bullets, and blindly sprayed the area around the corner. The captain took the full force of the burst as the bullets ripped across his stomach, almost cutting him in two.

Kamigami instantly returned fire, the sound of his three rounds blending in with the sharp bark of the AK-47. A scream erupted from the guard as all three rounds struck home. He squeezed off three more rounds to certify the kill as the C4 charge blew the door down. The flash framed a frozen still life as the team hesitated, appalled by the sight of their dead captain doubled back on himself in a grotesque contortion of death. The shock lasted for two seconds, not long by normal human standards but an eternity in the world of special operations. Then Kamigami assumed command. "Move," he snapped. "Do it." The first four men barged through the door, moving toward the command bunker. Kamigami led the next three men in and headed for Chiang's office.

Fastback Three, the team of four men assigned the task of taking the cell block, made it to the door leading into the cell block unopposed. The lead man gingerly tested the door handle and found it unlocked. He nodded at his high man, the shooter who closely followed him to clear an area by firing over his shoulder. The high man unsnapped a baseball-sized flash-bang grenade from his harness and pulled the pin. The lead threw the door open, the high man tossed the grenade inside, and the door was slammed shut. A bright flash and ear-shattering bang erupted inside the cell block. The lead threw open the door and the high man went in at an oblique angle. The lead followed him but at the opposite angle. They both knew where the other man was and they raked the room with gunfire, clearing it. But they missed.

Only one guard was in the room, lying stunned on the floor. The high man walked over to him and shot him in the head. The next two men were already through the room and into the cell block. "Americans!" the first one shouted when he saw the four cagelike cells. "Dana! Ricky! Drop!"

"Oh my God," DC whimpered. "We're alone. We're alone."

The second man into the cell block flicked the beam of his flashlight across the cells. Both DC and Ricky were curled up in tight balls on the floor covered with their pallets. They could hear more gunfire as the other teams cleared the compound. The team's lead man tested the doors. Both were locked. "We'll have you out in a few moments," he said. "Hold tight." DC only nodded but Ricky rolled up tighter as he started to wail and cry. "Damn," the lead said, testing the cell doors, "we'll have to blow 'em."

"No we won't," the high man said, throwing him a set of keys. "The guard had them." The doors were thrown open and DC was helped out, gaining strength as she started to move. But Ricky stayed rolled up in a fetal position.

"Carry him," the lead ordered. He keyed his radio to talk to Mackay. "Fastback Three has Claridge and Martel," he radioed. "Ready to move."

Mackay's voice was calm and clear. "Bring 'em out. Egress as planned." Mackay checked his watch. They were ahead of schedule.

The lead again spoke into his radio. "Fastback Three withdrawing as planned. Repeat, withdrawing as planned." Then the men were moving down the corridor, running for the hole they had blasted in the wall.

The team called Bigfoot Three reached their objective, the guest house where the Colombian-Germans had been staying. It had taken a direct hit by a single sixty-millimeter mortar round and the men could hear moaning and cries coming from inside. "Service 'em," the team leader growled. The men entered the wrecked building.

Sergeant Jim Isahata was leading Fastback Two, the team tasked with finding Heather. They followed their noses into the brightly lighted kitchen. The four men used the center work island as cover as they crossed into the main hall that led into the servants' quarters. They were looking for the fourth room on their left. A huge, bald-headed man stepped out of a bedroom. The man's potbelly hung over his loincloth and he glared at them as he swung a long sword. "What the shit!" Isahata barked as he blocked the cut with his MP5. The sword knocked the submachine gun out of his hands and Isahata fell to the ground as his high man cut the executioner down.

"If you were much slower," the high man growled, "you'd be in two pieces." Isahata didn't contradict him as he inspected his weapon. It had a deep cut just above the trigger guard where he had parried the sword cut. He threw the ruined submachine gun into a corner and drew his Browning automatic.

"In here," the third man called. He had found Heather Courtland under her bed, still wearing a party dress.

Isahata spoke into his mike. "Fastback Two has Courtland. Coming out."

The hall leading to Chiang's office was empty and dark. The three men following Kamigami could not believe how quietly and rapidly the big man could move. He was little more than a fast-moving shadow. When he saw the open door that led into the office, he halted and listened. Nothing. Then he went through the doorway at an oblique angle, ready to fire. But the office was empty. He keyed his radio. "No joy on Chiang," he reported to Mackay.

The reply was "Search the area. You've got seventy-five seconds." The four men split in two and each pair started a systematic search in opposite directions. Kamigami heard Isahata's radio report that they had Heather and were coming out.

The loud and strong pounding of a machine gun echoed through the building. Kamigami calculated that it was one of the 12.7-millimeter DShK heavy machine guns that were reported guarding the corridor to the command bunker from behind heavily armored firing ports. He ignored it. Then a deafening explosion shook the villa. The team covering the entrance to the command bunker had placed a massive C4 charge against a load-bearing wall and blew the roof of the bunker down. The guards manning the machine gun ports were buried under tons of rubble and cement. That problem solved, Kamigami thought as he swept through a third room. His internal clock warned him that he had only seconds left to find Chiang before Mackay ordered a withdrawal.

The radio cracked a sharp command. "Bingo time! Bingo time." It was Mackay ordering them to withdraw. The clock had run out and now they had to begin the complicated task of re-joining and leaving. The escape route and timing had been as carefully prepared and practiced as the attack and each man knew where he had to be at a specified second and whom he would join up with to egress the compound. Anyone not at the right place at the right time might be shot at by a friendly mistaking him for the enemy. It was the way they deconflicted their fire. Kamigami's team rejoined as planned and made for the villa's entrance. The team guarding their escape route passed them through, right behind the team that had blown the ceiling down on the command bunker. Satisfied that everyone who had gone in had come out, they followed Kamigami. The first faint hint of the approaching dawn could be seen to the east. It was definitely time to go.

Bigboot had copied the command "Bingo time" over their radios and started into their egress drill. As the covering force, they would be the last to pull back from the compound. One of the two-man teams guarding the main road leading to the compound were twenty-two seconds short of abandoning their position when they heard the rumble of a large truck coming toward them. They reported the traffic and waited. With exactly eight seconds to go, they saw the truck. It was moving fast with its headlights out. The driver obviously knew the road and had practiced driving it without lights many times. The two men waited as the truck drove over the antivehicle mine they had planted in the road. The explosion blew the truck over and it burst into fire. Five soldiers staggered out the back of the truck and into team's field of fire. Short bursts cut them down.

"Where did those fuckers come from?"

"Beats the shit out of me, but there's another truck coming." Neither man was too worried and they had planted two more mines farther down the road. They reported in on their radio and withdrew eleven seconds late.

The elements of Fastback came together as they egressed through the service gate. Two men were carrying what was left of their captain wrapped in a poncho. They loaded their burden into the back of the lead truck, which had now been turned around. Fastback Two came out leading a dazed and obedient Heather. A sergeant told Kamigami that all of Fastback was accounted for. "What about Bigboot?" Kamigami asked.

"One's unaccounted for" came the reply. "Captain Woodward's missing. All the rest are out. Bigboot's road team destroyed two trucks on the main road moving toward the compound."

"Probably soldiers who are billeted in the village," Kamigami said. "Their reaction time is slower than we anticipated." Then they heard the explosion of another antivehicle mine. Kamigami hesitated.

"Fastback is all accounted for," the sergeant doing the second head count told him. "It's time to go." Kamigami still didn't move.

Woodward stepped out of the shadows. "Sergeant Major, I believe Chiang is in the bunker. Courtland may know another way in."

"Sounds fair to me," Kamigami replied. "Miss Courtland," he asked the girl, "can you help us?" She only stared at him, not answering. "We want to take Chiang out and make him stand trial," Kamigami said, his voice low and soothing. A flicker of interest crossed Heather's face. "But we need to find him first. Is there another way into the bunker?"

"There's a hidden entrance," she said. "Go to the pool over there," she gestured to one corner of the garden. "Behind the waterfall there's a grotto. Inside, lift the cushions and you'll see it. But it's locked from the inside. You can't open it from the outside."

"I can blow it," Jim Isahata said. "Let me at it."

"No," Kamigami decided. "We need Baulck. If anyone can do it, he can. You take care of Courtland. Get her to Mackay. Now." Isahata did as he was ordered while Kamigami spoke into his radio, calling for Andy Baulck to join them. Then he told the sergeant monitoring the withdrawal, "Move 'em out. Leave a truck for us at the rendezvous point with Mackay. We'll join up with you at the LZ. But don't wait for us." Baulck came running up carrying his demo bag.

The three men ran back into the compound, now clearly visible in the growing light. Electricity to the pump driving the waterfall had been cut and they had no trouble seeing the entrance to the grotto. Kamigami slid into the pool and waded through the opening. Baulck was right behind him, almost up to his chest but holding his bag of explosives above his head. At one point he slipped and disappeared below the surface with only his hands still holding the bag up, keeping it dry. Woodward pulled him back to his feet and pushed him through the narrow entrance.

Kamigami had found the hatch and was studying it when Baulck reached him. Baulck ran his fingers around the edge, studying it. "Recessed hinges," he said. Then he swept the grotto with his flashlight. "This is going to be tricky," he allowed, "blowing the hatch without bringing the roof down." He set to work, carving small hunks off a block of C4 and positioning them on one side of the hatch. He motioned Kamigami and Woodward to withdraw, pulled the detonator and followed them out of the grotto.

"You back us up here while we go in," Kamigami told Baulck. A dull explosion from inside the grotto served as punctuation. Woodward darted back through the entrance with Kamigami right behind him. "Fucking brilliant," Woodward said as he pushed the hatch out of the way and dropped into a small chamber sealed with a heavy door. He gingerly inspected the door and threw the levers at the side to open it. "Decontamination chamber," he told Kamigami. "It may have muffled the explosion." The two men entered the bunker.

Silently, they moved down a darkened corridor as their eyes adjusted to the light. At one point, they saw a flicker of light coming toward them from around a corner. Woodward's left hand shot out behind him at waist level telling Kamigami to stop. He bobbed his head around the corner and flashed the sign for "enemy." Then he pointed into the shadows. They drew back and waited. A soldier came past them with a flashlight. Woodward's hand reached out and snared his chin, jerking his head back while he cut the man's throat. He dropped the body to the floor and they moved into the main corridor.

When they reached the main command room, Woodward motioned Kamigami to stop while he crouched at the doorway. Kamigami moved silently into position behind him and patted him on the top of his head. Woodward sprang across the open doorway as Kamigami moved into his old position and fired into the room at an angle, his silenced MP5 making a soft popping sound as the roller action bolt clattered and spent cartridges fell to the floor. Woodward fired into the room from the opposite side of the door. Between them, they cleared the room. Kamigami darted inside while Woodward guarded the corridor. Within moments, Kamigami was back. "He's not here," the sergeant said.

Mackay heard the distinctive sound of the MH-53 as it approached the LZ to land. Compulsively, he rechecked his watch. They were withdrawing according to plan and right on schedule. The black, ungainly shape of Gillespie's aircraft moved over them, barely clearing the jungle canopy as it came into view, and settled gracefully to the ground. The men ran toward the rear of the MH-53 as one of the helicopter's gunners marshaled them on board and counted heads. His count would have to agree with Delta's before they took off.

"One dead and three unaccounted for," a sergeant told him, reconfirming what he already knew. "We're almost loaded and ready to go."

Again, Mackay checked his watch as the second hand continued its unrelenting countdown. "Damn," he muttered to himself. Why had Kamigami and Woodward gone back in with the ISA agent? They of all people knew better. He calculated he could wait another three minutes before ordering the helicopter to lift off. "Have Captain Gillespie check in with Hammer to update our status," he told the sergeant. "Also, have him confirm Bigboot is airborne and egressing." The sergeant hurried over to the helicopter.

Two men carried the dead captain on board and gently laid the poncho-wrapped body on the ramp. A sour bitterness swept over Mackay as he ran the mental arithmetic peculiar to special operations: one dead, three unaccounted for, and no Chiang versus all the hostages safe. Is this par for the course? Do I cut my losses and run? A glance at his watch confirmed that it was almost time to go. The same sergeant returned. "Captain Gillespie has checked in with Hammer," he said. "Bigboot is safely airborne and out of the area." He paused. "Captain Gillespie wants to talk to you, Colonel. He's got an idea."

1944

RAF Hunsdon, Hertfordshire, England

"I can't believe this," Ruffy groaned when he saw the propellers for Pickard's Mossie, *F for Freddie*, start to turn. "It's on." The radio was mute since 140 Wing always maintained radio silence during a launch. They assumed that German monitoring posts, which were less than a hundred miles away across the English Channel, would hear them. "It's an absolute swine of a day and they want us to go up and play." Zack grunted and motioned to the ground crew that he was going to start engines. "My God!" Ruffy continued. "The ceiling can't be more than a hundred feet, if that." Sleet and snow was still dusting the nineteen Mosquitoes sitting in the dispersals at RAF Hunsdon and an occasional gust would obscure the aircraft at the end of the line.

"A bit hard to maintain formation," Zack told him. Hunsdon came alive as ignition after ignition cracked and blue flames spat out the exhaust stubs. Engines hesitated and then coughed to life as whirling propellers cut into the snow. A wave of turbulent sound broke over the field as the Merlins snarled and sent gusts of snow across the base. Zack switched on the ignition and pressed the starter and booster-coil buttons for the port engine. Brian, the ground crew mechanic, stroked the priming pump with demonic fury. Since they were using high-volatility fuel, the engine roared to life on the sixth stroke. Brian gave it four more strokes to continue the priming until it picked up on the carburetor. With the engine smoothly on line, Zack started the starboard engine. Brian worked furiously to screw down the priming pump and button up the priming panels.

Then the mechanic stepped back and listened to the sound of the big Merlins and, satisfied that all was well, gave Zack a thumbs-up signal. "The Film Production Unit Mossie doesn't look like it's going to make it," Zack said. The nineteenth Mosquito that was going along to film the raid had not started engines and a mechanic had the cowling on the right engine open.

"The death and glory boys," Ruffy mumbled, "will not regret sitting this one out." He was not happy with the way the mission was developing.

Zack ran the magneto drop check. "She's purring like a kitten," Zack consoled Ruffy. He gave Brian the chocks-out signal and the mechanic gave them a salute as they moved out of dispersal.

"Brian would be most unhappy if we brought his child back in," Ruffy said, giving in to the inevitability of the mission. "He'd probably accuse you or me of buggering it up so we wouldn't have to fly in this muck." Zack joined the other five Mosquitoes of his squadron as they taxied down the track to the runway. Their squadron leader, Wing Commander "Black" Smith, taxied out onto the runway and they followed, lining up in pairs. The other two squadrons held on the taxipath in a long line. 140 Wing was ready to launch. Now with their engines fully warmed up and ready to go, they shut down and waited for the clock to run out. Ruffy popped the hatch and dropped the ladder. "My bladder is remarkably weak at times like this," he said. Zack joined him at the side of the runway as they christened a bare spot of ground. They crawled back into the cramped cockpit and watched the minute hand on their watches move with maddening slowness toward the twelve. At exactly 1058, the propellers of their squadron leader's Mosquito cranked over as he started engines. Zack followed suit.

With the last-minute checks complete, they watched the first two Mosquitoes run up and start their takeoff roll. Zack motioned to his wingman and they pushed their throttles up. When the first two aircraft were three hundred feet down the runway, they released brakes and followed in a formation takeoff. *K for King* responded like a thoroughbred and charged after the lead pair. Snow and sleet beat against the perspex windscreen, almost defeating the windscreen wiper. The tail wheel came up. "I've lost them in this muck," Ruffy told Zack. Their squadron leader, Black Smith, had broken ground and disappeared immediately into the overcast with his wingman.

Zack felt the Mosquito start to fly but held it on the ground until the airspeed touched 130 miles-per-hour. He eased back on the stick and they came unglued from the ground. He snapped the undercarriage lever to the up position and held his altitude until the airspeed reached 170. Then he honked back on the stick and climbed briskly to fifteen hundred feet, his wingman glued to his wing. Ruffy gave him the first heading to the southern coast of England for their rendezvous with the Typhoons over Little-hampton. A lone dark image materialized in front of and slightly below them. "That's Black's Mossie," Ruffy said, identifying their leader. "He seems to have lost his number two." Zack maintained radio silence and joined up on Black Smith's right wing in a loose formation.

"Christ," Ruffy groused. "We'll never make the rendezvous with the Tiffies." Then: "We've got company." Another Mosquito from their squadron joined up on their squadron leader's left wing and, miraculously, eight of the twelve scheduled Typhoons appeared above them. "The chaps are doing well today," Ruffy allowed. "Time to start our descent." Zack held a constant 270 as the four Mosquitoes descended, the Typhoons following. Sweat streaked their faces as they ground down through the weather, bouncing and twisting through the muck. It was a hard, jolting ride that would quickly wear a pilot down. His leader would disappear into the weather and then pop back out. Zack kept his eyes riveted on Smith as Ruffy read the gauges off to him. They hit an open patch and, for a brief moment, he could see the entire formation. "Descending through one hundred feet," Ruffy called. "Seventy-five feet."

"Brave soul," Zack muttered. They had to get below fifty feet if they were to avoid being picked up on German radar.

Finally, they were flying straight and level, still in the weather. The hard ride continued to pound the aircraft and throw them against their lap and shoulder harnesses. "Twenty feet," Ruffy said as a patch of iron-gray water flashed below them.

"I can't believe this," Zack said. He had to keep jockeying the throttles to avoid outrunning the other aircraft. "Brian's magic has improved," he said. Suddenly, his inner alarm clanged furiously and he eased back on the stick, gaining another twenty feet of altitude. The gray and green shape of a Mosquito flashed under him, right into the space he would have been had he not pulled up. His natural reactions took over and he firewalled the throttles and pulled up as the airframe shuddered and the engines howled. "Who . . . I barely saw the bugger. . . . My God! That's *F for Freddie!*" *F for Freddie* was Pickard's aircraft. Only that strange sixth sense and the fine tune of *K for King* had saved them from a midair collision.

The weather continued to pound them as they flew across the channel and the clouds and sea merged into a gray blanket. A series of violent jolts shook them and *K for King* shuddered as if a giant hand were batting them about, testing the sturdy aircraft. Their harnesses cut into them as Zack fought for control. He tasted a heavy bile at the back of his throat and, for a fraction of a second, he was certain they would slam into the sea. Then, as if the weather gods were done with them and satisfied that they had proved themselves worthy, the hand released them. The turbulent air smoothed and visibility improved. He caught a glimpse of the sun and considered that a good omen. "I do believe Met was right for once," Zack allowed. He could clearly see the three other aircraft in their formation.

"And here's *B for Beer*," Ruffy told him as the fifth Mosquito from their squadron joined on them. They were still short one aircraft. "I hope the Tiffies are still with us." Zack strained to see into the weather that was definitely improving, wanting to see the Typhoons. They would be needed if the "boys from Abbeville" put in an appearance while they were on the bomb run. Nothing. Their leader maintained radio silence, certain that the Germans could now monitor any radio transmission. "Coasting in now," Ruffy announced as they flew low over white-capped breakers that were rolling against the French coastline. He studied the land for some recognizable feature to fix their position. The five aircraft screamed over the low dunes and a concrete lookout bunker. "Jerry knows we're here now," Ruffy said as Zack pushed up the throttles. Their airspeed hovered on 295 and their altimeters held them at a scant fifty feet above the ground.

The weather had improved and a strong winter sun gave sharp definition to features on the ground. Zack could see their shadows streaking over the snow-covered landscape, making him think of a golden eagle's shadow he had once seen as it swooped down on a hapless rabbit. "The boys from Abbeville will be up and about," he said.

Ruffy grunted an answer. Then: "Right, I've got our position. We're about a mile south of course." On cue, the lead Mosquito altered course to the north and the formation climbed to five thousand feet. They wanted the Germans to see them and think they were on a deep-penetration mission before they turned toward Amiens. They raced over a series of easily identifiable checkpoints. "Maitland did his job well," Ruffy said. "Expect a descent in thirty seconds." They would be pointed away from Amiens while they descended and dropped from radar coverage. "We don't want the penny to drop yet for Jerry."

Radio silence no longer mattered and the radio crackled to life. "Hello, this is Dypeg leader." It was their squadron leader, Black Smith, calling using the call sign they had been assigned for the mission. "Descend now. *K for King* take spacing and follow us in." Zack acknowledged the call and slowed to 270 as his wingman joined on his right. He started a weave as they descended to gain the separation they would need for the attack.

A cool voice came over the radio. "Dypeg, this is Garlic." The Typhoons that were tasked to fly cover for them while they were over the target and most vulnerable to attack by enemy fighters checked in. "We are approaching the target from the west."

"They are never where you want them," Ruffy complained. But relief was evident in his voice.

Zack had the spacing he wanted from the three lead aircraft; he stopped his weave and pushed the throttles up as they leveled off at fifty feet above the ground. Now they turned to the south and arced toward the northeastern side of Amiens. Far in the distance, they could barely see the distinctive spires of the thirteenth-century Gothic cathedral in the center of town—proof they had found their target. "Coming up on the Albert–Amiens road," Ruffy said over the intercom. His voice was a rapid staccato. Both men strained to find the road that led directly to the prison. "That row of poplars, that's it."

"Got it," Zack told him. He angled toward the trees that lined the road to avoid making a hard turn. He led the turn and rolled out on a westerly heading as they flashed over the road. His wingman crossed over the top and fell into place on his left wing for the run-in. A lone figure on a bicycle had stopped in the middle of the road and waved furiously at them. Both aircraft kicked up a rooster tail of snow as they raced over the open fields. They still could not see the prison.

"It's on the nose," Ruffy reassured him.

A dark form took shape in front of them and Zack keyed his radio. "Tallyho the prison! Let's slow it down." He retarded the throttles and a Typhoon flashed by in front of them and pulled up, wagging its wings. "That's reassuring. Bomb doors open."

Ruffy hit the switch. "Bomb doors open," he said as bright bursts of light punctuated the landscape in front of them. The first three Mosquitoes had hit the prison.

Now Pickard's distinctive voice came over the radio as he called the Australians who would attack after Zack and his wingman had dropped their bombs. "Cannon, I do not have you in sight.

The first element of Dypeg is off the target, second element of Dypeg is inbound. Say your position."

"Cannon is four minutes out," came the crisp reply. "On course."

Pickard was unbelievably cool as he coordinated the attack. "*K for King,* continue your run." Ruffy buried his head in the bomb sight. The prison walls were ahead of them. "Come left," he ordered. "Easy, easy, hold it." The cross hairs were aligned on the walls. Zack's breathing was labored as he concentrated on flying directly at the eastern wall of the prison. A strong wind was blowing out of the east, knocking down the smoke from the earlier bombs. Zack killed the drift with a combination of rudder and aileron. "Indicies are moving," Ruffy told him. At exactly seventy yards short of the walls, the indicies crossed and two bombs separated cleanly from the Mosquito. Shed of a thousand pounds, the agile aircraft ballooned as Zack firewalled the throttles and climbed to clear the prison. He could see dark figures running across the yard—soldiers.

"The walls!" Zack shouted. "I didn't see any holes!" He couldn't tell if the first element's bombs had done their job.

"Oh shit!" Ruffy yelled. One of their bombs had bounced over the walls and was skipping over the courtyard below them. "Pull up!" Zack saw the bomb and hauled back on the yoke, climbing to six hundred feet as the bomb slammed into the west wall and exploded. Then they dropped back to the deck and flew over the town.

"Dypeg is off the target," Zack radioed. "Results unknown. We will reattack." He turned to the right, circling back onto the prison.

"Roger, Dypeg," Pickard answered. "Cannon, do you have the target in sight?"

"Roger," Wing Commander Bob Iredale answered. The cool Australian was leading 464 Squadron and attacking from the north.

"Continue," Pickard ordered. "*K for King,*" he told Zack, "have another go at the walls after Cannon clears the target."

"Roger," Zack answered.

Another voice came over the radio. "*K for King,* sorry we're late. Had some trouble on engine start. Mind if we follow you in?" It was the Film Production Unit pilot. Zack grunted an answer. He never remembered what he told them.

Ruffy twisted in his seat to check their deep right. "Tallyho the death and glory boys," he said. He could clearly see the cameraman in the perspex nose of the Film Production Unit Mosquito as it closed on them. "They must want to record all this for posterity."

Zack turned back toward the prison and sandwiched between the two elements that made up the second wave and were attacking from the north at a right angle to their first run-in. The Mosquitoes in front of him slowed, lifted over the walls, and dropped back down. They were going after the guards' barracks. Ruffy had his head back over the bomb sight. It was harder for Zack to kill their drift since they were now in a crosswind. Billows of smoke erupted from the prison and obscured the target. He hadn't expected that and skidded *K for King* to the left to clear the smoke. "Aim for the right side of the wall," he told Ruffy.

"Got it," Ruffy shouted. "Steady, steady, bombs gone." Free of its bomb load, the Mosquito streaked over the walls.

The radio cracked. "*K for King,* would you mind going around again? That last footage looked very good." It was the Film Unit pilot who was still in tight formation with *K for King.*

"Can do," Zack answered.

"Have you gone around the twist?" Ruffy complained. "What ever happened to the daytime rules?"

But the request was exactly what Zack wanted to hear. He wrenched the Mosquito back around to fall in behind the last element of inbound Australians. He could see both Pickard's Mosquito orbiting to the east and the Mosquitoes that were bearing down on the prison. The Film Unit Mosquito was still with him. Two Focke-Wulfs dropped down out of the overcast and cut across the town, apparently not seeing the attacking Mosquitoes.

Zack hit the radio transmit button. "Two bandits over the town. Focke-Wulfs."

"Heads up, gentlemen," Pickard answered as the last element of 464 Squadron worked the prison over. Flames and smoke belched from the main building.

"*K for King,*" the pilot of the filming crew radioed, "are you continuing the run?"

"Roger," Zack answered. "Stay with us." He desperately wanted to see if prisoners were escaping and perhaps identify on film if any were women.

"Bonkers, you've gone bloody bonkers," Ruffy said. Zack dropped back onto the deck and flew a tight arc to the north as he turned back toward the prison. The film Mossie fell behind, not able to match *K for King*'s speed. Both Zack and Ruffy saw Pickard's *F for Freddie* as it flew by the prison, surveying the damage. Pickard's jubilant voice came over the radio. "Mission accomplished. Repeat, mission accomplished. Let's go home." Pickard had seen numerous prisoners running from the building and would not send the third squadron in.

The radios squawked as pilots reported being engaged by Focke-Wulfs. One voice reported being hit by ground fire and going in. "My God!" Ruffy shouted. "That's McRitchie. Time to break it off," the navigator pleaded. "What's Pick doing?" He had caught a glimpse of *F for Freddie* circling to the east.

"Might as well have a last look at the prison since we're almost there," Zack told him. He rooted the airspeed on 300. Running across the field in front of the wall was a line of German soldiers. "Right-fucking-on!" Zack gritted, his words giving sound to his intent. There was a viciousness in his voice Ruffy had never heard before. The Englishman had lived with Zack for almost three years and had come to know the power in the man's voice, how he could charm and cheer, cajole and convince. But this was new and its meaning was clear—Zack wanted to kill.

Ruffy cast a sideways glance at his pilot and fear shot through the Englishman. He did not sit side by side with Zack but slightly aft and could see Zack's face in full profile. He had never seen a true killing rage in a man before and what he saw was terrifying. Zack's head was thrust slightly forward and the oxygen mask he wore appeared for all the world as a raptor's beak, ready to shred its prey. His skin was taut and drawn around the edges of his mask. He was totally focused and it came to Ruffy that Zack would kill deliberately and with malice. This was not his friend beside him but a different being, the spawn of war, all that he hated in the enemy. And he was part of it.

Zack wanted to kill. He tapped the rudder pedals and skidded the Mosquito until he had the line of soldiers in his gunsight. He mashed the firing button for the machine guns. Bursts of snow kicked up as he walked the shells through the soldiers. Every dark figure fell to the ground. Ruffy caught a glimpse of prisoners darting out of the hole they had inadvertently blasted in the west wall. Some were running across the road and he saw figures motioning them to safety. Zack lifted *K for King* over the wall and zoomed over the prison as he peeled off to the east, turning in the direction to where they had last seen Pickard.

Ahead of them, two Focke-Wulfs were rolling in on a Mosquito. "Pick!" Zack shouted over the radio. "Break right! Bandits at your six o'clock!" But the warning was too late. The lead Focke-Wulf was in the saddle, its guns firing, chewing the tail, then the right wing of the Mosquito away from the fuselage. *F for Freddie* pitched into the ground going over 300 mph.

"Come . . . to . . . Jesus," Zack growled, biting off each word, as he hit the switch that injected nitrous oxide into the carburetors, overboosting the Merlins. The Mosquito shrieked in vengeance as it closed on the trailing Focke-Wulf.

"Damn!" Ruffy shouted as the two Focke-Wulfs pitched back toward *K for King*. Zack's inner warning alarm that had never failed him was quiet and he pressed the attack, not knowing that he was facing one of the most accomplished and dangerous fighter pilots in the world—Generalmajor Adolf Galland.

FIFTEEN

The Golden Triangle, Burma

"Time to go," Kamigami said.

Woodward paused, taking one last look around the command room deep in Chiang's bunker. "He's got to be here," he grumbled.

"He is," Kamigami answered. "But we don't have time to root the bastard out." He couldn't hide the disappointment in his voice. He wanted to find Chiang and make the mission a total success. They did not curse their bad luck for neither believed in it. For them, a victory was earned by hard training, planning for as many contingencies as possible, and then violent execution. But luck had become a factor because they were still wet from wading through the pool to get into the grotto. "Do you feel that?" Kamigami asked. A slight, almost imperceptible movement of cool air brushed against them. They would have never noticed it if they had been dry.

"An open vent," Woodward answered. He moved back into the command room. Low against the wall, they saw the grill of an air vent. Woodward held his hand out. Nothing. They quickly worked around the room, testing the vents until Woodward found the source of the air. Woodward pulled the grill aside and probed the darkness with his flashlight. "Here's his bolt hole," he said. "In we go." He crawled into the air shaft. Ahead and around a bend, they could hear scrambling. "Tallyho," the captain said as he scooted down the duct. Kamigami contemplated the opening and shook his head. There was no way he could fit into the opening. He moved to the door to discourage any unwelcome guests. The only sound he heard was a series of dull thuds coming from the air shaft followed by a dragging sound. Kamigami unsnapped his canteen and took a long pull, needing the drink. "Do you mind lending a hand?" Woodward called from the opening as he backed out. Kamigami hurried over and helped him drag an unconscious Chiang out of the shaft. "The bloody bastard didn't want to come," Woodward explained. "So I had to give him the needle." He felt the side of his face that had the making of a bad bruise.

"That looks about boot-sized," Kamigami observed.

"It is. His."

"Where did you inject him?"

"The foot. Where else?"

Kamigami picked Chiang up in a fireman's carry. "You lead," was all he said. They retraced their steps out of the bunker.

Fastback's teams were aboard Gillespie's helicopter, Rascal One, and strapped in. The security team holding the LZ had pulled in and were ready to board. The two sergeants responsible for making sure no one was left behind told Mackay that "three are unaccounted for" as he made his way forward. On the flight deck, Gillespie was sitting in the right seat with his night vision goggles in his lap. He didn't need them in the growing light. He turned in his seat while Mackay slipped on a headset. "Colonel, we've got to launch, there's some unfriendly Gomers out there. Saw 'em when we came in. But leaving three men behind sucks. . . ."

"Launch," Mackay said. The clock had run out.

Gillespie nodded and told the gunners to board the security team. A crisp "All on board and ready to go," came seconds later from the rear. Gillespie reached for the throttles and they lifted into the air.

"Colonel," Gillespie said as they gained speed, "this fuckin' A sucks. I think we should hit E-Squared for a refueling, find a safe place to orbit, and try to establish radio contact with the men still on the ground. What the hell, we can call Spectre in if we need some industrial strength firepower and stay in the area until the backup Pave Low gets on station. Colonel, if they can make it to an open area, we can get them out."

"Let me talk to Hammer," Mackay said. The copilot turned Mackay's wafer switch so he could transmit on the Have Quick radio and talk to the two colonels on board E-Squared's MC-130.

"Be advised," Mallard radioed after hearing Mackay's proposal, "that Bigboot has two WIA and Rascal Two must return to base at this time. Situation critical."

Mackay acknowledged the transmission. At least one of the WIA, wounded in action, was very serious. "They aren't going to go for it," he told Gillespie. He was wrong. Mallard came back on the radio and told them to rendezvous with the MC-130 for a refueling. Fourteen minutes later, Gillespie moved into the receive position behind E-Squared's dark Combat Talon MC-130. He hummed "Try a Little Tenderness" as they plugged into the trailing refueling drogue for a drink of much needed fuel.

Andy Baulck was waiting for Kamigami and Woodward as they came up the ladder into the grotto. "Trucks are in the compound," he warned. He led them out of the grotto and through the garden. "I think the best way out is through the cell block," he said. Woodward jerked his head in agreement and the three men worked their way around the compound and through the shadows until they reached the low building containing the cells where DC and Ricky had been held. They were almost to the last heavy steel door between them and the hole that Baulck had blown in the outer wall when they heard noises behind them.

"Coming our way," Kamigami said. "They need a little discouragement."

The British captain nodded, pushed the door open, and dove through it. "Clear," he whispered. Baulck waited until Kamigami had pushed through with his burden before he followed. Woodward half-closed the door as a shield and screwed on the silencer to his submachine gun. He pointed to a grenade on Baulck's LBE and gave him the ready sign. The sounds of running feet on the other side of the door were much louder. Woodward thrust the muzzle of his MP5 around the edge of the door and mashed the trigger. Only the muffled, distinctive clatter of the submachine gun carried down the hall. "Don't need the grenade," he said.

"Shame to waste it," Baulck said. He quickly tied one end of a length of copper wire around the grenade's detonator, holding it in place, while he rigged the other end to the door. Within seconds, the booby trap was set and he followed the other two men through the breach in the wall.

"Hammer, how copy?" Kamigami transmitted over his hand-held radio. The three were in the truck Fastback had left for them and Baulck was driving, going at full throttle down the road.

A scratchy voice came over the radio. "This is Hammer. Say call sign." It was Trimler.

Relief showed on Kamigami's normally impassive face but he had a problem—he didn't have a call sign. "This is the ground element of Fastback. Over." He waited.

"Roger, Fastback Ground," came the reply. They now had a call sign. "Say status," Trimler said.

Kamigami allowed a smile. "Clear of objective and moving," he answered. He was afraid to say too much in case they were being monitored but he had to tell Fastback that they had Chiang. "Mission accomplished and no casualties. Our next objective is Blue Four." Blue Four was one of the backup landing zones that had been identified during the planning stages of Jericho.

"Copy all, Fastback Ground," Trimler replied. "Remain this frequency."

"They got the message," Kamigami told the other two.

"Company is on the way," Woodward said, motioning back down the road. "Many guests coming our way and I do believe they have a complaint." He seemed unconcerned as he studied his map. "Interesting choice, Blue Four. We should abandon the truck about here." He pointed to a spot on the map and punched coordinates into his GPS monitor. The digital readout gave him a direction and distance to the place where he wanted to ditch the truck. "About eight more kilometers," he calculated. The GPS gave him straight line distance and the road was any-thing but straight as it twisted and turned through the jungle high-lands. "Then I make it three kilometers through the jungle to the bottom of the karst. It will be a hard scramble to the top but it should be an easy pickup." The landing zone Kamigami had picked was located on top of one of the high limestone ridges called karsts, that rose out of the jungle. This particular karst formation had steep sides and a relative flat top that was over five hundred feet above the surrounding jungle. It looked much like a badlands mesa in the middle of a jungle.

The White House, Washington, D.C.

The green light above the door of the Situation Room had been on for three minutes, signifying that the President was on his way. Mazie stood when the door opened and Pontowski entered. He was followed by Cox and Burke. She was struck by how haggard he looked and, for the first time, fully realized that he was an old man. Yet age had not diminished his intellectual abilities and only his body had worn out. Mazie waited until he sat down before she dropped her plump figure back into her chair. She waited for him to speak.

"What's the news, Mazie?" Pontowski had no trouble reading her face.

"Mostly good, sir," she answered. "All of the hostages have been rescued and are on their way out of Burma. The helicopters should be in Thailand's airspace now. One of the team was killed, two wounded, one of whom is very serious, and three unaccounted for. We didn't get Chiang."

Pontowski stared at the wall.

"Mr. President," his chief of staff, Leo Cox, said. "That's an acceptable trade-off for a mission of this type."

Burke said, "Now's the time to cut and run, Mr. President."

The President still said nothing. Mazie watched as he drew on some deep inner resource and put the concern for his wife on hold. "Who are missing?" he asked.

Mazie's face paled and she forced an iron will over her voice. She did not want to crack now. "Command Sergeant Major Kamigami and Captain Woodward, the British exchange officer, and an ISA operator, Andrew Baulck."

"What was Woodward doing there?" Burke snapped.

"Unknown at this time," Mazie answered. Her voice was stiff and controlled. "But we'll find out."

The President's eyes were locked on her. "Please tell me the details," he said. Mazie shuffled the papers in front of her, marshaling her thoughts. When she started talking, her voice was matter-of-fact and normal but her face was still drained of all color. Within moments, she had recapped the situation.

"That's all we have for now," Mazie said. The lieutenant colonel running the Situation Room handed her a new message. She scanned it and blood raced to her cheeks. She was glowing when she looked up at the President. "The mission commander has reported that Captain Woodward, Sergeant Kamigami, and Baulck have escaped from the compound with Chiang in custody. They are moving toward a pickup point. The command ship is staying in the area with one helicopter and Spectre to try for an extraction."

"Was this planned for?" Cox asked. Mazie shook her head. "Sir, we're up against many unknowns," he reasoned. "We need at least one backup helicopter, preferably two, before we go into an unknown situation like this for an extraction. Otherwise, we compound the danger of losing the one helicopter, not to mention the people on the ground. I think we should hold off until we can get our forces lined up."

"Take the time to position our forces and do it right?" Pontowski asked.

"Yes, sir," Cox answered.

"I agree," Burke chimed in.

"Do we have the time?" Pontowski asked, remembering when the clock had run out for Operation Jericho years before.

"That's an unknown," Cox answered. "We're only talking about a few hours' delay."

Do we have the few hours? Pontowski thought. What was the best course of action now? He didn't know. He looked at Mazie, studying her face before he spoke.

The Golden Triangle, Burma

Time had become lost in motion as Baulck tried to match Woodward's relentless pace through the jungle. It amazed him that Kamigami was still carrying Chiang over his shoulders and keeping up, sandwiched in the middle. The sergeant called a halt and dumped Chiang on the ground. "He's coming around," Kamigami told them. Chiang was regaining consciousness from the knockout injection Woodward had given him and was blinking, trying to focus his eyes. He shook his head and finally saw Kamigami. It wasn't a pleasant or reassuring sight to wake up to. "Stand," Kamigami commanded.

Chiang struggled to his feet and looked confused. "Water," he rasped. His throat was raw and dry. Woodward handed him a canteen and let him take a long drink.

"Captain," Kamigami said, "you lead. Baulck, you follow with

Chiang. I'll bring up the rear." He swung his MP5 to the ready and waited until they had disappeared into the underbrush before he followed.

"Move it," Baulck said, pushing Chiang after Woodward. But the general stumbled and fell. Baulck bent over him. "You don't seem to understand the rules, fuckhead," he growled. "I'm not a nice guy like the CSM who didn't mind carrying your yellow ass around." He pulled his knife and drew the razor-sharp blade across Chiang's neck. "I do mind and won't do it. But I won't cut your throat like the nice sergeant. I'll gut you and stake you out belly down on an anthill, like that one over there." He grabbed Chiang's shirt and rolled him over onto his back and cut his belt and the waistband of his pants.

"I'll keep up," Chiang whispered. Baulck let him get to his feet.

"Would you quit futzing around," Kamigami said from the underbrush.

"Just explaining things to the general," Baulck replied.

The foliage started to thin as the ground rose in front of them. Chiang was panting for breath when a sharp stitch jabbed at his side, causing him to flinch in pain. He paused, shot a look at Baulck, who had again drawn his knife, and rushed ahead, falling farther behind Woodward as the slope grew more steep. The faint sound of pursuers crashing through the underbrush behind and below them was growing louder. Then his left calf muscle cramped and he fell to the ground as slivers of pain shot up his leg. Baulck closed on him, ready to make good his promise. But Kamigami was right behind and pushed the ISA operator out of the way. He scooped Chiang up in a fireman's carry and followed Woodward. Slowly, the sounds of their pursuers faded as the three men set a killing pace, now moving more parallel along the slope than up it.

"Thank you, Sergeant," Chiang said, believing that only Kamigami was protecting him from Baulck. "I think I can walk on my own now," Kamigami dropped him onto his feet and he took a few hesitant steps before moving faster.

Woodward waited until they caught up with him. "The steepest part of the karst starts about two hundred meters ahead," he said. "Don't need those blokes chasing us when we go scampering up to the top."

Kamigami nodded and the three men quickly redistributed their remaining grenades. "See you on top," he said and turned back toward their pursuers.

"Time to do it," Woodward said and led them up the last part of their climb, using the vegetation for handholds.

Mallard listened to the metallic voice coming over the SatCom radio, the computer-driven encryption and decryption stripping away its human qualities. But the transmission gave him hope. "You are cleared to proceed with the extraction per your recommendations," the voice said. "Minimize casualties and expedite."

"We're still in the driver's seat!" Mallard was exultant.

"With some very big restrictions," Trimler added. "But I think we can do it." With a big slug of luck, he mentally added.

Moving downslope proved to be easy as Kamigami retraced his steps. The terrain was familiar and allowed him to mentally work the problem. He had to, first, close on their pursuers without being seen and, second, lay an ambush that allowed him to escape. He had no illusions about his chances nor did he intend to needlessly sacrifice his own life. He paused when he came to the edge of a small clearing they had skirted earlier. The grass was ragged and barely knee-high. The recent rains had knocked much of it down and allowed little hope of concealment. This is the place, he thought. He listened for a moment, before he plunged into the open, running through the grass in a zigzag pattern. Then he was in the shelter of the trees on the other side. Again he listened. Nothing. Aware that a gentle breeze was blowing in his face, he sniffed the air. Still nothing. But he knew that they had to be nearby. He searched the foliage until he found what he wanted, a long thin branch. He carefully cut the branch free, making sure not to leave any signs of his work, before he cut it into four sections about two feet long.

He moved back into the clearing and retraced his steps, making the trail even more obvious. About two thirds of the way across, he reached the most open part where the grass was the lowest. This was the optimum place to set the ambush. He planted two sticks in the grass eight feet apart and parallel to his trail. The sticks were set back as far as he could reach without leaving the path. Then he stretched a length of thin wire between them to serve as a trip wire and tied a grenade to the base of one of the

400 Richard Herman, Jr.

sticks. He carefully extracted the pin and used one end of the trip wire to hold the grenade's actuator handle in place. It was a delicate operation and even a strong gust of wind could move the grass enough to set it off. Anyone even brushing against the wire would detonate the grenade. He set up a similar trap on the other side of the trail before he moved into the safety of the jungle. He moved into cover where he could see the trail.

He didn't have long to wait before the first shadowy movement appeared on the far side of the clearing. They're good, he thought, trying to get a head count on his pursuers. Come on, take the bait, he urged. Slowly, a single soldier moved onto the trail, working his way cautiously forward. As expected, Kamigami thought. His face was impassive as he sized the man up. How good are you? he wondered. He set down his submachine gun and drew his black Bowie knife as the man made his way across the clearing, past the booby trap he had set.

When the soldier reached the trees, he was less than twelve feet from Kamigami's hiding place. He carefully studied the underbrush and at one point, looked directly at the American, not seeing him. Satisfied that all was well, he stepped out into the clearing and motioned for the rest of his troop to follow him across. Then he moved back into the underbrush to provide cover. You are very good, Kamigami decided, but not good enough. He studied the soldier's movements and noticed he was concentrating on the surrounding edge of the clearing, expecting a threat from that quarter. Kamigami rose out of his hiding place and moved like a ghost across the few feet that separated them. Pure instinct caught at the soldier's awareness and he turned around, not really sure why. He hadn't heard a thing. The last thing he saw was Kamigami's big knife slashing at him.

With an easy motion, Kamigami caught the dead man and lowered him to the ground. He had to move quickly for the next man was already past the ambush point. He retrieved his MP5 and squeezed off a burst. The bullets struck the lead soldier in the upper torso and blew out large chunks of his back. The two men directly behind him dove off the trail and hit the trip wires. A few seconds later, the grenades went off and a high-pitched scream cut the air. Kamigami moved away and fired a quick burst of fire across the clearing taking out one other man. Then all was quiet.

There's more over there, he thought. They need some more discouragement. He moved over the dead soldier he had taken out with his knife and examined his equipment. He drew the man's knife and decided it was long enough to do the job. He held the body up against the trunk of a tree and drove the knife through its chest, just under the sternum, and out the back to pin the body to the tree, its feet dangling clear of the ground. He knew his pursuers would get the message—go slowly and use caution. He could hear shouted commands from across the clearing as he hurried after Woodward, Baulck, and Chiang. They aren't going to be discouraged easily, he thought. He plotted his next tactic, thinking about the terrain in front of him.

Then it came to him. It was too easy. "These guys are seasoned jungle fighters," he mumbled to himself. This was their backyard and they had to know the terrain like the back of their hands. Their pursuers had to know where they were heading. He had to warn Woodward. Without stopping, he keyed his radio. "Expect some company on top," he warned the British captain.

The reply was a terse "We're on top and have them in sight."

Damn, he raged, they were herding us. And how did they get around us so fast? He forced himself to concentrate as he pulled his way up the steep, almost clifflike face of the mesalike karst. It was easy to follow Woodward's path. Less than twenty-five meters below the rim, the vegetation gave out where the eroded rock face of the karst was the steepest. Below him he heard a muffled crash—one of his pursuers had slipped and fallen down the steep slope. Those muthas are fast, he thought. And good.

"Hammer," Gillespie transmitted over the radio, "we're in contact with Fastback Ground. They're pinned down on the top edge of the karst approximately a hundred meters short of the LZ. Request clearance to go in after them."

"Say location of hostiles," Trimler asked, trying to evaluate the situation on the ground.

"Apparently a squad-strength group is in front of them on top of the karst and an unknown number are pushing them from the rear."

On board the MC-130, the two colonels conferred. They both knew that they were running out of time. "Spectre is inbound," Mallard said, "and should be on station in fifteen minutes."

Trimler studied the chart in front of him. "They haven't got fifteen minutes," he said. "Rascal One has got to go in now if we're to get them out." He waited for Mallard to make the decision. As the ground commander, he had told Mallard what had to be done. But it was Mallard's decision to commit the MH-53 with its six-man crew, thirty-five-man Delta contingent and Heather Courtland in order to rescue three people.

"We go in," Mallard said.

Both Kamigami and Woodward copied Gillespie's radio call that he was inbound and would be overhead their position in two minutes. "Can you pop a smoke grenade and direct my fire?" Gillespie asked.

"Can oblige," Woodward answered.

Kamigami's eyes drew into narrow slits as he considered his next move. He was still twenty-five meters below the rim and could now hear movement directly below him. There was no way he could get across the open area and reach the top now without being seen. But that worked both ways. He pulled back into a shallow depression that offered some concealment and waited. Moments later, the first of his pursuers came into view and stopped, studying the open area ahead of him. Then he was joined by two more men. They crouched and talked in low tones, not realizing that Kamigami was only a few meters behind them. Their decision made, the leader started across the open area, climbing for the rim and Woodward's location. The two men followed him at five-meter intervals.

I hope that's all of you muthas, Kamigami thought. He could hear the distinctive beat of the helicopter's rotor as it approached. The three men in the open stopped, frozen by the sound. They were not sure if they should press ahead or retreat. Kamigami made the decision for them. He pushed the snout of his MP5 clear of the depression and fired off a short burst. The man closest to him screamed and toppled down the slope. A second burst took out the middle man while their leader scrambled for the safety of the rim a few meters above his head. Woodward was waiting for him.

Kamigami broke from his cover and made for the top as fast as he could while Woodward turned his attention to the men in front of him. Below Kamigami, hidden in the underbrush, the man who had fallen down the slope only moments before carefully sighted his AK-47 at Kamigami's back.

"Smoke in sight," Gillespie radioed when he saw Woodward's smoke grenade pop. "Say your position."

"We are between the smoke and the edge of the karst," Woodward transmitted, his voice amazingly calm. "Your target is approximately ten meters the other side of the smoke from our position."

"Damn blokes would rather die than sound bad on the radios," Gillespie told his copilot.

"Turn right," Woodward transmitted. He watched as the helicopter started a right turn. "Roll out and you'll pass right over us."

Gillespie did as he commanded and saw three figures crouched in the low underbrush between him and the smoke. "I have you at my twelve o'clock. No joy on the target." He veered away so his right gunner could bring his fifty-caliber machine gun to bear on the area that Woodward had identified.

Kamigami's feet were scrambling, trying to get a foothold in the rotten limestone just below the top edge of the ridgeline. The fingers of his left hand dug in when they found a narrow crevice on the lip. Just as he heaved his bulk up, a short burst of submachine-gun fire cut across his back. One bullet ripped into the fleshy meat of his left side and another grazed the right side of his head, knocking his boonie hat off and momentarily stunning him.

The shooter had not been able to control the hard-rising motion of the AK-47 and most of the burst went high and wide. Kamigami rolled down the steep incline and crashed into his assailant. Now the two bodies jarred against each other as they skidded and fell farther down the slope. Kamigami's right hand tore at the man, gouging at his face and eyes while his left groped for a handhold. Finally, he snared an exposed root and clamped it tight, jerking to a halt, letting the smaller-framed man break free. But Kamigami had him by the neck. For a full minute, they hung there, frozen in a grotesque tableau of death while Kamigami squeezed. The big American heard throat cartilage crack and felt it separate as his fingers dug deep into the man's neck. Then he shook the lifeless body free and watched it roll down the steep slope into the more dense underbrush below him.

For a moment, he hung there breathing deeply. He glanced down at his legs, not surprised to see streaks of blood. You've been wounded before, he thought, so stop the bleeding and get to the top. He tested his legs, surprised to feel them respond. More blood than damage, he reasoned. Slowly, and then with increasing confidence, he moved his boots until he found a secure foothold and could release his grip on the root. Since his left leg was more bloody than his right, he examined the left side of his body, certain that shock was keeping him from feeling the wound. His fingers found the hole the 7.62-millimeter slug had punched into his back. "Right in the love handle," he mumbled. He unsnapped his first aid kit and pulled out a compress bandage. Too big, he thought and ripped it apart with his teeth. Then he shoved a wad into the bullet hole. Rest, he told himself. He still needed to bandage his head.

Above him, he could hear the familiar heavy humping of a fifty-caliber machine gun as the helicopter orbited overhead.

"No joy on the target," Gillespie radioed to Woodward as his right gunner worked over the area.

"You've got the area bracketed," Woodward replied. "Keep firing."

"Captain!" the rear gunner shouted over the intercom. "I've got Kamigami in sight. He's on the open part of the slope just below the rim. I think he's in trouble." Then he saw the distinctive smoke trail of an SA-7 Grail streak toward them. "Break left! Break left! SAM! SAM!"

Gillespie wrenched the big helicopter into a hard downward left turn as the copilot popped a chain of flares behind them in an attempt to decoy the infrared seeker head of the Soviet-made, shoulder-fired missile. It almost worked. The Grail missed the fuselage and flew into the rotor's arc. The tip of one of the six rapidly rotating blades hit the Grail and cut it in two. But the impact snapped off the outer six feet of the blade, throwing it out of balance with the other five blades.

The vibration that shook the helicopter made it impossible to see the instruments or move—it was simply a matter of holding on. Gillespie reacted with pure instinct as he fought at the controls, trying to make the aircraft respond. His small frame chafed and jerked against his shoulder harness as the vibration slammed him around. Then he sensed what was wrong as he traded off altitude for control. "Gear down!" he yelled at the copilot. It all came together as he honked back on the cyclic and pulled up on the collective for a landing flare. Two feet above the ground, he cut the throttles to stop the vibration and let his aircraft smack into the hard crust of the flat shelf that capped the top of the ridge.

"You are one lucky son of a bitch," he told himself as the rotor spun down. They had landed a hundred meters from the edge where the slope turned into a sheer five-hundred-foot cliff face. The helicopter's three machine guns started to fire as Delta rapidly evacuated out the back.

*   *   *

The sharp crack of the AK-47 carried a message of worry as it echoed over Woodward. But he trusted Kamigami to handle the problem, not that he had a choice. He was fully occupied with the threat in front of him as the helicopter came down. He zeroed in on the source of the Grail and sent a long burst of fire in that direction, but the range was too great for the close-in MP5. Before he could radio the threat to the helicopter, men erupted from the back of the helicopter and fanned out, quickly securing the area.

Two men ran toward the British captain. Mackay and his RTO. "The sergeant major," Mackay yelled, gesturing at the edge.

Woodward sprinted ahead of them, went over the rim and scrambled down to Kamigami. "Rope," he yelled. He looped an arm around the wounded sergeant's back and held him against the steep face of the karst formation. "You'll be all right now, mate," he said.

Kamigami raised his head and looked up at Mackay who was feeding a rope down to them. In the distance, he could hear the sound of gunfire and the dull whomp of grenades as Delta cleaned out the last of Chiang's soldiers who had reached the top of the ridge. "I'm okay," he told Woodward. A more important thought came to him. "Casualties?" he asked. He had to know for he was still taking care of his men, the first and last responsibility of a sergeant major, the responsibility that dominated his life and gave meaning to his existence.

"How the bloody hell would I know," Woodward replied. "I'm down here, aren't I?"

"Well," Kamigami said, "you've got us into one hell of a mess, Captain. Looks like I've got to get us out of it." He grabbed the rope and started to scramble up the slope.

"Cheeky bastard," Woodward allowed. He had seen it before and knew the sergeant's will was more than a match for his wounds.

Anger tore at Mackay and he turned it on Kamigami and Woodward as they emerged over the edge and scrambled onto level ground. "Damn," he swore. "We shouldn't be here." But it didn't help. His face was a granite mask as he buried his feelings and focused his thinking, making himself concentrate on the more immediate problem. "Captain Gillespie," he said, his voice now flat and unemotional, "can it fly?"

"No way, Colonel," Gillespie answered. "We lost about six feet of a blade, which throws the whole rotor out of balance.

Makes for one hell of a vibration. We were lucky, being so close to the ground when we took the hit."

Sweat etched Mackay's face, catching in the cracks and crevices of his pock-marked complexion and giving him a dark, evil look. "We've got to get out of here soonest," he said. His gut was telling him that more trouble was on the way.

"I'll work on it," Gillespie said. He turned and ran back to the helicopter, calling for his flight engineer.

Mackay checked with his team leaders to determine their status. The top of the ridge was secure and clear of Chiang's soldiers but a reconnaissance patrol had reported the discovery of a well-marked and improved trail on the far side. Satisfied that was how the soldiers had been able to reach the top so quickly, Mackay directed a team to establish a defensive fire position to block the head of the trail and discourage any more unwelcome visitors. You had better be worried, he told himself. Chiang's men had proven themselves to be tough and determined and they weren't about to go away. He motioned for his RTO to hand him the handset.

"Hammer," Mackay transmitted, "Fastback and Rascal One are on the ground at Blue Four." He quickly relayed their situation and requested a backup helicopter for an extraction. After a short pause, Mallard told him that the gunship was inbound and should be overhead their position in five minutes to provide a protective cover. There was no mention of the helicopter.

"Colonel"—Gillespie panted as he ran up to Mackay—"we might be able to fix this beast." He pointed to his flight engineer who was climbing up the side of helicopter. Another sergeant was waiting to pass a four-foot breaker bar to him. "We're going to remove the broken blade and two others to get the rotor back in balance. That'll give us three balanced blades."

"You think three blades can give enough lift?" Mackay asked.

Gillespie said, "Beats me, Colonel. No one has ever tried it before and there's nothing in the tech manuals about it. Worth a try. We're going to strip the goat clean to lighten the load. Tell your men they'll have to do the same." Orders were given and the Pave Low helicopter was stripped clean. Even the three 50-caliber machine guns and all ammunition were removed. "I'll punch off the external fuel tanks when we're airborne," he told the copilot. "That'll shed a lot of weight."

The tech sergeant who served as Gillespie's flight engineer fixed a socket wrench on the first of the eight bolts that held the broken blade to the rotor head. He slipped the breaker bar over the handle for an extension, braced his feet against the blade and heaved, straining to break the 2,460 pounds of torque that held the nut. His face turned red under the strain and, for a moment, nothing happened. Then he heaved for all he was worth and the nut broke free. Seven more times he repeated the process, freeing the 371-pound blade from the rotor head. He was hunched over, gasping for breath and in pain, when four men lifted the blade free. Then he skipped a blade and started to work on the next one.

"How long do you think it will take?" Mackay asked.

"Maybe twenty more minutes," Gillespie replied.

Mackay's radio crackled to life. "Fastback, this is Spectre." It was the Beezer. "Inbound your position. We are monitoring movement on the slope below you. Suspect hostiles coming your way." The sensor operator in the booth on the AC-130's gun deck had detected numerous small targets on his highly sensitive infrared sensors. "We'll see if we can discourage them."

"Copy all," Mackay answered. He turned to Gillespie. "I don't think we've got twenty minutes." Then he spoke into his radio to warn his small force. Delta sprang into action and the men ran an emergency action drill they had practiced many times as the first mortar round screamed down on them. "We need a fix on that incoming," he said into the radio. He made sure his men were dispersed as Gillespie's flight engineer worked feverishly at the second blade. Then he saw Heather and motioned for her to join him. He handed her his poncho. "Wear this," he said, "and wait over there."

The girl slipped the poncho over her head. She looked up as the first heavy drops of rain started to fall. "I'll be okay," she promised. She hurried past the pile of equipment discarded off the Pave Low helicopter and paused, rummaging through a survival kit.

Four more mortar rounds walked across the top of the ridgeline. A quick check on Mackay's hand-held radio confirmed the rounds had impacted harmlessly. But no one had zeroed in on the source of the rounds. Overhead, he could hear the drone of the AC-130 as it circled above them in the clouds. The rain pounded down—hard. "Spectre," he radioed. "We're taking incoming mortar fire. No joy on the source."

"We're pop eye in the weather," the Beezer replied. His

breathing was labored and sweat was pouring down his face as he tried to bring his fire control systems to bear. But the jagged terrain and weather were defeating him.

"Beezer," E-Squared transmitted from the command MC-130, "lay your fire on the lower part of the slope. If nothing else, you'll keep their heads down."

"A short round will hit the top," the Beezer said. The possibility of his friendly fire causing casualties among the men on top of the small plateau was very real.

"Do it," Mackay ordered as two more mortar rounds slammed into the plateau. "I'll call you off if you get too close." The drone of the AC-130's turboprop engines grew closer as the Beezer set up a firing orbit. Mackay ordered everyone to take cover and to immediately shout if any friendly rounds came their way.

The dull whomps of Spectre's forty-millimeter Bofors cannon echoed over them as the high-explosive shells chewed up the jungle below their position. The radio silence indicated that the Beezer had not hit the Americans. Again, the Beezer circled the ridge, pouring down a hail of twenty-millimeter cannon fire. Now the radios came alive as three fire teams reported movement coming up the slope toward them. Mackay keyed his radio and told Spectre and Hammer that an assault was starting.

Gillespie sprinted across to Mackay and flopped down beside him. "We got the blades off," he panted. The incoming mortar rounds had spurred on the flight engineer and he had finished the job in less than ten minutes. "I'm going to start engines and see what happens. We'll fire a flare and use the radios to tell you to board." Heavy gunfire came from the far side of the plateau.

"Make it quick," Mackay growled. "Get the girl and Chiang on board now. If you have to, take off without us. We can E and E out of here."

"I don't think escape and evasion is the answer," Gillespie shot back. He pushed himself to his feet and sprinted back to the helicopter. He shouted at his gunners to get the two on board as he ran through the cargo deck to the cockpit. Within seconds, the high-pitched whine of the number two engine split the air as it wound up and came on line. Then the left engine came to life. With both engines running, he unlocked the rotor brake to the turbines and the three blades started to turn. Gingerly, he tested the controls.

"Throttles one hundred three percent," Gillespie ordered. Again, he tested the controls.

"Any lift?" his copilot shouted.

Was there lift? Every rational thought told him no. But his instincts said yes. "Fire a flare," he shouted over the intercom. "It's time to get the hell out of Dodge."

Heather stared at Chiang as he fumbled for the seat belts on the parachute jump seat that were rigged alongside the cargo deck. She reached under her poncho and felt the knife she had found in a survival kit. The handle felt as if it belonged in her hand. Her face was expressionless as she stood and took the four steps across the cargo compartment to reach Chiang. Without emotion, she jabbed the knife into his throat. Astonishment flashed in his eyes. She was surprised that the knife penetrated less than an inch. With a hard push, she drove it deep into his neck. Heather made no attempt to pull it out and walked calmly back to her seat, leaving the knife protruding from his neck as blood gushed around the hilt.

"Captain!" one of the gunners screamed over the intercom. "The broad cut the old guy's throat!"

"What!" Gillespie yelled back as Delta pulled in and streamed on board. The helicopter shook as the men ran up the ramp.

"The girl jammed a Gerber into Chiang's throat. He's deader than a fuckin' doornail."

"Christ," Gillespie groaned. "Tie her down and make sure she doesn't hurt anyone else."

"She's just sitting there smiling," the gunner replied. Then the word came that all were aboard. The captain's left hand reached up to the throttle quadrant and moved the controls full forward. "Come on, baby," he said, pulling on the collective.

The blades cut into the air as he changed the pitch. He was certain the goat wanted to fly. "Come on," he urged, gritting his teeth. But they were still too heavy. "Damn," he shouted, wishing they didn't have so much fuel. Then it came to him—he could jettison the external fuel tanks on the ground. He hoped they would fall free and not rupture, spilling fuel and creating the makings for a huge inferno. His left hand flashed over the center control console and he flipped the guarded jettison switches open and flicked the toggle switches forward.

"The tanks are clear," a gunner yelled over the intercom.

He pulled on the collective, taking a bite out of the air. The goat was willing to hover-taxi but did not want to fly. From the rear, Gillespie could hear the sound of submachine-gun fire. The first of the soldiers had reached the top of the plateau and were rushing the helicopter. "Captain!" his rear gunner shouted. "GO!"

Gillespie hit the rudder pedals and cyclic, turning the goat toward the edge of the cliff. Over the side was an instant five hundred feet of altitude. He inched up the collective and the big helicopter moved toward the edge. Behind him he could hear loud popping sounds and the grinding of metal as round after round tore into the fuselage. Sweat streamed down his face. He was gambling that they could clear the edge of the plateau and the rotor would gain lift as he traded altitude for airspeed.

Kamigami had a death grip on the alloy frame of the webbed bench he was sitting on. He squinted through the smoke and dust at Mackay who was clamping his headset against his ears, trying to talk into the boom mike. The helicopter bounced over the ground and banged him against the side of the fuselage. He sensed that they only had moments before Chiang's men would be in a position to bring effective fire to bear and might even nail them with another Grail. His actions blurred in the smoke and din as he released his lap belt and ran out the back of the helicopter. The sudden loss of 260 pounds combined with its increasing momentum and the helicopter leapt into the air, this time sustaining flight for a few seconds before bumping back down.

A burst of gunfire ripped the air above Kamigami's head and he sprinted for a discarded pile of equipment that had been stripped out of the helicopter. He rolled behind the small mound of equipment, taking a little cover and found what he wanted— an M-203 rifle and grenade launcher. He grabbed a bag of the forty-millimeter grenade cartridges that fired from the single-shot grenade launcher grafted under the barrel of an M-16, and jammed a fresh clip into the rifle. He fired off a short burst and lobbed a grenade in the direction of the gunfire. A satisfying scream followed the grenade's detonation and he bobbed his head up in time to see two men working around him. One was carrying a shoulder-held Grail. The helicopter would be an easy target for the antiaircraft missile.

Kamigami came to his feet, a yell filling his throat. What came out bore no resemblance to his normal soft voice. It was a war cry, a rage that could fill a football stadium, and it was the stuff of warriors, a samurai. It froze the enemy as he charged.

"It ain't gonna fly!" Gillespie's copilot shouted.

But Gillespie had the measure of the goat and knew that if he could clear the cliff's edge, and go through the translational lift point, the goat would fly. "Come on!" he urged and they half-floated, half-taxied over the edge of the cliff.

Kamigami saw the helicopter clear the edge and disappear below the rim as the man in front of him fired his Grail. His head twisted around as he followed the deadly missile streaking after the helicopter. But it went ballistic, its seeker head not able to find the heat signature of the MH-53 that had now disappeared below the rim of the plateau. He jammed another grenade into the launcher and fired on the run.

"Rascal's airborne," Gillespie radioed.

"SAM! SAM!" Gillespie's rear gunner yelled, carrying over the pilot's hot mike and going out over the radio. "Six o'clock! Coming from the LZ!"

"Roger," the Beezer said, drawing out the word. The top of the plateau exploded as he raked the plateau with high-explosive twenty-millimeter fire from the AC-130's two gatling guns.

"We ain't gonna make it," Gillespie's copilot rasped as they lost altitude. They were still too heavy and dropping slowly onto the heavy jungle canopy below them.

"Jettison anything you can," Gillespie shouted over the intercom. He could feel the men move about through the controls as they raced to throw what was left of their personal equipment overboard. "Dump fuel," he ordered. The copilot did not hesitate and hit the fuel dump switches on center console. Fuel streamed out the fuel dump tubes near the helicopter's tail.

"Sweet Jesus," the flight engineer gasped as their rate of descent slowed, "we're gonna do it." The three men could not wrench their eyes free of the altimeter as it stabilized with maddening slowness.

"Stop dumping fuel," Gillespie ordered when he was sure they could maintain their altitude. They were barely two hundred feet above the thick treetops. "We need to find a place to put her down," he said.

"Make it quick, Captain," the flight engineer told him. "The fuel gauges are showing empty."

Gillespie keyed his radio and relayed their situation to Hammer. "We're close to flameout," he told the command ship.

"Turn on your IFF," E-Squared said.

"Roger," Gillespie said. They had forgotten to turn on their radar transponder. At least the MC-130 could get a fix on them. Not that he had much hope of them surviving a crash landing into the trees. "At least they'll know where to look for the bodies," he told his copilot and flight engineer.

"We got to be flying on fumes," the flight engineer said.

"Everyone strap in and prepare for a crash landing," Gillespie ordered as he locked the inertial reel controlling his shoulder straps. All he could see below him was an unbroken expanse of treetops. Just great, he thought.

"Gotcha in sight," E-Squared radioed.

"What the . . ." Gillespie gasped. The MC-130 had dropped out of the heavy overcast above them and was joining on their right. "What the fuck you doing?" he radioed. E-Squared should not have chased them down when they were so close to the ground. He had put his crew and the command element on board at risk. Gillespie knew the answer when he saw Mallard's familiar face studying him from the left side cockpit window as E-Squared flew past and jockeyed the MC-130 into a refueling position ahead and slightly above him. The big Hercules had its flaps full down and landing gear extended so it could match the helicopter's slow airspeed. The refueling line played out from the tank on the left pylon and the basket drifted toward the helicopter. Now Gillespie had to maneuver to hook up.

The copilot glanced at their radar before he turned it to standby while they refueled. He saw a bright ground return three miles ahead of them that formed the point of a dark triangle on the upper part of the screen. The tip of the triangle was pointed at them. The bright radar return was the near side of a mountain that was bouncing the radar beam back to the helicopter. The deep shadow behind it meant the radar was not "seeing" over the mountain. They were flying directly into the side of a mountain. "Rascal's painting high terrain ahead," the copilot radioed.

Gillespie's left hand gently pressured the collective, sensing if he could get more lift. It wasn't there. "No way we can climb," he transmitted.

"Our radar," E-Squared radioed, "shows a break in the terrain to the left. We'll head for that. Make the hookup."

Gillespie concentrated on the visual reference points he had picked out on the Hercules during countless air-to-air refuelings as he closed on the drogue. The two aircraft moved in formation as they flew in and out of heavy mist and rain. The MC-130 would momentarily fade before popping back out into full view. His problem was compounded as E-Squared gently arced to the left, heading for the break in the high terrain ahead of them. Gillespie's hands and feet did not move as he maneuvered. His commands to the flight controls were little more than slight variances in pressure, a gentle contraction of his grip, a tensing of muscles. His breathing slowed as he concentrated on the drogue. He was balancing on a pinpoint, making the unstable helicopter respond to his will. The refueling probe eased into the basket on the first attempt.

"Contact," Gillespie radioed. "We can't take much," he said as fuel started to flow into their empty tanks.

"So we pump a little and you draft a little," E-Squared answered. He was playing with the throttles and had discovered that he could drag the helicopter along in his draft, or was he pulling it with the refueling drogue? Slowly, the two aircraft gained five knots of airspeed and fifty feet of altitude as they entered the high terrain and E-Squared's navigator guided them through a low canyon.

Mackay came forward and plugged his headset into the extension cord the flight engineer handed him. "Well done, Captain," he said. "Let me talk to Hammer." His face was impassive as he spoke into the boom mike and they headed out of Burma.

The White House, Washington, D.C.

Only Pontowski's fingers revealed his emotions, slowly contracting and then relaxing, only to clamp down again, as he listened to the voice on the telephone. He glanced at the clocks on the far wall of the Situation Room as he listened—9:14 P.M. local time, 0314 GMT, Greenwich mean time. How long had the mission been going on? One part of his mind calculated the answer— over thirty-seven hours—while he listened to Dr. Smithson. "Mr. President, your wife is failing very rapidly. I think your presence is needed . . . " His voice trailed off, choked with emotion.

"Thank you, Doctor," Pontowski said. "I'll be there shortly." He returned the phone to its cradle and sank back into his chair. God, I'm tired, he thought. But not as tired as the men out there. That thought rallied him and he shook off his fatigue, making his body respond to his will once more. Again, he split his attention, concentrating on the problem at hand while thinking about Tosh. You're tougher than they know, he told himself. You'll wait for me.

The big monitor screen beeped and flashed a WAIT—MESSAGE COMING signal to the occupants in the room. A jolt of anticipation flashed through Pontowski—every instinct shouted this was it, success or failure. "Where's Mazie?" he asked.

Cox looked up from the stack of papers he was working. "Getting something to eat, Mr. President. And probably freshening up. She's been here since the mission started."

The big monitor screen flashed and a message scrolled up.

OPERATION JERICHO SITREP
RASCAL ONE AIRBORNE FROM BLUE FOUR AT 0308z.

Smiles and congratulations from the men washed over him as he read the second part of the message that now flashed on the screen. Then it was finished. "Please find Miss Kamigami," he said. "I'll tell her."

Three minutes later, Mazie was ushered in through the door. Fatigue etched her round face and her short dumpy body shook with each breath. The President of the United States was alone in the room. And she knew. Slowly, Pontowski came to his feet and took a step toward her. "Mazie," he began. "Your father . . . thanks to him the mission was a success. But there's bad news." He took a breath, studying the young woman who had served him so well. *Whatever gave me the right to demand so much of these people?* he asked himself. "Your father is missing in action. He fought off an attacking force and allowed the helicopter to take off. . . . He was the rear guard."

Mazie slumped into a chair, her knees too weak to support her. She looked up, her eyes dry. At first the words wouldn't come. "That's the way he would have wanted it," she whispered. Then, more strongly: "Thank you for telling me, sir. I know . . ."

Pontowski reached out and touched her cheek. "I'm sorry."

"Sir, your wife . . ."

The President nodded and left the room, hurrying for the waiting helicopter that would take him to Tosh.

1944

Amiens, France

The flight had been a welcome return to sanity for General major Adolf Galland and for the first time in months, he was reaffirming his credo that a leader, above all else, be first in combat. It was not a virtue practiced among the high command of the Luftwaffe and Goering had forbidden him to fly in combat. But the chance to actually take off in one of Kurt Tank's Focke-Wulf 190s with Josef "Fips" Priller, the Kommodore of Jagdgeschwader 26, on his wing had been too much of a temptation for the thirty-two-year-old general to turn down.

The two men had launched on a routine patrol and Galland had easily fallen back into the routine of flying in a *rotte,* a two-plane formation. For a few brief minutes, he stopped thinking about his chief adversary and counterpart across the Channel, Major General James H. Doolittle, the commander of the Eighth U.S. Army Air Force. Galland knew that as soon as the abysmal winter weather broke, an aluminum cloud of aircraft would launch out of England to rain a hail of explosive death on his country, and that unless he could employ his own fighters properly, he could not stop it. Galland's problem was compounded because Doolittle knew how to use fighter aircraft in combat and his superiors had the intelligence and resolve to let Doolittle do it. How many times had he raged in fruitless anger for Goering to let him do the same and let his pilots seek out and destroy enemy fighters before going after the bombers? But his superiors dithered in their incompetence and tied his hands, ordering him to go only after the bombers and ignore the fighters. It was an order that ensured the ultimate destruction of his Luftwaffe.

The flight with JG-26, his old unit, better known as "the boys from Abbeville," breathed life back into Galland and he felt the old, very familiar, adrenaline rush when their controller vectored them into an engagement with marauding Mosquitoes in the vicinity of Amiens. It was the first time Galland had flown against the Mosquito, which had caused so much trouble. He had a few scores to settle. Fips Priller had stacked high into the sun as they approached Amiens and saw the Mosquito first. The two Focke-Wulfs swooped down on the Mosquito, using the dive to generate the speed they would need to engage the Mosquito. Since Fips had the first sighting on the fighter-bomber, he led the attack and skidded unseen into a firing position behind the Mosquito. With the skill borne out of a hundred aerial victories, Fips gunned *F for Freddie* out of the air. The Focke-Wulf 190 had earned its nickname, Wurger, Butcher Bird, for a good reason.

Galland had not lost any of his skills during his prolonged battles with the deskbound warriors at higher headquarters and

had been checking their six o'clock while Fips engaged the Mosquito. Luckily, he was looking to the right, the side with his good
eye, when he saw the second Mosquito turning on them. "Fips!"
he radioed. "Pitch back to your right. Moskito." Galland turned
hard to the left to meet the Mosquito head-on. He was astounded
by the speed of the Mosquito as it closed on them and impressed
by the courage of the pilot in taking on two Focke-Wulfs.

"They're good," Zack grunted as he turned into the Focke-
Wulf on his right: Fips Priller. The Merlins screamed in agony as
the two aircraft merged, guns firing. Ruffy's head twisted to the
right as they came off, trying to follow the Focke-Wulf as Zack
zoomed into the sun and rolled, looking for the other Focke-Wulf
that he assumed would be going for a sandwich on him.

But Galland had lost sight of *K for King* in the sun and had
reasoned it was a hit-and-run attack. When he heard Fips radio,
"I'm shaking apart—shutting the engine down," he broke off his
counterturn on the Mosquito and flew cover for his old friend.
His head twisted back and forth as he strained to see if the Mosquito would return. Nothing. "I'm heading for that field," Fips
radioed as his prop feathered. Galland circled above Fips as he
dropped the Focke-Wulf onto the snow-covered field and skidded
to a halt in a shower of snow. The crash landing banged Fips
unmercifully about the cockpit and he ripped open his right thigh.
Later on he would discover that a single bullet had shattered the
tip of a blade and threw the propeller out of balance, setting up
a hellish vibration. The Focke-Wulf would be repaired and flying
two days later.

"Where are they?" Zack rasped as he turned back toward the
west and cut off the flow of nitrous oxide to the engines. The
Merlins ceased their heart-cracking wail.

"I've lost them," Ruffy said, wishing Zack would break off the
engagement. He had never seen the American so possessed.

"We'll find them," Zack growled. He checked his engine instruments and satisfied that the Merlins were still in one piece,
jammed the throttles forward as he dove toward the ground. If
he was going to reengage two Focke-Wulfs, he wanted it to be
on his terms where the Mosquito excelled.

They circled for three minutes. "Tallyho!" Zack shouted when
he saw Fips's Focke-Wulf kick up a shower of snow as he crash-
landed. He headed for the downed German and climbed to five
hundred feet, the killing rage still on him. "Gotcha, you bastard!"
He could see the German pilot limping away from the downed

Focke-Wulf. He lined up for a strafing pass. The pilot fell on the ground, obviously hurt.

"No!" Ruffy shouted when he realized that Zack was going after the German pilot. Zack ignored him as he concentrated on the lighted ring on his gunsight. He saw the other Focke-Wulf coming to his six o'clock and snorted. The years of flying in combat had honed the pilot's situational awareness to a fine edge and he flushed with elation, knowing the attacker was still too far out of position. Thanks to the speed of the Mosquito, he could make the strafing pass and then outrun the other German—if he wanted to.

Ruffy hesitated then settled the issue. The navigator's left hand flashed out and hit the arm switch, returning it to the safe position, disarming the guns. "Not with me!" he shouted. "Not with me!"

The simple words hit home with a force Zack couldn't believe and they scarred his soul. He had temporarily lost his humanity in a killing rage and had almost machine-gunned a wounded man. As they overflew the German pilot, Zack wagged the wings in tribute to the man's survival and pulled off. It saved their lives. Galland had broken off the stern conversion he had started and was going for a high-angle deflection gun shot to drive away the Mosquito that was about to strafe his old friend. When he saw the Mosquito's wing wag, he hesitated, improving the angle for the shot and also clearing Fips. He mashed the trigger. At that same instant, Zack jinked to the left, Galland's blind side. Two of Galland's thirteen-millimeter bullets hit *K for King*'s right wingtip, splintering it.

Zack tightened his turn and dove for the ground, trying to brush his antagonist off on a treetop. It was not to be. He did manage to kick the Focke-Wulf out enough in the turn to deny the German another shot. When he saw his pursuer, he pulled back on the stick and hit the nitrous oxide switch again. The Merlins bellowed in pain but responded as they outdistanced the Focke-Wulf in the climb. Zack had every intention of separating, gaining distance and altitude, and then reversing to reengage the Focke-Wulf. And the general was more than willing to continue the engagement. He waited.

But Zack had asked too much from the engines and the number twelve piston on the left engine collapsed from the overpressure. The gudgeon pin that held the piston to the connecting rod sheared and the rod fell free. The rest of the engine still continued to generate over fifteen hundred horsepower—thanks to the supercharger and nitrous oxide. The crankshaft rotated the connecting rod and on the next stroke the end of the rod gouged the side of the cylinder. On the following stroke, the tip of the connecting rod caught in the gouge and was driven through the cylinder wall. The jolting pressure transferred down the connecting rod to the crankshaft and loaded the rear main bearing. The bearing cap that held the main bearing and crankshaft together exploded under the pressure and the crankshaft literally twisted free of the engine.

The engine exploded in a mass of flames and smoke.

Galland's face was frozen into a rigid mask as he closed.

Zack's hands automatically flew through the tasks he had practiced so many times in the quiet of his room: feather the dead prop, close the throttle, close the radiator flap switch. At the same time he yelled, "Fire extinguisher! Port engine." Ruffy hit the button on top of junction box B on the right wall of the cockpit and discharged the Graviner extinguisher into the left engine. "Hold together, baby," Zack pleaded as he rolled and ruddered *K for King* over to the right, into the good engine, and dove for the ground.

The eruption of smoke and flames from the Mosquito's left engine and the sudden course reversal broke Galland's tracking solution and he had to follow the Mosquito around. He made a mental note to mention the admirable single-engine performance of the British warbird in his combat report. He fell in behind.

"Bandit! Six o'clock!" Ruffy shouted.

Galland squeezed off a short burst of twenty-millimeter cannon rounds just as Zack pulled up and skidded the Mosquito to the right, destroying the shot. The general swore when the cannons stopped firing; he released the trigger and mashed it again. Nothing. Jammed. An electrical or mechanical fault, he reasoned. He selected the two MG-131 machine guns mounted over the engine and squeezed off another short burst. This time, the guns worked properly and he watched the shells rip into the aft fuselage and tail fin of the Mosquito. But nothing happened. He could plainly see the holes the shells had punched into the fuselage with little apparent damage. That would not have happened with the twenties. He nudged the controls and repositioned for another pass, this time aiming for the cockpit.

But Zack had other ideas and Galland was learning from firsthand experience why his pilots were having so much trouble with the Mosquito. In many respects, the twin-engine aircraft was the high-tech wonder of its day: fast, light, maneuverable, long-ranged, and capable of carrying out numerous different missions. But at the same time, it was an anachronism—hopelessly out of step with modern aircraft because it was made of wood. Yet it could take certain types of battle damage and still fly because of the inherent strength and unique qualities of wood. Galland's small-caliber shells had splintered and punched holes in the fuselage and tail, but the wooden structure had not ripped or sheared as would a similar metal-framed aircraft. And even on one engine, the Mosquito was still flying at over 210 mph.

Zack timed his maneuver to perfection. When he judged the Focke-Wulf was about to fire, he ripped the throttle full aft and barrel-rolled into the good engine. As he came over the top, he jammed the throttle forward and hit the nitrous oxide button again. How much more could the Merlin take?

Galland could not credit the maneuver but dealt with it to avoid being shot out in front of the Mosquito. He rolled with the Mosquito but his depth perception was off. While he caught the sudden deceleration of the Mosquito, he missed its surge in speed as it came down the back side of the roll and then continued on under and accelerated for the deck.

He gave out a very English "Goddamn" as he flung his Focke-Wulf around to the left and chased the Mosquito. Much to his amazement, the pilot aerobatted the Mosquito again and was bringing his nose around to bear on him! Galland saw the cannons flash from underneath the nose but knew it was a wild shot, more to discourage him than anything else. The general broke hard to the right and then pulled up. He would come over the top to get behind the Mosquito. He clearly made out the letters K and EG on the fuselage that told him the Mosquito was K for King from 487 Squadron. A Kiwi, he thought. Then he saw the Mosquito's objective. The pilot was running for the leading edge of the bad weather that was moving in off the Channel.

The general checked his rounds counter: two hundred rounds left, enough for two more healthy passes. But the Mosquito would probably reach the protective shelter of the clouds in front of them before he could make the second pass. He would have to make the next firing pass do. Again he closed, this time from the right rear quarter. He sent a stream of shells into the right rear side of the cockpit. He could see pieces of the fuselage shred into the slipstream and the perspex canopy shatter as the Mosquito twisted away.

The shells tore into the rear of the cockpit, most striking the armor plating behind Ruffy's seat. The remainder of the burst walked off to the right and ripped into the right side of the cockpit, destroying junction box B in a shower of electrical sparks. The bomb sight seemed to explode in Ruffy's face and metals shards cut into Zack's chest and face. The angle of the bullets' trajectory was from the rear right to the front left and bullets shredded Ruffy's right leg and the instrument panel. The carnage behind the seats was total and the ammunition boxes in the nose were punctured. But luckily, nothing exploded. Zack fought for control as gas fumes filled the cockpit. One of the pipes in the fuel gallery underneath the floorboards had been cut. *K for King* responded.

Galland let out another "Goddamn!" The Mosquito was still flying! Determined now to make the kill, he chased *K for King* into the clouds.

Dark gray wrapped around *K for King* as they penetrated the cloud. A light turbulence buffeted the aircraft and water streamed into the cockpit from the numerous bullet holes that had riddled the cockpit and fuselage. Zack hauled the throttle back and checked the flight instruments. No altimeter and no airspeed. The artificial horizon was tilted at a crazy angle that indicated they were going straight up. Only a hole remained where the direction indicator had been. At least the climb and descent indicator seemed to be functioning along with the turn and bank gauge. The lower left of the instrument panel was okay; he had the rpm, oil pressure and temperature, coolant temperature, and the boost pressure gauges. But most important, he still had the compass sitting untouched, nestled safely in front of the throttles.

He decided to trust the climb and descent and turn and bank indicators. They were flying straight and level in the soup probably at about twenty-five hundred feet. He mentally calculated their airspeed using rpm and boost pressure. The airspeed should be about 150, he reasoned. Only when he was sure the aircraft was under control did he turn his attention to Ruffy. It was a matter of doing first things first and nothing would kill them quicker than an out of control aircraft.

Ruffy's condition was horrific and at first he doubted if his friend was still alive. His face was a mass of hanging flesh and blood. Zack felt for his neck, trying to feel a pulse. It was there, weak but steady. Zack reached down beside the seat and jerked the first aid kit free and pulled it into his lap. He opened the lid and pulled out a compress bandage. By holding the stick between his knees, he was able to tie up the gushing wound on Ruffy's right leg. But the bandage was immediately soaked with blood. He had heard too many stories of wounded crew members bleeding to death and pulled out the tourniquet strap. His hands were slippery with blood as he set the tourniquet. Then he wrapped another bandage over the first one. The worst bleeding had stopped.

He was wrapping a bandage around Ruffy's face when the dark gray that had wrapped them in a welcome obscurity lightened and they punched out of the cloud. Zack jammed the throttle full forward and looked frantically around him for the Focke-Wulf. His inner alarm, that strange sixth sense that had warned him of impending danger was clanging at full volume. Then the Focke-Wulf followed them out of the cloud, less than a half mile behind. For a fraction of a second, Zack considered turning hard into the Focke-Wulf and retreating into the cloud. But that was the wrong way and led back into France. He raced for the next bank of clouds, which appeared to be thicker and more developed. And that was the way home. He hit the nitrous oxide button and again the Merlin responded, screaming in anguish at the overboost. *K for King* accelerated and then suddenly, the wailing engine returned to its normal pitch. The nitrous oxide bottle was dry.

Zack did the only thing he could think of. He nosed the Mossie over and headed for the deck. How much altitude did he have to give away? he thought. Maybe his pursuer might give him a clue by breaking out of the dive. He bumped the rpm up to 3,100 and raced for safety. For a fraction of a moment, he thought they were going to make it. He saw the Focke-Wulf close and sawed at the rudder pedals, skidding across the sky and then rolling. But Galland would not be denied and he sent a stream of shells into the right wing. In desperation, Zack turned into his dead wing, anything to break the German's aim. It worked and the bullets walked off the right wingtip.

Galland pulled up and away and then rolled to his left to check on the Mosquito. He clinically analyzed the destruction he had wrought on the aircraft and seriously wondered if *K for King* had some sort of special relationship with the gods of war. He watched as four feet of the right wingtip ripped away. There was a huge hole on the right side of the fuselage just aft of the cockpit that a man could crawl through and that was getting bigger. Then the Mosquito disappeared once more into the clouds. He glanced at his rounds counter—six left. Could he find the Mosquito again and shoot it down with only six rounds? *"Vielleicht ein anderes mal,"* maybe another time, he muttered. He turned and headed for Abbeville.

Blood was streaming down the right side of Zack's face and blinding his right eye when he eased the throttle back and dropped the rpm down to 2,650 and set the boost at seven pounds per square inch. His right leg burned and ached and his right foot felt warm and sticky. He wiped the blood out of his eye and removed his helmet and oxygen mask. He felt for the gashes on his head. He was hurt much worse than he had first thought. He looked down into the first aid kit that was still in his lap and felt dizzy. He had to do something about his own wounds before he passed out. He bandaged himself up as best he could, again holding the stick between his knees. His fingers explored his right leg, carefully working their way down. He found a long wooden splinter embedded in his calf just above the top of his flying boot. It stuck out on both sides and blood was seeping into his boot.

Only his training and experiences boxing in the Golden Gloves saved him from panic. He had been mauled before in the ring and had overcome cuts and blood. He didn't move the splinter and poked wadding around both sides, sealing off the blood. Carefully, he put his right foot back on the pedal and pressed. He could work the pedal without brushing the splinter. Then he checked on Ruffy. He was still unconscious and breathing regularly. But he was bleeding about the face. Nothing more he could do about that. He checked the tourniquet and bandage on the navigator's leg. No change.

"Now fly the goddamn airplane and get us home," he told himself. He worked the problem. Altitude—unknown but low. Should he climb? Probably. He eased back on the stick and started a gentle climb, watching the climb and descent gauge. The weather grew darker and the buffeting increased. He dropped back down into the lighter portion of the cloud. That was a definite improvement. Judging by what he could see below him, they were between layers. But how low were they? Don't worry about it. The turn and bank indicator was centered and they were not climbing or descending. They must be straight and level. The rpm and boost were still the same so their indicated airspeed had to be between 150 and 170.

But where were they? Must be over the Channel, he reasoned. He checked his compass heading. They were going almost due north. He tried to reconstruct what had happened during the fight. They had been on a northwesterly heading when they engaged the Focke-Wulfs and the fight had turned toward the northeast. How long had it lasted? Four or five minutes before they found refuge in the weather. They had probably coasted out between Abbeville and Dunkirk and were now headed directly for Manston on the coast of Kent.

A series of sharp jolts shook K for King and the gray beating against the windscreen turned five shades darker. Water poured into the cockpit and the Mosquito creaked and moaned, sending him a message. They had flown into a weather cell. He dropped a few feet of altitude and the jolting decreased. A few more feet and the ride smoothed and the water that was drenching them slowed. "Must have been in the bottom of it," he muttered. He strained to see ahead and was relieved to see a lighter shade of gray. They flew into an open patch of sky. Yes, they were definitely between layers. Now they were in and out of the weather. He listened to the Merlin and checked the engine instruments. All was well there. But where were they? Time for help. He slipped his helmet back on.

He dropped his left hand down to the radio controller for the number one set and punched the top button: the emergency frequency. Nothing. The radio was dead. He reached lower and hit the same button on the controller for the number two set. Light static and voices filled his headset. What was Manston's call sign? He couldn't remember. Ruffy always took care of that. "Manston," he radioed, "this is Dypeg. Mayday. Repeat Mayday." He waited. Would they acknowledge his call without the proper call sign of the day. Nothing. The bloody British, he raged to himself. They could be so damnably stubborn. Didn't they recognize a friendly transmission when they heard one? Still no reply so he repeated the Mayday call. Come on! he raged. He felt dizzy.

"Dypeg aircraft calling, please use correct call signs," a voice said.

"This is K for King . . ." He wracked his brain to remember the call signs. He couldn't. "Request a QDM. Wounded on board." A QDM was a vector to the base. No reply. "Goddamn it!" he bellowed into the radio. "Get us down, you bastard!"

"Understand, K for King" came the cool and collected answer. The British controller had reasoned that no self-respecting German would talk to a superior officer in that manner. "Give us a short count."

Zack counted to five over the radio while the direction finder at Manston homed on him.

"Sorry, *K for King,*" the controller said, "we cannot find you on radar or get a radio bearing. A longer count please." This time Zack counted to ten and then back to one. "Sorry, old chap, no joy. Can you climb a bit and try again."

"Will do," Zack answered. He nudged the throttle forward to increase power. The Merlin hesitated and coughed. Something was wrong and he wasn't about to change the power setting again. Fuel! he thought. One of the pipes from the main tanks that fed through the fuel gallery had been cut. Then he remembered. The outboard tanks could feed directly into their respective engines and did not feed through the fuel gallery. More coughs from the Merlin. He twisted the starboard engine fuel cock to outer tanks and the engine smoothed. What is the matter with me? he raged. But he knew the answer. Shock combined with the loss of blood was taking its toll.

He tried to climb but heavy turbulence knocked the aircraft up onto a wing and almost turned them over. His right leg banged the splinter against the frame and long flashes of pain streaked up his leg and into his lower body. He heard a loud snap from the fuselage behind him as he recovered. How much damage had the repeated machine-gunning caused? With a sure instinct, he knew the Mossie was dying and couldn't stay airborne much longer.

"Manston, this is *K for King,*" Zack transmitted. "I cannot climb at this time. Any joy on the QDM?"

"Negative," came the answer. "Your transmissions appear to be increasing in strength but the weather is giving us false bearings."

And our low altitude, Zack mentally added. If he could overfly the radio beacon with any precision or had something for an initial approach fix, he could fly a pattern to Manston's wide runway. But where are we? He glanced at Ruffy and a tight vise clamped on his heart. The navigator's face had gone deathly white and blood had pooled on the floorboards. He stared out into the gloom. They were skimming along on top of what looked like a fog bank with a heavy layer of clouds directly above them. He estimated his forward visibility was intermittently out to four miles. But he couldn't see the ground. Then they would be back into the muck. "Manston," he radioed, "help please. I've got to get on the ground."

"Roger, *K for King.* Turn to a westerly heading for five minutes. That should put you over land. Then reverse course and when on a heading out to sea, bail out."

Zack looked at his best friend. "Sorry, Manston. Out of the question. I need to get my nav down." Without any way to fly an approach, he would try to ditch blind in the Channel. At least it was a smooth surface and he didn't have to worry about smashing into obstacles. Had their dinghy been holed by the machine gun fire? Despair crashed down on him as he calculated their chances of survival. Even if he did get Ruffy into the dinghy, how long before they would be picked up? "Manston," he radioed, "I'm going to ditch in the Channel. Position unknown."

Then out of the gloom off his right wing tip a bright light captured the sky. It was the unmistakable signature of a lighthouse, Tory Chester's lighthouse, and for Zack, it was a beacon of hope. Again it raked the horizon and Zack knew where he was—he could find Manston. "Tory," he shouted over the radio, "Shut it down. I've got it!"

The reply was a simple, triumphant, "Come on home, lad." And again the bright light swept the sky.

EPILOGUE

1944

RAF Manston, Kent, England

Willi was sitting in the hospital ward, waiting for him when he woke up. "Well," she said, "I was wondering about you."

"How long have I been out?"

"Not quite twenty-four hours. You came out of surgery late yesterday afternoon and the doctors thought it would be best if you had a long sleep. You lost quite a bit of blood. The doctors say you do have a thing about hurting that right leg of yours and it's time you gave it a rest."

"Ruffy, how's Ruffy?"

She didn't look away and her eyes filled with tears. A slight shake of her head. "I'm sorry, Zack. They did everything they could."

A deep anguish welled up and threatened to drown him in a tidal wave of despair. He had killed his best friend. The thought wouldn't let him go. It had been his own driving hunger for revenge that had led him on. Even now, he could still feel the raw anger that had coursed through him on the first bomb run, when he had lined up on the guards to gun them down, and when Pickard had been clawed from the sky. He had wanted to kill the enemy, even after he had done what he had been ordered to do—breach the walls of the prison. Nor could he transfer the responsibility for Ruffy's death to the anonymous pilot of the Focke-Wulf. He had been the one to press the engagement. Only Ruffy had saved him from killing the wounded pilot he had shot down.

Andrew Ruffum had not lost his way among the wreckage of war.

"Was he still alive when we landed?" She gave a slight nod in answer. He turned and looked out the window. The day was cold and crisp. He wouldn't forget the lesson Ruffy had taught him. Never again would he lose sight of the guideposts that marked his path. "Was the raid worth it?" he finally asked. He suspected that she knew the answer.

Willi made no attempt to sidetrack the conversation. She wanted to shout at him, tell him that he couldn't set right all that was wrong with the world. She almost told him to be satisfied with what he had accomplished and that she loved him. She did say, "At last report, over two hundred and fifty prisoners escaped out of seven hundred. Over fifty of them were Resistance workers. At least fifty of the guards were killed, and that's not counting the thirty-some soldiers who were strafed outside the wall when they were caught in the open." She never took her eyes off him. "It's for you to decide."

"It will be a long time before I know the answer," he said.

She couldn't contain herself. "You helped save many Frenchmen who would have been shot today and because of you, a splendid lighthouse is still there, ready for this bloody war to end. Settle for that." Then another thought came to her. "Just how much do you expect to win from life?"

"You said the lighthouse. . . . Tory Chester . . . he's okay?"

"Yes, he's fine."

"The Germans didn't retaliate because he turned the beacon on?" he asked.

"Oh, they sent a Heinkel over to bomb him early this morning but it missed." A hint of a smile played at her lips. "It made him more angry than anything else. He does have the most colorful vocabulary when he's angry."

"No E-boat shelled him?"

"They haven't ventured across the Channel since you bombed them."

Silence. He looked out the window again, studying the dark clouds that were starting to scud across the sky. Another weather front was moving in from the west. He turned to look at Willi. She knew what was coming next and would not run from it. "You were at Hunsdon when we launched," he said. It was not a question.

"Yes."

"You passed the word to the French Maquis that the raid was on."

"Yes."

"And you knew Chantal was in the prison."

"Yes."

"Did she escape?"

"We don't know," she answered.

He couldn't help but think how beautiful and composed she was, sitting there, still the Ice Queen. He saw her right hand clench and slowly relax, then clench again. "Has this," she asked, her voice not betraying what she felt, "come between us?"

What is the truth of it? he thought. He answered her truthfully. "I don't know."

"Well then," she said, rising, "I must go. I do have work to do. Perhaps I'll see you before you leave."

"Perhaps," he said as she walked away. He didn't see her tears.

THE PRESENT

Fort Bragg, North Carolina

Sergeant First Class Dolores Villaneuva knocked on the door of Mackay's office. Mackay glanced up from the pile of papers, reports, and notes he was assembling into an after-action report and acknowledged the statuesque secretary. "Captain Woodward is here, sir," she told him.

Mackay's face was impassive and did not reveal what he felt. "Please show him in." Villaneuva nodded. Woodward entered the office and for a brief moment, she hesitated, hoping that Mackay would ask her to stay and take notes. She could feel the tension crackle between the two men and sensed that the real lessons of Operation Jericho were about to be learned. "That will be all, Sergeant," Mackay said. A rare disappointment registered on her face when she closed the door on the two men.

"Please sit down," Mackay said. His voice was hard and edged.

"Thank you for the time, Colonel. I didn't think you'd want to talk to me."

"Your written report was sufficient."

"It was a highly successful operation," Woodward continued, ignoring the hostility he could feel.

"Was it?" Mackay replied, steel in his voice. "It turned into a shambles at the end. All because of you and Kamigami; the two most capable and experienced men on the operation skylarking and putting the mission at risk. You of all people know how these missions are conducted. You don't go improvising. We were lucky we didn't take more casualties."

Woodward stared at the colonel. "One killed and one missing in action with two wounded on this type of mission is a gift. And we accomplished our objectives."

"Did we?" Mackay said. He pulled a file with medical reports out of the stack in front of him. He extracted a laboratory report. "We ran an autopsy on Chiang . . . here's the report. . . . It seems Chiang's blood tested positive for the HIV virus . . . AIDS." He let it sink in. "Miss Courtland was his mistress."

The British captain's lips compressed into a narrow line. "Has she tested positive?"

"No. Not yet. But she's living with a time bomb."

A hard silence filled the room.

"One thing your report does not make clear," Mackay continued. "Why did you choose to deviate from the plan and continue the search for Chiang when the order to withdraw had been given? And more importantly, why did the sergeant major go along with you?"

An unbidden smile cracked the grim lines of Woodward's face. "Colonel Mackay, you do ask the right questions." There was respect in his voice. He knew the American would listen to the answer and, more importantly, would understand it. Maybe not today, but later. He began. "It's a risky business we engage in. We minimize that risk by careful planning and running our operations on a strict time schedule. But there are times for taking chances—when the opportunity is there. You did when we were delayed thirty minutes in starting the attack." He let that sink in. "I was worried at first, fearing that the delay would mean Chiang's men would be able to react more smartly than we had planned. But that didn't happen. We were virtually unopposed in the attack and Bigboot had not yet reported movement in the compound. We had some time to search. Didn't have time for lengthy discussions, though. In short, we had an opening and I exploited it."

"And the sergeant major?" Mackay asked.

"He understood the situation."

Mackay was like a bulldog and would not let it go. "How could you both be so sure?"

"Instinct, Colonel. Comes with experience."

That wasn't the answer Mackay wanted to hear. He rocked back in his chair thinking about Kamigami. The sergeant major had been pure warrior, that rare breed of man who was totally focused on the profession of arms. Woodward was also of that breed. But was he? He certainly lacked the instinctive feel for a situation that had been so much a part of Kamigami's strength as a leader. In the final analysis, it was what Woodward was all about. And he had seen it in Captain Gillespie. Mackay accepted the truth that he did not have that instinct.

"Thank you, Captain Woodward, for coming in," Mackay finally said. "Have a safe journey home."

"Thank you," Woodward replied. He stood up and did something highly unusual for the British. He saluted without his hat. "I hope we can work together again, sir."

Mackay returned his salute and watched him disappear out the door. Then it came to him—he might not have the instincts of a Kamigami or Woodward, but he could do the job.

Navarre Sound, near Hurlburt Field, Florida

Captain S. Gerald Gillespie sat at the bar of the Pagoda and took in the sunset. A pair of F-15s from Eglin Air Force Base shrieked by and entered the landing pattern. Gillespie studied the turn and decided that he wanted none of it—he was happy flying the MH-53. Oh my God, he thought, I *am* a rotorhead. He liked the idea and sipped his beer. Loud shouting drew his attention to the two volleyball teams hammering away at each other. It was a good match and Donna's Dynamos were holding their own against Allison's Amazons. Finally, the beautiful Allison spiked the ball down onto Donna for the winning point, almost falling out of her skimpy halter top. Allison gave a provocative laugh as she tugged her large and firm breasts back into place.

"She is somethin' else," Mike the bartender said. "I hear you and her have a thing going. 'Nother beer?"

"No way," Gillespie said. "There's nothing there. No thanks on the beer." He was watching Donna walk away. "Oh, well," he said and slipped off the bar stool. "Gotta do what I gotta do."

"Gil," Allison smiled at him. "Care for a beer?"

"No thanks," he said and trotted after the retreating Donna. She had always been there, waiting for him, while he chased the flashy Allison. He had finally come to his senses on the return flight from Thailand when he had thought only of Donna and the way a pixie danced below her serious, and at times, very aggressive personality. And he liked the way she looked at him, seeing him for what he really was.

"Donna," he called, "Wait up for a second." She turned and waited for him. "Say, I was wondering . . . a good friend is getting married a week from Saturday . . . and would you like to go with me?" She said nothing and he started to stammer. "We call him E-Squared . . . her name is Leanne Vokel. . . . I think you'd like them."

Relief flooded over Donna. "I may have totally misjudged you." Then she decided to let him off the hook. "I would love to go," she said, smiling.

Bethesda Naval Hospital, Maryland

The hushed night sounds of the hospital whispered around Pontowski and the reading lamp next to the comfortable arm chair was turned low. His eyes were closed but he wasn't asleep. As usual, he was working over the day's events and sifting through the flood of information he was inundated with. Still no trace of Mazie's father, he thought. A true missing in action. I wonder what happened to him? But a successful operation—at least the press thinks so. And we are going to get Courtland, if the Senate comes through. But will the Senate Ethics Committee disregard Tina Stanley's testimony about how they had bribed a CIA staff member and then leaked the information to the press? But there's more to it than that. Did Bobby Burke have anything to do with all this—those two deaths on Chesapeake Bay and the discovery of Stanley and Mado on that yacht? Is Burke overstepping his bounds as director of central intelligence? Will I have to solve that problem? And what do I do about Heather Courtland murdering Chiang?

Questions.

He glanced over at his sleeping wife. How much longer, Tosh?

Then he closed his eyes again. He heard the door to the room open and cracked an eyelid. It was Edith Washington, the head nurse. He watched as she entered the room and checked on Tosh. Then she moved over to him and covered him with a blanket.

"Edith, I could have sworn I asked not to be disturbed," he said.

"Shush, Mr. President. This is my floor and I'm in charge here. Your wife is still resting comfortably."

"How much longer, Edith?"

A gentle look lit the nurse's dark face and she shook her head, not knowing the answer. "Lord, she is a fighter." She moved to the door. "We have a bed next door, Mr. President."

"Thank you, but I'll stay here." The nurse nodded and closed the door behind her.

A whispered "Zack" came from the bed and at first he wasn't sure he had heard it.

"I'm here, love," he said, coming to her side and gently taking her hand in his.

"Talk to me," she whispered. It was the old Tosh and he started to speak, talking about the things she loved: their family, the turn of world events, the common things that made life predictable, the personalities that moved on their stage, all the rich and mundane matters that played out in the White House.

"Courtland?" she asked. The single word was so weak he barely heard it. But he knew her mind was there, the vibrancy that had enchanted him so long ago. Now it was coming to an end.

"We got them out." He felt her hand move. She was still with him. "But it was another Mosquito run. We won—and lost."

Her fingers contracted, softly squeezing and then relaxing. Slowly, she slipped into unconsciousness and her breath slowed. Pontowski felt the tears course down his cheeks and he clasped her still hand with both of his. And then she rallied one last time and the words came, her English accent weak but clear. "Zack," she whispered, "we won so much."

GOLDEN TRIANGLE

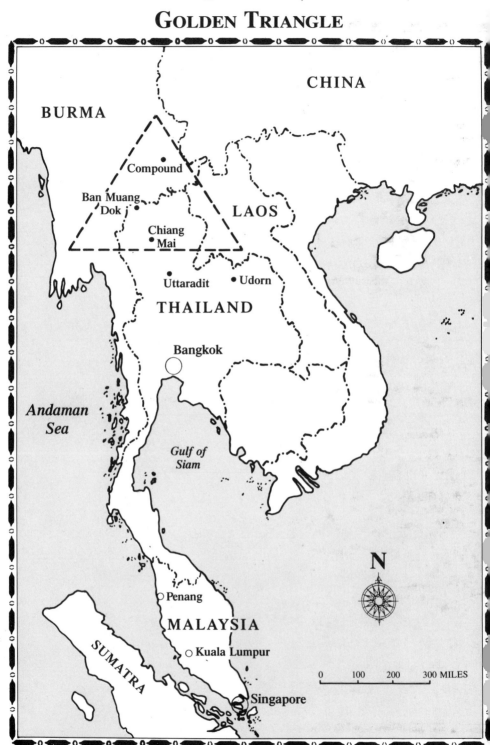